# BECAUSE OF THE DARK

THE DARK SERIES *Book Four*

# A NOTE FROM THE AUTHOR

*Trust Wes and King.*

**Each book in The Dark Series is unique to its main characters. They write the story; I'm just along for the ride. As they get older, their characters grow throughout the series, make mistakes that can have you either relate to, like, or dislike (possibly even hate) them. They are raw and flawed, but we love them anyway.**

***Because of the Dark*** (BOTD) features Wes's story. While the romance in BOTD is a standalone, the plot is a continuation of events that began in ***The Dark Series Trilogy***. **It is strongly recommended to read the previous books prior to reading BOTD.**

**Wes's story within The Dark Series is set two years after the last chapter (not epilogue) in *Of Light and Dark* (Book Three).**

This series is intended for **MATURE (18+)** readers. *Because of the Dark* is a dark, new adult, contemporary, suspense romance and features strong language, violence, sexual scenes, and situations that may be considered **TRIGGERS** for some. **Reader discretion is advised.**

*(For a more detailed list of potential triggers and tropes in this book, scan the below QR code.)*

Scan be barcode below to listen to the *Because of the Dark* playlist on Spotify.

## PROLOGUE

### WES

MY HARLEY STREET BOB VIBRATES UNDER ME AS I WAIT FOR the light to turn. I'm still in disbelief about how Kai finished the entire bottle of Patrón and was still standing upright when I walked through the door of our shared townhouse. The guy has a capacity for liquor I've never seen before and is still fully functional. But of course, I'm stuck replacing it once we run out. Allowing him behind the wheel of his Rover—functioning or not —is not something I can do with a good conscience. Thankfully, this task has become easier since June, when I turned twenty-one, and I no longer have to rely on a fake ID or bribes.

The red finally switches to green, and I'm moving again. Two more blocks until The Moose's Head. After almost twenty-four long-ass (and most of them cold as fuck) months, I'm still dumb-struck by the names of bars, restaurants, or local shops. You'd think just because we're in the Treasure State, surrounded by mountains and wildlife, we'd still have something like Whole Foods or Binney's. No, we have *The Farmer* and *The Moose's Head* —TMH for the locals.

Turning off the ignition in front of the liquor store, I take in the decked-out Jeep MOAB next to me. The car screams badass. Matte black, five-percent tint all-around, black rims, light bar, chrome tube steps—that's what I call a sweet ride.

I take a step toward the double doors when a familiar ping sounds in my wireless headphones.

"Message from Rhys McGuire."

*Fuck me. As if my day isn't already bad enough.*

"Wes, bro, you can't avoid us forever. It's been two years. We know you got the invitation. Calla misses you. Call us," the robotic female voice reads me the text from my former best friend.

*You bet your rich ass I can keep avoiding you.*

They're the reason my life turned into this dumpster fire. I don't bother pulling out my phone. Seeing the words will only result in me sending it flying, and I can't afford a new one. Instead, I walk into The Moose's Head and veer toward the aisle with the hard stuff.

After this, I really need to replenish our stash. Thank fuck I brought the hiking backpack. That way, I can load up triple time.

Getting everything I need, I add a pack of Big League Chew to my liquid purchase—never heard of that shit until arriving in Podunk, Montana, but it's addicting, and now I buy it whenever I come here.

I head back to my bike, bottles clinking together on my back despite the layers of paper bags I ordered the flannel-clad clerk to wrap around them. My gaze sweeps over the Jeep. After the text, I forgot all about it.

*I wonder who owns this baby.*


I'm standing at the light right off of TMH's parking lot, waiting for it to turn, when I see the Jeep pull out of its spot in my side mirror.

*Weird. I didn't notice anyone leaving the store behind me.*

"Radioactive" by Bullet For My Valentine blares through my headphones as I drive down 19th to our house on the south side, near the university. I approach another intersection just as it turns red, and I slow the bike down. Almost stopped, I glance in the mirror and spot the Jeep speeding toward me.

*What the—?*

I'm about to abandon my Harley to save my ass when the driver hits the brakes and brings the car to a standstill about a foot from my rear tire, leaving skid marks on the asphalt.

Adrenaline is pulsating through my body, and my hands tighten around the handlebar. This dude is asking for it. Still riled up from the text, I wouldn't mind planting my fist in someone's face. I'm about to get off my bike to march toward the MOAB when the light switches and the jerk beeps at me.

*Lucky motherfucker.*

I've never been a hothead. Rhys used to be the one who tended to lose his temper in our friendship. Not that I was a pussy; I simply didn't have the desire to pick a fight. I was the jokester—the person no one took seriously—until everything was ripped from under me. The day I punched my best friend across the face...that was when I changed.

The Jeep drives behind me with less than the mandated safety distance, and I clench my jaw.

*Give me a reason, fuckface.*

I switch lanes as I approach Bear Court, where I have to turn left—yup, even the streets have ridiculous names here. The dick navigating the Jeep follows suit and comes even closer. Fast.

At the last moment, the Jeep moves back into the right lane and halts next to me. The light turns green, but neither of us moves. I glower at the blacked-out driver's side through my visor —equally tinted—when the window suddenly lowers about halfway. My heart stutters when a girl with wavy, dark-blonde hair comes into view. Wayfarers cover half of her face that's visible, and despite not seeing her eyes, I can feel her gaze on me. Somehow, I know that she is stunningly beautiful. My body is instantly buzzing with...recognition?

*Have I seen her before?*

I hold my breath as something in her expression changes. She is smirking. The crinkle around her eyes is noticeable, even though most of her face is hidden from me. Lifting a hand, MOAB Girl salutes and takes off with screeching tires.

Stunned, I remain at the intersection until I can no longer see her lights down the road.

I have no idea what just happened, but the thudding beat of my heart tells me that it was the most exciting thing since exiting the plane two years ago.

## CHAPTER ONE

**KING**

*FUCK, FUCK, FUCK.*

I hit the steering wheel until my palm hurts. Pushing the gas pedal down, the distance between my Jeep and the Harley rapidly increases. I need to get out of here.

Checking the dash, I realize I'm going almost eighty—twenty over the speed limit allowed for this stretch of road leading out of town. Great. The last thing I need today is to get pulled over.

"Argh!" A growl bursts out of me, and my hands grip the wheel so hard the skin over my knuckles turns white. Goddamn it, why did I do that? I glance in the rearview mirror once more. He's still standing in the middle of 19th, straddling his bike and making no indication to move on. Despite his visor being blacked out, I can sense his stare on my car. On me. A wave of goose bumps runs down my spine, and I shiver.

*Weston Sheats, this is not how we were supposed to meet.*

The road turns, and I chance one last look. He's still there.

.  .  .

MY LITTLE STUNT turns into a twenty-five-minute detour. I could've done a U-ey and saved myself the headache of being late for work, but at the slim chance of running into Wes again, my stomach revolts like when Rae had dared me to eat the dead cockroach we found in the kitchen when I was eight. Of course, I had followed through. I never shied away from a dare—especially not from my big sister—but as soon as I had swallowed the disgusting thing, I barfed everything back up. Needless to say, there is not much that unsettles me or makes me nervous these days—not after everything I've gone through in my twenty-two years—but at the mere thought of seeing him again...*him seeing me*...my snack of a protein shake and leftover Chinese threatens to make a reappearance.

I slow the car and grab my phone from the passenger seat. Swiping up, my last message is still on the screen. I quickly type out a text to Mags before placing the device in the cup holder.

**Running late. Cover 4 me plz!**

My phone buzzes almost instantly, and I'm not surprised. I should've been at the bar by now. After all, it's only a few blocks from The Moose's Head.

My best friend, Mags, had asked me to pick up the booze for tomorrow's party, which was how I ended up at TMH before my shift. I was about to let her know that I had gotten everything she ordered for her little sister's twenty-first birthday when *he* pulled into the lot. I almost choked on my saliva and had to pound my chest multiple times. What was he doing there? He had practice today. He should have been home.

Yes, I know his schedule. Am I a stalker? Nope. I simply like to be informed. And that includes where Weston Sheats is at any given time, so I can avoid him. Well, avoid in the sense of me watching him without him knowing I am there. Okay, fine. I do totally stalk him—except for tonight.

I had held my breath as Wes climbed off his bike. Thank God the Jeep was tinted as fuck. He suddenly stopped and tilted his helmet-clad head slightly to the side as if he was listening to something, his shoulders going rigid. He ripped the helmet off with so much force that I jumped in my seat. Wha—? I spotted his EarPods, and understanding set in. He must've gotten a call or message he didn't like.

I should have left. I even started the car but then turned it back off. I rarely got to watch him openly, but in the security of my Jeep, I was safe.

Wes walked out of the double doors less than ten minutes later, his backpack looking like it was going to burst out of its seams. How much alcohol did he need? He drank, but nothing like his roommate. Kai must've gone on a bender again. That was it. I snapped my finger at my deductive skills. God, this was messed up. My knowledge of Weston Sheats bordered on obsessive, and I knew it. He was my distraction. My daydream. A dream that would never come true, which is why I indulged in it whenever I could.

And that obsession was the reason I had followed him and pushed his buttons by speeding up to his bike, wanting to get a reaction out of him. He's developed a temper over the year I've been hiding in the shadows, and I wanted to see what he would do. Would he engage? Deep down, I craved for him to notice me.

What a stupid fucking thing to do.

Everything is going to change. I can feel it.

THE REST of the night turns into a complete shit show. I'm lucky Mags was working, or I would've had to look for a new job by morning. I serve half my customers the wrong drinks, and my friend eyes me suspiciously. I don't make mistakes like that. I know that. She knows that. Hell, most of our patrons know it. Customers come to this place because of my bartending skills. I'm the best at my job—no point in being modest. It was one of the side habits I picked up at my previous place of occupation. It wasn't my main gig, but hanging out at the bar during breaks has now paid off.

Mags stays back after she's technically done for the night, and I'm fully aware that she'll grill me later. I am good at pretending—great, actually—but my BFF is not only intuitive; she also studied psychology and human behavior. And I'm her favorite subject to analyze.

I MET her during my second week in town. I didn't mean to stay more than a month, two tops. I knew the drill. Don't put down roots. Don't get attached. All that went to shit in a couple of days. I was walking the MPU campus, looking for easy prey. There was always a dude (or dudette—who am I to discrimi-nate?) who wanted to spot a meal for a pretty girl. I learned early on in life how to use my genetically blessed appearance to my advantage.

Apparently, Mags had been watching me since the minute I showed up on campus. I had just set my sights on a preppy-looking guy in a red-and-black jersey when she intercepted me—stepped right in my path. When I attempted to walk around her, she blocked me. I let my gaze travel up and down her body, giving her my best don't-mess-with-me glare. *Who the fuck was this bitch? How dare she stand between me and my meal of the day.* I wasn't opposed to using physical force, since the burrito yester-day's victim bought me had long since left my system. I was *hangry*. But instead of being intimidated, Mags cocked an eyebrow at me. "Let's go!"

*Huh?*

When I stared at her in disbelief, she grabbed my hand and dragged me in the opposite direction—away from my meal ticket. "What the fuck? Let go!" I dug in my heels. I couldn't remember the last time someone had gotten the best of me in *that* way. I didn't let anyone touch me. Ever. And this chick was not just able to surprise me, but also manhandled me away from any bystander without a problem.

"Stop fighting me. You're hungry, and I have the solution," she barked. But despite it being a command, there was kindness in her tone. Understanding. So, I let her.

That was a year ago and how I ended up at *The Grizz Pub*—literally.

She had brought me to a dingy-looking place off Main Street. The only reason I went inside was that I had no doubt I could take her. Granted, a whole gang bang of mountain men could've been waiting for me in there, but I always carried at least one of my two knives with me. And today, I had both. Being ambidextrous gave me a slight (insert sarcasm) advantage when I had to fend off unwanted *contact*. I was going to be okay.

In the end, it was an empty bar. Surprisingly clean and... shocker: inviting. A mix between Montana rustic and mid-century-modern college bar. Not what I would have expected based on the exterior of the building. The place was all dark-tone wood everywhere, with MPU memorabilia displayed along the walls and on shelves. All the lamps held these fancy Edison light bulbs that cost ten bucks a pop. Who the fuck pays ten dollars for one light bulb when you could get eight regular ones for the same price? Glancing around, there were at least a hundred in this place. The owner must have made good money to afford this. We certainly didn't have this ambiance at—nope, that was in the past. I wasn't going there. I scanned more of the room. The actual bar was massive, with mirrored glass shelves all the way to the ceiling. Absolutely nothing I would have expected to find in a Montana college town. I liked it.

After depositing me on one of the stools lining the counter, Mags disappeared through a door that I assumed led to the kitchen. When she didn't come back out for several minutes, unease started to build in my belly. What was I doing? I didn't walk into an unknown space without thorough recon. I knew better. Biting the inside of my cheek, I contemplated my options. I was outta here. Plus, I needed food. Between the prickly sensation on the back of my neck and my growling stomach, it was time to leave. I was bordering on the verge of nausea from hunger, and if this was some sort of trap... I slid off the stool.

Halfway to the door, Mags's voice stopped me. "Where do you think you're going?"

I pivoted on my heels, and this time, it was my turn to raise a brow. The girl that had just led me halfway across town stood behind the bar, placing a gigantic plate down. My mouth started salivating at the sight of one of the biggest sandwiches I had ever seen, and don't even get me started on the side of chips, fresh veggies, and dipping sauces.

"Sit down and eat. Then, we'll talk."

*What the fuck was going on here?*

The food made the choice for me, though. Who knew when I would get that amount of nourishment in one sitting again?

While I was wolfing down everything on the plate, Mags presented me with two offers that day. The first was a job. An actual legit and legal job. The second made my eyes nearly pop out of their sockets: a place to live.

"Why?" was my extremely intelligent reply.

I didn't even question her intentions, though my first thought was that she must have been high. Who the hell drags a stranger—who, by the way, was about to con food out of some poor college kid—to their place of employment, feeds them, and then offers for them to rent a bedroom? Was this for real? I glanced over my shoulder, expecting someone to push through the front door, screaming, "Gotcha!"

"Listen, girl. What's your name, by the way?" There was the quirked eyebrow again.

"Uh, King?" *Why do I sound like I'm asking her?*

"King." She considered that for a moment. "I dig it! So, King...I've been watching you since yesterday. You don't fit in here."

"Thank you very much," I mumbled, interrupting her.

"No offense, girly." She laughed. A genuine laugh. She wasn't making fun of me. "I'm really good at reading people. My little sister calls it my sixth sense. Anywho, I've watched you. You don't want to cheat meals out of some poor schmuck who only sees your great tits."

At that statement, I sprayed the water I was in the midst of drinking across the bar top.

"I'm also very direct." The girl in front of me shrugged nonchalantly.

"N-no shit." I was still coughing, pounding my palm against my chest.

"I want to help you."

"Why?" I asked her again. This still made no sense to me.

"Call it my good deed for the week."

"The week?"

Another shrug. "I just have this feeling that you could use a friend."

"And you want to be that friend? *My* friend. You don't even know me. Who says I won't rob you the second your back is turned?" I was actually boycotting my way to legal employment and a stable home. What was wrong with me?

"If you would do something like that, you wouldn't just trick one meal out of a person. You would hang around until they figured out that you were using them—however long that might be. And you would use"—she waved up and down my body —"*this* to get the max out of the situation."

She wasn't wrong with her assumption. *Damn, she is good at reading people.*

"Let's say I would agree to this arrangement. What guarantees me that you won't murder me in my sleep?" Yup, I had to up it one more notch.

Mags pursed her lips. "You can lock your door. Get a dog. Whatever makes you feel safe. I just want to help. I lost my roommate; she graduated and moved away. I could use the cash.

Grizz pays great as long as you do your job. You'd kill two birds with one stone."

"I didn't plan on sticking around," I admitted. Her brutal honesty was contagious.

"We'll figure it out when the time comes," she replied casually while picking up my plate and balled-up napkin. "So? What do you say?"

I didn't have anything to lose. It wasn't like sleeping in my car, constantly being on the move, and looking over my shoulder was any less dangerous than moving in with a bossy girl I knew all of forty-five minutes. I'd done dumber shit in my life.

"Let's give it a try."

AFTER MY SHIFT FROM HELL, I'm wiping down the counter while Grizz, the owner, is chatting with some stragglers. I peer over at him and remember the day we met.

It was the same afternoon Mags had introduced herself, aka lunch-napped me. My first thought was that Grizz represented the stereotypical mountain man: a buff, bearded, tatted tank of a guy with a man bun. Then, I took a closer look. His clothes didn't match his rugged demeanor. He wore jeans and a flannel, but everything was high end—name brands you couldn't buy in a town like this.

He was in his late twenties to early thirties, and his appearance and young age were not what I would've expected from the person who owned this bar.

However, the biggest surprise was when Mags told him I would be working here from now on, and he simply nodded. Grizz barely spoke a word until it was time for my interview—if you could have called it that. The way he watched me while I chatted with Mags about our new living arrangement unnerved me. But once he started quizzing me on mixology, the odd tension evaporated. We fell into an easy conversation, and I passed with flying colors. By the end, I felt as comfortable in his presence as if I had known him for years.

I didn't get to analyze this new development further because when I entered his office to fill out my paperwork, I stopped short at the sight. His office was full of monitors and TV screens. Grizz was a trader by day and bar owner by night. That explained how he could afford this place and those fancy clothes. He wasn't in need of money. How he ended up in Stonebriar, though, I still had no idea. There was no way he was a native Montanan.

The front door swings open, and I'm ripped out of the memory.

My boss is about to bark at whoever decides to walk in at almost two in the morning, but stops when he recognizes the intruder.

"What are you doing here?" I grin broadly.

"What? I can't come by and make sure my girl gets home safe?" Kiwi smirks as he walks around the bar and pulls me into a hug.

"Of course you can, you idiot!" I smack him against his chest. "But didn't you have plans tonight?"

"Plans changed," he replies. I catch the brief flash of disappointment flitter across his features. I know him better than he knows himself.

"Kiwinski!" Grizz snarls. "Stop distracting my employee from her job. I want to close up."

Grizz refuses to call Kiwi by his nickname—or his first name, for that matter—and to anyone who didn't know my boss, this outburst would've resulted in an immediate release of the bladder.

"Finally!" Mags rounds the corner. "I texted you hours ago."

I glance between them. "What's going on?" I ask suspiciously. It's never a good sign when Mags calls Kiwi for backup.

She plants herself on a stool right in front of me, and Kiwi drapes his arm over my shoulder. "Mags here said something was off with you. You served someone a Missouri Mule instead of a Moscow Mule."

Mags opens her arms as if to say, "See?"

"So..." Kiwi places a kiss on my temple. "Spill. What's going on?"

My gaze drops to my feet, and my heart immediately starts hammering in my chest as I remember my dumbass move a few hours ago.

"He saw me," I whisper, not making eye contact.

"Fuck!"

"Shit."

# CHAPTER TWO

## WES

THANK FUCK WE DON'T HAVE REGULAR PRACTICE TODAY. Monday is the team's rest day—rest meaning easy weight training and a three-mile jog around campus. I haven't had a full day off in...no clue. But that's exactly what I need. No downtime means no time to think.

I'm sitting in my last class before I have to head to the field house. Next to me, Kai's cheek rests on his arms, and he's snoring softly.

I flick his ear. "Wake up, fucker!"

I peer toward the front of the room to make sure the prof hasn't noticed my roommate sleeping again through the lecture. Half the time, Kai is hammered or sleeps in class, yet he still passes all his coursework.

Kaiden Raynolds is the son and sole heir to Raynolds Publishing, one of the first big publishing houses out of Europe and number three worldwide. He's on the team, but unlike me, he's playing for the fun of it. He calls it a good workout. To me, it's *my future*. A future that was taken from me two years ago, and I'm fighting to take it back.

"Duuuuude," he moans and swats at my hand, which gets Professor Rank's attention.

"Mr. Raynolds!" his voice booms through the massive room.

My spine stiffens. Great. *I* don't need the unwanted attention.

Kai slowly sits up and rubs his eyes lazily. "Sir?"

"Would you please repeat, in ten words or less, what this lecture is about?" Rank crosses his arms over his chest and lets them rest on his protruding keg belly. He looks at us down his nose, and I know what he thinks: dumb-as-a-rock jocks.

To everyone's surprise—except mine—Kai recaps today's topic in nine words. I bite the inside of my cheek, hiding my grin. He may be plastered or passed out most of the time, but what no one outside of his inner circle knows is that Kai has a photographic memory. He looks at the schedule on the first day of the semester and can repeat it verbatim three months later when you wake him up out of a drunken coma. Yes, a couple of us had started doing that for our own entertainment until Kai put a second lock on his door—on the inside.

With a huff, Professor Rank resumes the monologue Kai and I had interrupted, and when I glance to the side, my roommate smirks. Shaking my head, I laugh and pull my phone out of my backpack. I tap the screen: three new messages—two from BK and one from my mother.

Unlocking the device, I read my mother's first. She reminds me to call her to talk about my plans for the holidays. It's the end of September. But ever since I stopped coming home, she starts earlier to make plans—attempts to make plans.

Next, I click on the ones from my last remaining friend from my old life.

**BK: If u don't call me back today, I have no other choice than to jump on the next plane and kick you in the back of the knee.**

**BK: And u know I fucking hate the cold. Call me! LY**

My mouth turns up of its own volition. I've avoided her calls since the unwelcome text I received last week. I'm positive she was aware of my ex-best friend, her BFF's fiancé, reaching out—a topic I refuse to discuss, no matter how hard she's tried the last couple of years.

Instead, I replayed the *incident* after TMH over and over in my head. I even dreamed of MOAB Girl Saturday night. I never saw her full face, but why did she look so familiar?

I start typing, then pause. She's going to ask if I got the wedding invitation—the one I burned in our firepit. Do they really think I would simply forget everything and be the best man?

When my jaw starts cramping, I realize I am grinding my teeth—a habit I developed and repeat whenever I'm reminded of why I am currently not at my dream school with a future in the NFL.

I draw in a deep breath and respond.

**Me: Call u this week. I could never forgive myself if ur sexy ass freezes to death. ;) LY2**

The three dots immediately start dancing on the screen, and I roll my eyes, smiling. Of course, she's been waiting for my reply.

"BK?" Kai asks from the side.

I nod and show him the message. I don't get many texts that trigger the upward motion of my mouth.

"Why did you tell her not to come? I like her ass," he whines jokingly, then adds, "and I'd totally warm her up."

Ignoring him, I focus back on my screen just as another bubble pops up.

**BK: U got 24 hrs, or I am on that plane, Sheats. Miss u!**

The thought of her getting on a plane makes my pulse accelerate. I miss my friend—the one I didn't sucker punch in the face. I saw her briefly over the summer when she came to visit, but that was not nearly long enough.

**Me: Miss u 2, BK.**

**BK: U better not still have me in ur fucking phone like that. I can't believe u've been referring to me as Bulldog for years. Change it. NOW!**

My shoulders shake with silent laughter at her written outburst. I can picture her pissed-off expression perfectly, which is exactly why I've never changed it in my contacts. Riling her up is too much fun.

**Me: I would never do that to u, Ms. Keller. ;)**

**BK: Fuck you, Sheats.**

She follows that message with the red-faced cursing emoji, and I reply with a kissing emoji—which she instantly reciprocates. The brief exchange improves my mood until I back out of the text and see Rhys's name three messages below.

*Fuck!*

I LET my mind wander back to August, two years ago.

The Babysitter was taken into custody the previous week, and the nine-month-long nightmare was over. He admitted to kidnapping five girls over the course of ten years, and to say it caused a nationwide scandal would have been an understatement of epic proportions, especially with who he was and when Lilly took the stage, announcing her *involvement*.

Lilly had stumbled over the news article of his latest victim while doing research for a journalism assignment. The girls were abducted in one part of the country and dropped off somewhere else a few weeks later, completely unharmed. It was all a random string of fucked-up coincidences, but it led her to her family's secret—*her* secret. The one they had kept from her for a decade. Ten. Years. She couldn't remember any of it until she had gotten her first "*migraine.*" And whenever a memory hit, she would be crippled with excruciating pain. Toward the end, she even passed out. Lilly was supposed to see a neurologist, but before she could, the shit hit the fan. Nothing turned out as it appeared at first, including my friendship with Rhys.

Starting our senior year at Westbridge High, I never—in my craziest dreams—anticipated how things would change over the next twelve months. Rhys and I had been best friends for years. I would've trusted him with my life. Hell, he basically lived with me. That was how it had been since the beginning of our sophomore year. Before that, it was Lilly, Rhys, and me. The three of us used to be joined at the hip since we were kids—until Rhys changed that.

He and I had spent the summer before our sophomore year at football camp. The minute he got on the bus, something was off, but he wouldn't tell me what happened. After we got back, he wouldn't acknowledge Lilly. If she was in the same room, he'd leave. When we saw her in the hallway between classes, he'd make a show out of tongue diving down Katherine Rosenfield's throat. Kat was the head cheerleader and the queen bitch of Westbridge High. No one crossed her or took what was hers. And Rhys was hers now. Over time, Lilly became a stranger. It was Den and Lilly against Rhys and me—a war driven by secrets I was kept in the dark from.

Fast-forward to said August, *after* our senior year. Rhys would barely leave Lilly's side long enough for her to use the bathroom, and Den had become one of my closest friends.

I would've never considered that anything could tear the four of us apart—not after what we'd been through. We were still in Los Angeles, and Lilly and Rhys had settled into her mini-mansion and had no intention of leaving. Den and I were about to return to Westbridge, Virginia, to prepare for the coming year. Lilly and Den had finished their junior year, but Lilly would graduate online ahead of schedule, thanks to her summer school credits. Rhys declined his scholarship on the East Coast to stay with her, Den had another year of high school to finish, and I was due to leave for my dream college in less than two weeks.

Then, a call from my mother changed everything.

I was halfway to the motor pool where the other three were waiting for me. "Mom, what's up? We're about to head out to—"

"Wes, we have to talk."

Her words stopped me dead in my tracks, dizziness forcing me to lean against the wall. The one and only time my free-spirited mother had *to talk* to me was when I had climbed into my high school girlfriend's window, not knowing that her grandmother was visiting and sleeping in her room. Mom did not appreciate the call she got at one in the morning.

"What happened?" I held my breath, waiting.

A heavy sigh traveled through the earpiece. "You got a letter from UG. I opened it to make sure you're not missing any deadlines for school."

When she didn't elaborate, my patience snapped. "Well, what did it say?"

She sniffled, and I couldn't breathe. Laura Sheats didn't cry.

"M-mom?" I choked.

"They took your scholarship back." My mother barely got the words out. "I'll send you a picture of the letter." Her voice broke, and she paused. "We will figure it out, baby. I promise."

My legs were suddenly too weak to support my weight, and I sank to the floor. My scholarship was gone. How was that possible? I sat on my ass, back against the wall and knees tucked close. Mom hung up. The phone was still pressed to my ear, unable to move my hand, when the vibration announced an incoming text. I forced myself to pull the device away and opened the message. It was a picture of the letter.

*DEAR MR. SHEATS,*

*We regret to inform you that due to unforeseen circumstances, the scholarship funds for the UG football scholarship had to be reevaluated, and we are no longer able to offer you a spot on the UG football team.*

*You may contact the university's admissions department for alternative options on attending our school.*

*We appreciate your interest in our program and wish you the best for your future.*

*Sincerely,*
*Nicolas McLowen*
*Scholarship Committee*

THAT WAS IT? That was all they had to say? Covering my mouth with my hand, I read the three sentences over and over.

*What the fuck?*

"Sheats, what's taking—" Den's voice penetrated through my wall of disbelief, and I turned my head, locking eyes with her.

"What's happened?" She stood in the doorway to the garage, taking in my position and my probably ashen face. I was going to throw up. I'd worked toward this for as long as I could remember. It was not just a dream; it was what I was meant to do. I didn't have a school to go to. My professional football career, my future, was...*gone.*

I held my phone out, and she took it without a word. She scanned the screen for what seemed an eternity.

"What does that mean?" Her voice was barely audible. She full well knew what it meant.

"You guys, where are you?" Rhys's question drifted into the hallway.

A silent communication passed between D and me—something we had developed over the last few months since all our lives had been turned upside down. Besides what happened to Lilly, Den had lost her longtime boyfriend, and I had found out that Lilly hadn't been the only one lied to. Rhys had kept me in the dark as well, and used our friendship to his advantage.

Den turned toward the opening. "Go ahead. Sheats needs to take a shit. We'll take one of the other cars and meet you."

I couldn't even muster a remark to her *excuse*.

"You sure?" Lilly called, concerned. She wasn't stupid.

"Positive, babe. See you in a few." D faced me again and held out her hand. I grabbed it without a word and let her pull me up.

We never met up with Rhys and Lilly that day.

After the initial shock had worn off, I started making calls.

Den and I were sitting on the bed in my room—one of the many guest rooms the place held. "How can they just *reevaluate* the funds? You were their number one player. That's what your coach kept telling you since you got signed for the team," she asked out loud what had been reverberating through my head. I wanted to know the same fucking thing.

Scrolling through my contacts, I pulled up Jonah's number. I had met some of the players during an early meet and greet a few months ago. I hit dial and waited.

After three rings, my ear was assaulted by bass and word fragments I had to piece together in my head to complete the sentence.

"Wes—...—fuck happened? How—...—tell us—...—off the team," he yelled into the phone. "Catfish Billy" by YelaWolf was blaring in the background.

"Turn that shit down, asshole." Probably not the politest greeting since I wanted something from him, but I had zero patience left. Jonah and I had hit it off during the M&G, so I knew he wouldn't hold it against me.

The music cut off, but was replaced by several female giggles. "Be right back, ladies," his muffled voice came through the earpiece, and I curled my lips.

"Sorry, man. You kinda interrupted something." The smirk on his face was audible.

"Well, I feel honored that you still answered," I replied, forcing a lightness into my voice that I didn't feel.

Jonah laughed. "After what happened to you, of course I answered."

*What happened to me?*

"What are you talking about?"

"Dude, you serious? The Babysitter? Lilly McGuire? Ring a bell? Your name was mentioned several times in the news. The friend of... Coach almost had an aneurysm."

*What the—?*

Jonah continued, oblivious to my rapidly increasing heart rate. "When the school found out, they had an emergency meeting. Coach left in the middle of us running drills. You would've thought his ass was on fire."

The sophomore, junior, and senior players had already started practice a few weeks ago. The freshmen were supposed to arrive in a couple of days. "The next day, he called all of us into the locker room, announcing that you're off the team. Duuude, you should've seen the guys. They almost started to cry. You were supposed to bring us the title this year. Coach refused to give us anything else, but it wasn't hard to figure out. Dex is banging this chick who works at the office."

J paused, and my free hand balled into a fist. "Spit it out!"

My *former* teammate drew in a long breath. "The school doesn't want any bad press. And you being associated—well, more than associated"–Jonah chuckled–"with the case and people involved, you would bring a lot of negative attention to us. Star player and all."

I pressed the phone harder against my ear, as if causing pain would make me un-hear his words. Make them not true.

When I didn't say anything, Jonah sighed, "I'm sorry, man. If you ask me, it's complete bull—"

I ended the call before he finished his sentence.

I lost everything I had worked for because of my...friends.

I didn't leave my room the rest of that day. Den made up

excuses, which everyone knew were horseshit, but no one questioned The Bulldog.

D stayed with me. She only left to grab us food, then she returned to her spot next to me on the mattress. The light faded, and the silence was pressing on me like someone had dropped a hundred-pound weight on my chest.

Eventually, she interlaced our hands. "We'll figure it out, okay?"

That one sentence made me snap. "Figure what out?" I barked at her. "I can't afford anything beyond community college without a scholarship."

My family wasn't poor, but we also were not rich enough for my parents to send me to any school on their dime. And that was okay; I had been working toward this scholarship for years. I never worried about my future because I knew I could do it on my own.

*Not anymore.* How could this have happened?

Initially, I blamed them—my friends—anger and frustration clouding my judgment. I'd been there for them—loyal to a fault. I had helped Rhys hide from his family—from Lilly. Yet, he never revealed the real reason to me, and I let him. I thought he'd tell me eventually, but he never did—not until he was forced.

Was that friendship?

Lilly's search for answers had put everyone at risk. She became a target, and not just to the real villain hiding in the shadows. She found out who she was. To Rhys. To the people she thought were her family. None of that was her fault. Shitty fucking circumstances were the reason, but...Lilly ended up in the spotlight. Half the country felt for her; the other half crucified her. And I chose to stand by her side.

Big mistake, as it turned out.

I lost my future while they'd be living their happily ever after. I couldn't afford UG's tuition. Not that I wanted to attend that school after they dropped me. My dream school, since I was a little kid, had shown me the middle finger. Well, fuck them.


The next day, I went to find Rhys and Lilly in the kitchen. Lilly was in the process of making her signature Earl Grey while Rhys was sitting at the island, scrolling through his phone. Both turned as I entered, and there might as well have been a flashing neon sign hanging from the ceiling. They knew.

*Fuck. Me!*

"D told you?" I didn't think she would, but how else—

"UG posted an article that their biggest prospect would not be joining the team next year as planned. Jager texted this morning, asking what happened," Rhys elaborated with hollowed cheeks.

Double fuck me. It was already out? And Jager, of all people. He used to be one of our teammates in high school until the first article about Lilly hit the pages. Jager ran his mouth, and Rhys let his temper get the best of him. We were on neutral terms with him those days, but that didn't change the humiliation choking me that he was the one that had found out first.

"UG took the funds for my scholarship away," I explained in a flat tone.

"What?" The shrill pitch in Lilly's one-word explosion made me flinch. She slammed her Yeti on the countertop and spun around.

"Why?" Rhys slanted his head and watched me as I dropped down onto the bench of the breakfast nook.

I placed my hands, palms down on the tabletop, and repeated the phone conversation with Jonah without looking at them. Den joined us a few minutes into my recap and slid in next to me, her leg pressed against my thigh in silent support. The more I talked, the more my chest compressed.

"They can't do that!" Lilly exclaimed, outraged when I finished.

"Bro, is that even legal?" Rhys looked between all of us.

"It is." That was the first thing I checked yesterday.

"I'll give you the money for school. Just pick where you want to go," Lilly said calmly.

My head jerked in her direction, and I felt my eyebrows near my hairline. "Excuse me?"

Before Lilly could respond, Rhys interjected, "Of course. I mean, uh..."—he glanced at his girlfriend—"it's Calla's money, but..." He trailed off. Rhys never used Lilly's given name anymore. It was either babe or Calla, the nickname he had given her years ago—before their *falling out*—and now picked back up again.

Lilly rolled her eyes at him, then focused back on me. "I have more money than I can ever spend, I'll pay for your—"

"NO!" I interrupted, and Den jumped in her seat next to me.

"Why not?" Rhys stared at me incredulously.

*Of course he doesn't get it.*

The association with Lilly had already cost me my future. Who the fuck knew what would happen if it came out that she —her family's money—paid for my education? My reputation—if I would even get a chance for a professional football career— would be a joke. Everyone would assume I bought my athletic career.

"Just...no." I emphasized my refusal by pushing myself upright, leaning forward on the table.

"But—"

"Leave it, McGuire," Den barked at Rhys.

He glanced at Lilly, ready to push more, but she shook her head.

NO ONE TALKED about the topic for two days. Not until I received another call. I didn't recognize the number and therefore let it go to voice mail. When I later listened to the message, my mouth went dry. The longer the caller spoke, the faster my pulse thrashed in my veins.

"Mr. Sheats, this is Harrison Brown. I am on the admissions board of Pine Hill University in Texas. We would like to offer you a spot on our football team with a full scholarship to attend our institution. Please give me a call back so we can discuss our offer further. You can reach me at—" I pulled my phone away from my ear and gaped at the screen.

Pine Hill? They were a private university known for their athletic programs. You couldn't even apply to the school; it was by invite only. They scouted their prospects for years before offering them a spot. My initial excitement turned to suspicion. Something wasn't right.

With my phone in hand, I headed toward the basement. Lilly and Rhys, with the help of her new security shadow, Marcus, had converted the lower level into a state-of-the-art gym. It was the time of day they would be down there, and I heard the punches before I reached the bottom step.

With George, her family's head of security, being out of town, Marcus was in charge of her safety and training. Not that he normally wasn't. Marcus was in his early thirties and had been working for George for years. A couple of weeks ago, he fully took over for G as Lilly's personal bodyguard. George's focus had shifted to the Babysitter case and overseeing the legalities. That was when Marcus moved in. He was around twenty-four seven since Lilly, thanks to the media harassment, couldn't go out on her own anywhere—hence his nickname, Shadow.

Marcus held the large rectangular pads strapped to his fore-arms while Rhys kept punching and kicking. Lilly was nowhere in sight. Neither was Den.

"Hey!" I called out, and Rhys halted.

"Yo. What's up?" He wiped the sweat off his forehead with his taped hand.

I held up my phone as if that would explain everything. "Did you have anything to do with this?"

Rhys clapped Marcus on the shoulder. "Give us a sec," he said before walking toward me. "To do with what?" He was breathing heavily.

"Pine Hill offered me a spot on their team." I kept my tone unemotional, assessing his reaction in explicit detail.

"Dude, that's awesome! How did that happen?" Rhys's face lit up, and I cocked my head, trying to gauge the sincerity.

"No clue, man." I was not convinced that a university like Pine Hill would just offer me a full ride after a regular college dropped me for potential bad press.

Rhys hooked his arm over my shoulder. "Either way, we need to celebrate. Plus, Texas is way closer than UG. We can hang all the time."

"I guess," I replied, staring at my feet as he led me up the stairs. My gut was telling me that something wasn't right.

Den was ecstatic when she heard the news. Lilly smiled and gave me a hug, but I knew her too well. The girl couldn't act or lie for shit, and the way she fidgeted next to Rhys told me more than words. I kept watching her throughout the night. We got takeout, and Den talked us into opening one of the ancient bottles from the wine cellar. Not that I particularly like red wine, but that was what we had on hand. And according to D, the bottle was worth more than my 4Runner.

I returned Mr. Brown's call the next day, and we spoke for forty-five minutes. He assured me that they had been following me for a long time but could not move forward, as I had signed with UG during the early signing period. He would be emailing me all the paperwork to finalize my spot at Pine Hill.

Whenever the four of us were in the same room, Rhys would be *über*happy, as if overcompensating for his girlfriend's lack of participation. Lilly was keeping something from me, and I was a hundred percent certain she was keeping it from Den as well. D would've told me otherwise, no matter her loyalty to her best friend.

A few days later, Den and I were headed to the airport.

Marcus was driving, with Rhys in the passenger seat, Lilly and Den in the middle, and me in the third row. My phone rang, and recognizing the number, I answered. "Mr. Brown. Did I forget to fill something out?"

"Good afternoon, Mr. Sheats. No, no. We have everything we need. I was just wondering if you could provide me with the financial adviser's number for Miss—"

My entire body tensed at *financial adviser*, and I interrupted him without thinking. "Excuse me?"

Brown coughed. "I seem to have misplaced the number. He asked me to provide him with a receipt once the funds for your scholarship were received."

"My scholarship," I repeated slowly and zeroed in on Rhys as he turned around.

*I fucking knew it.*

I hung up the phone without waiting for another reply. They went behind my back. My spot at Pine Hill was bought. The school was never interested in me. My friends fucking lied to me —*after* I told them that I didn't want the money. It had to have been Rhys's idea, and Lilly went along with it. Did he think I was an idiot? This would've come out eventually. And then what? Rhys didn't care about anything but himself. He'd been using me for years, and now he was using his girlfriend's money to ease *his guilt*.

We were about ten minutes out from the airfield, and with every passing minute, the rage building in my core grew. I could feel the muscles in my jaw tic. Digging my nails into the palms of my hands, I needed something to keep my temper subdued. Unfortunately—or maybe not— the sting was not able to outweigh the betrayal. The girls missed the entire exchange, engrossed in some type of Westbridge High drama that had been unfolding over the summer.

When the SUV halted, Rhys got out and opened the door for Lilly and Den. My fists were curled tightly, the skin over my knuckles white, and I watched my friend through slitted eyes as

I exited the vehicle last. He was not prepared for my next move. Lilly was engrossed in a conversation with Marcus, with Den standing slightly behind her, ignoring Marcus as usual. As soon as my feet hit the polished concrete of the private hangar, I took a step to the side and allowed Rhys to close the door. He was about to face me when I drew my arm back and let my fist shoot forward. I clocked him in the jaw, and his head snapped to the side. Rhys caught himself against the side of the car. Behind me, Lilly shrieked in shock, and Den called my name. But everything was muffled over the hammering in my ears.

*They fucking lied to me. I asked him, and he lied to my face.*

I grabbed Rhys by the shirt and slammed him back against the car. A pair of arms latched onto my torso and pulled me away. Not letting go of his shirt, it ripped.

"HOW COULD YOU?!" I roared in his face, spit flying. I probably looked deranged, but I didn't care. I had covered for him for years while he kept secret after secret from me. I was there for him. For both of them. I told them I didn't want the money.

Lilly stood warily next to her treacherous boyfriend, who rubbed his jaw, not saying a word.

I was sure it was his idea to ignore what I had said, but she provided the funds for this farce. I would've been a fucking joke at Pine Hill.

Marcus dragged me away, and I struggled against his hold. I wanted to get another punch in. Not that I could have, now that Rhys was prepared. But in my rage-filled mind, that was all that counted.

"Wes! What the hell?" Den grabbed my hand as Lilly's shadow tightened his arms further. "Marcus, let go of him!" she shouted.

"No can do," was growled into my ear.

"You fucking went behind my back, you asshole. I told you I didn't want her money. And you? You probably guilted her into forking over what? A couple hundred grand? You knew I wouldn't take it. I've been by your side for years, and what do you do? You fucking betray me!"

"Wes—" Lilly took a step forward, but Rhys grasped her hand before she could get any closer.

I barked out a cynical laugh. "What? You think I'd hit her, too?"

Rhys still wouldn't say anything, but the guilt was written in bold letters on his forehead.

"Rhys, get Lilly in the car and wait for me," Marcus ordered from behind.

"But—" Lilly tried once more.

"Football has always been your dream. We just wanted to help," Rhys finally spoke up.

"FUCK. YOU!" I spat at them. "You turned me—*my dream*—into a fraud." I attempted to shrug Marcus off. "Let me go, Shadow! I'm done here."

Lilly nodded at her security detail, and he loosened his grip. Shaking him off, I turned on my heel and marched toward the jet. Not that I wanted to take this damn thing home now, but I couldn't afford a commercial ticket—not if I wanted to find a way to still go to school.

# CHAPTER THREE

### KING

MY ALARM IS BLARING. *WHYYY*, MY FOGGY BRAIN WHINES IN confusion. I run through all the scenarios in my head. There's no class today—not that I would be held accountable if I didn't show up.

*Why the hell is my alarm going off?*

After confessing my stupid fucking actions to my friends, I didn't get to bed until the sun was coming over the mountain range.

A sound between a groan, a curse, and a frustrated whimper escapes me as I untangle myself from my covers and try to locate the obnoxious sound between my discarded clothes on the floor. Dead on my feet, it seems I didn't bother plugging my phone in last night. I simply stripped and let everything fall where I was standing. It's a miracle my phone is still working.

"Why aren't you dead as usual?" I grumble to myself.

"Bitch, turn that off!" Mags's voice echoes through the apartment. My door flies open as I hang halfway off the bed, digging through what seems like my entire wardrobe. I peer up at my roommate, who is already showered and dressed. Of course she is.

She stalks toward me, her hand disappearing under the shirt I was about to lift next and pulls out—I squint. Whose phone is that? She silences it, then shoves it in my face.

Closing my hand carefully around the unknown device, I let myself fall onto the pillow, hitting something hard with the back of my head.

"Ow!" comes a rumble from behind me.

I shriek and jump out of bed. "What the fuck?" In shock, I stare at Kiwi, who is sprawled out on two-thirds of my queen mattress. The comforter is halfway off the bed, exposing his muscular bare chest, and a visible tent makes my duvet stick up.

*Jesus Christ.*

Mags is doubled over, gasping for air, laughing, while he combs his long fingers through his messy midnight-brown curls, blinking up at me sleepily.

"Are those panties new?" Kiwi drawls. "Love the color, Roe-Roe. Brings out your eyes."

"Argh!" Pulling the pillow out from under his head, he flops down. I throw it at his face. "What are you doing in my bed?" I fake outrage. It's not like we haven't shared a bed before. Hell, Kiwi and I have probably shared the same bed more than I have slept alone. But I don't like surprises, and he knows that. I didn't expect to find my best friend in my bed this morning.

"I drove with you home, remember? It was way too late, so I crashed here," he mumbles while he rubs his eyes.

"Plus, you asked him to stay," Mags adds helpfully. "Oh, and I agree with our bestie on your attire. You didn't tell me you finally went to Victoria's Secret." She slaps my ass before walking out.

I yelp at the sting and take a step forward. My foot tangles in a pair of jeans—the massive pile seemingly containing Kiwi's shirt and pants as well—and I stumble, hitting my shin on the bed frame.

"Fuck!"

Losing balance, I ungracefully land on top of the guy in my bed.

"Roe-Roe, you could've just asked for a hug. You know I always oblige," he laughs and wraps his arms around me.

I let my forehead rest on his collarbone. "I drank last night, didn't I?"

He squeezes me tighter. "Yes, you did."

Now that the sleepy haze is gone, bits and pieces are coming back. After I admitted my colossal fuckup to my two best friends, Mags made Grizz bust out a bottle from his private stash—the good stuff, as we call it.

I hardly ever drink, which results in me having zero tolerance. I get trashed from one beer, and whatever Grizz produced must've been much more potent than the 105 proof we serve our customers.

Growing up, I didn't have the luxury of being a regular teenager. I didn't go to parties or sneak out with my friends after raiding our parents' liquor cabinet. I never built up a tolerance. By the time my classmates reached that age, I had two jobs and took care of my sick mother. Neither allowed me to have any free time until I finally decided to drop out of school altogether. It was that or be homeless—Mom couldn't work anymore. Finishing my high school degree at a later date seemed the reasonable solution.

It wasn't always like that, though. The first half of my life wasn't so bad. I'd had the best mom. She was always there for my sister, Rae, and me. She made sure we were clothed and fed, put little notes in my lunch bag, the whole nine yards. I never felt not loved.

Dad...that was a whole different story. He wasn't around much, and we were used to it just being the three of us most of the time. Then, on my seventh birthday, he left for good. Thinking back, I don't understand how my mother didn't see it coming; the signs were all there. Digging through my muddled childhood memories now, it was clear as day. But she loved him with every fiber of her being, which was why it destroyed her when the realization hit that he would not return this time. He was gone.

It took almost a year before my shell of a mother was semi-functional again. She continued to go to work, but Rae, who was older than me, became my stand-in mother. She took a part-time job to help pay the bills and made sure I would go to school. When Mom wasn't buried in her two minimum-wage jobs, she would lock herself in her bedroom and cry herself to sleep. Even between her working herself to death and Rae helping out, our power still got shut off every other month. If it hadn't been for Kiwi and his grandmother, who lived in the apartment below ours...well, you can probably guess.

Mom did her best, and I will always be grateful. Sadly, Rae didn't see it that way. She and Mom never got along, which I didn't understand until years later—the day I buried my mother next to my father.

Four years after we lost Dad, Rae left as well. She had put her life on hold long enough, as she declared in the letter I found on her bed one day in fifth grade after coming home from school.

At age eleven, it made no sense to me. How could they both have left us? In a completely different manner, but they were gone nonetheless. How could one just abandon their family? That night, Mom crawled into my twin bed with me, hugged me tight, and told me that, no matter what, we'd be okay. We always had each other—always being seven more years. Then, she left me as well, and all I had was Kiwi.

He's been with me ever since, followed me wherever I went. The only time we were apart was when I was moving around, but once I settled into my new home, he packed his belongings and showed up within a week.

"You seemed to have slept okay?" My best friend's question brings my attention back to the present.

With my hands stacked, I prop my chin on top and peer into

his brown eyes. I smile softly at him. He knows me too well. "I did." After a pause, I add, "You know I always sleep better when you're with me. Even when I have no clue you're in my bed." I wink at him teasingly.

His brow furrows. "Roe-Roe, how bad is it?"

Instead of answering, I avert my gaze and stare at the wall beside the bed.

"King." He tries to get my attention by using my actual name, but I refuse to look at him. He would see immediately that I hadn't been able to sleep through the night in weeks.

"Kingsley Monroe." Kiwi's tone is hard, commanding, and a lone tear runs down my face.

"Awww, shit, sweetie." His arms tighten around me, and I return his embrace. Shoving my hands between his back and the mattress, I sob into his chest.

He lets me cry myself out. Between not getting enough rest and Wes being aware of me since last night, my emotions are all over the place. I hate it. Kingsley Monroe is not whiney or vulnerable. I buried that girl with my mother four years ago. Kiwi was there, at my side.

I sniff one final time and lock eyes with Devon "Kiwi" Kiwinski—the last link to my past.

"Guys! Get your asses out of bed. We have guests coming in a few hours," Mags yells from somewhere in the apartment. "If I didn't know better, I'd think King is making use of your morning wood you had on display, Kiwi."

Kiwi lets go of me and covers his face with both hands, shaking his head. "Good Lord, where did you find this girl again?" he mumbles through his palms.

I burst out laughing. "She found me, remember?"

AFTER A LONG, hot shower and a cup of coffee, I am finally ready to tackle whatever grueling tasks my roommate has planned for me. Kiwi bailed with the excuse that he had to go home to change but would be back later to help, which means he'll show up in time for the party.

Mags has left me with the glamorous task of setting up the extra folding tables we borrowed from our neighbors across the street (a bunch of MPU juniors) when my boss walks in through the side gate, carrying two crates of beer.

I knit my brows. "What's this?"

"My contribution," he grumbles as he walks toward the back door of our first-floor apartment.

I cackle a laugh, unfolding the legs of the upside-down table in front of me. By contribution, he means Mags ordered him to bring it over.

My friend has been an open book with me from day one, which is why—besides Kiwi—she is the one other person who knows the full truth about me—what I did and how I ended up in Stonebriar, Montana. But Grizz...he is the one topic Mags refuses to talk about, no matter how hard I've tried these last twelve months. And I've tried. They have a relationship I can't put my finger on. I'm ninety-nine percent certain nothing is going on between them, yet there is an underlying tension that everyone who spends more than five minutes in the same room with them basically gets slapped in the face with.

Grizz disappears inside, and I finish up without any further interruptions.

Later, we are bringing the last of the snack bowls outside when Chelsea and her boyfriend, Mack, enter the yard through the patio door.

"I dropped my purse in your bedroom," she informs her big sister.

Mags nods and continues to rearrange the beer bottles. Ever since Grizz left, her mood has taken a dive.

"Happy birthday." I hug the guest of honor as she takes in the transformed backyard. Lanterns and fairy lights adorn the trees, and we actually mowed the lawn for once. Not that we don't take care of it, but we're usually a week or two behind our neighbors, and one of the boys takes pity on our green patch of grass.

"Where is Echo?" Chelsea looks around.

"Grizz is keeping her for the weekend," I explain the absence of my three-year-old German wirehaired pointer.

I never had a pet before her. When I was little, we couldn't afford another mouth to feed, and as I got older...pretty much the same applied. Plus, I didn't have the time. But when Mags made the comment in her "move in with me" speech, the seed was planted.

*You can lock your door. Get a dog. Whatever makes you feel safe.*

I don't need Echo to make me feel safe; I can do that on my own. But the thought of having a dog appealed to me.

I let the idea fester for a few weeks, and every time I thought of reasons why I couldn't have one, I came up with none. I had a steady job and a home, so why not?

One evening, after Kiwi got to town, we were sitting on the back patio, and I confessed to my friends that I wanted to adopt a dog. Little did I know, one of Mags's classmates was looking for a home for her pointer, as she was moving and couldn't take Echo with her. Echo was trained as a bird dog—not that I knew anything about hunting, but it was something I was open to taking up.

Chelsea nods in understanding. Echo is the perfect dog, but she is also very protective of me. With so many people going in and out, I didn't want to chance it.

Mack veers directly to the sound dock and plugs his phone in. "Let's get this party started!" he shouts and hits play. "Last Resort" by Papa Roach starts blaring through the backyard, and I shake my head as Chelsea jumps into his arms and squeals. If the cops don't shut us down tonight, I'll be surprised.

· · ·

As PREDICTED, Kiwi shows up an hour after we're finished setting up and the first guests have arrived. I'm not mad, though. He has done more for me than I can ever repay him for. I'm chatting with Chelsea when arms envelop me from the back.

His touch is as familiar as my own. If it had been anyone other than my childhood friend, my body would've reacted of its own volition, which is why I left my knives in my room tonight. I don't fuck around. I may have dropped some of my guard over the last year, but I still don't let anyone touch me.

"Hi, Roe-Roe." Kiwi places a kiss on my cheek, and I twist in his embrace to give him a droll glare.

"I thought you were going to help." He knows I'm teasing.

"I landed a new project and had to go get supplies."

That makes me turn in his arms and drop the angry charade. "You did?" I'm beaming so hard my cheeks hurt. "That's awesome. Your business is totally taking off."

Kiwi loves art, and he can draw like no other, but what he enjoys more is building things—and he is fucking amazing at it. Shortly after arriving in Stonebriar, he met a guy who owned a welding business. It didn't take long, and they joined forces. They expanded the original business to incorporate woodwork, and together, they produce the most amazing furniture.

Kiwi grins down at me. "Who would've known that you going on the run and settling in the middle of nowhere would end up being good for me?"

"Shhhh!" I hiss and peer over my shoulder at Mags's sister. Mags knows why I'm here, but that doesn't mean I'm advertising it.

"Oh hush, she's preoccupied. Look," he placates me and nods his chin in the direction I hear a multitude of voices suddenly come from.

I glance toward the commotion, and my heart stops. "Shit." I push against Kiwi's chest, urging him to move toward the back door.

"What?" His confused gaze ping-pongs between the group that entered the yard and me.

Chelsea's friend Morgan arrived with a bunch of football players in tow. Is she dating one of them now? I keep shoving, and realization must've set in because Kiwi finally lets me go, and I dart around him into the house.

Mags is about to leave the house, and we collide, almost knocking each other over.

"What's gotten into you?" she asks, exasperated.

"Morgan brought a bunch of football players with her."

Mags's attitude instantly switches to alarm, and she peers around me. Chelsea's boyfriend, Mack, is on the team, but he has no clue about my little, uh... *fascination* with Wes. I didn't expect anyone else from the team to show up. This is Mags's sister's party. I try to move deeper into the house, but she grabs my arm to stop me. "He's not here."

Air leaves my lungs, and it's like a massive weight is lifted off my chest. I can breathe again.

*He's not here.*

Why would he be? Wes has never been seen at a house party. His sole focus is on football. He and Kai throw parties, but even during those, he keeps to himself. At least, that's what I've heard. I haven't had the guts to actually crash one.

I scan the group that is now engaged in a game of cornhole. She's right. It's only Morgan with Jasper—a guy she's had her sights on for weeks—and Zeke. Jasper is a sophomore, and Zeke is a senior. Wes is a junior. Not that it matters; they all still hang out together, but I know that neither of them is in Wes's minuscule inner circle of one, aka Kai.

"I think I'll hang back anyway," I mumble and pull my hand from my friend's.

"King," Mags calls out after me, but I'm already halfway to my room.

Between last night and this almost-encounter, I need a break.

I've been a loner my entire life, which has changed some since settling here, but it still becomes too much at times.

Kiwi has taken like a fish to water with the friends I made. He'll come find me if he needs to. Lying on my bed, I plug my headphones in and press play. With "Seven Nation Army" by the White Stripes assaulting my eardrums, I close my eyes.

## CHAPTER FOUR

**WES**

"IT'S ABOUT TIME. YOU HAD A LITTLE UNDER TWO HOURS LEFT. I already pulled up the airline page." Her irritation makes the corners of my mouth twitch.

Straddling my bike, I'm parked in front of the field house, about to head to practice. I'm holding on to the bike with one hand, flipping the lid of my wireless headphones open and shut with the thumb of my free hand. I laugh, glancing over the handlebar. "Awww, D, you know I would never miss one of your deadlines. I was busy with class and training."

"Bullshit, Weston. You don't have practice on Mondays. I expected your call yesterday. The twenty-four hours was a courtesy," Den sneers.

She's got me there, and I can't even be pissed at her for calling me out on my cowardliness. I avoided her as long as possible, but knowing I'd miss her allotted cutoff if I'd waited until after practice, I finally hit the dial button.

When I don't reply, her voice softens. "You don't want me to bring *them* up."

My jaw clenches, and I have to force my teeth apart to respond. "You know I don't."

It takes a Herculean amount of strength to keep my voice steady. I'd rather get a root canal without anesthetics than talk about my former friends.

"It's been two years, Wes," she says calmly. Den sided with me when Rhys used Lilly's money and bought my way into Pine Hill—that much I found out over time. Lilly wasn't a hundred-percent on board with her boyfriend's *good deed*, but she also didn't stop him. My anger toward her has slightly lessened, but the betrayal that makes my throat burn and every muscle in my body tense is as strong as ever.

Am I overreacting? According to Den and my mother...yes.

Do I care? Hell no.

My sole focus is on getting my lost future back. Everything—and *almost* everyone—else is of no interest to me.

FAST-FORWARD TO THE PRESENT, and I'm still in shock that MPU let me in. Through sheer luck, one of Mom's oldest friends had recently moved to Montana and taken a job in the school's administration department. She connected me with Coach Still-water the same day Mom called her. And to my even bigger surprise, Coach wanted to talk to me. He never listened to gossip, as he informed me during our first meeting. He was born and raised in Stonebriar. His father was the head coach before him, and he'd had a professional career in his future until a minor injury set him back. He was dropped overnight, never given a chance again. If he took me on to piss in fate's pretty face or because he truly believed in my talent, I don't know. I want to think it's the latter. Either way, I will always be grateful to him.

"D, let it go." I hate fighting with her, and I know it will end in one of us hanging up on the other. "Please."

"Just tell me if you got the invitation so I can let Lilly know." Her frustration comes through the speaker in waves.

My hand drops from the handlebar to my thigh, fingers curling into my leg and squeezing tight. They damn well know I did. Rhys said as much in his message. "I did."

*Fuck, my jaw hurts.*

"Are you going to RSVP?"

Now she's pushing it, and I bark out a sarcastic laugh. "Sure, and while I'm at it, I'll ask for Marcus's number so we can get matching mani-pedis."

It's a low blow, but I need her to stop the harassment. And Marcus is the only way I know she'll drop the topic. The same way I haven't forgiven my former friends, Den is still at war with Lilly's shadow. Him manhandling her on the jet in LA two years ago was a shitty move, but something tells me there is more going on. A secret my best friend has not let me in on—yet.

"I'm coming to visit you for Thanksgiving." She switches gears, and I have to replay it in my head before I comprehend her words.

My heart skips a beat, but I can't shake the feeling of there being an ulterior motive. "Uh, why?" Den always travels with her parents and Oli over the holidays—a tradition the Kellers have had ever since I've known her.

"Oli and Elena are spending this year at her parents' house."

"And your parents?"

"I might have told them that you invited me to spend Turkey Day with you in the snow. Go sledding and all the other winter stuff you mountain people do."

I crack up. "And they bought it?" I ask incredulously.

Everyone knows that Den would rather wear workout clothes to Lilly's big day than spend a day in the cold.

"They did." I can picture her shrugging nonchalantly, but the knowledge that her parents believed it makes my chest ache for her.

I've distanced myself from everyone over the last two years and have refused to visit Westbridge, simply to not be reminded of the past and my broken friendships, but I talk to my parents several times a week. They are fully aware of everything I'm doing—training for the most part—and they know what's going on in my life. What I like and enjoy, and what I don't.

"I'm sorry, D. We'll have a good time," I say and add with a smirk, "Kai is staying this year as well."

I wait for her reaction. Kai and Den get along just fine, but his relentless attempts to get into her pants even drive me nuts.

*Three, two—*

"Oh, fuck no, Sheats. I'm sleeping in your room or getting a hotel. I am not waking up to him jerking off again," Den barks.

*One.*

A wide grin spreads across my face. "Sure thing. We'll figure out an arrangement that'll make everyone happy," I tease.

"Wes," she growls.

"Chill. I'm joking. I would never let you go through that traumatic experience again." It was hilarious, though. I wish I could've seen her face.

Last spring, Den was in town for a few days. It was the first time Kai had stuck around during a school break. They had seen each other many times in the past when she and I video chatted, but Kai meeting her in person...I had never seen my roommate dumbstruck over a girl before.

During her previous visits, I gave her my bed and slept in Kai's room. Fully aware of what went on in there, there was no way I would have made D sleep on that mattress. But with Kai around, she said she'd take the couch in the media room—our converted third bedroom. The couches were too short for either of our six-foot-plus frames, but it worked out for her.

On the second morning, I was ripped out of a deep sleep by my shrieking friend and a cursing roommate.

"WHAT THE FUCK, YOU CREEP!"

"Chill, woman, I was just—owww!"

Kai swore all he did was watch a muted show while D was sleeping, but his raging boner tenting his pajama pants said something different. Den attacked him with a game controller, which resulted in a massive shiner for Kai and a broken controller I had to replace to appease him. Asking Den to pay for it would've resulted in another shiner—on my face. No, thank you.

So, Den visiting over Thanksgiving would be the first time in over two years we'd share a bed. We used to all the time when we were in LA, but that was *before*...

THAT NIGHT STARTS PLAYING in front of my mind's eye. I haven't thought about it recently, but every so often, the memory still breaks through. I don't regret it. At the same time, though, it probably shouldn't have happened. Talk about conflicting feelings.

After getting back from LA, I was in a bad headspace. The loss of two of my three close friends, combined with having no athletic future, had been too much and turned me into a hateful piece of shit. I refused to talk to anyone, including my parents. If someone attempted to address me, I lost it on them. I had never been a hothead, but I had reached my limit. After almost a week, on the day I was supposed to have left for college, Den showed up and dragged me out of the house.

"I don't give a flying fuck. You're coming with me," she announced, pulling me past my mother, who stood by, watching me get *kidnapped*.

Granted, I hadn't left my room in six days and had neglected personal hygiene for just as long. I'm sure Mom was glad to have me out of the house for a while.

After a pit stop at Magnolia's, where Den somehow convinced the barista to make me a turmeric and cinnamon hot cocoa in the middle of August, we went through a local drive-through and ended up at her house. I followed her to her room, where a bottle of her dad's Pappy Van Winkle was already waiting for us.

"This is your way of cheering me up?" I arched an eyebrow at her, still holding the take-out bag she handed to me in the car.

"Shut up." She faced me with her hands on her hips and chin tilted up. "Since I'm the only one who can tolerate going near your reeking body—which, by the way, is quickly losing its defin-ition—this is what we're doing. You get one last night of wallow-ing, then you pull your head out of your sexy ass and fight for your dream. We'll eat crap, get drunk out of our minds, and regret every minute of it tomorrow. But that's what I'll do for my best friend." In a softer tone, she adds, "I can't stand by and watch you suffer any longer."

That was what we did. And much more. And neither of us has acknowledged the "*more*" since I walked out the next morning.

By the time we had finished the food, I had a major buzz going, and Den wasn't far behind. Scratch that; she was way ahead. She downed the amber liquid like I did my cocoa. One could say we drowned our sorrows that night.

Denielle "Den" Keller had the reputation of being The Bull-dog, but she cared like everyone else—probably more, because she was so protective over the people she loved. She wouldn't often show her feelings, but over the last few months, she had let her guard down around me. She was hurting, even though she barely talked about what had happened over spring break. Finding your longtime boyfriend at a frat orgy, pounding another girl, would've broken anyone's trust in the opposite sex. Not once had Charlie tried to contact her after she *donated* all her cheating boyfriend's crap to Goodwill. I always knew he was a pussy, but I never expected him to be such a fucking coward. He owed her an apology, and one day, I would see to it that she got it.

That evening, though, we used each other to forget for a while. We were lying on Den's king-size bed. I was propped against the headboard with her nuzzled into the crook of my arm while she was watching...whatever it was. My attention span had exited several Pappy's before. I don't remember when or how, but I caught myself playing with her dark locks, curling and uncurling them around my fingers. The sudden realization made me pause, but then Den shifted, and the hand that, until then, had been tucked between us slowly slipped under the hem of my shirt.

*What the hell was she doing?*

Holding my breath, I waited. At first, her hand was splayed out on my lower belly, unmoving, but the sensation of her skin on mine stirred a flutter deep inside of me that had no business being there. This was Den, for fuck's sake. The one friend I had left.

Involuntarily, my abs flexed, and she jerked her hand away. When I didn't move and instead threaded my fingers in her hair again—I was so blaming that on Van Winkle—she started tracing every muscle of my abdomen with her fingertips.

My heart thumped in my throat, and my mouth ran dry. "D?"

The movement halted, and I instantly missed it. She was silent for so long that I thought this was it. "Yes?"

*I should stop this, but do I want to?*

Den was still dealing with the Charlie aftermath, not to mention what we went through in LA a few months ago and the letter that took my future away the previous week.

Instead, I remained mute, and her fingers started their pattern again, leaving a trail of heat where they connected with my skin.

The bourbon was muddling my rational thinking, and I closed my eyes, losing track of what I was going to say.

*Fuck!*

The fire spreading through my veins, combined with the burn in my stomach, felt so good after days of being trapped in a cold void. I angled myself slightly toward her, letting my free hand rest on her hip. Den's face was now in the crook of my neck, and I could feel her rapid breathing against my collarbone.

Goose bumps broke out on my entire body, and my groin

responded in kind with the pulsing, tensing flex of urges awakening in me. When she made no indication of stopping us, I nudged my leg between hers, slowly tracing figure eights inside the crook between her pelvis and hip bone—God, her skin was so soft. Her exhales sped up, and I took that as her approval to keep going. My hand glided up her arm to her neck. With my thumb caressing her cheek, I could feel her thudding pulse under my palm.

*I shouldn't be this turned on.*

Den's hand moved to my back, and she ground herself against my thigh. This was the best and, at the same time, most surreal moment of the last few months—and that said a lot. When the tips of her fingers slipped underneath the waistband of my sweats, and her nails dug into my ass, all bets were off. This was a really bad idea, but holy shit, I needed this.

With my forefinger under her chin, I tilted her head up and met her gaze. Her lids were hooded, and our noses touched, her warm breath fanning over my lips.

"Last chance, Bulldog." My tone was raspy, and I was giving her an out.

She visibly shivered instead of going off on me for using her much-hated nickname. I rarely called her by it to her face, but somehow, it felt right. She was in charge of the situation.

Instead of responding, pulling away, or making any other attempt to end this—whatever this was—she closed the distance.

At the feel of her mouth on mine, my body went into autopilot. I pulled her on top of me, one hand in her hair, the other squeezing her firm ass through her yoga pants. I'd joked so many times about her well-defined butt—just to get a rise out of her— but actually having my hand on it was a whole different story. Den rubbed herself against my raging hard-on, and every muscle inside coiled at the sensory overload. It had been too long.

As soon as she parted her lips in a moan, my tongue slid inside. There was no more waiting. I let go of the long strands of her hair, and my hand slapped her other ass cheek. I didn't think I had ever done that to a girl, but the frantic kiss and the need took over my actions. Her tongue tangling with mine in perfect synchronization set every cell inside of me on fire.

*Yes!*

I sat us up and grasped the hem of her shirt. Den lifted her arms, and in one swift motion, I threw the fabric off to the side. The instant it dropped from my hands, they were back on the girl straddling my lap. My eyes could barely focus, thanks to my intoxication, but I was able to make out enough for my cock to get even harder. Finding her breasts covered in the sexiest black bra, I traced the lace border with my index finger, the swell of her breast rising and falling with her labored breathing.

"Your turn." She leaned in and exhaled the words against my ear. Den mimicked my actions, pulling my tee over my head and dropping it off to the side.

I drew her into me again so that our bodies were flush against each other. The heat radiating off her burned my naked chest in the best possible way. Her lips were back on mine, and I thrust up, grinding myself against her like a horny teenager in heat—all of which I was.

Trailing kisses along her jawline and down her neck, I pulled the straps of her bra down, freeing her perky tits.

"Fuck, you're gorgeous," I mumbled before swiping my tongue over one of her nipples.

"Wes." My name on her lips spurred me on even more. Never in a million years would I've thought I'd have a half-naked Denielle Keller sitting on my cock.

I cupped her other breast while I captured her hard bud between my tongue and top teeth with a gentle tug and rolled it between them.

A loud moan escaped her throat. "If you don't fuck me soon, I am going to take matters into my own hands, Sheats." Her crass words were the biggest turn-on, and I pulled her hips forward against my erection. She leaned into me, and when she bit down on my shoulder, I flipped her on her back in one fluid move.

I had no clue I was into this kind of foreplay, but holy hell, the sting from the bite pushed my need to be inside of her to a whole new level.

Hovering above her, we stared at each other for a long moment, both breathing erratically. The alcohol had somewhat left my system, but not enough for me to want to stop us—unless she put the brakes on. I was too far gone. Plus, my dick would've never forgiven me.

I sat back on my heels on the bed and curled my fingers into the waistband of her leggings. Slowly peeling the tight fabric off her toned legs, my breath hitched when I discovered that she was going commando.

Her eyes twinkled with mischief, and I smirked. "A girl after my own heart."

She quirked one of her perfectly shaped eyebrows, and I stood up on the bed—slightly wobbly between the shifting mattress and the remaining bourbon in my system—and shoved my sweats down, my dick springing free.

Den licked her lips, and I was about to blow just at the sight of her tongue darting out and the thought of her taking me into her mouth. She must've read my mind, because she shifted to her knees, wrapping her hand around me.

"Fuck," I hissed incoherently.

Her mouth was less than an inch from the tip of my cock. At the warmth and moisture from her breath against my head, I closed my eyes, ready for—

Den's phone started blaring "Good Goodbye" by Linkin Park somewhere in the room, and it was like a bucket of ice had been poured over my head. Both of them. Not only was that Lilly's ringtone, but it also sobered me up enough for sanity to start shouting in my head about what I was thinking.

I was about to fuck my best (female) friend. Being trashed or not, this could've ruined everything. The song cut off, and the call either went to voice mail or she hung up. Not that I cared. What I did care about, though, was the girl whose swollen lips were way too close to my painfully hard dick. He didn't get the memo that this would've been a disastrous idea.

This was Den. Not one of the girls I used to make out with at a party. I loved her, but not in that way. Just as the realization hit, D sat back and looked up through her dark lashes. We stared at each other for a long time, her hand still wrapped around me.

I slowly lowered myself back down to the mattress, taking hold of her wrist and interlacing our fingers as we sat mostly naked in front of each other.

In an attempt to not make this beyond awkward and lose my last friend, I let a smirk creep up my face. After a second, she mimicked my expression. There was no embarrassment, but we were on the same page.

"Friends?" I asked. *Please say yes.*

She cocked her head, thinking for a moment. "Best friends."

With that, she leaned off to the side, hanging half off the bed, and retrieved her shirt. I followed suit, and we dressed without another word. Fully covered, I settled back against the headboard and lifted my arm, indicating for her to come close again.

"Hey, D."

"Hmm?" She was suddenly extremely interested in the TV again.

"Would a best friend take care of my blue balls—the ones *she* caused?" I made my tone drip innocence.

"Ha!" she barked out a laugh, but that was all the response I got. Guess they'd be the aching reminder of what almost happened between us.

I stayed the night in her bed. Despite being sobered up, neither of us was capable of driving. But that was the last time we shared a bed. And we never spoke of what had almost happened.

. . .

After the phone call and my trip down memory lane, the last thing I want to do is go to practice. But at the same time, it is the distraction I need from Lilly and Rhys's upcoming wedding. Or the fact that D and I would be sharing a bed in a few weeks. Whenever I do think about that night, I always come to the same conclusion: I'm fucking glad we got interrupted. I don't believe I would've lost her as my friend, but things would've changed. And I don't want things to change for us. There has been too much change already. I'd almost say, not fucking each other's brains out in a drunken haze has brought us even closer.

D and I text a few more times over the following days to talk about her visit. She actually seems excited to come during the winter.

Friday after practice, Zeke, one of the seniors on the team, hollers from his shower stall that he and the guys are going for drinks. All I want is to crash, but Kai immediately pulls his head out of his locker, calling that he's in. Fuck me. Knowing that my roommate will annoy me the entire weekend if I go home at nine o'clock on a Friday, I relent. Guess we're going out.

Kai follows me home, and we drop off my bike and his Rover and take an Uber back downtown.

"What is this place?" I glance at the sign above the door—another place with one of those ridiculous names.

"Oh, get over it. You've been here long enough." Kai laughs and slaps me on the shoulder. "Zeke met this dude at a party last weekend, and he wants to scope out the situation."

My brow furrows. "Scope out how?"

"The guy was all over some chick at the party. Hugging and kissing her." Kai shrugs.

That's...odd. Zeke doesn't make a secret out of his orientation. Why would he not ask the dude out when he had the chance?

"Well, let's figure out if Zeke stands a chance against a random girl."

One hour, then I'll find a way to bail.

I follow Kai into the place and am pleasantly surprised. This was not what I expected based on the name or the exterior. I can make this work.

"There they are," Kai shouts over his shoulder, and I follow along, making sure I don't lose him. The bar is packed with MPU students.

We come to a halt next to Zeke and Jasper, who's being mauled by his new girlfriend. Zeke is chatting with a guy a little shorter than him with dark hair. They're laughing, and my teammate touches the guy's arm. It seems they got it sorted out which way he swings.

"This is Devon," Zeke calls our way.

Devon's eyes land on me and nearly bulge out of their sockets.

*What the—?*

Just then, the music cuts off and "S&M" by Rihanna suddenly blasts through the speakers. The whole bar erupts into cheers, and Devon drops his head in resignation. When he lifts his chin again, he looks straight at me. I'm about to ask him what his fucking problem is when a movement to my left catches my attention.

Two girls are climbing on top of the bar, singing along and dancing in a way that probably gives every guy in the room an instant boner.

The brunette reminds me of D for a second, and I smile. She'll like this place. Then, my gaze wanders to the other dancer. She is blonde and holding a bottle of tequila in one hand and a glass in the other. Shaking her hips, she pours a drink and hands it to someone lining the bar. I let my gaze wander up her long legs barely covered by cutoff jeans that show part of her ass. Moving up, I take in her cropped white shirt with the bar's logo stretched over her chest. I linger on her tits for a moment before finally looking at her face.

That's when my heart falters, and my jaw drops. No. Fucking. Way!

The girl twirls expertly on the narrow bar, and when she faces the main room again, her eyes find mine. How the hell she is able to spot me in a place packed to the max, I have no clue. But she does. Her lips part in shock, and everything fades into the background. We stare at each other for God knows how long when she suddenly thrusts the bottle at the other girl, whose gaze is also on me, frozen in surprise.

MOAB Girl scrambles off the bar and disappears through the nearest door.

My heart is pounding in my chest, and I have no clue what to do.

I force my gaze away from the bar and search for Devon, who clearly expected this to happen, but he is nowhere in sight.

*What the fuck is going on?*

## CHAPTER FIVE

### KING

"It's almost time," Mags shouts over the music, and I nod without taking my eyes off the bottles in front of me, tapping my index finger to my chin.

Over the last few months, I started making my own drinks. A customer would tell me a flavor they liked, what type of alcohol (also, what they didn't want), and I mixed up a cocktail. It'd gotten so popular that Grizz hired another bartender to work twice a week so I could solely concentrate on my creations. One of those nights is Friday, when Mags and I also put on our *Coyote Ugly* show, as we've dubbed it. I had never heard of the movie until Mags made me watch it five times in a row last winter.

She knew I could dance—not through professional lessons, but I knew how to move. You could say I was self-taught. You learned quickly to adapt when you were, more or less, forced into the job I did for almost four years.

"We should do that. Grizz would shit his pants." I was mostly joking, though I did miss the dancing part in my current gig. It was great exercise and, if I was honest with myself, fun— as long as I wasn't groped doing it.

Mags beamed like I had told her she was getting all my tips for the next week while covering her shift as well as my own. "Hell, yeah! Let's do it."

"Uh." A fluttery feeling in my stomach forced me to swallow hard. Why was I nervous? I had danced in front of complete strangers six nights a week—sometimes seven if money was tight or another collection popped up. But dancing in front of my... friends—I even considered Grizz part of that group—the mere thought made my mouth run dry. "I don't know if that's such a good idea. Grizz wouldn't like us scratching up his precious bar."

*Excuses, excuses*, my inner voice laughed at me.

But that wasn't even a lie or too far-fetched. One night, when we sat down after a shift, Grizz opened up a teensy-tiny bit. It wasn't anything about his private life (which was still very much a secret) but how he ended up choosing everything for the bar. For my boss, this was almost as intimate as if I were to confess how I ended up in Stonebriar. The bar top was some super-rare reclaimed black walnut from...I don't remember. In short, it cost a shit ton of capital, and scuffing it up with shoes was the last thing I wanted to have on my conscience.

"Boo hoo. I'll take care of it. Don't worry your sexy behind over it." Mags shoulder bumped me, sitting next to me on the couch while the credits for the movie were rolling across the screen.

I scowled at her. "One of these days, you're going to tell me what the story behind you and Grizz is."

She still hasn't let me in on it.

I grab the Ki No Bi Sei off the shelf. "That will go well with what I have in mind," I mumble to myself—not that anyone would've heard me over Kid Cudi's "The Mood."

I tap my cell, which is lying on the backside of the bar, for the exact time and pause. Eight texts from Kiwi.

*What the—*

The song cuts off, and I know what comes next. We always

dance to the same song—the same song she first made me dance to after telling her what I used to do for a living.

Rhianna's voice comes through the speaker, and my mouth automatically pulls up in a wide grin. Who am I kidding? I fucking love these four minutes and three seconds on top of the bar each week. For 243 seconds, I am neither Kingsley Monroe, the girl who rents Mags's spare bedroom in Stonebriar, Montana, nor King, the star attraction of The Pole. I'm...me.

I'd have to message Kiwi back after the number to see what is going on. He's supposed to have a date tonight.

Toeing my shoes off, I grab the tequila and a shot glass from under the bar and climb on top. Moving my hips to the rhythm, I lip-sync the lyrics and pour one of the many free drinks we hand out during our performance—probably another reason Friday is now bringing in double the customers. I spin on the tips of my toes and am about to hand the guy in front of me the glass when my gaze is drawn to the far side of the room. I usually never look around. Dancing on top of a narrow bar is challenging enough, and doing so while not paying attention...rookie mistake. But it's like a magnetic pull, and the instant my eyes lock on their target, it is as if someone has swiped the bar out from under me. Adrenaline surges through my body.

*No, no, no.*

What is he doing here? His mouth falls open, and I know this is it. He recognizes me. Recognizes me because I exposed myself to him a week ago.

*Oh, God.*

I need to get out of here. Turning toward Mags, who has also noticed him, I thrust the bottle and glass at her with so much force that the tequila spills over both of us. Not that I care.

Scrambling off the bar, I beeline for the nearest door. I don't stop in the small storage room that holds our inventory that doesn't get displayed on the mirrored glass shelves. Instead, I pull the door to the back hallway open.

Halting in my tracks, I look around. My mind is racing a

million miles a second. What do I do? Is that why Kiwi blew up my phone in the middle of my shift? My phone. Shit, shit, shit. I left it behind the bar. I need to go. Thank fuck my purse—including my car keys—is in my locker. I can drive home and wait for Mags to finish her shift. Kiwi will bring me my phone. He'll help me figure out what to do. I have to leave town. God, I don't want to move again—be *on the move.* I fell in love with this place the minute I exited the highway. Back then, I had no intention of staying, but that was before I met my friends. My heart is hammering in my chest, and with every step toward our employee lounge, my stomach sinks. I'll be on the run again. I don't have a choice. Weston Sheats knows I exist—something that never should've happened. I draw in a deep breath. Kiwi will understand. He can stay. He doesn't have to follow me.

I throw open the door to the break room and beeline to my locker. My vision turns blurry as I fumble with the combination lock. When it doesn't open, I let out a frustrated scream. "Arrrrrgh!"

A hand covers mine as I ferociously pull on the lock. I yelp in surprise and whirl around.

"Roe-Roe, it's me." As I take in Kiwi's concern, my tears spill over.

"He saw m-me," I whisper.

Kiwi dips his head in confirmation, then turns to my locker and spins the dial in quick succession, pulling the door open. Of course he knows the combination. Kiwi knows everything about me.

Grabbing my bag and jean jacket, I face my best friend.

"Go. I'll meet you at your place. I'll help Mags finish up." Relief spreads through me, and I could kiss him.

I'm about to turn away when he takes my hand.

"Don't do it, King." Kiwi using my real name tells me how serious he is, and I smash my lips together. "Roe-Roe," he presses.

Shuffling my feet, my gaze dips to the floor between us. I

can't lie to him. Never could. A finger touches under my chin and gently tilts my head back up. "Do not leave me. If you need to move on, I am coming with you. Do we understand each other?" His tone is low, and his usual joking demeanor is nowhere in sight.

I briefly close my eyes. When I let my lids flutter open, I hold his gaze. "Yes."

Kiwi nods and lets go of me. I spin on my heels and dash out the door and down the corridor leading to the parking lot behind the building.

I lean against the metal door with my shoulder, applying more force than necessary. It flies open and slams into the brick wall behind it.

*Shit.*

As I walk toward my Jeep, my head is down while I dig through my bag in search of my car keys. "Where the fuck are you?"

"Leaving early?" The one voice I've craved to hear directed toward me for over a year yet never wanted to be addressed with makes my step falter.

*Oh, please no.*

I slowly lift my gaze and find him leaning against the side of my Jeep.

I swallow hard, and there is a shift deep inside of me. My self-preservation mode slams into gear, and I let it happen, even though I swore to Kiwi I would never become that person again. But it's the only way, no matter what my heart wants.

I let the numbness spread through every cell of my body—a trick I adapted years ago. When you don't feel, you can't get hurt. Physically or emotionally. You're an empty shell. I set my face, void of any emotion, and force the words out. "Do I know you?"

Wes arches an eyebrow in a perfect semicircle and folds his arms over his chest. His bulging biceps stretch the fabric of his white T-shirt to the max, and I wouldn't have been surprised to hear a ripping sound. And why does the possibility excite me so much? He looks nothing like the kid who was plastered all over the papers and internet when the news of the Babysitter case broke.

Back then, the gossip sites had a field day when it became public knowledge that UG had dropped him because of his association and friendship with Lilly. I dug up every single article I could get my hands on after the day I ran into him—literally.

My mind drifts to that day last October.

Besides flirting free meals out of innocent college students while on the move, I also sat in on several lectures a week. I chose my temporary homes based on the schools and if they offered the subjects I needed. Not that I would get credits for them—I couldn't afford a degree—but that didn't stop me. One day I would be able to, when I saved up enough to go to a real school and pursue my dream. Which was why I continued the habit after I settled in Stonebriar.

Mags had *intercepted* me three days earlier. I had moved my meager belongings into her spare bedroom and started my bartending gig. For the first time in a long time, I felt somewhat normal—like I belonged.

I was leaving the criminology lecture and was late for the next class. Not that I had to be on time; I wasn't an official student at MPU. But being late would mean drawing attention—and that I didn't want. I made sure the professors knew I was in class, got their permission, and as long as I wouldn't disrupt the lectures, they let me sit in the back and take my notes. All in all, it was a great deal if I could ever make use of what I learned... *one day*.

I was speed walking out of the hall, head down, reading a text Kiwi had sent sometime during the last two hours, when I ran face—or more forehead—first into a hard chest. A very hard chest.

"Holy shit, girl, slow down," a laughing male voice said before moving around me.

"Sorry," I mumbled, then paused.

*Wait! I had heard that voice before. Where had I heard that voice?*

The guy was already moving on, and I jerked my head up to get a glimpse of whomever it was. I didn't know anyone in this town, which was why I chose it. His back was to me as he walked down the corridor next to a tall blond guy who looked like he had jumped out of a surfing magazine. The speaker was blond, tall, and built. I'd seen lots of guys like that over the years, but something was familiar. Then, he turned over his shoulder and peered back once more. Locking eyes with him, my heart thudded to a complete stop. How was this possible?

Rooted in place, I stared at Weston Sheats's retreating form. Wes, the best friend of Lilly McGuire. Holy fucking shit. Now it clicked why the voice was so familiar. I had seen some of the interviews after the case made national news, and of course, I followed the fallout. Everyone did. It was huge. Everyone who was part of the events for longer than thirty seconds was put under a microscope.

Then, life happened, also known as my power and cable got shut off. *Again*.

It took me a few extra shifts before I could pay the bill to turn the electricity back on, but the cable and internet was put on the back burner. Whenever I asked Kiwi, he refused to let me watch footage about the case. He was acting all weird and overprotective, which was somewhat understandable. Maybe he sensed my attraction toward Wes even then. But that was all it was. Wes was good-looking, and seeing him on the screen stirred something in my chest I wasn't used to. But I had other priorities.

By the time I could afford my internet access, the reports had trickled down to reruns of Lilly, and I lost interest.

Blinking, I followed Wes and the surfer dude around the corner.

*What the hell was he doing here?*

That day, I picked up my research on Weston Sheats, and my slight fascination became a very unhealthy obsession.

Almost one year later, I knew everything there was to know about MPU's tight end and former best friend of Lilly and Rhys. I found out that he hadn't seen them since he left LA two years ago, and I suspected it had something to do with why he ended up here. The only person from his past that showed up regularly was Denielle Keller. She visited him, but he never went back to Virginia—that much was apparent from her public social media account and her complaints about the cold in Montana. I hadn't been able to pinpoint their relationship. Was there something going on? Whenever I thought about that possibility, a burning sensation spread through my chest.

Wes grew out his blond hair, almost to chin length, with the sides shaved. He came back like that from winter break, which he had spent with Kai. He wore it in a man bun, and girls on campus flocked around him wherever he went. Not that I blamed them. Fuck that, I did blame them. I hated every single one of them for being able to talk to him openly, touch his arm in a flirtatious manner, and do whatever else they got to do to him.

A LOW GROWL comes out of my throat at the memory of the last time I witnessed exactly that, and I realize I had completely spaced out.

Fuck! Feeling my face heat, I focus again on the present and the guy still lounging against my car.

Wes's mouth quirks up at the corner and— *Why does he have to be so gorgeous?*

I fight the urge to slap my forehead. Focus! I lower my arm that is still holding up my bag from searching for my goddamn keys and widen my stance. I slant my head and give him my best bored-out-of-my-mind *impression.*

"I asked you a question." I lace my tone with annoyance. I can do this. I've done this for years. Just turn it off. My heartbeat is slowing the more I repeat my old mantra in my head, and I can sense the numbness creep through my body. This means nothing to me. *He* means nothing to me.

"I asked you a question first," he counters.

*What the fuck?*

Frustration eclipses the numbness, which is still better than me drooling at his feet. I need to get out of here. I take a step forward.

"Get off my car," I say, grinding the words out through clenched teeth.

"And if I don't?" he taunts.

I fight the urge to stomp like a toddler. An idea forms in my mind, and a slow smile spreads across my face. I tilt my head, reaching behind me. Wes follows the movement, and his eyes widen when he sees what I'm holding.

"You can't be serious." He glances between my CRKT Du Hoc and me. My CRKT Du Hoc fixed blade is one of the two knives I take everywhere for multiple reasons. Grizz's customers assume it's my fancy, eccentric way to cut their limes, not that this blade holds several memories for me—good and bad.

"I asked you nicely. I'm not repeating myself." All emotion has left me. This is the old King, the one I never wanted to be again. But if this is the way to get rid of him, I have to let her come out and play.

Wes stares at the curved blade for a long moment before pushing off the Jeep. I fight the urge to exhale in relief, but then he strides forward casually and steps right into my personal space. I have to crane my neck to look at him. Damn him for being so tall. He studies me, and the intensity of his stare makes me want to squirm. I've dreamed for a year of being this close to him, and now that I am, all I want is to run. People always want their dreams to come true, but it's better if this dream remains a dream. There is no Wes and King. There is only a Wes and a King on completely different playing fields.

Wes leans down until our noses almost touch, and I hold my breath. What the hell is he doing?

"I'm going to figure you out, MOAB Girl," he whispers, so close to my lips I can feel his warm breath mingle with mine. With that, he straightens and walks around me down the alley leading to the front of the bar.

I'm rooted in place, my legs too weak to move.

*What just happened?*

## CHAPTER SIX

**WES**

A KNIFE. SHE PULLED A FUCKING KNIFE ON ME. WHO THE HELL is this chick?

Common sense would tell you to stay the fuck away from this lunatic. First, she chases me down the freaking road, almost running into the back of my bike, then she bolts when she sees me, followed by threatening me with a blade that could gut a bear.

I've dealt with enough crazy shit to last me a lifetime, yet something deep inside of me stirs, wanting to peel back every single layer and expose who this girl is deep down. My intuition tells me the tough act is real, but there is a reason for it—a good reason—and I itch to figure out what it is. Plus, I can't shake the feeling that I've seen her before. But when or where?

There is no way I would've forgotten if she had been one of my drunken sexual escapades, as D calls them. Now that I have gotten a glimpse of her entire face, I got my confirmation that she is truly beautiful. Her eyes are the lightest blue I have ever seen; I definitely would've remembered those. She's around Den's height, her dark-blonde hair hangs in casual waves down her back, and her tan tells me she spends a lot of time outside—which is not hard, given where we live.

I stride casually to the front of the bar, not looking back. I know she's watching me, and no matter how badly I want to see her pale eyes again, I force myself to keep moving.

As I round the corner to the street, I almost smack into Kai, who apparently came looking for me. After she jumped off the bar, I raced out of The Grizz. Something told me she would make a run for it, and I was right. It was easy to spot her badass Jeep in the back parking lot. All I had to do was wait. I was not prepared for her, though.

*A. Knife.*

"Dude, what the fuck was that?" Kai is still holding his beer, and I grasp it out of his hand and take down half of it.

He frowns, pursing his lips, and I shrug. I didn't tell him about the strange encounter with her a week ago, so clearly, my behavior tonight borders on "he finally lost his mind."

"Let's go inside. I want to talk to Zeke's new flame," I say as I hold the bottle back out.

"Bro, I love you, you know that, but I draw the line at sharing a beer with you. I don't want your cooties." My roommate looks mortified.

"Ha!" I bark out a laugh. "I should be more worried about where your mouth has been."

Kai strokes his chin with his thumb and forefinger, grinning. "I guess that's a fair point. I did see Kennedy yesterday and—"

I punch him in the shoulder. "Shut the fuck up."

I pull the door open to the bar and walk inside. Zeke is still at the same table, but his boy toy is nowhere in sight.

"Where is Devon?" I yell over the music.

Rhianna has been replaced with "Antisocial" by Ed Sheeran and Travis Scott.

Zeke glances in my direction before pointing his chin toward the bar. I follow his gaze and find Devon now manning the bar with the brunette who was dancing with MOAB Girl earlier.

I turn to head in the direction of the guy who would give me answers, whether he wanted to or not, when Zeke grabs me by the arm. "What the fuck is going on?" He scowls.

I glance between his face and his hand on me, and he drops it quickly. I like Zeke, consider him a friend, but he knows that no one touches me without consequence. An unfortunate side effect of developing a temper, my fuse blows easily.

When I don't answer, he says, "Don't mess this up for me. Please."

Some of my *determination* lessens, and I dip my chin in confirmation.

As I reach the bar, Devon glances at me out of the corner of his eye, not showing any reaction. He is fully aware of why I am here, yet he doesn't seem to care.

*Interesting.*

The brunette stops in front of me. "What can I get you?"

Her tone is too cheery. I saw her mirrored shock when MOAB Girl noticed me—or more like I noticed her. They're friends; there is no question in my mind. But I won't play that card yet.

I nod my head in Devon's direction. "Him."

A smirk forms on her mouth. "Well, well, I didn't know that MPU's football star swings that way."

She wants to play games, then we shall play games. I put on an innocent pout, pretending to consider it. "I'm always open to trying new things."

I can see her fighting a smile. "I don't think you're his type."

I cock an eyebrow. "Oh yeah? Whose type am I?"

She bursts out laughing, then points a finger at me. "You're good, Weston Sheats. I'm not telling you shit." Then, she winks and saunters toward Devon. She places a hand on his shoulder, indicating for him to lean down, and whispers something in his ear. His eyes fly to mine, and he jerks his head up and down.

I plant my ass on one of the barstools and wait. They want to ignore me? Fine. I have time.

To my surprise, it only takes a few minutes before Devon makes his way over to me.

"Wes," he greets me with a blank expression.

I'm impressed as I see the same shift in him as I observed in MOAB Girl earlier. It's like they flip a switch and are a completely different person—one without personality.

"You know my name," I state.

"Zeke mentioned it." Most people probably wouldn't recognize the lie, but I do.

"Did he now?" I challenge him, calling bullshit.

"Did you want to order something? I have more customers." He sounds bored, and I fight the urge to applaud him. His performance is good.

"I wasn't aware that you work here. I thought you were on a date tonight," I push.

He picks up a glass from somewhere under the counter and starts polishing it with the hand towel he's holding. "Filling in for a friend."

"Yeah, she seemed to have to leave rather urgently." I nod thoughtfully.

Devon's shoulders slump, and he glances in the brunette's direction. I follow his gaze and find her watching us closely.

When he turns to me, his mouth is in a thin line. He's visibly fighting with himself. Opening and closing his mouth, he finally sighs, "You need to stay away from her."

I'm about to reply where he can shove his protectiveness when he adds, "She's not good for you."

*Wait, what?*

*She* is not good for *me*? That was not what I was expecting.

"Who is she?"

"She is my best friend. And I'll do whatever it takes to protect her."

"From me?" I ask incredulously.

"From herself." With that, he turns and walks to the other end of the bar.

The brunette heads back over to my side. After she peers over her shoulder, she plants both palms on the bar and levels me with a serious stare. "You won't get anything out of him."

"Why not?"

"Because he and King have been through hell together."

*King.* I school my features to not give away that she just provided me with more information than I hoped for.

"What's your name?" I redirect.

I expect her to refuse to answer. Instead, she holds out her hand. "Maggie. But I think you can call me Mags."

"You think?"

"My friends all call me Mags, and I'm sure I'll see you around."

After this bizarre encounter—all three of them—we stayed another thirty minutes before Kai had reached his public limit, and it was time to call it a night. He could finish at home, where I didn't have to watch him too closely. I would simply confiscate his car keys as usual and let him drown his...whatever his reason was that he always drank himself into oblivion.

I DUMP him on the sectional in the living room, and he lets his head fall back, eyes closed.

"Why did you chase the girl?" he mumbles, barely audible.

I peer back, assessing his ability to focus on the conversation if I were to tell him what happened a week ago.

Kai opens his eyes and peers at me sideways. "I'm not that drunk, asshole."

I huff out a laugh and make my way over. Dropping on the couch, I plant my feet on the fancy coffee table Kai—or more like his interior designer—furnished the place with.

He turns his head in my direction and waits.

Rubbing my hands over my face, I try to sort through it in my head. After another deep breath, I recount the event after TMH to him, followed by seeing her tonight and wanting to confront her in the parking lot. I tell him about the knife and her friend saying she was not good for me. The only thing I keep from Kai is that Mags slipped and revealed her name: King.

Just thinking her name stirs something in my jeans.

*What the fuck is wrong with me?*

"Dude, I could swear I know her from somewhere." That thought has driven me nuts for the past week.

With his eyes closed, Kai had been listening to me the entire time, and I debate if he had paid attention until he says, "You ran into her about a year ago."

*Excuse me, what?*

"What the fuck are you talking about?" His bombshell makes me jerk into an upright position.

"I don't remember the exact date, but you ran into her—literally," he says, as if he was reminding me we had pancakes for breakfast.

I glower at him, biting my tongue. If I lash out, he'll clam up to spite me.

Kai smirks. "You don't remember, do you?"

My fingers curl into fists. I could beat it out of him.

Thankfully, it doesn't come to that. He pushes himself into an upright position and lets his elbows rest on his thighs. He tips the side of his head with his forefinger. "Photographic memory, remember?" Then he smirks. "Or not."

*I'm going to pound his face.*

He must see that I'm about to snap. "Chill out, bro. We were on our way to class. She came out of Professor Steward's criminology lecture and ran into you because she wasn't paying attention."

I rack my brain but come up blank. "How do you know what lecture hall it was?" Neither one of us nor any of our teammates takes any criminology courses.

"This chick I banged took that course, and I walked her there a few times."

I scowl at him.

"Not your chick. Jesus, you're wound tightly about her." He looks exasperated.

"I'm not—"

"You are." He cuts me off. "Anyway, she ran into you and then watched you the entire time until we turned the corner. It was like she saw a ghost. Fucking weird."

Fucking weird is an understatement at this point. Who the hell is King, and how does she know me?

I will find out.

---

# CHAPTER SEVEN

**KING**

I LOST TRACK OF HOW LONG I STOOD IN THE PARKING LOT until my feet cooperated again. I made my way to my Jeep on shaky legs, my eyes not leaving the spot Wes had leaned on.

Unlocking my car was another challenge. I needed to start carrying a smaller bag. Though, then I wouldn't be able to have all my essentials with me in case...

PACING the living room for the hundredth time, I begin to second-guess my promise not to leave without Kiwi. He'd forgive me. I would have to grovel for a while, but we'd be okay in the end—we always are.

Echo follows me from her spot on the couch like she's watching a tennis match. It's past midnight. The Grizz doesn't close until two. This will be a long-ass night.

Suddenly, Echo sits up, perking her ears, and I stop mid-stride. What the—? I hear the key in the door and swivel on my heels, expecting Mags to walk in, but instead, I'm locking eyes with Kiwi. He spots me instantly and halts in the doorway. I stare at him with furrowed brows.

"Mags is closing up with Grizz. She sent me ahead to bring you your phone."

*Oh.*

When he hesitates and seconds turn to minutes, a knot forms in my belly. I can read him like an open book. "What is it?" I croak.

He closes the door and walks toward me without a word. Echo jumps off the couch to greet him, but he just absently pats her head. Clue number two: Kiwi would never not give my dog the attention she demands unless—

He holds out my phone, and I slowly lift my hand to take it. Dread builds in my core and spreads through every limb. My fingers tremble as I close them around the device. I hold Kiwi's stare as I pull my hand back and turn the screen toward me. It instantly lights up, and my eyes fly back to my best friend's. My free arm wraps around my stomach in an attempt to contain the dizziness—it's of no use.

Echo nudges me with her nose, whimpering. She senses when I'm upset.

"What does that mean?" I ask in a hushed tone more to myself. Kiwi wouldn't know the answer any more than I would.

"Roe-Roe, let's sit down." He's come closer, and I jump at his sudden nearness. I am too preoccupied with the letters taunting me from the screen.

I let him guide me to the couch, and I drop onto the cushion, unable to avert my eyes from the one name I haven't seen in years: Rae.

The last time I spoke to my sister was when Mom died. She refused to come to the funeral. It was a miracle she even answered my call.

Remembering, my heart rate speeds up, and my body tenses.

I still hear the conversation in my head like it was yesterday and not four years ago.

. . .

*"What do you want, Roe?"*

*I was crying so hard it took minutes to get the words out. "M-mom is d-dead."*

*There was a brief silence on her end. "What do you want me to do about that?" Her tone was like ice. I finally understood why Mom and Rae didn't get along, but she had still raised and cared for her. How could she not care?*

*"C-can you come t-to the funeral? It's this weekend." I wanted my sister there. I wanted my last living family member by my side.*

*"No. Don't call me again." She hung up.*

I HAD TRIED CONTACTING her a few times since, especially when I couldn't pay the mortgage because all my money went toward the hospital bills Mom left behind. Rae never picked up again.

"Do you want me to read it?" Kiwi's question snaps me out of my catatonic state.

*How long have I been sitting here?*

I shake my head and take a deep breath, holding it as I swipe open the message.

**Rae: Roe, he knows where you are. He's coming to get you. You should've kept moving.**

I read the text twice, and with every word, my breathing increases until I can't get the air in fast enough. Black spots appear in my vision. What's going on? How does she know about him? I only confided in Kiwi. I press my palm against my chest. Why can't I breathe?

"Roe-Roe, you need to calm down." Kiwi's voice sounds like I'm underwater.

Need. Air.

A paw touches my leg, followed by a second until Echo is fully crawling into my lap. Her warm tongue licking my chin is what snaps me out of it, and I drop my phone, not caring where it lands.

How did I survive before her? A pair of arms wraps around both of us, and Kiwi leans his cheek against my head. I keep my face burrowed in Echo's fur until I'm in control again.

*This night is getting worse and worse.*

THE CLOCK on the microwave shows that it's 1:32 a.m. Kiwi and I sit at the kitchen table with Echo at my feet. She hasn't left my side, always one part of her trim body pressed against me somewhere.

"I have to leave," I whisper.

I stare at my fingers threaded together with Kiwi's, unable to make eye contact with my friend.

"No, you don't," he says calmly.

*Why doesn't he get it?*

I force myself to meet his gaze. "I was supposed to keep moving. I can't let him come here. If he sees you—"

"Roe." His harsh tone makes me pause. "You know as much as me that I'm not the issue. He's not gonna touch me. The real reason you're losing it is Wes—what he might do to him if he finds out about your little, uh...obsession."

*Motherfucker.* He's right—on both accounts. He would never harm Kiwi. If he wanted to, he would've had the chance. Wes though...

I pry my hands out of his grasp and cover my face, inhaling deeply. At the thought of anything happening to Wes, I feel like I'm being choked. I swipe my hands up and into my hair, taking a fistful and pulling. "This is all my fault. He gave strict orders not to stay anywhere longer than a few weeks. But what did I do? Blew it all to hell because I ran into *Weston Sheats* and developed this unhealthy crush on the guy. I should've known better. *Weston. Sheats.* Look at me." I gesture wildly at myself, and Echo sits up, startled. "Who the fuck stalks a guy like this? Ask me anything about him; I probably know the answer. That fact alone would make anyone run for the hills. I'm a freaking nutca—"

"ENOUGH!"

I flinch at my best friend's outburst. He rarely raises his voice at me, and I don't like it. Kiwi is one of the few people I care about what he thinks of me.

Instead of responding, last week replays in my head like a movie.

*The adrenaline rushing through my veins as I pushed the gas pedal down, Wes's bike coming closer and closer.*

"King."

*As I skirted to a halt next to him, my finger pushed the button to roll the window down. When he saw me—really saw me...*

"KING!"

My head jerks toward Kiwi, who sits leaned back in his chair, arms crossed over his chest.

"WHAT?" I snap.

He cocks a brow and pointedly looks toward my hands. I follow his gaze, and my eyes widen. When did I get that out? I'm holding my Guardian Helix in a white-knuckling grip—with the blade out.

A whimper comes from under the table, and I drop my second favorite knife as if it had burned me.

*Oh, God.*

I wasn't carrying the GH tonight. I only had the Du Hoc with me earlier. My heart is racing in my chest. I haven't lost time in over a year. Not since—

"You had it in your boot." Kiwi's subdued tone penetrates my ears.

*I did?*

I glance down at my worn Doc Marten boots.

"Roe-Roe." My eyes begin to sting at his gentle tone. I'm such a basket case.

Suddenly, Kiwi stands up and pulls me out of my chair. I don't fight him as he drapes his arm over my shoulders and leads me to my room. Echo pads after us, her nails clicking softly on the hardwood floors.

Neither of us turns the light on. Kiwi lets go, pulls his shirt over his head, and unbuckles his jeans. When I continue standing in front of my bed, he takes over. He picks up the sleep shirt I discarded on the mattress this morning, pulls my The Grizz crop top over my head, followed by dressing me for bed like a toddler—arms up, shirt over my head.

He pops the button of my shorts, and inwardly I want to make a joke about how he's so good at opening a girl's pants, but I can't manage to form the words. I'm pretty sure a low chuckle escaped me, though.

If he heard it, he didn't show it. He pulls the comforter back, and before either of us can get in, my dog jumps up and moves to the far end of the mattress.

Kiwi sighs. "At least she's leaving enough space for both of us."

I get in first, and when we're both—all three—tucked in, Kiwi lies on his back, and I'm nestled into the crook of his arm.

*I have no idea what I'm going to do.*


*WHY IS it so fucking hot?*

We don't have AC in our apartment, but it's late September, which means the nights are in the low forties. I shouldn't wake up drenched in sweat. My attempt to turn is blocked from both sides. What the—?

I pause and assess the situation further. Usually, the inability to move would send me into an immediate sense of panic, but there is none. A body is pressed into my back, arms wrapped around my stomach while my face is pressed into...fur. Peace settles over me. I'm sandwiched between my dog and best friend, both radiating more heat than sitting in front of our firepit midday in August.

Last night begins to come back to me.

*Aw, fuck, there goes my happy place.*

I start pushing against Echo, and she grumbles at me—the dog seriously grumbled.

"Move over, girl." I shove harder, and she jumps up, bolting off the bed, but not before stepping on Kiwi and me in the process.

"Owww..." comes a groan from behind me.

Finally having more space, I pull away from the other heat source and sit up, swiping my tangled hair out of my face. My fingers touch something wet, and I let out a string of curses.

"Jeez, Roe-Roe, I know you're not a morning person, but this is a bit extreme, even for you." Kiwi turns on his back, rubbing his hands over his face.

"She drooled all over my hair," I whine. "I have dog slobber all over my head." I'm somewhere between losing my shit and crying. Still assessing if I can fix the damage with dry shampoo, my bedroom door opens, and out of the corner of my eye, I see Echo bolt out into the hallway, knowing precisely that she's the reason for my current mood. Mags appears, holding a mug between both hands, taking in the scene in front of her.

"You need to wash it." Her remark makes my frustration rise even more, and I fight the urge to kick my legs in a temper tantrum.

Of course she can read my mind.

I climb over Kiwi, who is now sprawled out with his hands behind his head, and pass my other friend on the way to the bathroom.

"Psych-major freak," I hiss at her in passing, which makes her grin as she brings her coffee to her lips.

I take my time, fully aware that Kiwi probably has to piss like a horse. But like he pointed out, I'm not a morning person. Actually, you could say I am diabolically evil in the morning— especially running on less than seven hours of sleep and zero caffeine.

Mags has the bedroom with an en suite, which leaves me to

use the hall bathroom. I'm not complaining; it beats living out of my Jeep or my living arrangement before that. I'm grateful for everything I have.

*How long will it last?*

I'm drying my face when someone—Kiwi—hammers against the door. "OPEN UP!"

"Go use Mags's bathroom. I'm not done," I shout back.

"Kingsley!" Kiwi's exasperated use of my full name makes me snicker. Mags doesn't let anyone use her bathroom, and I mean anyone—not even her own sister. She is a weirdo when it comes to that.

When I don't respond, a low thud sounds against the bathroom door. I picture him hitting his forehead against the wood. I count to twenty, being extra salty, before unlocking the door.

Kiwi immediately pushes in and stalks to the toilet.

"Jeez, you could at least wait to whip your dick out until I'm done," I laugh, following his movement in the mirror.

"Fuck you, Roe-Roe," he murmurs as he relieves himself, and it sounds like a waterfall in my small bathroom. "You've seen my dick more than anyone else," he adds when he tucks said man part back into his shorts.

I just shake my head as I rummage for my moisturizer in the cabinet next to the mirror. He's not lying, but it has never been in the way most girls see a dude's privates.

Growing up together, his grandma took care of me whenever Mom worked. I slept at his place, or he at mine, more nights than I slept alone. Especially after my sister... I refuse to go back there.

We'd gotten ready together in the mornings so much that we had a routine between who showered, who got the sink, etcetera. Neither of us wanted to get up earlier to have privacy. Kiwi's interest in his own gender was evident from an early age—the age when it would've become inappropriate for us to see each other naked—so neither parental figure in our lives objected.

Mom was glad I wasn't alone when she worked herself to death —literally.

Kiwi steps up behind me and waits for me to meet his gaze. "I'll wait for you in the kitchen so we can talk."

*Talk.*

I nod and watch him leave the room. My small bathroom suddenly seems like a vast black hole with no way out. A cold shiver runs down my spine, and I know I can't avoid it any longer.

*He is coming here.*

MAGS AND KIWI are sitting at the kitchen table with steaming mugs in front of them. I glance around. "Where's Echo?"

"Where do you think?" Mags huffs out a laugh, and I sigh. I don't have it in me to go back to my room and kick her out of my bed. Last night was an exception—a huuuge exception. I love my dog, but she is not allowed in my bed. She rolls around in the dirt whenever she can, no clue if that has anything to do with her breed or if she's simply a major slob, but I'm not having sand, twigs, and dried leaves in my bed.

I grab my favorite *I don't like mornings* mug, fill it to the rim with liquid energy, and sit down across from Mags at the table. Taking a sip, I look at her closely and tilt my head. "Spill it."

Mags's gaze jerks up.

*Yeah, bitch, I've learned some tricks from you over the last year.*

All the times I had to help her study micro-expressions and body language have started to pay off. Some of the shit stuck with me.

Thankfully, she doesn't try to be evasive or deny it. "I may have given Wes your name." Her admission is so low I have to strain my ears, but I hear it. My jaw drops, and before I can say anything—or lose my shit—she continues. "I didn't realize it until he walked away, and I thought about the conversation again. He tried to hide it, but there was a fraction of a second where he displayed surprise—when I mentioned your name."

*Micro-expressions, I'm telling you.*

My mind goes blank. I don't know what to do.

"I'm so sorry," Mags whispers, and I peer over at Kiwi.

He sits with a grim expression, both hands wrapped around his mug so tightly one would think he's trying to break it.

"Kiwi." I want him to look at me.

As his eyes find mine, the concern is written all over his face, like the neon billboard where my previous place of work advertised what we offered inside.

As we stare at each other, I search for the right words.

"King?" Mags draws my attention back to her.

I wrinkle my forehead in question. I'm still not happy that she revealed my name to Wes, but that's the least of my worries.

"I'm really sorry."

I know she is, and I'm not mad at her. She is not the whack job with stalkerish tendencies running from her past. I force a smile on my face. "It's fine. It wouldn't have been hard for him to find out anyway—he knows where I work."

"True. But still—"

I wave her off. "Wes is not important at the moment."

"Oh?" Her brows knit. "What else happened?"

"I got a message from my sister."

"Your sister? As in, the bitch who wouldn't come to her own mother's funeral? *That sister*?" She purses her lips.

"That's the one." Needing to do something and suddenly feeling extremely thirsty, I take a large sip of my coffee before continuing. "She warned me that *he* is on his way since I am no longer on the move."

"He?" Mags scowls as she repeats the word slowly. Kiwi and I never use his name because of who he is (you never know who is listening in), and Mags has adapted to our habit. She's the only other person I've confided in about my past and what I did. I wait for it to click. "OMG, *he*! What is he doing with your sister?

How? And why would she tell you? I thought you hadn't spoken to her in, uh...years." She doesn't mention my mother's death, and I appreciate that.

"I have no idea what's going on, Mags." I'm as confused as the rest in this room.

I glance over at Kiwi, and on cue, he says, "Roe-Roe wants to leave."

"What?" Mags's wide eyes ping-pong between us. "Why? Is it so bad that he's coming here? I mean, yes, you shouldn't have stayed, but—"

"He's not the most stable person," Kiwi interjects.

Mags ponders that. "What does that mean? I mean, besides all the shit he has done to you."

I sigh. "He's not going to like whose attention I have since last night." I really don't want to get further into my fucked-up past. I want it to stay there—buried.

"But he helped you," Mags tries again.

I scoff. "Just because he took care of E, doesn't mean he cares about me. He likes control. For all I know, he'll call it in as a favor, and God knows what that'll be."

## CHAPTER EIGHT

**WES**

*KING.*

She's all I can think of over the weekend. Who is this girl?

Saturday, I searched the student directory for hours. Not one female student with the first name King attends the school. Eventually, I resorted to compiling a list of every chick whose first name starts with a K and comparing them to social media accounts in Kai's friends list. With my online presence being limited to seventeen friends, one of them being Den and the rest teammates, I'm looking through my manwhore of a roommate's profile and followers now. There's no one named King or with a photo remotely resembling her or her other two friends: Maggie or Devon.

*Fuck.*

I want to go back to the bar, but we have a mandatory team meeting at Coach's house every last Saturday of the month. His way of keeping his players close (or in line, as the team jokes). But if I'm honest, I enjoy those evenings at his old log cabin-style house. It's outside of town and up a mountain, and you can only reach it with four-wheel drive and spiked tires once the first snow hits. I bought my bike when I arrived in Stonebriar, but after the first snow, my parents shipped me the 4Runner. I didn't want to bring it—being part of the past and all—but I needed a car that would work here, and I couldn't afford a new one.

Sunday, I inflict an extra-long torture session, aka running and weight lifting, on my body until I wobble to the locker room on shaky legs. But I needed to pass the time somehow until five when The Grizz opened.

Walking through the front door of the bar, my heart is hammering against my chest. My face is flushed, and I swipe my hands on my jeans in nervous anticipation. I'm acting like a complete idiot. She—King—almost plowed me over with her Jeep, then threatened me with a fucking knife. But here I am, tongue out like an obedient puppy, waiting for his treat.

*She would be a treat, that's for sure.*

The place is still mostly empty. Behind the counter are two dudes I haven't seen before. Neither King nor her friend is in sight. Shit.

I saunter up to the bar and plant my ass on one of the stools. The older guy walks over. He's tatted up his neck and down both arms, his long beard is way past the socially acceptable length of attractive, and his unwashed hair is tied back in what I learned is a man bun. Ever since I lost a bet to Kai over winter break, I have had the same *hairdo*. Losing the bet, I was supposed to shave my head, but thankfully we never defined how much, and I got away with the sides. But when I started tying the rest back, the jersey chasers got out of control. Chicks apparently get all wet for a guy with a girly hairstyle.

"What can I get you?"

He leans his tree trunk-like forearms on the bar top in front of me. This dude is in such a contrast to the high-end interior and the rest of the staff—all younger college-age kids, from what I've observed.

"I'm looking for King." I don't see a reason to beat around the bush. Plus, I don't play games.

His features shift, and I straighten my shoulders automatically. With his mouth pressed to a slit, I notice his fingers curl into fists.

A burning sensation spreads through my chest. Why is this guy reacting this way? Is there something going on between them? Why I care, I'm not sure—but I do.

"Why are you looking for my employee?"

*Employee?*

"You're the owner?" My eyebrows shoot up. I'm briefly distracted from my mission by this inked mountain being the owner of the place.

"You got any problem with that, *kid?*" he sneers at me.

I don't like the way he calls me kid, but going all alpha on him will get me booted out on the street.

"No problem at all." I relax my posture. "So, King? Is she working tonight?" I glance around as if she might jump out of the back room, arms extended like, *Here I am!*

"She is not here."

*No shit.*

It takes every ounce of self-control not to drop a sarcastic remark. "When is she scheduled to work?"

He cocks his head and gives me an up and down examination I haven't seen since Katherine Rosenfield, the fallen queen of Westbridge High.

*Mental note, I need to ask D if there is any new scoop on her.*

I wait for him to answer my question, but he never does. He turns to the side and calls out to the other guy, "Dean?"

"Boss?" Dean answers immediately.

"Give Wes here what he wants on the house, but that's it."

Translation: don't answer his questions. Wait, how does he know my name?

"Hey!" I call after the owner, but he ignores me and disappears into the back corridor.

Dean eventually makes his way over to my end, and I order a beer, not bothering to ask for King.

*Guess I'll be a regular here from now on.*

My hermit days at the townhome are over. Too bad.


I KEEP my eyes open on campus. Every time I see a dark-blonde head with long hair, my stomach vaults, then the girl turns, and the fluttery feeling turns into a clenched, *I got sucker punched in the stomach* sensation.

This is fucking ridiculous, but I can't help that my curiosity is growing with every waking moment I'm in the dark about her.

I spend the next few nights at The Grizz. I head there directly from practice, and Kai is starting to give me a weird look. He's probably not wrong with whatever he's thinking. I'm beginning to feel like a stalker, and for the first time in years, I almost wish I could ask Lilly, with her *skills,* for help. Almost.

On Tuesday, I took over a high top table in the back of the bar. It had great visibility of the entire room and gave me privacy. After getting approached by several girls the first evening, I decided on a low(*er*) profile. I started keeping my hood up, which made me feel even more like a creeper. But without my blond man bun on display, girls seemed to not be as interested. Glowering at every chick like a psycho may have helped as well. No one glances in my direction by Wednesday.

I've already been here my usual two hours, and I'm about to head out when the energy in the room changes. My eyes find her immediately, and my pulse speeds up as if I sprinted a mile. It's past ten, but The Grizz doesn't close until two. It seems she's covering the closing shift, or someone else had to leave.

*Jesus Christ, why do I put so much thought into this?*

King is wearing a similar top to the one she wore last week, but instead of shorts, her toned legs are covered by black skinny jeans, the look completed with black Doc Martens. My cock twitches in my jeans, and I shift in my seat. It appears he forgot the near-death experience we had meeting her the first—and second—time.

Her spine is stiff.

Grizz—Tattoo Guy's name, as I found out—probably called her the minute he left the front room on Sunday. It's so not weird to name a place after yourself in third person—*it totally is.*

She doesn't look around and, instead, heads straight to work. She greets some of the customers who immediately approach her —mostly males—and gets busy. When one of them leans over the counter to hug her, my hand clenches around my beer.

*What the hell?* I have never been the jealous type. I don't know her. Plus, she threatened me just a few days ago.

I watch her from my spot in the corner, knowing that if I approach her, it would end in me most likely getting banned from the bar. But witnessing her smile at one preppy college douche after another, after they basically eye-fuck her, is grating on my nerves. I'll need more beer if I stick around.

After about thirty minutes, I conclude she definitely knows what she's doing. She mixes the drinks without ever looking at a recipe book. And none of them look the same, yet the customers all look like she's handed them liquid gold—or flashed them her perky tits.

*I wouldn't mind that either.*

At one in the morning, I call it a night. I have an early practice and have fulfilled my need to spy. Every time she laughed at something the other bartender said or smiled at a customer, my chest straightened. Her entire face lit up, and I want that reaction directed at me.

Why? No fucking clue. I have other priorities right now, and girls—correction, a girl—was at the bottom of that list. I shake my head at my own idiocy, knowing very well I would be back tomorrow.

The need to uncover the mystery around King is consuming my every waking moment. I even slacked off in practice yesterday, which I haven't done in the last two years. How does she know me? Why does she carry a creepy knife? I peer back over at her—a knife she is currently using to carve an orange into fancy-looking spiral slices. Wait, no, that is a different creepy knife.

*Why does this get me even harder?*

I not so subtly readjust my groin region and get the side-eye from the chick a table over. I throw her my greasiest smirk and complete the show with a wink. She jerks away so fast she almost falls off her chair, and I fight the urge to high-five myself at the picture I'm displaying: dude lurking in a dark corner all night with his hood up and a hard-on.

Getting up, I walk past the bar without taking my eyes off King. When I'm about to pass her, her gaze flits up, and I hold her stare until I would have to walk backward. Neither of us makes any indication of knowing each other, yet I know with absolute certainty that she's as affected as I am. The increased rise and fall of her chest is a clear indicator.

*I'm going to figure you out, King.*


Pulling up to our townhouse, I'm surprised to find the light on the main floor still on.

Two scenarios play out in my head: Kai is either hammered and passed out on the couch, or he is currently banging a chick on the couch.

I take the stairs from the garage to the first floor, two steps at a time, while listening to any noise that would indicate me finding live porn being played out in my living room. When there is nothing, I push the door open and turn to head into the kitchen. I'm so ready to fall into bed and get my few hours of sleep before my alarm goes off at five thirty. I veer directly to the fridge, grabbing a bottle of water to help with my beer dehydration. I've consumed more alcohol in the last few days than since high school. And all of it because of one girl I know nothing about. Turning toward the living room area to shut off the lights, I take a step and—

"WHAT THE FUCK?" I clench the plastic bottle so hard it bursts.

"Hey, stranger."

Holding the remnants of my water bottle, my hand is dripping wet, and the water meant to hydrate me is spilled all over the kitchen floor.

Regretting not staying longer at The Grizz or maybe even attempting a conversation with King, I address the last person I want to have standing in my house, let alone in front of me. "What are you doing here, Rhys?"

My former best friend takes a step toward me, and all I can think of saying is, "Don't."

I lift both hands and cover my face.

*Fuck, I'm too tired for this.*

A growl escapes me, and I rake my fingers over my hair, inhaling slowly through my nose as I hold Rhys's gaze. Blood pounding in my ears, my brain fires memories from every direction at me. Rhys and me at parties all through high school. Us laughing together and playing ball or practicing new wrestling moves on each other. The three of us hanging out at the McGuire house. The confusion when Rhys suddenly refused to talk to Lilly and started sleeping over. The nights we spent talking until the sun came up, laughing at some shit Jager pulled during practice. The betrayal I felt when I found out what he had kept from me for all those years. The happiness for my friends when we finally were us again, and Den was no longer enemy number one. The fear when the nightmare started and the relief when it was over. Then, the letter came. I lost my future. Rhys tried to buy my way into a prestigious private school and then lied to my face. I don't know which is worse, that he went behind my back after I told him—them—that I didn't want anything to do with that money or that he lied to me. Again. With every reminder of the past twelve-plus years, my anger reaches a new height.

I don't want to fight him. Not here in my home. Not ever again. He was my best friend once, but that's in the past.

With my hands still on top of my head, I blow out a breath. "You need to leave." I force the words out calmly, despite the inner chaos raging havoc on my already wound-up emotions, thanks to a certain blonde.

"I came to talk," Rhys mimics my controlled tone.

My jaw clenches, and I force myself to relax it enough to respond. "You need to leave."

My restraint is slipping.

"Calla misses you. We both do. We want you to be at our—"

"LEAVE!"

There goes the last bit of composure.

Rhys stares at me for a long moment before he sighs and dips his chin.

"Okay." He slowly turns and walks to the front door. As he opens it, he pauses and turns one more time.

I meet his steady gaze.

"I'm sorry, Wes. I...I made a mistake. I was selfish and tried to get rid of my guilt about you losing your scholarship by buying your education with Lilly's money."

I'm waiting for his words to have an impact on how I feel, but there is nothing. Maybe it's too late. Maybe I need more time. I have no clue.

I dip my chin in acknowledgment and swivel on my heels, heading for my bedroom without turning the house security system on. At this point, I don't care if he leaves the front door wide open.

But just as I reach my bedroom, I hear the door shutting. I fall face-first on my mattress, not bothering to take my shoes or clothes off.

## CHAPTER NINE

### KING

AFTER GRIZZ'S MESSAGE THAT WES SHOWED UP AT THE BAR and asked for me by name, I called in sick for three of my shifts —including closing the bar on Sunday. My boss wasn't happy, and I promised to make it up to him. He has no clue why I'm avoiding Wes, but with him not divulging anything about his life, he seems to understand not to ask.

I also didn't go to class, which bugged me more than the loss of my income. Not that anyone missed me there, or that it would have any impact, but this week, we covered a topic in Professor Steward's criminology course that I had been looking forward to for months. I was simply too chickenshit to run into Wes.

I had enough saved up to afford the few days off, but not for much longer. I needed the money in case I had to move on. Or for something important—like a fake passport. One in my position never knew.

The mere thought of being confronted after going psycho on Wes and pulling a knife on the guy—Jesus, what was I thinking?

I had let the old King out to play—something I didn't like to do anymore. It was survival of the toughest back then, but I didn't have to be that girl here.

For the past three days, one thought kept replaying in my mind: Why was Wes looking for me? It even overshadowed the imminent arrival of the last person I wanted around. I tried calling Rae again. Her text had completely thrown me off. How did she know about him? And why were they together? But as expected, she didn't pick up.

Wes knew my name and place of work. If he wanted to press charges for reckless endangerment, he could send a cop to the bar. But instead, Wes had become a regular, as Grizz reported back.

Tonight is Wednesday, my scheduled night off, but Mags's time of the month came crashing in like a red tidal wave, and she is curled up on the couch. Initially, I refused. A few Advil and she would be as good as new (I would go to Friendship Hell for that), but when Leigh also called in that she couldn't close up today, I had no choice.

I waited as long as possible, but finally, I put on my big-girl panties and got dressed. Getting to the bar only took seven minutes, if all three traffic lights were red, which left me more than enough time.


PARKING the Jeep in my usual spot, I wipe my sweaty hands on my black skinny jeans.

*You can do this. Pretend he's not there.*

Inside, I stop in the doorway to Grizz's office and knock on the frame. He glances up from behind the multitude of monitors on his desk. "Hey."

My boss is a man of not-so-many words, which is how I prefer it.

"Hi."

We stare at each other for several—in my case, accelerated—heartbeats as I wait for him to tell me what I already know.

"He's camping out at the corner high top. Again."

I nod in acknowledgment and turn to leave.

"King?"

I glance over my shoulder.

"Say the word, and he's out."

Warmth grows in my chest. Besides Kiwi and my mom, I've never had anyone look out for me. Now, I have several people who have my back if I need them.

"Thank you." I give him a narrow smile, not wanting him to see how much his words affect me.

The lump in my throat has cleared by the time I enter the main room and is replaced by my stomach reeling like the one (and only) time I got on a roller coaster. Let's hope I won't puke my guts out after this *ride*.

I avoid scanning the crowd as I make my way behind the bar. *Pretend you have blinders on your eyes.*

I'm working the left side, Mags's usual spot, while Dean has the right. I greet him and then get busy mixing the drink orders.

At one point, Aiden, one of my regulars, appears in my line of vision, and I jump.

"King, baby!"

When I realize who it is, my body sags. Aiden leans over the counter to hug me, and it's like the room is suddenly charged with crackling electricity—not the good kind.

Keeping my head down, using my hair as a shield, I chance a glimpse toward the back corner for a fraction of a second. It's long enough for me to see that Wes is strangling his beer, glowering at Aiden's back. I avert my gaze before he catches me, but, oh my God, is he—? My breath catches. No, it can't be. There is no way Weston Sheats would be...jealous? That's ridiculous. I fucking threatened him with a knife. Yet, the still-present nausea is replaced by hundreds of butterflies, and hope fills my chest, just to be squashed by reality hitting me over the head with a baseball bat.

*Nothing can happen. Wes is a good guy. He would never accept who I am and what I've done.*

Aiden pulls back, and I force myself to smile at him in greeting. "Hey, A."

"I didn't know you were working tonight." He grins as if I had offered for him to take shots from between my tits. I can sense Wes's eyes on us and fight the urge to check on the corner table.

"I'm covering for Mags." I hold up the empty glasses I was about to place under the bar. "I gotta get going."

*Please stop talking to me.*

He gives me a fake pout. "Can you make me one of your specialties?"

I sigh inwardly but smirk. "Surprise you?" I know how to put on a show, and that's exactly what I'm doing.

Aiden winks. "You know it. You never disappoint me."

Usually, I enjoy his flirty behavior, but tonight, it annoys the ever-loving hell out of me. The last thing I want is for Wes to think I'm a psycho stalker *and* a whore.

After that, my shift runs smoothly. I am able to turn my Wes-obsessed brain off and focus on my job. I don't allow myself to acknowledge his presence and serve my customers their drinks.

I'm holding my Guardian Helix, about to slice a lime, when the atmosphere shifts. I purposefully didn't bring my usual curved blade tonight.

My eyes fly up of their own volition. It's as if someone—Wes —has called my name, and our gazes collide.

My breath hitches before the pulse in my veins takes off. I'm having flashbacks to the time I was put on Ritalin for suspected ADHD. Needless to say, my attention deficit was caused by my homelife falling to pieces and the counselor I was forced to see being an incompetent asshole. He took the easy way out, and in addition to misdiagnosing me, he also overprescribed the shit.

No one at twelve years old should think they are having a heart attack.

I hold Wes's impassive stare as he saunters by, trying desperately to steady my breathing. He has his hood over his head, his features expressionless. His entire body language screams alpha, and my thighs clench together.

I scold myself internally, but can't help the desire building in my core. I've had a crush on this guy for so long that him acknowledging me makes my vagina break out in a cha-cha.

Following his exit, I have a hard time concentrating. Thankfully, no one orders anything too extravagant for my last hour, and I manage to finish the night and get home without any further incidents.

THURSDAY IS Mags's night off, but knowing that Wes will most likely be at The Grizz, she talked Kiwi into moving his date to our place of work. She hates hanging out at a table alone.

During breakfast this morning, I downplayed how Wes's presence caused complete emotional havoc in me, but she gave me her therapist look, and I spilled my guts, recounting every last detail.

As I got to what *I thought* I saw when Aiden hugged me, she grinned and shrugged casually. "He wants to fuck you."

"Shut up!" Heat crept up my cheeks. "You know that can never happen."

She rolled her eyes. "Why not? You don't have to tell him what you did. But you need to get your lady parts serviced. They have cobwebs."

"Jesus Christ, what did I walk in on this time?" Grizz is standing in the patio door with Echo slightly behind him.

What the—? How didn't I notice my dog wasn't in the house? Good Lord, what kind of dog mom was I? I stared at my best friend in horror, and she understood immediately. Getting up from her chair, she walked over and hugged me while Grizz stepped to the side to let Echo in. My four-legged girl jumped in my lap and gave me her best good morning kiss. I couldn't even be upset about being covered in dog saliva. I didn't notice that she wasn't here when I woke up.

"Stop stressing out. I let her out, like, twenty minutes ago. It's all good," Mags whispered in my ear and kissed me on the crown of my head. "Thanks, big guy." She dismissed our boss, and once again, I wondered what their history was.

WATCHING my friends chatting at their table from my spot behind the bar, I can't help but feel guilty. Kiwi likes Zeke, but with my shit show of a life, he doesn't get to see him. I've been in constant need of my best friend—not that he would ever hold it against me. We made that pact when I was eleven and Kiwi was thirteen—on the day Rae left. We swore on a blood oath that we would never not be there for each other, and to this day, we have stuck to our promise. I look at the small scar across the pad of my thumb—one of my many links to him.

As expected, Wes walks in not twenty minutes after his practice ended. Zeke is not here yet, which means Wes must've been one of the first to leave. I'm not sure if that excites or freaks me out more.

I track his every move as he walks by my friends, meeting Kiwi's gaze and holding it. Neither of them looks away.

Wes's hair is still wet and tied back. He's wearing a red-and-black hoodie with the team's mascot on it and jeans that hug his ass like—God, why does he have to be sex on a stick?

*Maybe my lady parts do need to be dusted off.*

Nope, no, they don't. And if they do, not by Weston Sheats.

I find Mags's eyes, who was just waiting for me to look at her. Her usual smirk is missing, and she's psychoanalyzing me: *Is King going to make it through the night?*

I look back down to the glass that I've been polishing for several minutes. I need to ignore him. Maybe he'll leave.

*Yeah, like that's going to happen,* the old King laughs inside my head.

"Hey, Monroe." My head jerks up, and I lock eyes with Dean. *Huh?*

What is he doing here? He isn't scheduled until later. My brows furrow. He holds up his acoustic guitar, and a pit the size of the state I currently call home opens up in my stomach. I want to scream, cry, and rip my hair out at the same time.

Today? No, no, no. Not tonight of all nights.

Months ago, Dean caught me singing in the break room—something even Mags doesn't know about me. I don't perform in front of people. Dancing on top of the bar, no problem. Stripping at a dingy nightclub when I'm still more a pubescent teen than a woman, also no biggie. Singing? That is a whole different level of exposing myself. That's like baring my soul. Fuck. No.

I inherited my mother's talent—which was how she met my father in the first place. She was singing at a friend's birthday party held at a karaoke bar where daddy-not-so-dearest and some of his buddies were celebrating as well. Anyway, that story is so far in the past I buried it with my mother.

However, Mom always sang to me. She encouraged me from the day I was able to memorize lyrics to sing along. I can hold a note, and my voice doesn't sound too bad either (if it's the right song), which is why Dean harassed me for days until I caved and agreed to perform with him sometime—emphasis on *sometime*. I assumed it would be at a backyard barbecue or something low-key, and I could give Mags a heads-up—bring her as my backup in case I barf all over myself from nerves. *Not* during my shift and, most of all, *not* at The Grizz. My stomach begins to churn, and I place a hand on my belly.

*This will not end well.*

I peer over my shoulder to check that Leigh has the customers at the bar covered before making my way over to Dean.

"What the fuck, asshole? I'm not singing here." I glower at him and gesture at the room around us.

He smirks sheepishly and shrugs. "Why not? Grizz thought it was cool."

"You talked to Grizz about it?" I shriek, then clamp a hand over my mouth. Whether it is to stop me from further yelling at my coworker or from keeping my late lunch inside me, I have no clue.

"Sure, I mean, it's his place. We needed his okay."

I draw my arm back and let it soar forward, punching him in the shoulder as hard as I can. Maybe he wouldn't be able to hold his damn guitar if I hurt him enough.

"Jesus Christ, Monroe. Overreacting much?" He rubs the spot my fist connected with. Out of my peripheral vision, movement diverts my attention. Kiwi is standing next to his table, waiting for my signal that I need him. Wes has shifted closer as well, and I want the earth to swallow me up. I'm causing a scene. I blink slowly at Kiwi, silently communicating that I'm okay. He dips his chin in acknowledgment, though he doesn't sit down.

"Not today, Dean. I'm not prepared. You can't throw something like this at me." My hands are trembling at my sides.

Dean purses his lips. "If I would've given you more than a five-minute heads-up, you would've bailed."

*Five minutes? Wha—*

The beating of my heart grows in speed, and I glance in the direction of my friends again. Zeke has joined them in the last few minutes, and my gaze connects with Wes's. He has abandoned his corner table and positioned himself slightly behind the others, hands shoved deep in the pockets of his faded jeans. His impassive features are in stark contrast to his pulled-back shoulders and wide stance. His entire frame is rigid. He's ready to pounce as he follows my exchange with Dean, yet no one else seems to notice. His temper is simmering right under the surface.

As we are locked in our stare down, a new emotion slowly

spreads through every cell of my body. I want him to hear me sing. My pulse calms, but instead of giving me the confidence I so clearly need to make it through this, this awareness sends me reeling.

"Monroe!" Dean calls out, and when I turn, I realize he is on his way to the stool set up for him next to the mic. My stomach rolls, and I fight the urge to turn around and run for the mountains—literally.

I close my eyes for a brief moment. Deep breaths. You can do this. Just pretend you are back in the break room.

*Yeah, not working.*

Slowly, I set one foot in front of the other. When I reach my position, I swivel on my heels and find Kiwi staring at me. Of course he knows I sing, but he also knows I don't do it publicly. Mags leans in and whispers something, but he ignores her.

The music cuts off, and everyone turns toward us. My arms are folded across my exposed stomach, and my fingers clasp the hem of my shirt. I clench the material in my fists. I can do this. I used to dance pretty much naked in front of *filth*.

*I can do this.*

I turn to Dean. "What song?"

"I figured we'd perform the track you sang the day I ran into you. I learned it, which is why it took me this long." He winks, and I fight to hit him again.

Of course he decided to play that one. My fucking luck. It's the song that has been stuck in my mind whenever I think about Weston Sheats. The lyrics I associate with him whenever I hear them.

I bob my head, unable to form words. Dean starts strumming a few notes, and everyone goes eerily quiet. I draw in slow breaths. I can do this.

He pauses for a beat, and then the melody of DIAMANTE's "Obvious" fills the room. I let go of my shirt and place my hands on the mic. I focus on a spot on the opposite wall. I put every bit of emotion into the lyrics, and as we reach the second verse,

I can't stop myself. I find him instantly, the one person I should not be looking at. I fumble, but then regain my composure and continue. His blue eyes are on me, but they seem darker than normal. Blazing with... The room fades into the background. It's just him and me. I'm baring my soul to the man I've cared about since I found out what happened to him, how his friendship with Lilly cost him everything. Something I can relate to all too well.

I sing the last words, and as Dean lets the melody drift away, reality crashes in.

The entire bar erupts in applause, and I peer at my friends for the first time. Kiwi radiates pride. He's pushed me to do this for years, but the more he pushed, the more I pulled away and retreated into my shell until he gave up. Mags has her hand in front of her mouth, her cheeks wet with tears.

*I need to get out of here.*

I spin on my heels and run down the hallway to the employee lounge. We have a bathroom in there so the staff doesn't have to use the same one as the customers, and I beeline straight for it.

Out of breath, I place my hands on the sink and drop my chin. Why did I do this? And that song of all the possibilities. How can he not know that every word was for him? Down to the other girl in his phone: Denielle Keller.

I bite the inside of my cheek until a metallic taste fills my mouth. Don't cry.

Suddenly, the door behind me opens, and my head snaps up. My vision is cloudy, but I don't have to see him to know. My eyes find Wes's in the mirror above the sink. He closes the door without breaking eye contact and slowly moves into the room until his front is almost touching my back. Heat radiates off his body, and I fight the urge to lean into him, to let his tall frame swallow my shorter one.

"King?" The way he says my name...a shiver runs down my spine. It's a question, yet it's not.

I hold his gaze, unable to form words. It takes all my concentration to continue bringing air into my lungs.

"You followed me from TMH," he states with a blank expression.

I jerk my head up and down.

"You threatened me with a knife." He shows zero emotion as he lists the things that would make me a psychotic stalker in anybody's book.

Another nod. *Where is he going with this?*

"You know who I am."

I draw in a sharp breath. He's not talking about him being MPU's star player, and I press my lips into a thin line, having no idea what to say.

Suddenly, his hands lightly touch my sides, right above the hem of my jeans, and a jolt of electricity runs through me. The sensation of his fingers on my bare skin is almost too much. I haven't been touched by a guy in so long—and this is Wes.

My body reacts of its own accord, and I press my back to his front.

He angles his head, studying my reflection. "Are you interested in me because of my friends?"

I gasp and try to move away, but his grip tightens, and his fingertips dig into my flesh. Heat begins to pool in my core, my lids fluttering closed.

"They are not your friends anymore," I whisper before I can stop myself.

*Oh God, what did I just say?*

I don't dare to move. Now I really sound like a stalker. What the actual fuck? How else would I know that he no longer speaks to Lilly and Rhys? I wait for him to shove me away, demand answers, ask how I know so much about him, or simply leave. He does none of that.

"You sing."

My eyes pop open, and my lips part. *Uh.*

"You sing," Wes repeats when I stare at him slack-jawed.

Why is he not calling me out? My heart beats through my chest, and I grip the rim of the sink.

"Not in public." I'm surprised at the steadiness in my reply, and a small smile creeps onto my face.

The corner of Wes's mouth twitches, and he steps closer into me, his fingers slowly moving from above my hips to my exposed stomach. I'm not sure if I'm happy or not about having turned my work shirt into a crop top. It gives him easy access, and at the same time, I'm terrified of how my body reacts to his. I'm all but panting as he leaves a scorching trail with his fingertips. I don't even want to think about what's going on inside my pants.

*Thank fuck I didn't go commando today.*

My eyes flutter closed, and as his pinkie stops right over the button of my jeans, I moan. If he keeps that up, I'm going to come without him even touching any of my sensitive spots.

His rumbled laughter vibrates against my back. He leans down, and his warm breath fans over my neck. "What would you call what you did then?"

My mind is completely blank as his thumb strokes up and down underneath my navel, and I turn my head ever so slightly so my cheek touches the side of his face. Of course he doesn't know that I basically sang for him.

*Dear Lord, how long have I wanted to be near this man?*

"Dean didn't give me much of a choice," I remark with my eyes still closed. I should be embarrassed by how breathy I sound.

"There is always a choice, MOAB Girl." His lips swipe along my neck, and I whimper.

*A goddamn whimper.*

What is he doing? There is no question about him sensing my out-of-control pulse where his lips hover over my skin. If I had worn anything but black jeans today, you could, without question, see how he affects me. My panties are soaked, and all I want is for him to continue. Let his hand glide all the way into my jeans and slip a finger deep inside of me.

One of his hands disappears from my stomach and takes my chin between his thumb and forefinger, turning me farther in his direction.

My hand leaves the sink and covers his that's still splayed out on my abs. His fingers spread apart, and I automatically interlace mine with his, Wes mimicking the movement and squeezing my hand.

His mouth hovers over mine, and all I want is for him to press his lips to mine and kiss me.

"Who are you, King?"

*No!*

This is the one question he shouldn't have asked. Dread fills my veins, and my eyes spring open. He stares down at me with a hooded yet curious gaze.

I drop his hand like he's burned me and step sideways out of his embrace. Pressing myself against the wall, I attempt to get as far away as possible in the small space.

"Don't touch me again!" I sound borderline hysterical. I probably look completely deranged.

His expression hardens, and he shoves his hands into his front pockets. Tilting his head, his stare bores into me, and he drawls, "And why is that?"

I could cry. I want nothing more than to move into his arms again, let him touch me, but instead, I take a deep breath. I don't want to be numb, not when it comes to him, but I have no choice. Do. Not. Feel.

As I exhale, I hiss, "Because I want nothing to do with you."

I pivot on my heels and leave the bathroom. Tears are already welling up, and I'm going to have to explain to Grizz once more why I bolted mid-shift. I grab my purse, which is still sitting on the table in the lounge. As I'm about to exit into the hallway, I hear one word echo after me.

"Liar."

## CHAPTER TEN

**KING**

*LIAR.*

Wes called me a fucking liar—and he's one-hundred-percent right. Fuck!

I'm sitting in my usual seat in the far back of Professor Steward's criminology class, but can't concentrate on a word he's saying—which frustrates me even more. The prof stopped me on my way in and asked where I was last week, a gesture that meant more to me than he could possibly understand. It feels good to be missed. I may not be one of his students, but we've shared several conversations before and after class about his lectures.

A while ago, he offered to put me in touch with the administration department managing the financial aid. I could be a real student, but with no idea how long I'll be around, I declined. I'd hate to let Steward down.

It's been five days since the incident. Five days in which Mags has not shut up about not having had a clue that her best friend could sing. One hundred and twenty hours in which Kiwi has told me countless times how proud he is of me. Seven thousand two hundred minutes since I bared my soul to Weston Sheats.

Four hundred thirty-two thousand seconds since I felt his hands on me and then pushed him away, declaring I wanted nothing to do with him.

*Liar.*

I've replayed everything a gazillion times in my head: the sensation of his fingers on my bare stomach, his lips feathering over the sensitive skin on my neck, the almost kiss. In my mind, Wes never asked the question that brought reality crashing down. In my vivid, Technicolor fantasy, he continued the exploration of my body with his mouth and hands. He unbuttoned my jeans and slipped his fingers into my pussy until I was riding his hand. I may even have played said fantasy out myself—with my own fingers. God, when was the last time I did that? I can't remember. But the thought of Wes and—

Great, I'm sitting in class and am about to come from a freaking daydream. My obsession has taken on a whole new level, and I have no idea what to do.

Professor Steward concludes today's lecture, and everyone begins to pack up. I'm trying to steady my breath and hope to fucking God that no one noticed me panting in my seat. Most of the students have gotten used to me being here and nod as they leave the rows in front of mine.

I stuff my notepad in my bag. Sliding out of my seat, a tall figure lingering outside the doorway registers in my brain. My heart stumbles before my entire body starts buzzing with the remnants from my recent fantasy.

What the hell is he doing here?

I slowly approach the exit and stop in front of Wes. He stares down at me impassively. "MOAB Girl."

I take a deep breath and pray that the heat currently setting my body ablaze is not visible to him. "Tight End."

His lips twitch. "You know my position."

I shrug as casually as I can. "You are well known on campus."

*Liar.*

He grins at me indulgently, and I wait for him to call me out again. He doesn't.

Instead, he steps to the side and allows me to leave the room. I flatten myself against the opposite side of the doorframe, and I hear a snort from behind me. He's enjoying this way too much.

I start walking without a backward glance. On Mondays, I sit in two lectures, and I have to hurry to make it to the other class on time. Most students wouldn't take these classes in the same year and therefore wouldn't have this issue, but I attend as many lectures as I can or am allowed to. Having missed most of my high school experience, I am now soaking up all the knowledge I can get.

Wes matches my hurried strides, and I peer at him from my peripheral vision. "What are you doing?" A few days ago, I quite loudly *informed* him that I wanted nothing to do with him.

"Not sure what you mean." He keeps his eyes forward as he responds.

I stop in my tracks and swivel to face him. He follows my lead, and we're facing off in the middle of the corridor with students passing us on both sides.

"Why are you here?" I gesture between us.

"Why were you at TMH?" he counters with a smirk.

His directness flusters me. I never expected him to engage. Everyone else would run as fast as they could. But then, Wes isn't your average person. His past has shaped him, and he probably is not fazed by much.

"I was picking up drinks for a party." I cock my head, waiting for his response.

He's about to say something when he stops, then pulls his phone out of his back pocket. He glances at the screen, and I fight the urge to pry.

He holds up a finger with his free hand and swipes with the other to answer the call. "Hey, D."

*D. Denielle.* My jaw locks. I should leave.

"Uh-huh."

Denielle says something, but I can't make out the words. Wes's entire demeanor changes. His *almost* playfulness is gone, his shoulders drawn back. "Yeah, stood in my fucking living room when I got home. Way to give me a heads-up."

Who is he talking about? I have so many questions, yet I know I have no right, nor should I want to.

I need to go.

More talking on the other end, and Wes rakes his hand through his hair, getting stopped by the hair tie in the back. As he glances up to the ceiling, about to respond, I see it as my chance. I start to bolt, but I'm not fast enough. A hand latches onto my wrist. "Not so fast, MOAB Girl."

I jerk around and gape at him, my gaze shifting between him and the device pressed to his ear.

"D, I gotta go." Pause. "None of your business." Another pause. "No, you knew he was coming, and you didn't warn me."

He? Oh my God, Rhys was here. In Stonebriar. Now his anger makes sense.

"I already told you that's none of your business. Jesus, D—" I take a step back, but Wes's hand tightens on my wrist, and he is shaking his head. I could easily dislodge his hand—one of the first lessons I learned working in my old job—but I don't want to. Instead, I wait. His eyes never leave mine.

"Sure, I'll call you tonight." Denielle says something else, and his features soften. "Love you, too. Yeah, bye."

My chest constricts, and I suck in a breath. Hearing those words out of his mouth...directed at another girl...

Wes hangs up and pockets his phone. He stares down at me as if he wants to say something, but then stops himself.

I inwardly squirm from the way he studies me.

He changes his grip and interlaces our fingers. "Let's go."

As he takes a step, I'm rooted to the floor, gaping at our joined hands. My heart is thundering. What is he doing? What am *I* doing? I need to stay away from him.

"King?" His tone is gentle. For the first time, there is no smug taunt.

I can't form words. The feel of his rough palm in mine... I swallow over the lump in my throat and meet his eyes.

"I'm only walking you to class."

Is he saying that for my benefit? Why would he need to hold my hand to walk me? Is this a game? What if someone sees us?

I should let go of Wes for so many reasons. None of them matter as he waits for me. Does he expect me to push him away?

I inhale deeply and whisper, "Okay."

He nods, and we turn in the direction of my next lecture simultaneously.

As we make our way down the hallway and out of the building, curious eyes follow us. Girls give me their best elevator glance. Boys who never noticed me suddenly pay attention—everyone knows Wes. He squeezes my hand, and I tighten my fingers around his.

*This will end badly.*

I'M PLACING four cocktails on the bar—one cosmo, one appletini, and two strawberry daiquiris. Gag. It is a miracle I serve them with a straight face to the platinum-blonde bimbos ogling Wes. He's been camped out at his usual table for the past hour. Shortly after he arrived, Kai also made an appearance. The two are now chatting as if they have always hung out at The Grizz.

I glance over to him as I pour a beer from the tap, and Wes's eyes immediately find mine. My stomach somersaults, but I force the grin threatening to overtake my features down.

*Nope, do not show how much today has affected you.*

AFTER HE HAD WALKED me to my class, I expected that to be it. But no, as soon as I came out of the lecture, he was leaning on the wall to the right of the door, arms crossed over his chest, one foot against the wall, acting as if that was the most natural thing in the world.

Noticing him there, I stopped short, as if I'd run into an invisible barrier, making some of the actual students bump into me in the process.

When I didn't move and the curses behind me got louder, he pushed off the wall and wrapped an arm around my shoulder, guiding me out of the way. "Ready?"

Unable to stop myself or ask questions, I let him lead me outside. With the weight of his arm over my shoulders and the heat radiating off his body, my lady parts didn't know what to do: close up shop in a nervous panic or prepare for a possible...for what, really? I felt as if I was being pulled into opposite directions by two Humvees. What was he doing?

Outside in the main quad, I finally regained some control and dug my heels in.

"Stop!" My command was shrill, and several heads turned. Shit.

Wes obeyed but didn't remove his hold, peering down at me.

"I..." I disentangled myself from him and rubbed my palms over my face. Dropping my arms to my sides, I stared past him. What was I going to say? "I..." I started again, then drew in a deep breath. "I told you that I want nothing to do with you. Why won't you leave me alone, Weston?"

Calling him by his full name sounded weird, but I had to put distance between us somehow.

Wes cocked his head and rubbed his chin with his thumb and forefinger before stuffing his hand into the front pocket of his MPU hoodie. "That's a great question."

*Uh, what?*

My brows furrowed, and he barked out a laugh. I involuntarily smiled at his genuine display of emotion, a tingling sensation spreading through my every limb until I almost felt weightless. How odd. Was that...happiness?

My reaction seemed to be what he was waiting for, because he grinned from ear to ear. This guy was so confusing to me.

My smile dimmed a little. "I'm serious, Wes." My voice was lower now. "What are you doing?"

He shrugged, his lips still quirked up. "I have no fucking clue, MOAB Girl." After a pause, he added, "I guess you intrigue me."

"Intrigue? Jesus Christ, you're more messed up than I am. And what's with you addressing me with the model of my car?" I giggled like a little girl. What the hell? He brought out a side of me I forgot existed.

"Never said I wasn't." He sobered a little. "King."

When he called me by my name, not MOAB Girl, something shifted again. It was like he formed a connection between us, and before I could stop myself, I said, "My name is Kingsley. Kingsley Monroe." Quickly I added, "But everyone calls me King. Besides Kiwi, but that's a whole different story. We've known each other—"

*Oh, God, what was I doing?*

My eyes bulged in shock as I realized all that I just laid out for him. I glanced around in an almost wild panic. What if he gave my name to Lilly? She could easily find out—

"Hey."

Fuck, now I really needed to leave and—

Two large hands landed on my shoulders. "King."

I focused on Wes, and concern was shining in his blues. I pressed my lips together to keep from spilling more details about myself.

He seemed to understand, and his hands moved upward until he framed my face. He stepped closer until we were mere inches apart. I squeezed my eyes shut and fought the urge to lean into him.

*This was not how this was supposed to go.*

"Look at me, please."

I could smell the cocoa he must've had while I was in class. I slowly peeled my lids back and found him studying me.

"There you are." He huffed out a laugh. "Listen..." He glanced to the side before focusing back on me. "Let's see what happens."

*See what happens?*

He continued, "I have no idea what's going on. Why you followed me, or who you are. How you know so much about me. But if I'm honest—and I have thought about it a lot since you stood on top of that bar—I don't give a flying fuck."

I burst out laughing at the absurdity of this.

"Wes, you need to stay away from me. I'm not good for you." I sighed. "I should've never followed you from TMH."

His thumb caressed my cheek. "I've heard that already."

My eyebrows jolted up. "Oh?"

He chuckled. "Yeah, Devon—or Kiwi, as you call him—made that clear the night you bailed from the bar."

*That little shit*, I cursed inwardly. "He didn't tell me."

"I figured."

His grip on my head tightened, and I wanted to lean my forehead against his chest, but I forced myself to hold his gaze.

"Let's see what happens, 'kay?"

My eyes bounced between his. I should have said no. Every cell in my body screamed in wild terror to say no.

"Okay," I whispered.

# CHAPTER ELEVEN

## WES

"Dude! Pay attention."

I slowly turn my head toward my roommate. I can't help but watch her. She is completely in her element behind that bar.

*Kingsley Monroe, what am I going to do with you?*

"SHEATS!"

Fingers snap in front of me, way too close for my liking, and I jerk back, scowling.

"You need to fuck that chick out of your system already." Kai laughs like a hyena, and I fight the urge to clock him. Him calling King *that chick* triggers an extreme sense of violence in me.

Showing up outside her criminology lecture—a lecture she is not officially a part of, as I found out—was a spur-of-the-moment decision. My class was canceled, and I was already on campus.

Plus, I hadn't seen her since she ran out on me last Thursday. After that, I took a break from hanging out at The Grizz. I would've fingerbanged her in that bathroom if she hadn't put a stop to it. I certainly wanted to do a lot more. I don't think she noticed in her panic how rock hard I was against her sexy ass.

I focus on Kai. "Don't talk about her like that." My tone is way more hostile than necessary, but this girl causes all kinds of emotions in me that I've never felt before.

Kai lifts his hands in surrender. "Man, she did a number on you. Didn't peg you for going for the stalker kind."

"Kai." His name holds a warning, but he's already too intoxicated to get it.

"I mean, didn't she follow you from TMH? Then, she runs from you the other night. Something is seriously off with her."

"KAI."

"What?"

"Shut the fuck up." One more word, and I'm going to find myself a new seat.

Suddenly, the hairs on my neck stand up, and I automatically turn my head, finding her looking at me. My pulse picks up, and all I can think about is dragging her back to that room and finishing what we started last week. Jesus. I don't even know her.

One would think after everything that went down two and a half years ago, I would want to find myself a nice, boring girl-friend. No, I go for the one that has more secrets than Lilly's head of security has assault rifles—and the dude has a lot.

King's mouth quirks at the corner, and I can't help but smile back. My view gets blocked by a bunch of sorority girls that came over to the table earlier. Now armed with colorful cock-tails, all of them close in on us once more, and I groan inwardly. Please don't.

As they move forward, King becomes visible again. She's glaring daggers at the airheads approaching us—as if I would ever be interested in one of them for more than a quick lay. And even for those, I am pickier.

Her displeasure is visible, like a blinking neon sign in the dead of night, and I can't deny the satisfaction that stirs inside of me. The realization that I want her to be jealous is jarring.

When did I get so involved in this? But then again, I did come close to rearranging that preppy douchebag's mug last week when he had his fingers all over her.

Kai straightens in his chair, probably calculating which—or how many of them—he can *entertain* tonight. They've almost reached the table when I jump up and walk past them like they're not even there. I ignore Kai's, "Uh, bro?" and zero in on the only girl I am interested in. Her eyes grow wider with every step I take in her direction, and I let the grin that I've been trying to suppress show. Screw "*Let's see what happens.*"

Her gaze darts left and right like a deer in the headlights, and before she can make a run for it—again—I lean over the counter. Reaching for her, I grab her by the back of the neck, pulling her close. She's about to protest when I bring my mouth down on hers. King stiffens as our lips make contact, and I keep my eyes on hers. I let my tongue swipe over her bottom lip, urging her to let me in. When her lids flutter closed, I know I've *won*.

She melts in my grip, and her hands lift to frame my face, returning the kiss. My primal craving for her sets every cell of my body on fire. I didn't plan for that to happen. I didn't even think I wanted to pursue anything deeper with her. She caught my curiosity, intrigued me, but then instinct took over. I want everyone in this damn place to understand that she is mine—and I am hers. Am I? *Hers?*

A low moan escapes her throat, and that's all I need. I tighten my hand at her neck and pull her close until she kneels on top of the bar. Whistles and shouts erupt around us, but I couldn't care less. At the velvety sensation of King's tongue tangling with mine, my cock grows rock hard. I fight the urge to pull her across the unwanted barrier and dry hump her right here in front of everyone. I've never met a girl that has caused such a reaction inside of me. She nips at my bottom lip, and I groan at the sting.

*So good.*

Reluctantly, I force both of us to slow our pace. I got my

point across to The Grizz's customers. Not losing contact, I place one more kiss on her lips and then let my forehead rest against hers.

"What was that?" she whispers so only I can hear it.

"This"—I bring my mouth back to hers for a small peck—"is making sure that all the dicks in this place, who have been eye fucking you every night, see that you're not interested."

She chuckles, and her eyes open for the first time, finding mine. With an amused smirk, she challenges me. "I'm not?"

I let my mouth glide along her jawline to her ear and growl lightly, followed by gently biting the lobe of her ear. "You're not. There is only one dick you'll be riding anytime soon, and we both know whose—"

"You have some explaining to do, Sheats!" a female voice that should not be here breaks me out of my haze, and I drop my hands from King like I'm doing something wrong. I spin around in shock and gape.

"What are you doing here?"

My gaze flickers back to King, who is scrambling off the bar, not taking her eyes off the brown-haired girl in four-inch heels, skintight jeans, and a white lace blouse. She commands this place like she has with every room since junior high.

"BK!" Kai's voice breaks our stare down as he envelops D from behind to lift and twirl her around.

"Ahhh!" she shrieks, but nevertheless laughs.

She's not mad that he called her by the name she forbade *me* to use under the penalty of being impaled by her Louboutin.

Once he sets her down, she regards me with her head tilted. "Wes?"

Hesitantly, I open my arms, and Den steps into me like she belongs there, which she did until recently. She used to be the only girl I let in or come close in years. Now, it feels like I'm cheating. I hug my best friend, peering behind me so I can see King. She stands with her back pressed against the glass shelves on the other side as if she is trying to get as far away as possible.

Her lips are pursed, and I want to assure her that it's not how it appears.

Den pulls back, and with her heels, we're almost at the same eye level. She studies me intently before looking behind me. "Who's this, Sheats?" Her tone is neutral, but I know her better than anyone—the bulldog is in the house.

I throw Kai a pleading glance and hope he is not too drunk to understand what I want him to do. I need Den out of here so I can talk to King. Then, I'll have a conversation with my best friend away from prying eyes. Half the customers probably think she's my girlfriend.

Thank the sobriety gods, Kai is coherent enough to get the message and wraps his arm around Den.

"D, let's get you home and continue the party there."

She's ready to argue, but Kai has her halfway out the door before anyone can blink. I'm impressed.

Seeing it as my chance, I whirl around to address King when I find her in deep conversation with a customer. She laughs at something he says, and my fists ball at my sides.

I move closer, waiting for her to look at me, but she never does. What the fuck?

"King?"

She holds up a finger, signaling "one moment" without averting her eyes. The asshole flicks his gaze to me before focusing back on King's tits, and I'm coming close to introducing my fist to his nose.

Fuck this shit.

I stalk to our high top table. Dropping several bills on it, I grab my hoodie from the back of the chair and leave. As I pass King, our eyes connect for a fraction of a second, and all I see is the girl with the knife from last week.


Den is in the back of Kai's Rover with him in the driver's seat. I walk around and open his door. He glowers, probably hoping I won't embarrass him in front of D, but I don't give two shits. He is not driving my best friend while intoxicated. Usually, I couldn't care less. His tolerance is incomparable. Most of the time, he is the one functioning better than me with ten times the amount of booze in his system, but not tonight. I had barely two sips of my beer while he had...I lost count after four. Kai sighs dramatically and slides out of the SUV, walking around to the passenger side.

No one speaks as we make the short drive to the townhouse. I peer at D in the rearview mirror and am fixed with a glare she reserves for the Katherine Rosenfields of the world.

Fucking great. Now my best friend *and* my girlfriend are pissed at me. Wait, what? Girlfriend? Do I even like King that way? Jesus fucking Christ, when did my life become such a mess again?

Kai is the first to exit with a huff and is up the stairs before I can turn in my seat. Den sits with her arms crossed, surveying me with a mix of curiosity and something I can't pinpoint.

"Can we talk upstairs?" I mutter, suddenly beyond tired. I just want to get to bed.

"Sure." She doesn't smile, but some of the hardness melts off of her.

She pulls a small overnight bag from the seat beside her as she slides out, and I frown. "Is this it?" I don't think I've ever seen her travel with less than two large suitcases.

"I'm heading back tomorrow," she explains as I take the bag from her.

"I see." *I don't.*

Upstairs, she aims straight for my bedroom, and I pause. Maybe I should take the media room. My neck instantly protests, remembering the one time I accidentally fell asleep on that tiny-ass couch. I had a kink in my neck for days and had to go see the team's physician.

Guess we're co-sleeping—not waiting for Thanksgiving. By

the time I close my door behind me, she is in the bathroom, and I hear the shower come on.

Resigned, I sit down on the edge of the bed. Putting my head in my hands, I prop my elbows on my thighs. She doesn't take as long as I expected, but when she emerges in a cloud of steam, I choke on my saliva and start coughing. Pounding my chest, I can't take my eyes off my friend.

"Why do you have my shirt on?" Another cough. "And please tell me you're wearing something under it."

She narrows her eyes and lifts the hem enough to reveal her hot-pink lace underwear. "I don't think that is much better," I deadpan.

Den snorts. "Dude, like you and I would ever go there again. Your shirts are the size of two of mine, maybe three—so much comfier to sleep in."

With that, the weird tension evaporates. I give her my sauciest grin and open my arms to her.

Closing the distance, Den straddles my lap, her pretty much bare pussy rubbing against my jeans and...nothing. My dick doesn't twitch. He only wants one girl—if she still wants us after tonight. Does King know who Den is? She seemed to be informed about my other friends. Former friends. Fuck. I shake my head. Not going there.

Instead, I focus on my surprise visitor. "What are you doing here?"

I look into her eyes as she rests her arms on my shoulders.

"I felt bad for not warning you about Rhys. I texted Kai asking where you were when no one answered the door," she pauses for a beat. "Lilly made me promise not to tell you because he wanted to talk face-to-face. And we both know that you would've bailed and hidden somewhere."

She's correct in that assumption.

"I kicked him out," I snarl, not wanting to rehash that evening.

"So I've heard." Den sighs.

I wrap my hands around her waist. "Can we not do this?"

I hold my breath and count to seven before she replies, "Okay."

Climbing off me, she crawls over the bed to the other side and pulls the covers down to slide in. "Go shower."

I don't immediately move, so D amends, "You stink. And I want to hear all about the blonde you tongue fucked earlier."

I SPEND about five times as long under the hot spray, hoping Den would fall asleep. No dice. She sits in the middle of my bed, propped up against every single pillow I own. Her ferocious typing indicates that she's anything but happy.

"Comfy?"

Her eyes snap to mine, and she attempts to school her features. Too late.

"Very. Are these the pillows I ordered for you when you moved out here?"

"Who pissed in your egg whites?" Her regular breakfast.

She lets the device drop on my comforter. "Don't get mad."

*What now?*

"Lilly is picking me up with the jet tomorrow morning."

My spine is so stiff it feels like it's going to snap in half. I inhale slowly through my nose, not breaking eye contact. Den is fidgeting with the duvet, and I wait for the punch line.

"Is she now?" I force my response out between clenched teeth. I normally don't get this worked up about them anymore, but after what went down with King earlier—the wrong girl is in my bed, Rhys was standing in my living room less than a week ago, and now Lilly is coming into town—my adrenaline level skyrockets.

"G was supposed to be with her, but he had to leave Colorado unexpectedly, and now it's just Marcus." She doesn't have to say much more. Marcus became Lilly's security when George was handling the legalities surrounding her case, but even back then, when Lilly traveled, G was with her. George would've been the buffer D needed. Marcus by himself...

"You want me to come with you to the airport." I don't have to ask.

"Yes," she whispers. I would act as the distraction until they were in the air, then she was on her own.

Addressing the actual issue—what goes on between her and Marcus—would be a moot point. She'd evade me as usual. "Why did George leave?" That is more interesting to me. He would never abandon his charge unless it was a situation of life and—

"Is Rhys okay?"

*Why am I asking?*

"Yes. She said it was a family emergency." D's gaze mimics my own confusion.

"Fam—what? George doesn't have family, does he?" I realize I never bothered to ask; I simply assumed.

"Your guess is as good as mine."

"And now *the shadow* is going to be with her." Her lips turn to a scowl.

"Under one condition." I'm an asshole, but I don't care.

"Oh?"

"I'm not ready to talk about King."

She smirks. "King, is it?"

I tilt my head, and she pretends to zip her mouth. She reorganizes the pillows so that both of us have four and scoots over to the far side.

*That was too easy.*

"We'll talk in the morning," she says in the sweetest tone as she settles into bed, facing away from me.

# CHAPTER TWELVE

## KING

WES HASN'T BEEN BACK TO THE BAR SINCE HE LEFT THE Grizz. That was last Tuesday. Today is Monday. To say I have not been obsessing about it would be like trying to make someone believe I had a normal childhood.

I know from Kiwi, who was told by Zeke, that Wes missed Wednesday practice because he took Denielle to the airport. Why has he not been back? Maybe I shouldn't have ignored him, but my armor of indifference and self-preservation immediately snapped into place as soon as he wrapped his arms around the dark-haired girl. I've seen pictures of her on social media and also a video in which a flock of paps had been following her and Lilly. But encountering her in real life...how can I stand a chance against what she and Wes have? Even if it would just be friendship (which it certainly didn't look like). Maybe he would eventually accept me. Denielle never would.

The last few days, I kept myself busy with work. I took on two extra shifts to be distracted, with a small part of me clinging to the sliver of hope that Wes would walk in. He didn't.

Saturday evening, Kiwi showed up with Zeke, and during one

of my breaks, I finally caved and asked Zeke about Wes. The glance he gave my best friend was everything I needed to know, and I didn't stay for his answer. Kiwi tried intercepting me several times before they left, but I...couldn't.

I got it. Wes realized what a nutcase I was and checked out.

So, with my extra shifts from this week, I texted Grizz Sunday morning and asked for the night off. He called me back about an hour later to tell me it was no problem and he'd see me Monday night.

With that, I packed up the Jeep and was walking the last supplies out as Mags pulled into the driveway.

"Where are you going?" she called out, exiting her car.

"Taking a break. I'll be back tomorrow." Hoping she'd drop it, I turned toward the open door. "ECHO! Let's go, girl."

After a few seconds, my dog shot out of the house and straight into the Jeep, sitting down expectantly on the passenger side. We'd taken a few girls' trips like this since I got her, but not in the last few weeks.

Mags came closer until she was in my personal bubble, and I fought the impulse to step back. "Everything okay?" Her tone was wary, and she scanned me up and down—days like this, I cursed her choice of education.

I rolled my eyes. "Of course." The words pitched like one of those blonde sorority bimbos yapping about the newest designer shoe Daddy's credit card bought them.

Mags pursed her lips, not buying my Broadway-worthy performance one bit.

"Echo complained that I've neglected her, so I'm making it up to my baby." It wasn't a complete lie; I had spent less time with her because I had been too wrapped up in my own personal Weston Sheats soap opera.

But now that it was over, it was time to get back to reality—work, squatting in classes I didn't belong in, and saving as much money as possible.

Mags stared at me expressionless but then miraculously dropped it. "Okay."

"Okay?" Now I was the one with the jaw on the ground. Who was this girl, and what had she done with my roommate?

"Close your mouth before you catch a fly," she chuckled, then leaned in for a hug. "Are you going to your usual spot?"

I nodded, and she gave me a forced smile. Mags didn't like when I was out of reach, which I would be. There was no cell reception once you crossed into dirt-road territory, as we called it.

About an hour and a half out of town, there was a small lake in a forested bowl at the base of the mountains. If you didn't know about it, you would never expect it to be there. One of Mags's friends had told me about it, and during my first need to escape, I drove up there. About halfway, I thought I would die the way the road (I'm using the term loosely) was laid out—or not laid out, for that matter. But once you got there, holy shit, it was like something out of a fairy tale. There was a small camp-ground nearby, but that was about it. You lost service less than a mile after leaving the paved roads, and that was still seven miles before you reached your destination. My personal place of mental peace was the epitome of "off the grid." A few more weeks, and the road would close for the winter.

"When are you back?" Knowing my roommate, she'd wait on the doorstep for my return to make sure I was safe. Even after all this time, it was still new to me to have people in my life that were this concerned about my well-being.

"Before my shift tomorrow." I settled into the car, and Echo circled in her seat once before getting comfy. I blew Mags a kiss through the window and watched her get smaller in the rearview mirror until I turned at the end of our street.


THE NIGHT away was exactly what I needed.

After setting up camp, Echo and I hiked and then settled on

the edge of the lake. Wrapped in my heavy jacket and a blanket around my legs, I watched the sun go down while my dog tried to catch critters.

With my floodlight-style flashlight Kiwi bought me after I brought him with me one time, Echo and I made our way back to camp and ate dinner. Lying in my tent, Wes crossed my mind, and I briefly let my mind wander. What could happen inside these thin walls if he were up here with me? My sleeping bag quickly felt like I was wrapped in a heating blanket, and I had to pull my beanie off to cool down.

Throwing my hat across the tent, I balled my fists. "It doesn't fucking matter. There is no Wes and King."

Echo lifted her head from her paws and stared at me with her head tilted. Tears started pooling in my eyes, and I dug the heels of my hands into them. I came here to escape, not to be reminded that the words Wes whispered in my ear at the bar last week would never come true.

Something dropped into my lap, and I let my hands fall on it. Echo had brought my beanie back over. I took her snout between both hands and planted a kiss on her wet nose. "Thanks, girl."

She settled next to me, and I covered her with her own sleeping bag.

Oblivion thankfully came, and in the morning, I felt better. The Wes phase was over. So what if Sheats lived in the same town? At least now I didn't have to worry about "*him*" coming. For a hot second, I was afraid of what he would do if he found me with Wes.

Echo and I went on another hike before packing up, and by the time I reach the *Welcome to Stonebriar* sign, I have formed a new plan. Finish this semester and move on. Kiwi can stay, and I would come back to visit him and Mags. It's better than—

"What the fuck?" I bring the Jeep to an abrupt stop in the middle of my street. The front of our house is in full view, Mags's car is gone, and in its place sits a Harley.

*His Harley.*

My heart stutters, and I glance left and right as if I'd find the answer of what to do outside the Jeep. I could turn around and pretend I was never here. Go straight to work. He'll have to leave eventually. But what am I going to do with Echo? Out of the corner of my eye, I see my dog *scrutinizing* me as if asking why we're stopped.

I inhale deeply and slowly ease off the brake. I don't press the gas pedal down and instead roll at a snail's pace until I am in my parking spot. I peer to the side, scanning the bike. It's his. Every bit of doubt I was building up in my head is eradicated and stomped on like the roach I once found in one of my old places.

*Fuck!*

Opening my door, Echo squeezes between me and the steering wheel and races to the side door we usually enter the house through.

My childhood Ritalin experience floods my mind as I try to slow my thrashing pulse—unsuccessfully. I slowly slide one leg out of the car and let my foot hover over the cracked concrete. Drawing in a deep breath, I close my eyes. This is my house. My home. I'm not letting him chase me from that.

With more determination, I get out and follow my dog, who is now dancing on her paws.

"Calm down, girl. Why are you so excited?"

I twist the knob, and before I can open the door all the way, she pushes forward, racing inside.

"ECHO! Heel!" But she's gone. "Shit."

I bite the inside of my cheek. I could leave. She's in the house.

Before I can talk myself into running, I walk farther inside. There is no sign of Wes in the kitchen or living room. That leaves only...

I push the door to my room open and—fucking hell.

My treacherous dog has her front paws on Wes's chest—who

is sitting on *my* bed—and licking his face like he's the most delicious treat.

*She's not wrong there. Damn it!*

I watch as his full attention is on Echo. His belly laugh is infectious as he fends off her doggy kisses. Warmth unfurls through my chest, taking in his interaction with her, and for a brief moment, time stands still.

"Whoa. Hey, hey, slo—" He falls backward, and Echo is immediately on top, pinning him to the mattress. He's shit outta luck now. She knows how to use her fifty-eight pounds to hold you captive.

"Echo, heel." I keep my voice low but use the commanding tone her previous owner taught me. My girl immediately swivels her head, and when she takes in my expression, she is off our guest in no time and by my side.

Wes raises himself onto his elbows, and our eyes lock. Taking him in on my bed, my breathing accelerates, and all my good intentions to move on from him and Stonebriar are out the window.

I envision myself walking over slowly and straddling his legs, pressing my already needy core to his—nope, not going there. I shake my head at myself, and Wes quirks a brow.

Neither of us says anything, and I use the elongated silence to calm my racing heart. It's time to let the old King out again. Maybe if I remind him of my knives, he'll leave.

I tilt my head and scan him up and down. She snaps into place, and I let the numbness spread through every cell Wes's presence has sent into disarray.

"What are you doing here?" Most guys would flinch when she comes out to play, but not Wes. He is not impressed.

"I was looking for you." He makes no indication of abandoning his comfortable position.

I snort, crossing my arms over my chest. "And what gives you the right to invade my home?"

Wes's eyes drop to my boobs, which are—thanks to my

motion—pushed up and halfway out of my low-cut tank top. When I packed, I went for comfort and did not consider who I might encounter upon my return. This shirt is one of my favorites and is oversized. It hangs loose and low on my frame, and my unzipped hoodie doesn't help to cover anything up either.

"Eyes up here!" I bark. Not that I don't enjoy them on me. The slickness in my panties definitely contradicts my attitude, but I need to keep up the charade.

"I didn't invade your home." Wes finally sits up and scoots to the edge of the bed. "Your roommate let me in."

*I'm going to kill her.*

I hollow my cheeks, signaling him that I'm not buying it. I know he's telling the truth, but he doesn't need to know that.

"I got here when she was on her way out," he elaborates. "She said you should be back soon, and I could wait inside."

"Inside did not mean on my bed." I grind the words out between clenched teeth, propping my hands on my hips.

Wes shrugs, and I want to throttle him for his nonchalant attitude.

I pull my phone out of my back pocket and tap the screen. "I have to get ready for work." Maybe switching gears will help.

"Okay."

I'm starting to lose my patience. Not because of him, but because my body wants him here while I change and maybe him touching me...

"Get out!" I cut my internal thought process off, and instead of stomping like a toddler, I channel my pent-up (sexual) frustration toward Wes.

He slowly pushes himself off the mattress and saunters over. He stops next to me, but I keep my eyes forward as he leans down, whispering, "I'll be waiting outside."

His breath against the shell of my ear... His arm brushing against mine as he moves on... Even the old King pants like a dog in heat.

I remain in place as Wes walks down the hallway.

"Echo, come keep me company." His voice travels through the house, and before I can stop her, my dog dashes after him.

"Motherfucker!" I whisper-screech, stomping my foot. What is he doing here? I don't understand.

The creak of the back door, followed by it swinging shut, signals that Wes took Echo outside. I drop my arms, and the breath I was holding leaves me with a whooshing sound. Resigned, I pad to my closet and pull my medium-wash skinny jeans off the hanger. I'm so glad Grizz doesn't care what we wear as long as it's paired with the bar's T-shirt. This particular pair has seen better days, and the ripped material over the knees and up the thighs reveals more skin than my self-cropped work tops. I glance behind me at the open door, then decide that I don't care. This is my house. Plus, he's outside.

Despite my non-caring pretense, I change quicker than usual, then head to the bathroom to apply mascara and pull my hair up in a messy bun. It's the best I can do after sleeping in a beanie last night.

Through the glass of the back door, I see Wes throwing Echo's favorite ball. She chases after it and brings it back. He repeats the motion a few more times before he calls out, "Are you coming outside, or are you gonna keep ogling me?"

His question is muffled by the barrier between us, but it's obvious he's enjoying himself.

I open the door, and the immature child in me wants to make Echo heel so that he can no longer play with her. I stop myself, though. This is getting ridiculous.

I put the old King back into the dark corner of my mind that she calls home and slowly walk across the lawn. With every step that takes me closer to Wes, I force my racing pulse to slow more. Whatever happened this past week after he kissed me, after he left with Denielle, none of what I was dealing with was his fault. He doesn't owe me anything, and for once, I want to be the adult my mother raised me to be. I stop several feet away, and Echo saunters over, pressing her trim body against my leg. I lean down and scratch behind her ear, not breaking eye contact with Wes.

He is the first to speak. "Can we talk?" His earlier cockiness is gone.

I focus on the far end of the yard, collecting my thoughts. It's exactly what I was hoping to hear from him last week as I waited. Flicking my gaze back to his, I ignore the fluttery feeling in my chest. "I need to go to work."

The corners of his mouth turn down, and I want to forget everything between our kiss and this moment—pretend it never happened. That I didn't ignore him and that he didn't leave with Denielle.

Wes nods once. "What time do you get off tonight?"

*He still wants to see me?*

"Ten."

"I'll see you here at ten thirty." He comes closer until we're toe to toe. I have to crane my neck to see his face, but I don't step back. His gaze searches my eyes, and he lifts his hand to cup my cheek. His thumb strokes back and forth, and I lean into the caress, shivering at the sensation.

There is no way in hell I can leave this man voluntarily. The mere thought of moving on after this semester is a joke. What was I thinking?

Wes lowers his head, and for a fraction of a second, I think he'll kiss me again. Instead, his lips graze my other cheek, and he whispers, "I'm sorry."

Before I can ask for what exactly, he turns and walks out of the gate. I'm rooted in place, listening to the engine of his bike come to life and slowly fade as he leaves the neighborhood.

# CHAPTER THIRTEEN

### KING

*Fuck, fuck, fuck.*

*I glance at the dashboard. It's almost four in the morning, and now I'm going to get to bed even later—or earlier, however you want to see it. Of course I forget my damn cell the one time I don't have to be back for a full forty-eight hours—which is, like, every six months.*

*I rub my stinging eyes for the hundredth time. The smoke in the club is going to make me blind one day. As I pull into the parking lot, I notice E's car in its usual spot—that's odd. My breathing becomes erratic. I could've sworn he left before me. Only one of the security guys was there when I headed out thirty minutes ago.*

*My hands tighten around the steering wheel. Whatever he's doing here, maybe he won't notice me if I'm quiet.* Yeah, right, *my inner voice clucks at me. Even if the alarm is not triggered, the cameras that monitor every inch of the place will pick up on the movement. There is nothing that is not being recorded here. Insurance policy, as my boss calls it. Or live porn.*

*Shit. Why today of all days? I could already be in bed.*

*Something is off. My gut is never wrong. A cold feeling snakes its way across my skin, and my stomach clenches. A voice in my head begs me to* turn around. I can make do without my phone for two days. Who's calling me anyway? Besides Kiwi, I have no one left. Kiwi. I promised him I would message him when I got home. He'll lose it if he doesn't hear from me. He hates my job.

I stare at the back entrance for several minutes in a failed attempt to get the sudden onslaught of terror under control. What the hell is going on? I'm not scared of E, but if he has one of his guards in there, that's a whole different story—some of them have tried to cop a feel before. My heartbeat accelerates to an almost intolerable speed, and I let one hand glide down my exposed leg down to my Doc Marten boot. It's there. Why wouldn't it be? I never go anywhere without my knives. Even when I dance, at least one is tucked into my knee-high patent-leather boots or strapped to my hip as an eccentric accessory to my thong, garter, and lace bra. Sometimes the blade is all I wear.

I'm going to be fine. In and out. It won't take more than two minutes.

I open the door and step out of my Jeep. My legs tremble for a second. After pulling a double shift in four-inch heels all day, it's a miracle I can stay upright.

I approach the back door, and with every step, the hair on my neck stands more. I glance at the camera above the entrance, the red light taunting me. I hold my breath and carefully try the knob. It turns without resistance. He's definitely here.

Pulling the door open, my ears are assaulted by Niykee Heaton's "Nexus". The club is soundproof, including all the doors. No wonder I didn't notice it until I was inside.

The strobe light is flashing in the main room. What the hell? The dressing room is to my right, but instead of being smart, grabbing my phone, and leaving, my feet carry me toward the commotion. The song gets louder, yet it is dulled by the thrashing pulse in my ears. The closer I get, the more sounds filter through the music.

At first, I think it's moaning. Maybe my boss is having an after-party at the club. Then, the words become clearer. "No. Please don't. No, no, no. P-pleeease." Whoever is begging is in tears and nearly hysterical. Between the pleas, the sobbing gets louder the farther I creep down the corridor. I've almost reached the small archway separating the stage room from the *back. Dizziness is taking over my body, and I'm supporting myself with my hand pressed against the wall.*

*"Oh God, please stop," the female voice wails, followed by a slap and a scream.*

*What the fuck is going on here? It's too late to turn around. I remain hidden in the shadows of the hallway but have a full view of the stage.*

Jesus Christ.

*The back of my hand flies to my mouth, and I gag as I take in the scene in front of me. A girl, fully naked, is bent over the edge of the stage, her chest pressed on the polished wooden floor, while her ass is bared. One of E's guards is standing on the stage with his boot on her back, and my boss is pounding into her from behind. There is absolutely nothing consensual about this.*

*I'm breathing so fast that black spots appear in my vision. There is no way I can leave this girl to their mercy. When she lifts her head slightly, I can see through the strands plastered on her face that she's the dancer who was supposed to start next week. Is he doing this to all the new girls? He's never touched me. I need to do something. Oh God, I can't take on both of them, though. Or can I? I have to.*

*They are violating this poor girl, who's probably not much older than me. I bend down and pull my Du Hoc blade out of my boot. This blade was a gift, and despite everything it represents, I have kept it safe for over a decade. Tonight, it will finally come in use.*

*I creep one inch closer at a time, staying to the edge of the room that is still mostly shrouded in shadow thanks to the lingering smoke. I need to get rid of E's guard first, but there is no way I can get to him undetected. Plus, E's favorite gun is laying on the stage—within his reach. E has to go first. I can only pray that, once his paycheck is gone, his guard's loyalty will shift.*

I'm so dead.

*My jaw hurts from clenching it, but I won't allow myself to breathe through my mouth and potentially end up giving myself away—by screaming or something equally stupid. When I get to the point where I have to step away from the wall to reach my raping pig of a boss, I drop to all fours and move from one seating area to the next, never letting the guy on the stage out of my sight. He almost looks bored and pays E no attention as he assaults the girl in the most vile way. His hand is now fisted in her matted hair, and her head is pulled back. From my angle, I can't see her face, but I don't have to. Her whimpers are perfectly audible over the music, which has changed to a quieter tune.*

*I'm behind the booth facing the stage, with a direct view of my employer's pale, naked ass as he thrusts forward more forcefully every time. If I'd been on my feet, my knees would've given out by now. I keep swallowing over the bile forcing its way up. I haven't eaten in hours, so I'm not concerned about throwing up anything of value—like nourishment.*

*E begins to grunt, and goose bumps erupt all over my body. He's about to be done, and I have no clue what'll happen next. I need to act now. With my heart beating in my throat, I swallow one more time, clench my knife, and leap over the back of the booth. It all happens so quickly. I use the cushioned seat to propel me forward and reach him in three strides. With a scream, I lift my arm and plunge the curved blade into the side of my boss's neck—*

"KING! PRINCESS, WAKE UP. KING!"

I sit up with a start and immediately wrap my arms around my stomach. No, no, no. Not again. Someone touches my shoulder, and the scream—the same sound that came out of my mouth when I killed E—erupts from my lungs.

I squeeze my eyes shut and scramble away from whoever is in my bed. Where is Echo?

The door flies open, and the ceiling light illuminates the room. The mattress dips, and hands touch my face.

"I'm here. Take a breath. It was a dream. You're safe." Mags repeats the same words over and over, stroking my cheek while I sit cross-legged on my mattress, rocking back and forth.

"What is going on? What's wrong with her?" another voice filters through to my brain.

"You need to leave," Mags commands to whoever is talking.

"The fuck I am."

*Wes. Oh God, Wes is here. Why is he here?*

I blink through the tears and turn my head in the direction of his voice. Wes stands in the middle of my small room, wearing only briefs. His hair is tousled, and his hands are clasped on top of his head. He locks eyes with mine, and his concern is my undoing. I cover my mouth with my hands to muffle the sob threatening to burst out.

Mags touches my chin and nudges me to look at her. "Do you want him to leave? I can call Grizz if—"

I shake my head.

Her tone is calm. She's been through this with me too many times to count. One of the many reasons I love this girl.

Wes waited for me when I got home from work, like he said he would. But instead of talking about the past week, we watched a movie in the living room. The last thing I remember is him taking my hand and resting my head on his shoulder. The comfort and feeling of safety let me relax.

I slowly drop my hands back to my lap and draw in a hiccuped breath. "N-no. It's okay."

"You sure?"

"You heard her. Stop being a b—" Wes's angry remark gets interrupted by my other girl pushing past him and jumping on the bed.

"Hey, sweet girl. Where were you?" I nuzzle my nose in her fur as she climbs in my lap. Echo also has seen me like this— many times.

"I had just let her out when you screamed," Mags explains. "I must've left the back door open when I came running."

I look at my best friend. "Thank you."

She strokes my cheek one more time. "Of course. Do you need anything?"

I shake my head, and Mags stands slowly. When she's in front of Wes, she tilts her head up. "Do not push her to give you answers she's not ready to give." Her tone doesn't leave room for negotiation. Wes dips his head once in acknowledgment, then walks around my friend to the bed. Without hesitation, he climbs back under the covers. He sits against the headboard and lifts an arm.

I scoot closer with my dog still in my lap and lean into him. Echo shifts to be tucked between us, and I feel cocooned between Wes's embrace and my furry girl.

"Do you want to talk about it?" Wes asks after a beat of silence.

*Do I?*

I don't want him to know this side of me, but I owe him an explanation as to what he witnessed.

"In the morning?" I lift my head slightly to glance at the alarm clock on my nightstand. It's almost three, which explains why Mags was letting Echo out. She always does it when she gets home from her shift.

Wes tightens his hold for a second before letting go, and I expect him to push me away and leave. Instead, he starts drawing circles on my upper arm, and I wish right about now that we didn't have a chaperone dog between us.

My eyelids begin to droop, and eventually, I am lulled to sleep by his caress. My last thought is that I never fall back asleep when I've had that dream.

# CHAPTER FOURTEEN

## WES

I GOT ZERO SHUT-EYE AFTER KING'S...WHAT THE FUCK WAS that? How could I? The last time I saw someone that scared, one of my best friends was—*fuck*.

I had sat on King's front porch for over an hour, waiting for her to get back from work. Why I was so early, hell if I knew. I owed her an explanation for disappearing for almost a week—at least that was how I justified it. Then, she pulled up, and I saw how tired she was, so I suggested watching a movie. We could always talk in the morning.

I expected her to cross-examine me. Every other girl I'd ever dated would have. But King is so far from those chicks that I wasn't surprised that she instantly agreed. When she dozed off on the couch, I carried her to her bedroom, and in a spur-of-the-moment decision, I stayed. I'd been away from her for far too long, fighting my own demons, and it was time to change that.

What I didn't expect was getting jolted out of a deep sleep by *her demons*.

After she calmed back down, I was the one who wanted to

demand answers. I knew she had damage, but witnessing the... the terror in her eyes, the need to hold her was overpowering.

Seeing all the tension leave her features reminded me of watching Den sleep in LA—the one time she was truly relaxed during those days.

King is still out when I slip out of bed at seven. I have to move. Think. I pull on my jeans, and Echo trails after me. I take that as her signal that she has to take care of business. After opening the back door, I watch her run around the yard.

*What am I doing here?*

My focus should be on training, but instead, I've let this girl completely consume me. It's been weeks, and I know jack shit about her. This is so not me. I used to be in it for fun, not drama. And after what I saw a few hours ago, there is a lot of that in King's life.

"You're up."

I jerk around and find Mags in her pajamas, standing in the doorframe to the kitchen. Her hair is a mess, and she covers her mouth as she yawns.

"Didn't go back to sleep." Why downplay the situation? From what I gathered, Mags is familiar with...whatever that was.

She nods and makes her way over to the Keurig. "I can never sleep past seven, no matter what time I go to bed. Which is why I hate closing the bar."

Is she making small talk? Echo plows back in and straight to her water bowl before disappearing down the hallway.

"Ha," King's best friend guffaws. "She is totally abusing this."

I cock an eyebrow, and she elaborates, "King doesn't let her in her bed."

*Oh.*

"Where is King?" Leaning away from the counter, she peers down the hallway.

"Still out cold."

She whips her head around so quickly I take a step back. Whoa.

"What do you mean she's out cold? What did you do?"

*Huh?*

"What do you think I mean?" This conversation is getting ridiculous.

Mags shakes her head. "You don't understand. She never goes back to sleep after…"

"The nightmare?" I supply helpfully.

She purses her lips and glances between me and the hallway. "It wasn't a nightmare."

"Excuse me?"

"It was a memory. She relives it over and over, and it always ends…like last night."

*Oh, Jesus Christ.*

"Did she tell you anything?"

I want to say yes to keep her talking, but at the same time, I can't do that to King. I know all too well what it's like to have your trust betrayed, and I would never do that to her.

"No, we were going to talk this morning."

"Okay." She picks up her steaming coffee and ejects the cartridge out of the coffee maker. On her way out, she pauses and rotates back to me. "Thank you."

My brows shoot up. "For?"

"Being there for her. She doesn't let many get close. In fact, no one besides Kiwi or me."

I nod, unsure what to respond, and she disappears back down the hall.

I'M SITTING at the kitchen table, staring at my cold coffee. I hate that black murky-looking water substitute, but I need to have something in front of me to hold on to as I sort through my thoughts.

I still haven't told Den about King. Maybe I'm worried she'd be my voice of reason. Reason that I've shoved so far down then covered up by whatever I could find just so I don't have to admit to myself what's becoming more and more obvious. Something is wrong with King.

"Hey." Her hesitant greeting snaps me out of my internal battle, and I turn my head.

She is wearing my T-shirt, and my cock immediately twitches at the sight. I scan her bare legs and let my gaze trail back up until our eyes meet.

"My clothes were grimy from...and it was laying on the floor. I hope it's okay. I can go chan—" She fidgets with the material. Her nervousness makes her look like a little girl.

"It's fine." I force a smile on my lips, despite not feeling the emotion. Holding my hand out, I say, "Come here."

She slowly comes closer, and I reach for her as soon as she's at arm's length. I wrap my arm around her middle and lean my head against her chest. Her heart is hammering out of control, and I tilt my head up, finding her staring out the window. She's stiff as a board, and her fear of my reaction makes the decision for me. Can I afford instability in my life? No. Should I run for the hills after everything that I've seen? That is an all-caps FUCK YES. Yet, I can't. Kingsley Monroe has captured my attention, and no matter what, I feel alive for the first time in years. I feel something besides anger and resentment, and I'm not willing to give that up. Yet.

I push my chair back and stand facing her. She dips her head back to meet my eyes.

"Let's go talk somewhere."

We get dressed in silence. As we leave the house, she holds out the keys to her Jeep. I frown at her offering, and my girl only shrugs.

*My girl.*

I have no clue what horror story she will divulge to me soon, and still, I claim her as mine. I've lost my mind.

I drive us to the reservoir thirty-five minutes out of town. It's in the mountains, and she fumbles with her curved blade the entire ride. I've noticed by now that she carries one of her two knives everywhere. She is never without one. Last night, it was sitting on her bedside table.

Exiting the car, she tucks the knife in a sheath in the back of her jeans, and I stare for a second. What have I gotten myself into?

We walk for a good ten minutes before she speaks. "It's always the same...*dream*." Her tone is low, and she hugs herself. A sour taste settles on my tongue, and she hasn't even started the actual story.

Her eyes remain trained on the ground, and I take that as her wanting to get it all out on her own terms.

"My mother got sick when I was fifteen. It was just the two of us. She could no longer work her two jobs, and I had to find a way to help out. I was working at a diner for a while. I took on every shift I could get, but between school and taking care of her, it was never enough. We constantly got our power shut off, or Kiwi's grandmother had to bring us food."

Instinctively, I pull her into me and place a kiss on the top of her head. No wonder she and Kiwi are so close.

"When I was sixteen, I started working at The Pole. I had dropped out of school the year before."

*The Pole?*

The name speaks for itself. I stop dead in my tracks, and my arm drops from her shoulders as she keeps walking. All I can do is gape at her. King holds my gaze, and my brain fires off one signal after another for me to turn around. Leave. Screw feeling alive. I had too much fucked-up shit in my past. This is my fresh start. But I can't. I'm already in too deep with this girl I know barely anything about—something that will change very soon.

She reaches for my hand. When her fingers make contact, my heart skips a beat. Feeling her skin against mine, her soft palm against my calloused one, there is no way I can walk away from her. After she drags me along for several feet, my legs finally start moving on their own again.

"The Pole was an exclusive strip club. Men had to drop half their paycheck to get in, but with that, they also got certain perks."

*Jesus Christ, I'm going to be sick.*

"I was one of E's best dancers, which was why I was solely on stage. The other girls had to work the floor as well as dance. I never did."

*Thank you, Lord.*

King doesn't look at me as she talks. "Almost two years ago, one night after a double shift, I forgot my phone at the club. It was in the middle of the night, and I should've simply left it there, but I had the next night off, and I didn't want to be without it for that long. I didn't notice until I was almost home. Kiwi was expecting my text, so I had to drive all the way back to get it. I didn't want to worry him. When I got to the club, E's car was there. He had left earlier, and I knew something wasn't right."

When she stops her recap, I peer at her sideways, not having the guts to face her head-on. It's obvious she'd rather forget the memory.

"If you'd look up the word *creep* in the dictionary, you'd find Isaiah Ellis's picture. He's everything you imagine a sleazy strip club owner to be: tall, scrawny but with a keg belly, ash-brown hair with a receding hairline, neon parachute joggers, and a white wife beater."

"Did he—?" I can't bring myself to form the words.

King understands immediately and rushes out, "No."

I exhale a sigh of relief, which is quickly replaced by another wave of nausea.

"But it seems I was the only one he didn't touch."

"WHAT?" My outburst makes several birds around us take flight.

King pivots toward me and takes my other hand as well. We

stand in the middle of the wooded walkway, and she studies me. "Do you want me to continue?"

*No. Yes. No. Fuck!*

Instead of responding, I slowly lean in and press my lips to hers. There is nothing sexual behind the kiss, not like the first time, just the slightest bit of pressure. King's soft lips part, and I let go of her hands, framing her face and deepening the connection. My heart rate accelerates, and I pull her into me until our bodies are flush against each other. Heat spreads all the way to my toes, and as King's tongue seeks entry, I break the kiss. Her lids are hooded, and I have to take a step back to not crash my mouth to hers again. I didn't mean for that to happen. This is as much for her as it is for me—a way to test me. Do I want her to continue? Do I feel...*something* for her?

I interlace our fingers and answer her question. "Yes."

She dips her chin, and we start walking again.

"I can stop anytime." Her fear of me pushing her away for whatever is coming is audible in her plea.

"Okay."

I almost think she has changed her mind when she speaks.

"As I said, apparently I was the only one he didn't touch." She draws in a slow breath. "Walking into the club that night, I knew something was off. No one should've been there. The Pole closes at three, and it was almost four. But the music was blaring through the speakers, and even the lights were on. When I got inside, I heard a girl..."

My hand involuntarily grips hers tighter, but she doesn't indicate that I'm hurting her. She's miles away, wherever this club was located.

"I...I went to check out what was going on—the sounds coming from the main room..."

"Keep going." I get the picture.

"What I saw there, Wes, God, I—I had to help her. But Vic... He was E's right-hand man and security. E was...and Vic, he held the girl—"

*Jesus fuck.*

"I killed him."

Those three words were spoken so low that it takes me longer than it should to comprehend them. King has stopped moving but won't look at me.

I wait.

"I surprised E from behind and stabbed him in the side of the neck. Here." She touches the side of her own neck with her free hand. "The blade slid in like a hot knife through butter, which was exactly what went through my mind. This was like slicing butter—until I hit...bone. But it wasn't butter that was spilling over my blade and hand."

Her voice is detached, and I don't dare interrupt her.

"The girl started screaming, and Vic noticed what I had done —he had been facing the other way. Like he didn't give two fucks what his boss was doing to this poor girl. She was supposed to start working at The Pole the following week. Vic...he—"

"Did he hurt you?" I can't stop myself. I scan every inch of visible skin for scars or signs of old injuries.

"No. He... Vic stared at me and then...left."

"He left?" *What the—*

"I couldn't focus on it at the time. I had to help the girl. She was bleeding from where E had hit her. His body was at our feet, and she was still naked. She went into shock, wouldn't talk or respond. I didn't know what to do. I had killed my boss. There were witnesses, not to mention the entire club was wired with cameras. I would go to jail." Her tears resemble a downpour against a pane of glass. "I wrapped the girl in a blanket and drove her to the emergency room. Once she was taken care of, I—"

Suddenly, King folds into herself. She kneels in the middle of the hiking path and rocks back and forth. She drops her head to her knees, and my lungs compress at the sight. I've seen this before. This was how Rhys reacted to finding Lilly's Jeep flipped upside down on the side of the road. I peer in either direction, but we're the only people up here.

*Fuck it.*

I sit down next to her and pull her into my lap. She curls into me, and I hold her tight, rocking both of us as one would soothe an upset child.

It takes her forever to regain some control. It could've been just a few minutes, but it sure as shit felt like hours.

"I drove back to the club. It was nearly six, and E was dead in the middle of the bar's main room. I did the only thing I could. I called the one person I knew would help me."

"Who—"

"Please don't ask," she cuts me off, and I swallow the remark on my tongue.

Who would she have been able to call who could make a dead body and a bunch of security videos disappear? I mean, I know who I'd call, but I doubt King has Lilly's or George's numbers. I have so many questions, and it's clear I won't get any answers to them.

"He told me to go home and wait for his call. He'd take care of everything. Then, he ordered me to run. I could not stay in one place for more than a few weeks until no one would be looking for E anymore. I left town before the club reopened that night. From what Kiwi told me, E was reported missing. I also never checked back on the girl. I should've gone back, but I was too scared."

"This is how you ended up in Stonebriar?"

King nods against my chest, and I hug her tighter.

"Why didn't you keep moving?" Deep down, I know the answer, which makes my stomach flip in a good and bad way at the same time.

"You."

# CHAPTER FIFTEEN

## WES

After that, uh, confession, we walk—both of us in our own thoughts. When I check my phone, I am shocked to see that it is almost two in the afternoon. I've missed my morning classes, and practice starts at four. It'll take us forty-five minutes to get back to town limits, and I don't have my gear with me. I can't afford to miss another practice.

After ditching last Wednesday and barely being present the rest of the week—thanks to my constant state of hangover—Coach will have my balls if I don't show. At the same time, I don't want to leave King.

Her confiding in me brought this—*us*—to a different playing field. I thought I would be able to walk away, despite what I witnessed last night. Now, there is no chance in hell I can leave her side again. Kingsley Monroe is one of the fiercest women I've ever met, and I know some strong fucking girls.

I squeeze her hand lightly. Her eyes are haunted, and I'm worried about what recalling the events after having the nightmare mere hours prior has done to her. I stop and spin her toward me. "We should probably head back."

The corners of her mouth draw down, and I realize how this came out. I close my eyes briefly. "Shit, no. That's not how I meant it."

I let go of her hands and pull her into me. She returns the embrace without hesitation, burying her nose in my shirt. The strain that I didn't realize had my muscles coiled melts away. I place a kiss on the crown of her head.

"I have to get back for practice, but I want to see you later," I murmur against her hair, inhaling the fragrance of her shampoo. I halt mid-sniff. *When did I start smelling a girl's hair?*

King draws back slightly and peers up at me. "You do?" A laugh bursts out at the astonishment in her voice.

"What? You thought stabbing this motherfucker would change my mind? Make me want you less? Did you forget who my friends are?" *Were.*

Their actions never were the issue. It was the betrayal that ruined everything.

Something I can't decipher flashes across her face, and her eyes become watery. It's gone as quickly as it appeared, and I chalk it up to this day being an emotional mindfuck.

When a lone tear spills over, I untangle my arms from her and brush it away with my thumb. Her sadness chokes me, and I want to take her pain from her.

I open my mouth to start explaining why I had disappeared for almost a week when she shifts and hooks her arms around my neck. Her grip tightens, and I automatically engage my neck muscles against the sudden force. I don't fight as she yanks me to her, and our lips connect.

My brain short-circuits as her tongue strokes mine and—*holy shit!* It's not our first kiss, or second, but this is...any coherent thought leaves me. At the bar, I was marking my territory when I didn't have a right to—yet. But I had to make sure everyone knew that she was mine before *I* admitted to myself that she was. This time, she is claiming me.

My pulse speeds up, and my cock is rock hard within

seconds. I thrust my hips against her as her tongue tangles with mine. I drop my hands and glide them down her sides until I find her ass—her very firm ass. How many times have I watched her in her skintight jeans stalk around the bar, endured with clenched fists as every guy's eyes also followed the sway of her hips as she moved past?

*Mine*, a voice inside my head growls, even though I am the only one here.

Yes, she's mine.

I lift her up, and King wraps her legs around my body as soon as her feet leave the ground. Grinding her hips against me, I groan at the friction she causes. Despite the cool air up here in the mountains, a sheen of sweat covers me from head to toe. *Too hot.* The limited space inside my pants becomes smaller, and I want nothing more than to press her against the nearest tree and fuck her senseless.

She moans against my mouth, and my fingers dig into her butt. She tastes like heaven, and I wonder if she tastes this good in other places.

Fuck, I need to stop, or I really won't make it to practice.

I slow the kiss, and she whimpers in protest, applying more pressure against the back of my neck, wanting to hold me in place.

"Princess..." I try to get the words out when she nips at my bottom lip, and my control is about to snap. A metallic taste fills my mouth. She's drawn blood—this little devil. Instead of being bothered by it, I swipe the tip of my tongue against the spot and close my eyes at the sting. What the hell has gotten into me?

I let go of her ass, and she slides down my torso. As soon as she hits the ground, I take a step away, lifting my hands as if to hold off an assailant. King looks at me through her lashes, her chest rising and falling rapidly, mimicking my own breathing.

God, she is so fucking beautiful.

"Why did you stop?" Her question is breathy, and I huff out a laugh.

"Because I was this close"—I hold my thumb and forefinger about half an inch apart—"to fucking you in the middle of the woods."

Her bottom lip sticks out, and her pouting evokes a fierce need to jerk her to me and continue what we (almost) started. How can I deny her?

"I have practice, and you're scheduled to work," I reason with her as much as I do with my protesting cock. I swear, the profanities he's hurling at me inside my head would make Kai proud.

*Yeah, I'm not happy either*, but I have enough common sense left not to want our first time to be in the middle of the forest with me pounding King against tree bark and making her back-side bleed.

I reach for her and intertwine our fingers. She squeezes my hand in return and steps closer. I don't stop her now that the hormonal crisis has been averted.

Leaning down, I place a gentle kiss against her still-scowling mouth. Before straightening, I whisper, "Don't worry. You will get thoroughly fucked—very soon."

Her eyes widen, and her lips part. Her tongue darts out ever so slightly, and I can't stop the groan escaping me. I turn and stalk in the direction we came from, dragging her behind me by our clasped hands.

"We need to go." My gruff tone is met with a chuckle, and for the first time in my life, I have the urge to spank a female.

This girl will be the death of me.


I MADE it to practice on time. My performance was still shit, though. I was fully sober, but my mind kept wandering to King every few minutes, and every fucking time, my cock would stand at half-mast. At one point, Zeke took a double take at my pants, and I pulled a total girl move. "Eyes up here!"

My outburst, of course, brought everyone's attention to me,

and I followed my emasculating display with face-palming my forehead. Zeke doubled over, howling like a hyena, and the rest stared like I had lost my mind. I probably did. I left it in the woods by the reservoir when I raced to the Jeep with the last bit of self-control I could muster.

I am the first out of the locker room, and Kai whistles after me. "Finally came to your senses, huh?"

I flip him the bird, not bothering to turn around, and pull my phone out with my other hand. King has a couple more hours of work. I contemplate showing up at the bar but then decide to send her a text instead.

**Me: Can I pick you up after your shift?**

I don't expect her to respond, but when the little bubble pops up a second later, I hold my breath.

**King: I drove, and I need the Jeep in the morning to make it to class on time.**

*Is she making an excuse not to meet me?*

I decide to pull one from Kai's playbook.

**Me: So, that's a yes?**

**King: Ha ha. Meet me at my place at 11:15?**

I send her a thumbs-up emoji in return.

**King: Oh, come on now. Like you are not grinning from ear to ear. Don't start acting cool all of a sudden.**

I realize she is right when my cheeks pinch, and I glance over my shoulder, making sure she is not anywhere in the vicinity.

**Me: I. Am. Cool! Are you stalking me again, MOAB Girl?**

**King: You wish, Sheats.**

**Me: Maybe I am. I'm getting used to it. Something is missing when I don't have one of your knives near me.**

What the fuck am I even saying? When she doesn't respond, my first thought is that I pushed it too far. She has a reason to always be armed. I should've asked her if she's scared someone will come after her for killing her boss. The mere thought of the raping son of a bitch... What he did, what King witnessed, makes my throat go dry and my breath increase. If she hadn't already killed him, my first call would be to George. Not that I would ask him to do the deed, but I would need his help in covering it up.

I stare off toward the other end of the parking lot as my phone vibrates in my palm, and King's name lights up the display.

**King: Sorry, Grizz came out front. Need to get back to work. See you later?**

**Me: Yes. See you soon.**

Glancing at my watch, I have time to head home for a bit.

As I pull into the garage, an incoming call is announced through my ear pods. I smile to myself and answer. "Took you long enough to call me."

"Well, according to Kai, you've been in a drunken stupor for the past week."

"Talking to my roommate now, are you, D?" My smile is gone. I do not need to be reminded of last week or why I ended up drowning myself in Kai's liquor stash, which could keep our entire campus intoxicated for a week.

"Well, you didn't answer. I was worried." The second part is spoken softly, and I know what she is referring to.

"I needed to think." About a lot.

"Come to any results?" My best friend sounds hopeful.

"Not yet." I try not to be an asshole, but I can't just decide that the last two-plus years didn't happen. "How was the flight?" If she pushes the topic I don't want to talk about, I can do the same.

There is silence on the other end, and I check if the call is still connected. "D?"

"It was fine."

Which means it wasn't. "What did he do now?"

If I didn't like Lilly's shadow so much, or if he wasn't always armed to the teeth like his boss, I would beat his pretty mug in one of these days.

"I don't want to talk about it. He...he was his usual self." She sighs.

It's a complete mystery to me why Marcus treats Den the way he does. Yes, they didn't have the best of starts, given the fact that he manhandled her onto the jet in LA and basically had to hold her down the entire flight to Virginia, but still. He's a cool dude but a major dick to Den. I wonder if Lilly and Rhys know.

"Tell me about blondie. You never elaborated on what I walked in on last week." She doesn't sound smug or condescending, just curious. Den knows about pretty much all the girls I've hooked up with over the years. She's taken Rhys's place when it comes to guy talk, which is another reason I love her to death. Despite what almost happened between us, she is my best friend and only my best friend. She is hot as hell, and I'm sure the sex would've been phenomenal, but in the end, we wouldn't have worked out as a couple. We are too much alike and probably would've killed each other in the first six months—figuratively speaking.

"I don't want to talk about it." I throw her statement back at her and hear an intake of breath on the other end. "What?"

"You're serious about her?" Her shock is audible.

*Am I?*

"I have no clue, D." I pause before adding, "There is a lot I still have to figure out."

On so many levels.

"Wes?"

"Yes?"

"If she hurts you, I will hunt her down and shave her pretty blonde hair. And I will bring G with me," Den deadpans.

I puff out my chest, not that my friend sees it. "You would need half of G's team to take King down."

"What does that mean?" Alarm rings in her voice. Shit.

"Nothing. Just..." I need to get off this call before I say something I shouldn't or may regret. "Listen, D, I'll call you this weekend, okay? I gotta go."

"Practice is over for the day, where are you—? Oh." She halts herself. "Okay, call me Saturday. I'm flying back to New York on Sunday."

"K. Love you, BK."

"Fuck you, Sheats." After a beat of silence, she continues, "Love you, too."


I GET to King's at 11:16 p.m.

It's getting too cold for my bike, and with the possibility of snow any day, I decide to take the 4Runner. I never took my spiked tires off in the spring. I simply switched to riding my bike everywhere.

If we need a car, I drive with Kai or take his Rover. He couldn't care less.

She sits on the front porch and immediately gets up when I stop in front of her driveway, dusting her jeans off. She's still wearing the same pair as earlier but changed out of her work shirt. Instead, she's covered in a fitted black hoodie and a leather jacket.

Wes Junior enjoys the outfit as well and instantly stands at attention. Though, King could wear a white bedsheet with cutout holes for the eyes, and I would have a raging hard-on in zero point three seconds. After all, there could be a chance of her being naked underneath.

When she pulls the passenger door open and slides in, I slant my head. "Are we going somewhere?"

She gives me an apologetic smile. "Yes. Mags got into it with Grizz. You don't want to be in there."

"What's their deal?" I've noticed their...dynamic, and it's more fucked up than Den and Marcus's.

"I wish I knew. She won't talk about it." King purses her lips.

"Can we hang out at your place?" She quickly adds, "I can drive myself so you don't have to bring me back later."

"Do you really think you will sleep alone tonight?" I let the question hang because it's clear what I'm insinuating.

A faint blush spreads over her cheeks, and I prop my elbow on the middle console, leaning over to her. Her eyes fly to my mouth, and I smirk.

King angles her body so her leg rests on the seat. Impatience taking over, I reach for her. She opens up without hesitation, and when her warm tongue connects with mine, my single-minded brain fast-forwards to what else she could do with her mouth tonight.

Jesus, I don't remember ever wanting someone this bad.

I let my hand glide from the nape of her neck to her cheek and break the kiss, leaning my forehead against hers. "Let's go."

"Hurry." King has her eyes closed and swipes her lips against mine as she says the word. Her tone is like a purr, and I shift in my seat. I should've worn sweatpants.

We both move back to our own seats, but she weaves our fingers together in the middle. Her head is slanted toward me, and a soft smile turns the corner of her mouth upward.

I reach over with my other hand to shift the truck into gear, not wanting to let go of her. Peering at her out of my peripheral vision, I say, "You look happy."

"I am." She squeezes my hand.

I draw in a deep breath, and as I slowly let the air out, all the tension I've held—for what feels like years—leaves my body. Where her skin is connected with mine, a tingling sensation begins to spread, and goose bumps erupt on my arm. Her thumb begins to stroke back and forth over my knuckles, and a sigh escapes me. I fight the urge to close my eyes and fully give in to the sensation.

. . .

WE REACH THE TOWNHOUSE, and I pull straight into the garage. I can't decide if I want to fuck this girl's brains out or simply fall asleep with her in my arms. The fierce need to protect her from everything and everyone makes my muscles coil, but at the same time, I haven't felt peace like this in...I don't know if I ever have.

With my hand in hers, I guide her from the garage up the stairs. Through the door leading onto the first floor, I hear laughter and someone hooting like a fucking lunatic. I frown.

"Sounds like Kai has company," King says quietly behind me, a pang of disappointment in her statement.

"At least it doesn't seem to be a full-blown party or mass orgy," I mumble to myself, but she hears it and snorts. "Are you sure about that?"

I'm spared the response as we enter the living room and find Kai, Mack, Zeke, and—

"Kiwi?" King's confusion mimics my surprise at finding her BFF in my living room.

"Hey, Roe-Roe." He grins, and I take in his leg pressed against Zeke's.

Mack cracks up out of nowhere, and I narrow my eyes.

What have we walked in on?

I wasn't gone that long. How the hell did this happen? The house was empty when I left.

I take in the beer bottles on the table and scan my roommate's face as he lifts his drink in my direction. "We're playing *what would you not be able to do when...?*"

"Huh?" I glance between the four guys spread out on the couch. Before I can ask anything else, King lets go of my hand, clapping hers together and jumping in place.

"Oh, oh, I wanna play!"

I stare at her incredulously. She rarely gets this animated unless she is pissed or—as I discovered—horny.

Her head swivels in my direction, and she beams. "It's something Kiwi and I used to play as kids to pass the time." Her excitement dims slightly. "Usually, it revolved more around topics like what would you do if our electricity would not be turned on again? Or what wouldn't you be able to do if—"

"Dude, that's fucking depressing," Mack exclaims as he lifts his beer to his lips.

"Well, hit me, then. What was your last would/wouldn't question?" my girl challenges him, and Kiwi's eyes widen. He shakes his head slightly, but I don't think anyone notices.

Kai leans forward and rests his forearms on his thighs, his bottle dangling between two fingers. "I asked the guys what they wouldn't be able to do anymore if they only had one hand."

*The fuck?*

"Oh, that's easy." King perks up, and all eyes are on her.

"Yeah? Let's hear it." Kai smirks.

"Well, you could masturbate, but you wouldn't be able to hold your phone and watch porn while you do it," she deadpans.

Zeke spits his beer across the couch table, and Kiwi breaks out in hysterical laughter. Mack gapes at her, slack-jawed, and Kai... I've never seen him this serious. King holds his stare, and I glance back and forth between them. I have no fucking clue what to say to this.

Suddenly, Kai stands up, walks over to us, and drops to his knees. King juts her eyebrows, and my roommate folds his hands like he's praying. "You're my queen!"

"Wha—?"

"You know what these douche canoes said?" He slowly stands up. "You wouldn't be able to braid your hair." He throws a glare of contempt at our teammates and Kiwi. "I mean, what the actual fuck? You, however..." He points a finger at King, still holding his drink by the neck. "*You* know what's important."

He turns so fast that I take a step back, pulling King with me by the belt loop of her jeans. Kai addresses the other three while still pointing at King. "This, gentlemen, is a woman who knows what's important. Let this be said: if our boy here doesn't stake his claim on Miss Monroe, I will!"

"Oh, Jesus Christ!" I roll my eyes while two of the three grin, and Mack still looks mystified.

I can't even be pissed at my roommate for his comment, because her answer was genius, and he's a hundred-percent right that I need to stake my claim.

## CHAPTER SIXTEEN

### KING

STILL GIGGLING, WES DRAGS ME DOWN THE HALL. THIS IS NOT how I thought this night would end. I was hoping for some more making out, maybe an explanation of where he was last week. But then again, the night is not over yet.

At Kai's declaration, aka challenge, against Wes, I fought to suppress my eager grin. Kiwi did not hold back. He gave me his toothiest smirk, and I rolled my eyes at him.

Maybe Wes needs the challenge to—

My train of thought breaks off when I realize where we are. The door clicks behind me, and my breath hitches. It's just the two of us. The sound of the others' laughter is muted, and with my pulse thumping inside my ears, it's barely noticeable. The room is illuminated by light spilling out from the adjoining bathroom, and I scan my surroundings. The furniture is high end. I heard a rumor that Kai's family's interior designer furnished the whole place. The color scheme is dark. Besides a desk, dresser, and nightstand, there is one more piece of furniture. I take in the massive king-size bed with its rumpled gray sheets and—I start counting—eight pillows? As if reading my mind, he elaborates, "A move-in present."

His arms wind around my midsection, and I lean my back against his front, resting my head against his collarbone. Placing my hands over his, he tightens his hold further. He bends down until his lips graze the shell of my ear. "Do you have any idea how many times I've envisioned having you here since last week?"

A shiver of pleasure runs down my spine, and I swallow over the saliva pooling in my mouth. I can feel him everywhere, even where our bodies are not connected—yet.

Then, a sobering thought strikes my brain. "Why did you disappear then?" I hate the vulnerability I'm allowing him to see.

His grip loosens, and I curse myself for ruining the mood. I shift to scan his face, expecting him to look angry, but instead, his gaze is toward the opposite wall, and I follow his line of sight. On his dresser is a framed picture that I hadn't noticed in the dimness before.

Wes steps away from me and reaches for my hand, leading me across the room. He picks the photo up with his other hand, holding it in front of us. I recognize the pictured individuals instantly. The picture was taken somewhere sunny and warm, judging by the palm trees in the background and the lack of clothes. The four are on a patio, scattered across various lounge chairs. Lilly and Denielle are in shorts and bikini tops. Lilly sits sideways on top of Rhys, his arms wrapped around her slender waist and her leaning into him. He is shirtless, only wearing green-camo cargo shorts. Denielle is on a chaise next to them with (what looks like) a cocktail in hand, ginormous glasses covering her eyes, and Wes sits with his elbows on his knees, leaning forward at the foot of Denielle's chair. They're all laughing.

Wes places the frame back on the dresser but doesn't move away. "This was taken a week before...you know what I'm talking about, right?" His head turns toward me, and I nod.

Of course I know. I've seen every single recording—numerous times.

"That day, everything was finally settled. All the paperwork was signed and filed—for Lilly." Wes adds the last two words when he sees my frown, and I understand. "We had one week to forget. Lilly had seven more days before they went public with the whole story, and for that limited time, we all pretended to be normal."

My stomach is in knots as he speaks about his friends.

"I haven't looked at this picture in years. I thought I threw it away. D brought it last week and must've set it on the dresser when I pulled the car around. I haven't been able to take it down, no matter how much I want to."

He pauses, and I'm not sure if he's done speaking.

"What happened?" I whisper, wanting him to keep talking, wanting so desperately to understand what happened to the funny, charming boy I saw in the media before arriving in Stonebriar.

"I saw Lilly last week."

I hold my breath, not sure what to say without revealing anything I know about him—or her, for that matter.

"It was the first time since I left LA two years ago. Rhys showed up at my place a few weeks earlier. They're getting married next spring."

Oh, wow.

"I refused to talk to Rhys, kicked him out of the house. But then Den asked me to take her to the airport. She has a complicated relationship with Lilly's bodyguard; that's all I can say. Lilly and I... We got into it. She asked—fuck, it's not important. Then, I found the picture on the dresser...and everything came crashing back. The betrayal and anger. I felt like I was being choked. I thought I was past it, had moved on, but...I'm not."

The grimace tells me that it's not easy for him to admit that out loud, showing vulnerability.

"That's why you went AWOL?" I ask hesitantly.

Instead of answering, Wes pulls me over to the bed and settles against his mountain of pillows. He pulls me down beside him, and I nestle into the crook of his arm, resting my head on his chest.

He starts talking, telling me everything that has happened and led him to be in Stonebriar. Parts of it I knew from my stalkerish tendencies and what I could piece together from different media reports, but that didn't even scratch the surface. My heart breaks for him when he describes how betrayed he felt, and understanding sets in. Rhys may have wanted to help, but the combination of him going behind Wes's back, having kept so many secrets from him for years, and Wes losing his dream was too much. It broke him.

"I needed to forget," Wes ends his recollection, explaining his absence with those four words.

I start drawing circles on his chest, and he sighs. I peer up at him through my lashes. His eyes are closed, and he relaxes in front of me. I drink in his gorgeous features.

"Do you miss them?" I ask softly.

He remains silent for so long that I think he might have fallen asleep. But then he says, "I do."

I look away from him as a tear escapes my eye. He lifts his hand, turning me back to him. "Why are you crying, Princess?"

*Princess.*

"Maybe it's time to forgive them?" I am ignoring the blaring alarm bells in my head. I'm probably overstepping every boundary there is. What right do I have to suggest that?

Wes tugs on me until I'm on top of him, our noses touching, and his eyes merge to one.

"Maybe I should." His words are low, and I have to strain my ears.

Before I can reply, he captures my mouth with his, and as before, it's like I'm meant to be here—in his arms, with his lips on me. Wes deepens the kiss, his tongue tangling with mine, and heat builds in my core. His hands wander along my spine, and his touch burns itself into every muscle. His fingers find the hem of my jeans and slip inside, squeezing my bare ass. My entire body becomes feverish at the sensation of his rough touch against my flesh, and wetness pools between my legs.

"You're not wearing underwear," he growls against my mouth and begins trailing kisses along my jaw until he reaches the lobe of my ear. "Naughty, naughty." He licks the sensitive skin underneath, and my eyes roll back inside my head.

*How can this feel so good?*

There are many days I forgo panties, always depending on what I'm wearing, but tonight I may have had an ulterior motive. I rock my hips into him, and he groans, nipping at me.

Unashamed, I continue the motion, fully aware I am dry humping Wes. The friction of his hard cock against my pussy—even with the barrier of two pairs of jeans between us—is like heaven.

He removes his hands from my ass and grasps the bottom of my shirt. I disentangle myself from him so he can pull it off my body. Wes sits both of us up, and I straddle his lap. My arms wrap around his shoulders, and I press my mouth back to his, the short break instantly starving me for him. With a swift movement, he unlatches the clasp of my bra and slides the straps down my shoulders until the material falls into our joined lap.

His hand cups my breast, and all my senses go into overdrive.

*Oh, God.*

When his mouth leaves me, I want to protest, until I realize what he's doing. His tongue makes contact with my pebbled nipple, and a moan escapes my throat.

I throw my head back and lean into his caress. When he bites down ever so slightly, I can't hold back.

"Fuck, yes!"

*Can one come from just getting their tits sucked on?*

It's that moment that Wes's door flies open. "Hey, Roe-Roe! I'm gonna—oh fuck!"

"WHAT THE HELL?" Wes roars, throwing me on the mattress behind him and shielding me with his body.

I squeak in surprise, covering myself with my arms. I peer around Wes at an extremely pale and wide-eyed Kiwi.

"Oh, uh...shit. I, um—" he stammers.

"Get. The. Fuck. Out!" Wes sounds lethal, and I stifle a laugh. Kiwi has seen me naked—several times. We grew up together, after all. But he has never seen me with a guy.

My best friend jerks around without another word, and the door slams shut.

Outside, we can hear the other guys ask what happened, and I let myself fall into Wes's obscene amount of pillows, unable to hold back any longer.

He rounds on me. "This is not funny. I'm sick of having blue balls when it comes to you."

His anger is half-hearted, and it makes me crack up even more.

WITH THE MOOD down the drain and it being almost one in the morning, I end up riding home with Kiwi. Wes wasn't too happy, but it also felt weird to sleep over—no matter how much I wanted to wake up in his arms.

Kiwi is oddly quiet on the drive, and when he stops in front of my house, he keeps his eyes forward.

I place my hand on his thigh and squeeze. "Hey, what's going on?"

After what feels like minutes, he looks at me, and what I see makes my heartbeat speed up. I'm not going to like what he has to say.

He stares past me into the darkness as he speaks. "You know I love you, Roe-Roe. And I only want the best for you." He pauses. "If someone deserves the world, it's you."

When he trails off, I have a suspicion where he is leading

with this. My throat goes dry, and words won't come out, so I jerk my head up and down.

*Please don't say it.*

"I hate being the asshole doing this, but I also feel it's my... obligation to watch out for you."

*He is going to say it.*

"I'm worried what will happen when you get in too deep with Wes." He quickly adds, "Don't get me wrong. I like the guy, I do, but—"

"But?" My one-word question is no more than a croak.

"What are you going to do when *he* shows up? You know he will. Can you leave Wes when it comes down to it?"

I blink rapidly against the moisture quickly clouding my vision. "I...fuck!" I cover my face with my palms. I don't want my best friend to see in my eyes what I, deep down, have known since Wes kissed me for the first time. I'm falling for him. No, I already have fallen. I have no clue what I'm going to do. I don't want to leave him, but inevitably, the day will come. Even if *he* doesn't force me to leave, someone in Wes's inner circle will eventually find out who I am.

Fingers wrap around my wrists, and Kiwi gently pulls my hands away. "You know I always have your back. Just promise me you will be careful."

I force myself to nod. Tugging a hand free, I swipe under my eyes and draw in a deep breath. How can my heart feel like it's breaking after Wes and I finally start to get closer?

If we continue this conversation, I don't know what I will do. If anyone can talk sense into me, it's my best friend. But for now, I want to enjoy my time with Wes—however long that may be.

AFTER KIWI DRIVES OFF, I stand in front of my house for a long time. Maybe I should leave now before we go even further.

I have myself almost talked into packing up the Jeep when my phone in my back pocket begins to vibrate.

I pull it out, and Wes's name flashes across the screen. Instantly, my chest is filled with a flock of hummingbirds, and my mind is back in his bedroom, Wes's mouth on me. God, his mouth.

I should let it go to voice mail. Instead, I swipe and hold the phone to my ear. "Hey."

One foot in front of the other, I slowly walk to the door.

"Hey." The sound of his voice makes everything that's wrong in my life right. I can't leave him. Not unless I have no other choice.

"Why are you not asleep?" I unlock the door and step inside the house. Before I can fully close it, Echo is by my side, pressing against my leg, and I scratch her ear.

"Well," he sighs exasperatedly, "see, there was this girl here earlier. She is... She has fucked with my head, and I have no clue what to do about her."

His admission catches me off guard, and I stop in the middle of the hallway, my dog bumping into me. "Oh?"

He chuckles. "Yes, what do you think I should do?"

I start moving again, past Mags's closed door, and let myself into my room. Echo races past me to her bed in the corner.

I sink onto the mattress, chewing on my thumbnail as I contemplate his words. "Does this girl reciprocate your feelings?"

There is silence on the other end, and my stomach rolls. Did he want to hear something else?

"I hope she does," he admits, and I understand how much it means for him to open up this way.

Any other girl might have started playing games to get more reassurance from him, but not me. I inhale deeply. Here goes nothing. "She does." I feel ridiculous talking about myself in the third person, so I amend, "I do."

My heart is pounding in my throat, waiting for his next words.

"Can I pick you up for class tomorrow?" He knows I don't go to MPU, yet he treats me like I'm any other student.

My stomach somersaults. "I, um...don't you have practice?"

"Not until late afternoon. I have to be there at two. We could grab lunch after your second class, and I can take you home before heading to the field house."

He even knows that I attend two lectures tomorrow. "Are you asking me on a date, Weston Sheats?"

"I guess I am, Kingsley Monroe." The laughter is audible in his reply.

I fall backward on my bed, letting out an inaudible squeal, and kick my legs like a lunatic. My free hand covers my face, and I look at the ceiling between my fingers.

"Yes."

"Good. I'll be out front at at eight thirty."

"Okay." No question, he can hear my ridiculously wide grin as my voice pitches.

A chuckle reaches my ear. Yup, he totally heard it. "I'll see you in a few hours."

I peer at my alarm clock. Oh shit, I'm gonna need a lot of caffeine.

"Night."

"Night, King."

# CHAPTER SEVENTEEN

## WES

*WHAT THE ACTUAL FUCK?*

I'm standing outside King's second class, rubbing my palms against my jeans. I don't remember ever being this nervous to see someone. Especially because Exhibit A: I've already seen her today. I picked her up only a few hours ago. And Exhibit B: I had my hands on her bare ass and her nipple in my mouth last night. So again, what the fuck?

The clock on the wall opposite me shows one minute to noon. The noise level inside the lecture hall gets louder, and I wait for the first student to exit.

When the door opens, I involuntarily hold my breath. Of course, it's some geek in khakis and a tucked-in, light-blue polo shirt. A black belt and brown loafers complete the cringe-worthy outfit. I fight the compulsion to take a picture for D—she would have an aneurysm at the color combination. Chuckling at the thought of her reaction, I miss my girl exiting until she is right in front of me.

"What are you laughing about?" She scrutinizes me with her head slanted, hands on her hips.

"Nothing, just admiring your classmates." I pull her to me until her body is flush with mine. She raises herself to her tiptoes, and I press my lips to hers.

Her arms wind around my neck, and I slip my fingers into the back pockets of her black jeans, rocking my already hard cock against her belly.

Drawing back far enough to meet her eyes, I murmur, "Have I told you this morning how hot your outfit is?"

King snorts and rolls her eyes. "I'm wearing jeans, an oversized hoodie, and my DMs. Your taste is lacking, Sheats."

"My taste is spot on." I place a kiss on her cheek. "For starters, you are wearing my hoodie." (When she was shivering in her thin, long-sleeve shirt this morning, I forced her to put my spare hoodie on that I always have in the car.) "Secondly, I don't think I have ever seen a sexier ass." To emphasize my point, I squeeze so hard that she yelps and shakes her head at me. "And thirdly, I would take your Doc Martens over those ridiculous heels"—I cock my head in the direction of a group of jersey chasers that are openly glaring at King—"anytime."

King places a kiss against my chin, and a wave of goose bumps runs down my spine. *This girl!*

"Denielle wears those heels," she points out, and I know what she's getting at. We still haven't talked about my relationship with D. King is aware we're friends, but I feel like I owe her more of an explanation.

"True," I concede, returning her kiss by leaning down and nipping on her neck. "But Den is not the one I want to fuck senseless."

"Fair point." King's response is a blend between a breathy moan and a purr, which makes my erection strain against my jeans.

"What do you say? We skip lunch and go to your place?" I'm blunt as hell, but my balls have taken on a permanently unhealthy tint, and I need to get that remedied sooner rather than later.

She holds my gaze for a moment, her lids already hooded, and her chest is rising rapidly. She peers to the side, where the chicks are now openly talking about us. A devilish smirk turns the corners of her mouth up, and I wrinkle my forehead.

She steps away, and I instantly crave her body against mine again. When she intertwines our fingers and turns in the group's direction, the one in the lead stumbles back. I'm dying to see what's going to happen next.

King guides me down the hall. We're about to pass them when she halts and swivels toward the herd of fake blondes. "Okay, so would you like him to strike a pose, or no? How do you want him?"

*Huh?*

The girls' perfectly plucked eyebrows draw together in unison, and I have to press my lips together to not laugh out loud at the picture.

The one in the lead props her arms on her hips. "What's that supposed to mean?" Her nasal tone is like nails on a chalkboard. It's my turn to scowl.

King shrugs, then lifts our joined hands. Pointing at them with her free one, she says, "Well, I figured you'd like to take a picture for visual aid when you pretend that it's his fingers touching you when you hide under your pink princess covers tonight."

The lead blonde makes a sound between a gasp and like someone who has accidentally inhaled water through their nose. Another one's jaw hangs down, and a third says, "My duvet is blush, not pink."

I can no longer hold back and double over, having to let go of King's hand.

"No photo, then? Okay, because this is the closest you'll get to my boyfriend. If I catch one of you *letter sluts* ogling him again or calling me a name when it's clear that I can hear you..." She trails off.

"What then?"

Dum-dum is actually challenging my girl.

From my crouched position, desperately attempting to get my side cramps under control, I see King unsheathe her blade, twirling it on her palm.

Gasps ring through the hallway.

"This bitch is psycho."

"Oh my God, why would he hang out with this?"

"Let's go!"

My wheezing laughter has finally subsided, and I straighten. I catch a glimpse of the group rounding the corner down the hall, and I face King.

She studies me impassively, waiting for my reaction.

"Boyfriend?" I smirk.

She shrugs, seemingly not satisfied with my response.

"Was this jealous, knife-wielding-girlfriend performance for them, or was it your attempt to scare me off?"

"Are you scared off?" Her tone is neutral, reminding me of the few times she showed me her other side.

I grin. "Fuck no, *girlfriend*." I step into her personal space. She retreats until her back hits the wall, but I prowl after her until my large frame swallows her shorter one. With my arms on either side, I lean in. "The only thing you achieved with this show is me getting rock hard, and if it wasn't our first time together, I'd fuck you in the nearest broom closet."

Her eyes bulge before she shoves me away. King takes me by the wrist and drags me out of the building toward the parking lot.

WITH KAI not having any classes today, I drive us straight to King's place. Neither of us speaks, and she fidgets with the hem of my hoodie the entire ride.

I park in front of their house, and she's out of the 4Runner before I can shut off the car. I follow close behind as she fumbles with the lock.

Cracking a smile at her eagerness, I wrap my arms around her waist from behind. "Calm down, Princess."

I take the key from her and insert it into the lock, letting us in. I don't break our connection as we enter the house. Leaning down, I nip on the skin below her ear, and she moans, pushing back into me. There is no doubt she knows how turned on I am. I trail kisses down her neck when the sound of retching meets my ear.

*What the—?*

We still, and when we hear it again, my stomach constricts. Please let it be the dog. We follow the noise to Mags's room. As soon as we clear the threshold, her feet are visible through the doorframe of her bathroom.

King takes off, all but dives over Mags's bed, and sinks to her knees next to her friend.

Raking my hand through my hair—I didn't bother tying it back today—I follow a little slower. Conflicted emotions between concern and my dick weeping in my pants are raging through my body.

"Mags, what happened?" King is holding back her friend's hair as she is draped over the porcelain bowl.

"I—" More gagging comes from Mags, and I stop right outside the doorframe, saliva pooling in my mouth. I've never been good with anyone *un-eating* around me, and I instantly feel like throwing up myself. I start reciting different stock values in my head to drown out the sounds coming from the brown-haired girl.

Eventually, the toilet flush signals Mags being done (for now). I take a step inside and lift my hands in front of my nose.

*I should've stayed outside.*

"It started a little bit ago. I had just made a snack when I got sick."

King swipes Mags's hair from her sweaty forehead. "Did you eat something bad?" She evaluates her carefully.

"I have no idea. I—" Mags swings back around and clings to the toilet as the retching begins once more.

King's eyes meet mine, and her mouth is in a thin line.

"Can I help with anything?" Anything to get me out of here.

"Can you get her a glass of water?" She smiles tentatively.

"Sure." I feel like a complete asshole for the relief flooding me as I make my exit and head to the kitchen.

Returning with the water, I find Mags curled up in King's lap on the floor. The poor girl looks miserable, and King is gently stroking her hair. I hand her the glass, and she sets it beside her leg on the tiles.

"I need to take care of her," she whispers.

"What can I do?" I want to help. I simply can't be around Mags expelling her guts.

King shakes her head and mouths, "I'm sorry."

"Call me if you need me, okay? Either of you." I keep my tone low, not sure if Mags has fallen asleep.

I want to lean down and at least kiss her goodbye, but that would probably be inappropriate, given Mag's current physical state and position. She nods, and I leave the two alone in the bathroom.


I HAVEN'T SEEN my girlfriend in four days. Girlfriend. The term feels as familiar on my tongue as George would look comfortable dressed in a designer suit—or better, a ball gown. When was the last time I had a girlfriend? Probably senior year—Kimberly. Yeah, that sounds about right. Fuck, is King my girlfriend? She called me her boyfriend in front of the sorority jersey chasers, but we haven't talked about it since.

And why am I questioning this? Rhys would laugh his ass off. Rhys. Between my inability to see King and still working through my encounter with Lilly, my ex-best friend has invaded my thoughts more and more. Is King right? Is it time to move on?

My foot is propped up on our couch table, the TV playing a tape from one of our last games. We promised Coach we'd review it over the weekend, and of course, we waited until the last minute. Do we love football? Hell to the yes! What I don't like is getting homework for it. We normally watch our tapes together at the field house, but apparently, Coach is taking a weekend trip to Yellowstone before a specific area of the park closes.

Kai is slumped in the seat next to me, a bottle of God knows what propped between his legs. Zeke is sprawled out on the other side of our sectional, with Kiwi at his feet. The two have been hanging out more, and with Zeke at our place half the time, Kiwi has become our fourth. I'm not complaining; he's King's best friend. That makes him automatically a good dude in my book.

After King took care of Mags all day Wednesday, she took over Mags's shift in the evening, then covered both her and Mags's shift Thursday and slept most of Friday until I had to report to practice. With Coach gone, the assistant coach tortured us extra, so by the time I finished, neither my legs nor my dick were interested in driving over to King's place, which tells you how bad it was.

Mags started to feel better but not nearly good enough to make it through the double she had previously signed up for on Saturday, which meant King also covered those. She promised she'd text me as soon as she knew when Grizz would let her head out Sunday. Today! I finally get to see her, and with some luck, I'll get to see all of her.

My phone vibrates next to me, and I pick it up, glancing at the screen. "Fucking finally!" I feel like doing the touchdown dance on our breakfast bar.

My roommate raises his eyebrows as I shoot to my feet. "Where the hell do you think you're going?"

"King is getting off in thirty."

"Getting off or getting off?" Kai makes some seriously questionable gestures, and I smack him over the head.

"Shut the fuck up, asshole!"

Zeke pipes in, "The shade of your face is answering that question." Since I can't reach him, I flip him off.

When my eyes meet Kiwi's, I pause. My back stiffens. I don't like what I see. He smirks at me, unblinking, but it's not a positive or genuine amusement.

I narrow my eyes. "What?"

He glances down, examining his nails in meticulous detail, before looking back at me. "I'm sure you care about Roe-Roe, and I know she cares about you—more than she should. So, let me tell you this: if you hurt my girl, I will tongue-punch your fart box until you beg for mercy, and believe me, I will enjoy that more than you." He follows this statement with a wink, and I stare at him.

*What. The. Actual. Fuck?*

Kai sprays his booze across the carpet, pounding his chest, and Zeke is curled up on the couch in hysterical silent laughter.

Kiwi cracks up himself, and I turn on my heels and leave.

I'm fucking speechless.

I'm WAITING in the parking lot behind the bar. When Grizz comes out the back door and spots me with my ass planted against King's Jeep, he halts for a second.

"You're waiting for King?"

I dip my chin in confirmation, not changing my stance with my hands in the pockets of my jeans and legs crossed at the ankles. I'm not sure what to make of the guy. He's about as secretive as Lilly's head of security, with the appearance of Ragnar Lodbrok in *Vikings,* and has more computer monitors on his desk than a certain someone.

"She's finishing up. Front's already locked. You can head on in." He surprises me. My narrowed brows must give it away, because he barks out a laugh.

"If someone can take care of herself, it's King. I'm not worried about her." He starts walking to a beat-up old truck. Before he climbs in, he turns one more time. "I'm more worried about you."

I frown at his retreating rear lights and can't help my fists clenching and unclenching in my pockets. What is it with everyone having a problem with King and me?

*Fuck this shit.*

I push off the Jeep. Grizz kept the door unlocked, and I hope it's because he knew I was going in. I don't like the idea of anyone walking in when King is alone inside the bar—no matter how many knives she has strapped to her body.

Letting it fall shut behind me, I'm not overly quiet. I prefer not to be stabbed because I startle her in the empty place.

"Princess?" I call out, making sure she's aware I'm here.

King appears in the opening of the hallway leading to the main room. There is a pause before she speaks. "Hey!" Her greeting is slightly breathy, and even though I can't see her expression in the dim light—most of them are already muted— her excitement is audible.

My heart stutters, and I increase my speed. The need to touch her overwhelms my senses. Every cell in my body is starved for her.

Reaching her, I scoop her up by the ass, and she automatically latches onto me like a koala.

*God, I've missed her.*

Her pussy connects with my dick as she wraps her legs around me, and despite the layers of fabric between us, I can already smell her arousal. How is this possible?

Before I can say anything else, her mouth is on mine. She nips at my bottom lip, followed by soothing the sting away with the tip of her tongue. My dick is throbbing with the need to be inside of her. I walk us into their employee lounge while King trails kisses along my jaw and neck.

A shiver runs down my spine when she reaches my shoulder, and she bites down. I've never been into any of that stuff (rough sex), but with her, I barely recognize myself.

# CHAPTER EIGHTEEN

## KING

I WASN'T PREPARED FOR HIM TO SHOW UP AT THE BAR. I thought we'd meet at his place—or mine. When the familiar clang of the metal back door reached me in the front, I figured Grizz had forgotten something. Wes calling out for me—*Princess* —instantly made the butterflies in my stomach act as if they had received a dose of dopamine, serotonin, and oxytocin all at once. My heart flipped inside my chest as I made my way toward the hallway, dropping the cloth I was using to wipe down the counter on the floor.

I find him at the end of the corridor, stance wide, thumbs tucked into his front pockets. His washed-out jeans hang low, the dark hoodie emphasizing his broad shoulders and bulging arms. Has he toned up more in the last few days? My mouth waters at the sight. His hair is tied back, a look that makes me clench my thighs every time. I never knew I was such a goner for a guy with a man bun until Weston Sheats.

. . .

HE CARRIES me to the break room. I fight the impulse to let go of him and tear his clothes off. The hunger to see him in all his glory has every nerve ending inside me humming. I let instinct take over as I rub my aching core against his hardening length and bite on his shoulder. A primal sound that could bring me to my orgasm then and there erupts in his throat.

Wes drops me on the couch situated on the far wall of the room, and as soon as my back hits the cushion, I let go of him and reach for his pants. They need to go. Now.

With his mouth on mine, his tongue assaults mine in the most delicious way, and I miss him unfastening my belt until my jeans are ripped off my legs.

"Jesus, Princess, do you ever wear panties?" His tone is low as he stares at my bare pussy.

My throat goes dry, and I attempt to close my legs, suddenly insecure about being exposed to him.

"Nuh-uh." Wes stops me, holding my knees and pushing my thighs even farther apart. "Don't you dare."

Before I can respond, his head is between my legs, and his tongue flicks my core. Holy— My hands grasp for his head, and my fingers dig into his scalp as he sucks on my clit.

*Oh, God.*

My eyes roll back inside my head as my legs begin to tremble. I can't stop the moan building inside of me. Need. More. He chuckles, and the cool air of his exhale is too much. A tingling sensation spreads through my belly, all the way down to my toes. I don't want to come yet. At the same time, I don't want him to stop. I've never experienced such a sensual overload, and I know it can only get better from here.

"D-Don't make me come," I beg.

Wes removes his talented mouth far enough to peer up at me. His lids are hooded, and glancing down his body, his own desire is visible by the bulge in his unfastened pants.

"Oh, but, Princess..." He smirks and licks the entire length of my pussy. "Who says you're done after this?"

"Fuck," I whimper, and his devilish grin tells me that I will be ruined for any other guy after tonight. Not that I want anyone else.

His lips are back on me, and as he slips not just one but two fingers inside at once, I cry out. "Oh, shit. Yes!" The sounds coming from me are a surprise to my own ears.

Wes starts pumping in and out, and my toes curl as the orgasm builds. My hips buck, which results in him using his free hand to drape it over my lower abdomen, holding me in place.

"Let go," he orders at the same time as he adds a third finger to it.

"Ahhh...*fuuuuck*!" My body follows his command, and fireworks explode behind my closed eyelids. I arch my back, and he removes his arm, sliding a hand under my shirt to squeeze my breast.

I ride out my orgasm, all while he continues the assault with his mouth and fingers. When the wave of pleasure begins to subside, he slows as well, and I'm boneless.

"Holy hell... That was—" I try to catch my breath.

"My turn."

My arm was draped over my face, which is how I missed that Wes had removed all his clothes. I gape at him as I take in his body. There is not one gram of fat on him. He is...perfect. I let my gaze drift lower until it reaches his... My mouth waters, and I lick my lips.

"Off," Wes growls as he reaches for my shirt. I force my spent body to sit up, and he pulls the material off me. As soon as my head is through the opening, I wrap my fingers around his cock. I watch him through my lashes, and he sucks in air between his teeth as I tighten my grip, stroking up and down his length.

I lean closer, letting my tongue dart out, and lick the precum off his tip.

"Fuck, Princess." His hands fist my ponytail. He guides me until I have to take him into my mouth, and—holy hell—I take him in until he hits the back of my throat. I fight against the gag reflex, but before I can do anything else, Wes withdraws and pushes me down to the couch. His mouth comes down on me once more, and I instantly open up for him—mouth and legs. He settles between my thighs as his tongue tangles with mine. He glides his lips in a featherlight caress along my jaw until he reaches my ear, his fast exhales making goose bumps erupt on my skin. "I need to be inside of you." His voice is almost desperate, and I cross my ankles behind his ass, guiding him forward.

I turn my head so I can meet his heated gaze. "Then fuck me already, Sheats."

His eyes flare before they narrow, and a devilish grin turns the corners of his mouth upward. "You have no idea how long I've waited for you to say that."

My retort is swallowed with his mouth on mine, and his hips thrust forward until he's fully sheathed inside of me.

I cry out at the sudden fullness, and a guttural groan comes from the guy on top of me.

"Fuck, you feel so good." He nips at my neck. My hands glide down his spine, my nails leaving marks on his skin. This man brings out a side of me I never knew I had, even with my history at The Pole. The connection between us is one of a kind, and I trust him with my body and soul. He would never hurt me—not in a way I wouldn't want him to. My teeth sink into his shoulder, and Wes grasps for my butt with both of his hands, squeezing hard, while driving his dick in and out.

I moan as he thrusts forward, filling me up, then withdrawing and repeating the motion. All I can do is hold on for the ride. And holy shit, what a ride it is. I had imagined sex with Wes so many times, but nothing prepared me for this. I'm on fire, my heart hammering in my chest, while I try to suck in the air my lungs so desperately demand to keep up with my panting. A sheen of sweat forms on his back, and I'm about to combust if I don't come soon.

"Harder," I breathe.

Wes increases his speed, and he thickens inside of me. He's as close as I am. He grunts, and his teeth find the flesh above my collarbone.

The climax hits like a wave, and I can't suppress my screams. My pussy clenches around his cock as he fills me up, and Wes's fingers dig into my ass as he drives into me one last time. My body jerks as I come down from the high, and he slumps on top of me, shuddering every few seconds.

"King-sley Mon-roe, you—" He sucks in more air.

"I what?" I giggle, loosening my grip on him and begin trailing the tips of my fingers up and down his spine.

He shivers, then sighs. "I forgot." Which makes me laugh more.

Propping himself on his elbows, our eyes meet.

He hovers above me, less than an inch of space between us. His lids close, and he whispers, "What are you doing to me?"

Our noses touch, and I let my lips feather over his. "The same thing you are doing to me."

He rests his head on my chest, and we stay like this until exhaustion pulls me to the brink of sleep. "We should probably get out of here," I murmur.

"Mhmm." He is as drowsy as I feel. Slowly, he pushes himself up, sitting on his haunches in front of the couch. Wes scans my body with such intensity that heat flares in my core once more—until he lands on a spot between my legs. He pales. "Shit."

"What?" I jackknife up, scanning my body for injuries of any kind. Then, I notice the sticky spot between my legs and understand. We didn't use a condom. Shit indeed.

My eyes fly to his, and he blurts out, "I'm clean, I swear. This, uh..." He won't look at me. "This is the first time this has ever happened."

I touch my finger to his chin and turn him to me. "I trust you. And I'm on birth control." I leave it at that. Nothing like ruining the best night I have had in years by telling him that I started taking the pill at sixteen out of fear of getting raped at my stripper job.

"You sure?" He studies me with a crease between his brows.

"Stop worrying. No harm done." I follow with a slow and gentle kiss.

He leans in, and we fall back onto the couch, his hands wandering from my hips to my breasts, and his thumb swipes over my hardening nipple.

"Wes?" I try to push against his chest, but he outweighs me by eighty-some pounds. Or more.

He trails kisses along my neck, and I feel him hardening against my core once more.

"Never mind," I breathe out, grip his ass, and force him forward.

WE DID it two more times that night, and I didn't get out of The Grizz until close to five that morning. The second and third times were nothing like the first. They were slow and tender. The complete opposite, yet just as mind blowing. Never in a million years would I've expected sex to be like this. The few times I'd had it was to scratch an itch, nothing more. There were no feelings involved. With Wes, I'm on constant emotional over-load. I almost blurted out the L-word that night, but thankfully stopped myself in time. Our relationship—if you can call it that—is on fragile ice at best. I called him my boyfriend when I was proving my point the other day. He said I was his girlfriend, but how can that be if everything we have is built on lies? Lies I choose to ignore with every passing day. I don't remember ever being this...happy? Does that make me selfish? Yes. Do I need to tell him eventually? Also, yes. But every time I promise myself today is the day I'll come clean, I chicken out as soon as I see him.

. . .

WES HAS two away games in a row. Of course, I knew before he mentioned them to me—previous WS-stalker and all. I had memorized the team's schedule weeks ago when Wes was still a daydream. What sucked the most was he asked me to come, and I had to decline because of work.

For the first game, Mags took time off. She was joining Chelsea, who wanted to support Mack, on the road. There was no way Mags was going to let her little sister drive by herself, not with the chance of snow. It was a two-hour drive, and the roads through the mountains were awful, especially at night and without spiked tires. I didn't bother asking Grizz. Instead, I promised Wes I'd request the following Friday off work and join Kiwi that weekend.

IT'S TUESDAY, and everyone is hanging out at The Grizz during my shift to celebrate Kiwi landing a new client. He and his business partner recently sold several pieces to the Mountain Club, a private community where the rich (and famous) settle in the area. It is *über*exclusive, and you can't even drive up to the properties without an invitation that puts you on "the list." I am so proud of him.

The bar is ridiculously packed, and I haven't had a chance to say hi to my friends—or boyfriend.

*Boyfriend. The concept is surreal to me.*

After an hour of pressing my thighs together and almost peeing my pants, I finally get to rush to the bathroom. One more minute, and I would've embarrassed myself. I'm speed walking out of the employee lounge, not wanting Leigh to be on her own for too long, when two arms grab me from behind.

I don't scream. Instinct takes over, and I elbow the assailant in the side. The hold loosens, and I spin around, ready to execute my next move, when Wes comes into view. His mouth is in a grimace, and he's hunched over. Oh, crap.

"Shit, I'm so sorry, baby." I place my hands on either side of his face, scanning his features. "What's wrong?" I didn't hit him that hard.

"I'm fine," he mumbles, but squeezes his eyes shut.

*Fine, my ass.*

I tighten my hold and force him to look at me. "What's wrong?" I sound harsher than necessary, but the knot in my stomach from seeing him in pain doesn't allow for patience.

"Mack tackled me at practice, and I landed wrong. It wasn't you who hurt me." He smirks.

For that remark alone, I want to punch him in the same spot again. "You're lucky I left the Helix behind the bar."

He stares at me like I said something idiotic. "Princess, do you think I would've approached you like that if I hadn't seen it on the cutting board?"

"What if I had the Du Hoc on me?" I challenge him.

He grins. "You left that one on my nightstand this morning."

*I did?* Well, shit!

Wes had talked me into spending the night at his place, and it was everything I ever imagined being *normal*. We ordered pizza, watched a movie with Kai, Zeke, and Kiwi, and then went to bed.

Well, not to sleep.

I SAT ON HIS MATTRESS, fidgeting with the duvet, my skin hypersensitive to the gazillion-thread-count sheet set. I'd never slept at a guy's place before—besides Kiwi's, but he didn't count. What if I kicked him in my sleep, or I had my nightmare and woke Kai up? I was sliding my legs back out of the bed when Wes entered from the bathroom.

"What are you doing?"

"I, um...maybe I should go home?"

"Why?" At his scowl, I wanted to pull the comforter over my head.

Why didn't he see it? I didn't want to spell it out.

Closing my eyes so I didn't have to see his reaction, I confessed, "I don't know what I'm doing, Wes. I've never been in a relationship. What if I wake up screaming? What are you going to tell Kai? I can't—"

He stopped me by pressing his lips to mine. Not having seen his approach coming, I fell backward into the mound of pillows, and my eyes popped open.

Pulling back, he studied me. "Do you think I know what I'm doing? I have never had a girlfriend." After a pause, he amended, "Not one I was serious about."

He was serious about me? My heart somersaulted at his admission, and at the same time, my throat closed up. I blinked against the building moisture.

"Hey." His gentle tone made it worse, and I stared at the ceiling above us. "Princess, wha—"

"Why do you call me princess?" I blurted out. I loved it, but it was not your typical endearment a twenty-some guy calls a girl.

"Because of your name: King. Maybe one day, I'll change it to Queen." He winked, breaking the somber mood, and I burst out laughing.

"You're such a dork."

"Don't I know it." He placed a kiss on my nose. "I thought that guy died a long time ago, but you brought him back."

With that, he captured my mouth with his, and I forced every negative thought out of my mind, making *love* for the first time at twenty-two years old.

# CHAPTER NINETEEN

## WES

*I'M HAPPY*, IS MY FIRST THOUGHT AS I WAKE UP NEXT TO KING for the third day in a row. What an odd sensation after such a long time.

After her almost-freak-out the first evening, she tried arguing with me again the second, using Echo as an excuse to go home after her shift. So, I did what every guy would do: I brought her dog to my house.

Wednesday was her night off, and I told her to meet me at the townhouse. Kai announced at practice that he would be spending the night at his newest bedwarmer's place, so I planned to pick up dinner and finally have some real alone time with King.

She and Echo followed me into the garage when I pulled in. Heading up the stairs, she made her way into the kitchen but stopped short, causing me to bump into her with the take-out bags. Her hands flew to her mouth, eyes bouncing back and forth between the food dishes on the floor and me. I had stopped quickly at the local pet store after my morning class, not wanting Echo to have to eat and drink out of our unused pots again for her meal.

Suddenly unsure if I had done the right thing, I attempted to downplay it. "It's just bowls."

She wrapped her arms around me, pressing her cheek against my chest. "Thank you."

*Had anyone ever done something nice for her?*

Still loaded with bags, I awkwardly hugged her back, mumbling, "It's nothing."

Being the amazing woman she was, she dropped the topic. We ate dinner, watched a movie on the couch—her lying on top of me, humming in contentment—and the rest of the night I spent buried deep inside of her.

Yup, I was happy.

MY MOOD TOOK a dive when I had to say goodbye to her on Friday. It was just for a night, but this entire week, she didn't have one nightmare. From what I gathered by eavesdropping on a conversation King had with Kiwi, this was unusual. The thought of her going back to her place and not being able to sleep made my chest constrict.

"I've been fine long before you came along, Sheats." She smirked at me, but the smile didn't meet her eyes. I placed a kiss on her forehead and made her promise to call if she woke up. I didn't spell it out, but it was clear what I meant.

She didn't call, and I didn't ask her when I got back Saturday afternoon, even though every cell in my body demanded to know. The fierce need to protect her from any harm had grown the more time we spent together.

WE'VE FALLEN INTO A ROUTINE, and I would be lying if I said I didn't like it. Is this too soon? Probably. But the inner peace she brings me outweighs any possible consequence. King and Echo spend every night at my house. Some nights, I pick Echo up while King is still at work. Others, they come over together.

I'm at practice when Coach blows the whistle in the middle of the sprint exercise. It's the day before our second away game, and he always tortures us a little extra for those. For what, I haven't been able to figure out.

"SHEATS!"

I stop short at my name and turn.

"Answer your freaking phone. It won't stop ringing."

I look around at my teammates, mentally taking count of whoever is *not* here. All the usual candidates are present, except—a hollow sensation settles in my chest, and I take off toward the bench where I had left my bag.

*King or Den.*

I pull it out from the side pocket, and the screen lights up automatically. Eight missed calls from King. Shit. I tap on her name and don't have to wait for more than two rings before my sobbing girlfriend answers the phone.

"Sh-she i-is in s-surgery," are the four words coming through the speaker.

I grip my hair with my free hand. Stay calm. Figure out what's going on. I've been through hell with my friends; I can do this. But hearing King nearly hysterical—

"She who? Princess, what's going on?" Deep breaths.

"E-Echo."

I close my eyes. Please no. "What's wrong with Echo?" As relieved as I am that King is okay, the dog has grown on me, and she means the world to King.

Footsteps in the background indicate that she is pacing. "S-she got hit by a c-car. She j-jumped out of the Jeep and—" I can picture the rest.

"Where are you?"

King gives me the address of the vet, and I'm on my way. Grabbing my bag, I yell in Coach's direction that there is an emergency, and I have to go. I don't wait for his response. Kai can tell me later if I'm benched tomorrow.

The drive takes ten minutes, and I burst through the door of the clinic, finding Mags walking back and forth in the waiting area. Her head snaps up. "Oh, thank God!"

King's best friend throws herself in my arms, and I pull her close, scanning the place for my girlfriend. "Where is she?"

Mags steps back. "She's through there. They told her she could wait outside the operating room."

I nod, unsure if I should follow or wait here. "What happened?" I ask without taking my eyes from the door Mags pointed at.

"One of the frat guys across the street backed out of his driveway and into ours to make the turn into the street."

*What?*

"He did what?" I try to picture the scene but come up blank.

"It's trash day, and one of the neighbors is moving. The street was packed with a truck, cars, and trash bins. Andrew couldn't turn into the street without hitting another car. So, he backed into our driveway to make it. It was an accident. Echo came around the Jeep—" Mags covers her mouth with her hands, fresh tears running down her face.

I press my lips together, preventing myself from asking where I can find said Andrew. Accident or no accident, we'd have a chat.

"I'm gonna go check on King. Are you okay here?" *And where the hell is Kiwi?*

"Yes, I'm fine. Go make sure she hasn't lost it yet. She was a mess when I got here, but they wouldn't let me wait with her." Mags squeezes my hand, and I return the gesture before making my way to the back.

I don't have to look far for King. The place is not big, and I find her after one more turn. She is leaning against the wall opposite a door. She has the Helix in one hand, arm crossed over her chest, and she's chewing on the thumb of the other.

"Princess," I whisper. I don't want to startle her.

Her eyes find me instantly, and her lips begin to tremble. I'm at her side in a few strides. Taking the blade from her hand—knowing where she keeps it—I tuck it in the sheath in the back of her jeans. I wrap my arms around her shoulders, drawing her close. She falls apart, and my heart breaks for her.

"Is there any news?" I murmur against her hair, but she shakes her head into my shirt.

"I'm sorry I made you leave practice." She peers through her wet lashes.

I study her before responding, hating that she feels the need to apologize. "Are you kidding me? You always call me, no matter what or when. Understood?"

A small smile appears. "I'm not used to relying on someone," she admits. Chewing on her bottom lip, she adds, "You were the first one I called. The only one I wanted with me. Not Kiwi. And he's always been *the one*."

Something inside of me snaps into place at her words, and I swallow over a new emotion clogging my throat. I know exactly what she means. She is the first one I want to talk to—no matter how trivial it is.

We wait for another hour before a middle-aged woman in bloody scrubs comes out of the OR. King is crushing my fingers in a vise grip as we listen to her explain about Echo's injuries. They were able to stop the internal bleeding. Through an utter miracle, she has no broken bones, but she would have to be kept as still as possible for the foreseeable future. Good luck with that—this dog is the Energizer Bunny on speed in a canine's body.

THE VET IS KEEPING Echo overnight to monitor her vitals and assures us she will let us know if there are any changes, but she believes she will remain stable.

We would be able to bring her home the following evening. I

want to argue with the woman because I won't be here tomorrow. Isn't there a way to get her home sooner? But then logic sets in; I am selfish in my need to take care of the two. Echo is part of King, and that makes her automatically important to me.

Once we are at my place and King is in the shower, I call Kiwi. He was supposed to join King at my away game the next day. Instead, he'll be staying back and driving King to pick up Echo.

It gives me some comfort but won't prevent me from checking in on them hourly, except when I am on the field.

We're in the locker room. Most of the guys have already left for the bus to take us to the hotel. Kai is waiting as I put my shoes on. Finished, I pull out my phone to check if there is any word about Echo.

"Bro, I don't know which pussy you're more whipped for, King's or Echo's."

Narrowing my eyes at him, annoyance laces my reply. "Do you listen to yourself? Half the shit that comes out of your mouth makes no sense."

My roommate curls his lips between his teeth.

"What?" I challenge him.

Kai keeps a steady gaze on me. He is rarely serious, and it's clear I went too far. "I'm worried about you. Just because I joke around—or drink myself into oblivion—doesn't mean I don't see what's going on."

I consider his words. The buzzing current that had been building since he blurted out his first comment disappears. "Explain."

Kai sighs. "Don't get me wrong, man. Your girl is badass, and I love her." My scowl makes him lift his hands in surrender. "Not in that way, bro. Chill out. What I'm trying to say is, something is off."

*Off?*

Kai doesn't know about King's past, what she did—had to do.

"She used to stalk you, Wes. She's always on edge, even when she seems relaxed. She watches you like a..." He rubs his palms over his face. "Like you're a ticking time bomb or some shit. I can't pinpoint it."

For him to have a conversation like this, he's truly concerned. But he also has no idea what King went through. Of course she's on edge. I blow out a sharp breath as the need to defend her bursts to the surface. I don't want to go off on him, but it's almost impossible to keep a steady tone.

"I—thanks." Kai scowls at me, and I bark out a laugh. His expression is not one I see too often. "I appreciate your concern, man. You've been a good friend to me the last couple of years. I haven't been the easiest person to share your house with."

A cocky smirk spreads over his face, one of his typical comebacks burning on his tongue.

I hold up a palm. It's my turn to be serious. "King has a past. One she doesn't talk about unless she has to, and it's the reason she is the way she is."

I'm as cryptic as Lilly's head of security when anyone asks him something about himself.

Kai places a hand on my shoulder. "Just...be careful."

I jerk my head in a nod as he says, "So, are you allowed to party with your friends tonight or what? I need some pussy to celebrate this win. Or a drink. Or both. In no particular order."

And just like that, my roommate is back.

WITH THE ENTRANCE to our townhome being up a flight of stairs, King decided that she and Echo would stay at her place. The backyard is right off the kitchen, and Echo would be able to go to the bathroom and come right back in without someone having to carry her.

So, as soon as we're back in town, I grab a bag, throw some

clothes in, and head to her apartment. I find King on the couch. Echo's head is on her lap, and she's stroking her fur.

"How are my girls?" I ask as I lower myself onto the cushion and place a kiss on King's temple.

"Glad you're back." She leans into me. Warmth radiates through my chest. It feels good to be wanted.

I scratch Echo behind the ear, and she glances up at me without moving. "We'll get you back on your feet in no time," I tell her.

Focusing on King, dark circles are visible under her light-blue eyes. "Have you slept?"

"Not much. I was too worried she would need something."

I nod in understanding. "Why don't you go lie down for a bit." I shift to lift Echo's head and take King's place.

She resists for a moment but then concedes, exhaustion winning out. "She needs the pain medicine in an hour. The bottle is in the kitchen. Give it to her with a little bit of peanut butter, but not too much, or she—"

"Princess."

"Yes?" She stares at me, chewing on her nail—a habit I've not seen on her until two days ago.

"I got this." I give her a reassuring smile.

"Okay."

"Okay." I wink.

King needed the rest. She doesn't reemerge until it's dark. We order food and spend the rest of the weekend with Echo, resting in her room or on the couch.

When it's time for her to go to work on Sunday, I assure King that I won't leave Echo's side. She's standing in the doorframe, gnawing on her bottom lip. I'm sitting on her bed with my laptop propped on my legs and Echo on her doggy bed right in front of me on the floor.

"We'll be here."

King walks back in and kneels in front of Echo, placing a kiss on her head. Standing up, she leans down to me, putting her mouth on mine, and I involuntarily let my tongue swipe across her lips. She opens up and deepens the connection. Heat shoots to my cock. Shit, I didn't mean for that to happen. All we've done since Echo's accident is cuddle and the occasional peck on the mouth. She sleeps in my arms, and I am content with it. As awful as the accident was, it brought us closer.

"I—" I break off, and King wrinkles her forehead. "I'll see you in a bit," I finish the sentence, and she searches my eyes.

*What was I about to say?*

THE VET DECLARES that Echo is healing nicely and that she'll be running around again in no time. I'm standing next to King as we get the news, and this time, it's me who squeezes her hand. She sags against me, and I let out a huge breath. I wrap my arm around her, drawing her close, the relief making my knees weak.

We continue our routine. Whenever King is at The Grizz, I stay with Echo, even as she begins to feel better and can walk around almost normally again—only a little slower.

On King's night off, we curl up in her bed, my laptop in front of us. We watch one of those new Netflix shows, and before we realize it, we've watched the entire season.

*So, this is what Rhys and Lilly always had with each other.* I never understood until now.

That night, I go to bed with a lightness behind my ribs I've never experienced before. Making sense of my friend's relationship also puts something else in perspective. Lilly didn't stop Rhys from his mistake, because they were a team. They may disagree on topics, but she trusts him with every fiber of her being.

*Maybe it's time to forgive them,* I hear King's words in my head.

# CHAPTER TWENTY

**KING**

"MAAAAGS!" My shout turns into a croak mid-scream. Heart pounding in my throat, sweat begins to build on my forehead. I'm going to throw up. No, no, no.

*How could this happen?*

My eyes fly back and forth between the calendar displayed on my phone and the two round boxes sitting next to it. One I started a week ago—seven pills gone—and the other one I had fished out of the large blue bin outside the house—talk about dumpster diving at its finest. One pill left. How? My mind is racing through the days. I don't understand. I've never missed one. Ever!

My calendar has several reminders. One for when to get more (having no health insurance, I always have money set aside. I'd rather be hungry for a few days than not be able to protect myself) and two daily reminders for when to take it (one at the time I should swallow the tiny pill and another, two hours later, in case I forget it). I have never forgotten it. Until now. I even have it marked when to start a new pack in my calendar, which I did without thinking or double-checking the old one a week ago.

Fuck! For once, I'm glad about my laziness with taking out the bathroom trash, which meant it was still outside.

Realizing what must've happened, I dove into the trash can like the time I was fifteen. Mom had been in the hospital for two weeks, and I was looking for something edible, not wanting Kiwi or his grandma to know how bad it was. They found out anyway.

I shake the memory and focus on the present. My best friend is still not here. Where the hell is this girl when I need her?

"MAAAAGS!" My voice now borders on hysterical.

The door flies open, and Mags stands in the threshold, frantically searching my small bathroom for the possible danger. Then, her eyes zero in on the vanity and instantly jerk back up, followed by dropping to my stomach. Understanding sets in, and she gasps, eyes bulging.

My throat closes up, and I swallow several times, but it's no use. The tears start pooling in my eyes until they spill over, and a sob bubbles up in my throat.

My best friend is at my side in two strides and wraps her arms around me. I cling to the front of her shirt while cries rack through my body. She strokes my hair, continuously murmuring, "I'm here. Let it out. It'll be okay," to me.

It feels like hours until my body begins to calm and numbness takes over. I pull back and meet Mags's concerned eyes.

"What am I gonna do?" My question breaks the silence in the room.

"Are you sure?"

She is asking if I have taken a test yet.

"I'm six days late, Mags." My voice cracks again at the end of the sentence.

"Stay here." She disappears and walks back in not thirty seconds later, holding a pink box.

Momentarily distracted from my situation, I frown. "Why do you have a pregnancy test handy?"

She completely ignores me and pulls out the test, holding it out to me. "Pee!"

"Gee, aren't we blunt today?" A half-hearted laugh escapes me, but Mags doesn't blink and shoves the little stick in my hand.

Not caring about modesty at this point, I drop my pants and sit down on the toilet.

*Aiming at this darn stick is harder than it looks.*

I cap the test and wipe the other end with toilet paper, setting it on the sink. Mags already started the timer, and we both stand there, staring down at the piece of plastic that will determine my future from here on out.

We wait two minutes before a faint second pink line starts forming. With every passing second, dizziness spreads through me further. By four minutes, the line is solid, and I clamp my hand in front of my mouth.

I'm pregnant.


SITTING on the couch with a glass of water in both hands, I stare at nothing. I expected to be upset. Being happy would be a stretch. I'm twenty-two years old, and the father of the baby is only twenty-one. A baby. But none of the emotions come. I'm numb. There is nothing.

Mags says I'm in shock or denial, but wouldn't denial mean I don't believe that the little stick displayed the truth?

"You need to tell him." Her words rip me out of my catatonic state, and I stare at her.

"Come again?" *Tell him what?*

"He deserves to know. He's been kept in the dark too much in his life. Don't make that same mistake."

Is she seriously psychoanalyzing my relationship right now? *There is an emotion.*

I stand up, squaring my shoulders at her. "Are you fucking serious? How do you think this will go over?"

"He is part of this, too," she pushes.

"Oh, sure." I throw my arms up. Heat is spreading through

my body, and I welcome the sensation. It's better than the void I was feeling for the last few hours. "So, I'll walk up to him and say, 'Hey, baby, guess what? I forgot to take my birth control the day I told you I'm a murderer. Congratulations! You're going to be a daddy.'" Sarcasm drips from my tone, and Mags crosses her arms over her chest, cocking her head.

She doesn't grace me with a reply, and I know what she is doing, which pisses me off even more. She is right. I can't keep this from him.

"King," her voice softens, which makes it worse.

The red haze still clouding my vision disintegrates, and her form becomes blurry in front of me.

Goddamn it, no more tears.

My phone begins to vibrate on the coffee table, and both of our heads jerk in the direction. Wes's picture lights up the screen, and I peer over at the clock over the TV. I missed my class, and he just figured it out. Shit.

I meet my roommate's concerned eyes. She also skipped her lecture to stay with me.

"Do you want me to answer?" She's trying to help.

"NO!" I screech. Covering my face with my hands, I look through my fingers. I steady my voice. "If you pick up, he'll immediately know something is wrong."

"So, what do we do?"

I draw in a deep breath. "I'll text him that I'll see him tonight after practice. He'll come by The Grizz with the team, and I'll have time to figure out how to break the news to him."

*How to ruin his life.*

Mags's expression morphs. She's proud of me. Standing a little bit taller, a small smile tugs on the corners of my mouth. I'm going to do the right thing. I move toward her, and she meets me halfway. I hug her, resting my chin on her shoulder. "I'll tell him tonight." She pats the back of my head. Pulling away, she plants a kiss on my cheek.

"Everything will be fine. Wes is not someone who will run for the hills, trust me."

I dip my chin, despite the nausea building in my throat again.

He may not abandon me for the unplanned pregnancy, but when he finds out what else I've kept from him, I'm going to lose him.


THE THOUGHT of running without coming clean crossed my mind several times as I got ready for my shift, but at the same time, I couldn't do that to Wes. I refuse to be like his friends who made decisions for him. I love him too much for that. Love. God, I never thought I would experience that emotion.

The first three hours at work keep me busy, and I don't have time to think about what's about to happen. All my concentration goes into mixing drinks, and one of my regulars compliments me that this is the best I've ever served him. The things I can do when avoiding reality at all costs.

Around nine, Kiwi walks in, and he only has to take one look at me to know something is up. Fuck. He sits down at my section of the bar instead of the table the guys have claimed as their own whenever they're here. After the first week, no one dared to sit at the high top in the corner anymore.

"Hey, Roe-Roe." Kiwi tries to catch my eye.

"Hey." I keep my gaze locked on the glasses I'm scrubbing in the bar sink.

When the barware is cleaner than it's ever been, I busy myself drying each glass meticulously. I'm at number three when a hand latches onto my wrist above the counter. I slowly trail the arm attached to the hand until I lock on my childhood best friend's glare. Great, he's pissed.

"Talk," he commands, and I cringe. For our entire lives together, he has never been harsh with me. His taut jaw relaxes ever so slightly when he takes in my reaction. "Roe, what's going on?"

I set the glass and dish towel down and square my shoulders. I want to confide in him more than anything, but not until I've had a chance to talk to Wes. "I can't talk about it right now. I'll explain later, 'kay?" I'm not asking him, and he understands. He's not happy, but we've been in this together for way too long.

"Is it Wes?" Kiwi pushes once more.

I purse my lips, and he exhales his resignation. "Fine, but I want to know what's going on before your man takes you home tonight."

*If he is still taking me home.*

I force my face to remain neutral and bob my head. "I promise."

As Kiwi makes his way to the high top, Mags steps to my side. "Did you tell him?"

"No," is all I say, and she moves back to her section.

Not thirty minutes later, the door swings open, and a hollered, "The man of the hour is here!" announces the team's arrival. Kai's entrance prompts my first genuine laugh today. This guy.

He is followed by Zeke, who aims straight for Kiwi, Mack with his arm around Chelsea—she waves at her sister and me— and Wes in the rear. His eyes zero in on me as soon as his foot is over the threshold.

My mouth waters as I drink him in. He's wearing his trademark jeans, paired with a black formfitting Henley, and his varsity jacket. A cocky smirk pulls his mouth up at the corner as he approaches me. My stomach flips with excitement until I remember what is growing inside my belly. The happy tingling sensation quickly morphs into barf-inducing dizziness, and Wes doesn't miss the shift.

He steps up to the counter and leans over, waiting for me to kiss him. Pressing my mouth to his, my throat thickens. How am I going to do this?

"Everything okay, Princess?"

"Sure," I answer way too quickly, and his furrowed brows say it all. Fuck. Shit. Fuck!

He angles his head, and an unspoken promise crosses between us. He wants me to talk to him, and I concede that I will confide in him later. My heart is jackhammering, but I don't let it show how I'm freaking out inwardly. There would be no way he'd let me finish.

After he joins his friends, I expel a long breath and meet Mags's eyes. I press my lips together to conceal the trembling.

*I can do this.*

An hour later, Mags sidles up next to me. "It's Friday."

Huh? Then it sinks in. Crap. Friday. Our performance.

"You think you're up for it? I can always pretend I sprained my ankle, and we can't do it," she offers, and I bark out a laugh. This is why I love this girl.

I peer at her. "It'll be good for me. I should let some of the emotions out. There's no better way than dancing, right?"

Mags's eyes light up. She loves our gig as much as I do. "Right!"

She puts her index and middle fingers of both hands into her mouth and whistles. My shoulders scrunch up to my ears. "Geez, bitch. You could've waited for me to move away." But she simply beams at me.

Dean, who is helping out by serving tonight, cuts the music, and instantly hoots fill the room. Everyone knows what's coming. I'm giddy, excitement buzzing through my veins, and I climb the bar as Rihanna's voice fills the room.

I glance toward the back and find Wes's heated gaze already on me. His smirk can't hide the desire blazing in his eyes.

Reaching down, I grab my usual props and begin my show. I let the music take over. This is exactly what I need to forget the impending confession.

*Confessions—plural*, my inner voice chides. But instead of reveling in the upcoming misery, I squash it down and shake my ass. Twirling on the narrow bar, I lean down and hand a guy one of the shots. He throws it back and holds the glass back up. Laughing, I shake my head and move on. I'm at number three when the music suddenly stops. What the—?

I glance around, and most of the customers mirror my confused gaze until my eyes land on Mags—who is grinning. Not good. I whip around to find Wes, but he's not at his table.

"Princess!" I almost fall off the bar when Wes calls me from behind the counter. What is he doing? He's holding something up to me, and it takes me a moment to comprehend what it is.

I scowl at the object he's extending. "What's this?"

Wes, in his lovable way, shrugs. "A mic."

I want to whack him with the mic right now.

Mags saunters over to me and leans in, saying, "Show us what you got." Before I can answer, she twirls her finger in the air, and "One Way Or Another" by Blondie comes through the speakers.

You got to be kidding me. I glower at both of them, who have equally mischievous expressions.

"You want me to perform this song right now?"

"You told me how much you love the scene from the movie. You can sing and dance, so..." Wes trails off, and I want to kick myself off the bar for letting him join us during movie night.

"I hate you guys," I hiss at them both.

"No, you don't," Mags deadpans and reaches for Wes to help her down.

He holds the mic up to me once more, and I take it, sighing exasperatedly. Shit, I guess I'm really doing this.

The entire bar erupts in cheers, and I can't help but laugh. Kiwi beams with pride, and my pulse quickens but, for once, not from nervousness.

I look for Dean and signal for him to start the song over. All eyes are on me, and as soon as the first notes fill the room, my hips begin to sway on their own accord. I belt out the lyrics like

I've done it a thousand times, and to my surprise, I love it. I lose myself in the song, close my eyes, and forget everything: my past, present, and future.

As the song comes to a close, I let reality flood back in. Everyone stares at me, slack-jawed, before a cacophony of noise nearly throws me backward. Claps, cheers, hollers. The bar is out of control, and I cover my mouth. I don't know what to do. I didn't expect *that*. Wes is in front of me, holding his arms high, signaling for me to jump.

"Are you crazy?" I laugh, shaking my head.

"Jump!" The grin on his face is contagious, and I let myself fall. Clinging to him with my arms and legs wrapped around him, I'm looking into Wes's eyes. I love this man with every fiber of my being.

His mouth is on mine before I can react, and I open up automatically. The few hours I avoided him today left me starved, and I can't get close enough. I all but grind myself on him, and he pulls back, chuckling. "Should we take a detour to the employee lounge?"

*The lounge. Where it happened.*

Wes narrows his eyes at me. "What's wrong, Princess?"

I draw my bottom lip between my teeth, biting down. The sting distracts me from the pain piercing my heart. I place a gentle kiss on his mouth and untangle myself.

"I'll check with Grizz to see if I can leave a little early and grab my stuff from Mags's car. I'll be right back." Before he can ask any questions, I weave through the crowd. I get stopped here and there, customers telling me how much they loved my rendition of the song. All I want is to be alone with Wes. I need to get it all out before I lose the last bit of courage I have left.

Grizz nods from behind his monitors, and I grab Mags's keys out of her purse to collect my backpack. I knew I would leave with Wes tonight, and hope made me pack an overnight bag—hope that he won't kick me out when I come clean.

I push through the back door and veer toward Mags's car,

clicking the key fob. In my mind, I go over possible ways to break the news to Wes when a voice stops me in my tracks.

"Hey, baby girl."

The blood in my veins turns to ice. No. Oh God, please no. My body begins to shake uncontrollably, and I drop the keys, the sound echoing in my ears like a wrecking ball demolishing a building.

My breath comes in shallow bursts as I slowly turn toward the one person that could make tonight even worse. He steps out of the shadow behind another car, and my eyes meet his ice-blue ones.

"What are you doing here?" I force my voice to remain steady when all I want is to break down in sobs.

"Didn't your sister tell you I was on my way?" His casual attitude overwrites my fear of anyone seeing us together.

"That was weeks ago," I bark at him.

"I had other things to do." His voice is low, and I can read between the lines.

"What other things?" The quiver is back, and I hate for him to hear it.

"I had a job to do. There is a lot you set in motion with your hasty action."

*Hasty action?*

He folds his arms over his chest, and I take him in. I haven't seen him in so long. He's gotten larger, more menacing than I remember. For years, *his lifestyle* had put a strain on his body, but something has changed. He's never been a good man, but I'm looking at a monster now.

"Hasty action?" My voice is shrill, and despite being aware of potentially drawing attention to myself, I can't stop. My fists ball, and I want to draw my blade. "How long should I have watched E rape that girl before it would've been appropriate for me to kill him?"

*Jesus, I'm openly confessing to murder.*

"You have no idea who Isaiah Ellis was, do you?" He scowls, stalking toward me, and I take a step back.

"He was my boss?" My reply sounds like a question, and my eyes dart around the parking lot. A cold shiver runs down my spine. What am I missing?

He steps closer and places a hand on my shoulder. The contact makes me flinch. He tightens his grip, his thumb pressing in the flesh under my collarbone. The pressure is almost too much, but I don't show him the pain he causes me.

"Ellis was your boss; that is correct. But he was also—"

"WHAT THE FUCK?" Wes's voice makes me jerk out of his grip. I spin on my heels, meeting the eyes of the man I...the man I just lost.

Wes is standing in the doorway of the bar, his ashen face visible even in the dark of night. His eyes swivel between me and the person behind me. I open my mouth to explain when he whispers, "Don't ever come near me again."

# CHAPTER TWENTY-ONE

## WES

This can't be happening. What. The. Hell. Is. Going. On? I need to get out of here, or I'm going to kill someone. How could I've been so blind? All her secretive behavior. The guy she called for help. Of course, if someone knows how to make a body disappear, it's him. JESUS FUCK!

I pound my fist into the nearest wall until the pain in my hand overtakes my senses. Anything is better than the betrayal. She was the first person to break down my carefully constructed barrier in years. I let out the roar that's been building since I found her standing in front of the last man I ever expected to see in the flesh—with his hands on my girlfriend. Correction: ex-girlfriend. I pound the wall one last time. My knuckles are bleeding, and I'm pretty sure I broke one or more bones in my hand.

"Wes, what's—"

I whirl around and have my forearm against Kiwi's throat before he can finish the sentence. A gurgling cough comes out of his mouth, but that's all he manages.

"Did you know?" My spit flies, but I couldn't care less at this point.

"Wha—" he rasps, and I remove some of the pressure.

"Did you know she was playing me all this time?" My force on his trachea increases again. The question is more of a growl than a coherent sentence, but he understood.

His eyes close, and I have my answer. A hollow emptiness begins to spread through my body that numbs even the agony in my hand. My arm drops from his neck, and I take a step back. Blood is roaring in my ears, and at the same time, it's like I'm falling into a black hole where I deny everything I just saw outside.

"Who is he to her?" I search Kiwi's face, not wanting to miss anything.

"He is my father," King answers for him from behind us.

Everything slows, and I turn to the girl who managed to thaw the ice around my heart, make me love her, and then destroyed me.

I blink once, twice. Her father? How is that even—? My mind catapults me back to LA, two and a half years ago. I'm standing next to Rhys and Denielle, watching him on the security feed carry an unconscious Lilly over his shoulder out of her house and throw her into the back seat of his stolen car. We had no idea if she was alive or if we would ever see her again.

"Monroe is my middle name—my mother's maiden name. My full name is Kingsley Monroe *Turner*." She hugs her midsection and stares at the ground as she speaks. Her light-blue eyes slowly lift to mine, and I instantly see the resemblance. I may have never met him in person, but I've seen enough pictures and videos of the guy.

"You know him as Gray," she finishes, holding my gaze.

*Kingsley Monroe Turner*. Gray. Francis Turner. She is Francis *fucking* Turner's daughter. The dead man who got past Lilly's security, kidnapped her, and almost got her killed.

Kiwi moves around me and to her side. "He's here?" He addresses her, but King won't look away from me.

"Please let me explain," she begs, with tears streaming down her face.

I slowly shake my head, taking one step backward, then another. This is too much. I can't— I need— She doesn't follow. While the fingers of my uninjured hand tremble from the adrenaline rush, the other hand begins to throb. When I'm near the entrance to the main room, I pivot and push through the throng of people. I ignore Kai and Zeke as they call out to me.



A KNOCK at the door forces me to lift my head off my pillow. "Go awa—ohhh fuuuck." I squeeze my eyes shut. My head feels like it's split in two. What the— I let it drop back onto the pillow.

Reality seeps in, and I remember her. I remember seeing her with Gray—no, Turner, whatever. Her fucking father. I fell in love with a criminal's daughter—a criminal who was part of ruining so many lives.

The knock comes again, more forcefully. I peel one lid back and peer at the half-empty bottle of amber-colored liquid sitting on my nightstand.

*That explains my headache.*

"Bro!" Kai's voice drifts into my room. The doorknob rattles, but he can't get in. Making sure no one would be able to enter, I propped a dining room chair against the door. "Sheats, open the fuck up!"

Hearing the slight panic in my roommate's calls should make me feel...something. Guilt for locking him out? No, I don't owe anyone shit anymore. She fucking played me. She knew who I was from day one. It probably was all a game. Did Gray put her up to it? But for what? Revenge? Well, that backfired.

*BANG. BANG, BANG.*

It sounds like he's about to break through the barrier, and I jerk to a sitting position, a movement I immediately regret as the room begins to fade in and out, and my stomach revolts. I glance toward my bathroom, but it's too late. Cold sweat is already running down my temple as I swallow hard. It's no use. All I can do is lean over the side of the mattress before I say hello to whatever I consumed after coming home. The retching subsides, and hanging over the edge of the bed, I make out my trash can and two more empty bottles on the floor.

*Did I drink all that?* is the only thought I manage before my body begins to shake uncontrollably, and I heave again.

Maybe I should open the door.

I must've managed to push myself back up somehow because, the next thing I know, something cold drenches my body. When my vision adjusts, I see Kai's furious mug staring down at me.

"What the fuck, asshole?" he barks, and I frown. How did he get in?

Kai's arm shoots out like a snake, and he pulls me up by the hair. "The fuck—?" I roar, trying to punch him in the junk, but my movement is sloppy, and all I manage is to clip his thigh. And even that is no more than a gentle pat my ninety-six-year-old great-grandma would laugh at.

He doesn't release the hold he has on me but shifts so I can see what's behind him—no, what used to be there.

"Where's my door?" My outrage isn't much more than a hoarse slur.

"Gone, motherfucker!" he bellows, as Zeke and Mack appear in the frame.

How the hell did they manage to take my door off?

My teammates look down at me with a mixture of concern and disgust. Following their gazes, I quickly understand why, and a new round of nausea hits me.

Kai finally releases me as I slam my hand over my mouth. This time, I make it to the bathroom before I start heaving. From what I could see in the remnants of my bedroom, I must've puked numerous times over however long I was in here —and missed the trash can half the time.

"It's Monday night, fuckwad," Kai answers my unspoken question from the threshold.

Did I ask that out loud? Wait. Monday? I lost...shit, almost three days.

I turn my head slightly. His earlier rage morphs into worry as he scans me up and down. "Bro, what happened?"

Zeke and Mack show up next to him, holding their sweater sleeves over their mouth and nose. "Dude, what the hell is going on?"

I eye Zeke suspiciously. "Where's your boyfriend?"

His brows shoot up. "At work. What's it to you?"

"Talk to him."

I push myself up, using the rim of the toilet bowl, and stumble back into my bedroom.

*Jesus Christ.*

It's my turn to cover my nose. This will take a while to clean up—or maybe we should burn it all and move.

WE DIDN'T BURN ANYTHING, but the process required a professional cleanup crew—courtesy of Kai with his rich-folk connections—and purchasing a new mattress and bedding.

Mack spent Monday night with me at the emergency room. My hand looked like one of those surgical gloves when you blow them up. Not taking care of it for three days, the bruises and scabbed knuckles emphasized my friends' argument that it needed to be checked out immediately. I wanted to wait until the morning, but Kai threatened to stuff me in the trunk in my vomit-covered state if I wouldn't concede.

By the time I washed off the remnants of my self-induced pity party, urgent care was closed, and my friends (the verdict on whether Zeke remains one is still out) refused to let me wait any longer to see a medical professional.

Kai oversaw the hazmat process at home, and when it came down to who would drive me to the hospital, I didn't give them a choice. I planted my ass in Mack's car without acknowledging Zeke's offer to drive. I couldn't be around him just yet, not with Kiwi being his fuck buddy.

Four hours later, the results were in, and I was ready to throw up again. I didn't break *break* my hand, but I managed to cause a hairline fracture in the trapezium and capitate of my right hand. I was out for the next six to eight weeks. Coach would kill me. Hell, I wanted to hurt myself. Practice was all I had left.

D called me almost daily, but I let it go to voice mail every single time. On day three, I shot her a text saying I was busy with practice—lie—to which she responded: **Just practice? ;)**

The two words managed to snap my carefully constructed self-control like a brittle twig. My good hand clenched around my phone, but no matter how hard I tried, the red haze would intensify. I was coiled so tightly my jaw began to cramp. I chucked the device across the room, where it slammed into the wall and fell behind my dresser. The screen was now cracked, and the sound buttons didn't work either. Add that to the list of things to replace—right after what was ripped out of my chest last week.

Every night, I saw King standing in the hallway, her arms wrapped around herself, confessing who Gray was to her. I wanted to believe that her anguish was real, that she didn't know, and she was hurting as bad as I was—or worse. At the same time, there was no freaking way it was a fucked-up string of coincidental events that led me to the girl who could've been the one. The fucking one. The joke was on me once again.

The only way to get some shut-eye was with the help of our in-house bar. I hadn't gone on another bender; Kai made sure of that by gluing himself to my side. However, I had a steady buzz going and became a regular at The Moose's Head. The clerk now greeted me by name, and it had been just ten days since my life got ripped from under me for the second time in less than three years.

Coach made it his personal mission to make me pay for my

*cock brain*—his words, not mine. I was his star player, head in the game, and all the shit, until I let my dick think for me because of a girl. I was about to snap at him that she wasn't just any girl when I remembered who she was and shut my trap.

After that, I took his punishment and promised him—and myself—that this would not happen again. I made a point to show up early and participate in everything that didn't require the use of my injured hand. In addition, I got signed up for extra cardio sessions and became the team's personal gopher—also part of my *sentence*. I deserved it. And as soon as I was done in the evenings, I went home to my liquid distraction.

Kai tried asking a few times what happened, but I ignored him until he mentioned *her*.

We were sitting on the couch, a game on the flat-screen TV —no clue who was playing because all I cared about was how much I could drink before Mr. Functioning Alcoholic cut me off. I was about to lift my drink to my lips when my roommate turned his head in my direction.

"I've waited long enough. I need some answers. You've gone off the fucking rails and become...me." He gestured at the glass in my hand. "Zeke's boy acts all fidgety around us, like he forgot to pull his favorite vibrator out of his ass. And no one has seen your girl since you fucked your football gig by pounding a wall. Seriously, what the—"

I was on him before he could finish that sentence. My fingers curled into a fist, and I drew my arm back. Tunnel vision took over, and all I saw was Gray's hand on King's shoulder. Adrenaline rushed through my veins, and my nails dug deeper into the palm of my hand. I was shaking from trying to hold back. A voice was screaming in my head that none of this was Kai's fault.

Suddenly, my wrist was in a vise. I was being lifted off Kai in one swift motion and dropped carelessly on the floor in front of the couch.

"What the fuck, Sheats?" Zeke roared at me. "Dude, are you okay?" That was directed at my roommate.

I blinked once, twice, and my surroundings came back into focus. Zeke was leaned over Kai, who was bending his head left and right as if I'd choked him.

*Shit, did I choke him?*

Mack was standing off to the side with his girlfriend tucked close. Her hand was covering her mouth, and her eyes were wide. Slightly behind them, I noticed the one person I did not want to see—Kiwi.

I wanted to kick the traitor out of my house, but logic set in, and I would have had to answer even more questions that I wouldn't acknowledge.

I pushed myself off the ground and stalked to my room, ignoring all of them, and slammed my door—which I finally got back two days ago.

SINCE THE INCIDENT in the living room, I stay in my bedroom whenever I'm home. I manage to avoid Kai and the others for almost a week. Not being able to train with the team during practice makes it laughably easy but also leaves me with nothing but my thoughts and my new favorite hydration method.

It's Wednesday evening. I'm sitting on my bed in the dark, a show playing on my laptop that I have zero interest in and a beer in hand. I close my eyes and lean my head back onto the *one* new pillow I purchased when the noise level in the house rises. God, I hope Kai is not throwing another party. I avoided the last one by escaping down the stairs to the garage and sleeping in my car —in front of King's place. Why? I refuse to analyze that. According to Kai, she's gone. No one has seen her.

Suddenly, my door flies open, and I blink against the light coming from the hallway. When my vision adjusts, I lock eyes with a tall female figure with dark, long, perfectly curled hair. She stares down at me with so much disdain that I hold my breath, waiting for her to rip me a new one.

*I forgot to pick up my best friend from the airport.*

Den folds her arms over her chest, making her tits push up in the top that is not Montana appropriate for the season, and I cock an eyebrow.

"If you so much as think about my breasts right now, Sheats, I'm going to shove my brand-new winter boot so far up your ass, you can admire the handmade details with your inner eye."

She delivers this with such a straight face that I can't keep it together. D props her hands on her hips, which makes it even worse. I can't stop the laughter, and within a few minutes, I'm wheezing. Den watches me from her spot, and when I regain control, I find myself smiling for the first time in weeks. My chest feels like a heavy weight has lifted off it, and I'm...almost happy.

I push myself up and walk over, wrapping my arms around her. "I'm sorry I didn't come to get you, D." I press my nose in her hair and inhale deeply. The signature scent of her black-bottled shampoo that costs more than my annual supply of hygiene products registers in my nose, and my body relaxes.

My best friend is here.

She returns the hug, and I tighten my hold. "I missed you, D." I didn't realize how lonely I felt until now.

She pulls back and frowns at me. "What's going on, Wes?"

Kai, who'd been lingering in the door, closes it after he gives me a brief nod. I guess I do owe the guy an apology for everything I've put him through.

I take Den's hand and lead her back to the bed, where we both settle against the headboard.

She waits patiently while I sort through my thoughts. I don't know how much I want to tell her, but at the same time, there is no question that I need to confide in someone. She is the only person that would truly understand.

"King—" My throat closes up, and I rub my hands over my face, digging my fingers into my hair. "Fuck!"

A hand lands on my thigh. "Talk to me." Den knows me too well, and she won't judge.

I wrap my arms around my midsection and turn my head to her. "King wasn't who I thought she was."

"What does that mean?" Her tone is hesitant, and after everything we've been through together, it's understandable.

"I fell for her, D. Hard," I confess, and my heart rate picks up. I admitted it as much for myself as I wanted to tell someone else.

Den's brows shoot to her hairline. "So why are you not with her?"

I draw in a deep breath, my pulse now so fast that it's almost painful. "Because she is Francis Turner's daughter."

# CHAPTER TWENTY-TWO

## KING

THE PASSING LANDSCAPE HAS LONG BEGUN TO BLUR TOGETHER. At first, the constant stream of tears impaired my vision. After that, it was simple disinterest. I didn't give a fuck where I ended up. I turned my phone off hours ago when Mags wouldn't stop calling.

*I guess she found my note.*

After Wes walked away and my world fell apart, I broke down right there.

Grizz found me hunched over and bawling hysterically next to a fist-size hole in the wall. He didn't ask questions, only nodded at my best friend, who stood helplessly beside me. Since I didn't have a car there and Mags was busy, Kiwi texted her that I had taken off. That gave me at least three hours.

My best friend watched me run through the apartment in an attempt to find all my belongings.

He pleaded with me not to do it. "You don't need to run. Has Francis said anything? Why can't you stay?"

Kiwi still called my father by his given name—the name we knew him by before he had *died*.

His car had gone through a side rail and crashed off a cliff on the Pacific Coast Highway when I was a child. My father was dead—at least, that was what the police officer had told my mother. What no one knew was that it was all a lie. He had faked his death—and for what?

I had no idea what to call the man who came back into my life a week after I buried my mom—by myself. He was neither my father nor Francis Turner to me, which was probably why I used his childhood nickname after the shock wore off: Gray.

I heard him mention it to Mom here and there, yet she was not allowed to use it. The first time I addressed him as Gray, he was livid. Thankfully, I was also pissed enough to hold my own. He had abandoned my mother—his wife—and his daughters for over a decade then leaned against my car in The Pole's parking lot like he used to when he came to pick me up from school. I lost it. I had been reliving my mother's last moments over and over in my head while I danced naked in front of middle-aged men for hours, hoping for enough tips to be able to pay the hospital bills eventually. How dare he show up like this. I punched him and cursed him out while tears streamed down my cheeks. He took it all—until I called him Gray.

His eyes had narrowed to slits, and he seethed, "Don't ever call me that again. Ever."

"Oh, yeah? Gray." I had propped my hands on my hips, eyeing him with a what-are-you-going-to-do look.

He had grabbed me by the shoulders and shook me. "NEVER, Kingsley! That's who *they* turned me into. Gray was never your father. I was. Am."

His reaction scared me, but not enough to back down. He had left us. I yelled until my voice gave out, hurled everything we went through because of his selfish actions at him. When his shoulders sank, I had won. But the victory didn't make it better. I was tired. At eighteen years old, I was exhausted from life.

That day, he became Gray to me. Gray may have never been my father, but neither had the man in front of me.

. . .

I STOPPED STUFFING my belongings into the duffel I had arrived with so many months ago and met Kiwi's eyes. "I can't stay here. Wes and I are over. We should've never started. I made a mistake. He knows who I am and what I've done. He thinks I betrayed him!" My words got louder toward the end, and I swallowed over the rock clogging my throat.

*I would never betray Weston Sheats, but he doesn't know that.*

"But you didn't!" Kiwi threw his arms up.

I let myself drop onto the mattress and covered my face with my hands. "You know that, and I know that. But no one will ever believe me." It came out mostly mumbled, but Kiwi understood, nonetheless.

Fingers wrapped around my wrists and pulled until I was forced to look at him. "Eventually, he has to listen." He tried to sound convincing, but we both knew Wes didn't have to listen to anything I had to say. I lost him the second he stepped out into that parking lot.

I sighed, and Kiwi held my gaze as I said, "No, he doesn't. What if he calls Lilly and Rhys? They could try to use me to get to Gray. I can't do that to our—" My eyes widened, and I cut myself off. This was the one secret my best friend was not aware of. I didn't get to tell Wes. There was no way I would reveal it— the baby—to Kiwi before its father found out.

"Then let me come with—"

"NO!" I jumped up and made him fall on his ass in the process. My outburst was louder than I intended, and I cringed. "I'm sorry, but...no."

"We said we'd always..." He peered up at me, and his plea was not just in his tone and words but carved onto his face. The only time Kiwi and I were not together was when I was on the move. I refused to tell him my location in case I got arrested.

"I'm not letting you give up your life. You have a job, one that makes actual money and you're good at. You have a boyfriend. I'm not allowing you to g-give th-that u-up." My speech ended in hiccuped sobs.

*Fuck, I didn't want to break down again.*

Kiwi stood up and drew me close. Clinging to his shirt, I buried my nose in his chest.

We were still in the same position when a new voice broke through the silence. "It's time to go, baby girl."

I jerked away from Kiwi and stared at the man hovering in my doorway. "How did you get in here?"

He slanted his head—stupid question.

Kiwi's eyes bulged in shock. "You're going with *him*?"

I ignored him and focused back on my bag. How could my life fit into one duffel bag?

Echo chose that moment to stride into my room and clumsily jumped on the bed. She had gotten a lot better over the last week, but she was still recovering. Her tongue hung out, and she tilted her head, looking at me expectantly. Crap. Echo. Fresh tears pooled in my eyes. I didn't want to leave my dog behind, but I had no idea where I'd be ending up. She still required regular checkups. Her stitches were being removed in a few days, and—

Kiwi must've read my mind because he propped one knee on the mattress, scratching Echo behind the ear. "Mags and I will take care of her until you can get her. Or I'll bring her to you."

It was obvious what he was doing. He wanted me to confirm that I would tell him where I was. I nodded and zipped up my life. Bending down to be on the same level with Echo, I placed a kiss on her head.

I was losing everyone I cared about tonight.

"Be good for Kiwi, baby. I'll see you again soon." *I hoped.* Straightening, I threaded my fingers through Kiwi's. "I'll call you as soon as I'm settled."

"Kingsley!" Gray barked, and my shoulders stiffened.

"I'm coming, *Gray*," I emphasized his name, and I heard a

low growl behind me. It still pissed him off, but I didn't give a shit.

I took one last look at them and followed my father out of the house and to my Jeep. He automatically went to the driver's side, leaving me standing several feet from my car. He didn't turn, and simply said, "You are in no condition to drive."

JOLTING AWAKE, I'm frantically glancing around. Where the fuck am I? Then, I see who is in the driver's seat of my Jeep—the Jeep he gave me years ago after he somehow found out that Mom's ancient car had broken down. I never questioned him how he knew, but I'm starting to gather that he's always been around.

Yesterday comes flooding back. The pregnancy test, my performance at The Grizz, the lightness I felt looking into Wes's eyes. How the visible affection eased the knot in my stomach, knowing that telling him about the baby would be the right thing. I trusted Wes with my heart. Then, *he* came back.

I peer at Gray—my father. "Where are we?" My throat is dry, and I start coughing.

Gray hands me a bottle of water from the console without averting his eyes from the road. "Almost at the Arizona border. You fell asleep before we hit Utah, and I had to get some shut-eye as well. Otherwise, we'd be farther by now." After a pause, he amends, "It's been a long day."

"No shit," I mumble, and Wes's face appears in my mind. I had never seen him look like that. Everything from betrayal to hurt to hatred flashed across his features. There was no way he would ever have listened to me.

A stabbing pain in my chest makes me press my palm to it—right above my heart—and I wince. My surroundings become blurry, and I cover my mouth with my other hand.

*I lost him.*

Gray jerks the car over to the side of the highway and comes to a screeching stop. "What's wrong, baby girl?"

I'm unable to respond. The cries rack through my body, and I wrap my arms around my stomach where I am carrying...our baby. My baby. Wes won't want anything to do with the grandchild of the man who almost murdered his friend.

A hand lands awkwardly on my shoulder. "Kingsley." Gray's tone is soft, the same way my dad used to talk to me when I was a little girl, and it's my undoing. I try to get away from his touch, but he holds me in place until I surrender. What will happen to me—to my baby? I shift in my seat and cling to my father, crying for everything he took from me when he left and the hope I lost when I buried my mom. I found friendship and love in Stonebriar—something I never expected to experience. Last night, it all got ripped out from under me when the reality of my life—of who I am—stepped out of the dark. The dark has overshadowed the light all my life, and just when I thought I'd escaped the shadows, it snuffed out my chance at happiness for good. Because of the dark, I am on my own once again.

"Why?" I sound hysterical as I fist his leather jacket in my hands. Pulling back, I make sure his focus is on me. "Why did you do this to me? To Mom?"

Gray turns his gaze out the windshield. "I made a lot of mistakes in my life."

His answer is void of emotion, yet the remorse as he studies me contradicts his tone.

Somewhat in control, I settle back in my seat. "Are you clean?" I scan him up and down. I noticed last night that he looked different, but I couldn't pinpoint what it was.

"Haven't touched anything since you called me."

My forehead wrinkles. "What changed?" I ask softly. This talk, the importance of this moment, is not lost on me. I have not spoken to my father since I was seven years old—not truly spoken to him.

He draws in a long breath and exhales slowly. "When I answered the phone that night, I was already on my way to you."

My heart stutters, realizing what that means. He knew I had killed E. How? I don't dare to interrupt him.

"Vic filled me in."

"VIC?" the name bursts from my lips, and I clamp my mouth shut. *So much for not interrupting.*

Gray nods. "He worked for me."

What the—?

He holds up a hand to stop me before I can start my interrogation. "When you started at The Pole, I paid Vic to watch over you. He'd been Ellis's guard dog for years. I made him mine." A sinister grin I've seen many times turns the corners of his mouth up. "He was the perfect choice. E had a reputation for how he *broke in* his dancers and kept them under control. There was no fucking way I'd risk him raping my daughter. He was a disgusting motherfucker. I admit I was quite impressed when Vic recalled what you'd done."

I scowl at the man in front of me, and he smirks.

"You look like Stephanie right now. She used to have the same frown."

Hearing my mother's name on his lips makes white-hot rage surge in the pit of my stomach, and my sorrow is replaced by something else. I welcome the shift and let it spread through every cell. Anything is better than the misery of losing the love of my life.

"Don't you dare speak her name! You don't deserve to—"

"I know." Those two words are like a punch to the gut. I'm getting whiplash between the man who used to be my father and loving husband to my mother and the criminal drug addict who abandoned us and did unforgivable things.

When I don't speak, he continues. "Ellis had been laundering money for businesses like your uncle's for years. E took over when his father died and added his own services into the mix. Anything from prostitution to small weapons deals. He had his hands in many ventures. He used drugs to keep his girls in line."

All I hear is *my uncle*.

I was aware from an early age that Uncle Ronnie, aka R.J. Turner—my father's older brother—was not a good man. He wasn't a bad man either. He was one of the worst. Everyone feared him, which was why I never met him. Gray kept my mother and me far away.

I woke up many nights as a child, listening to my parents fight. R.J. was a few years older and supplied my father with his drugs. Gray had also worked for him since he was a kid, even through his time in the military, which, in the end, cost him just that. He was dishonorably discharged for attacking a superior officer while he was high. But when my father died, so did the mention of his brother. I didn't find out why until later, when Gray came back.

"Uncle Ronnie has been dead since—"

"Since I killed him and faked my death, yes." Gray nods. "My brother deserved what he got." He doesn't show guilt. "Unfortunately, his business didn't die with him. His second-in-command took over. I didn't stick around, as you know, but when I got word that you walked into E's place and asked for a job, I made sure to get involved again. R.J.'s original team was still there, and they didn't suspect an ulterior motive for me to want in. I failed you and your mother because all I saw was the next fix. The drugs and alcohol fucked with my judgment for as long as I remember. R.J. made sure to get me hooked before I hit puberty. When I finally realized what it had done to me—to my family— it was too late. After that, I kept using to forget. I had nowhere else to go. I didn't exist on paper, but I would check on you whenever I was in the US for a job. When Stephanie died—"

His voice cracks for a second before he can compose himself. "I'm not a good man, baby girl. I will never be able to redeem myself. You know just the tip of the iceberg of what I've done in my life. I learned my lesson when the person I blindly followed betrayed me. Then, your name flashed across the screen. You asked for help." He chuckles. "I don't delude myself. I'm aware you only reached out because you had no other choice, but it was my...wake-up call. I wasn't near you. Vic took care of the body and erased the footage. I arrived later that night, drove eighteen hours straight. After we spoke, I made Vic lock me up until I was one-hundred-percent detoxed and no longer needed a fix to make it through the day."

I'm stunned by his recollection. I knew he wasn't there, but I also didn't ask who cleaned up after me. Gray had called me back, ordered me to pack a bag and leave town. I had been curled up in my bed. At every sound outside my door, I expected the cops to burst into my apartment and arrest me. So, when he told me to *run*, I did.

I have so many questions, yet only one will form. "How did Rae know where you were?"

"Your sister found me many years ago."

*She did?* "How?"

He doesn't answer. Instead, he says, "We're not far from our destination. Let's keep going."

WE DRIVE IN SILENCE, and I replay everything Gray has said in my head. Every so often, I glance over at him, trying to find evidence that he lied. That he's not gotten clean for me. But he looks good. He is less gaunt. He has a natural tan, and the gray tint he had for as long as I remembered, from the old pictures from my childhood, is gone.

"Why did Rae warn me that you were on your way to Stonebriar?" I hadn't heard from my sister in years. "Were you going to hurt Wes?"

Gray's gaze flickers over to me, and he snorts. Actually snorts. "No, baby girl. The Sheats boy is of no consequence to me. Do I like that my daughter has a boyfriend? No. But that would apply to anyone with a dick."

"Gray!" I exclaim in disgust. Hearing the word dick out of his mouth is...just no.

His expression sobers. "I came back because when you killed E, many people lost a lot of money. Your uncle's business wasn't E's most dangerous customer. You stopped moving, as I told you. I wasn't happy, but you were safe. Vic and I alternated watching you. It was his turn, then I got word that Vic was found with his throat slit."

*Holy shit!*

Something in my memory triggers. "Wait...was that the murder behind MPU's track?"

Gray nods, and I touch my hand to my throat while my other arm wraps around my belly. I heard two of my regulars at The Grizz talking about it a couple of weeks ago. This was big news for a small college town like Stonebriar. I didn't watch much news, so all I heard about it was from our customers. I never asked about who the victim was. I had lived through too much gruesome shit in my short life. I avoided the reality of the outside world, aka outside of my bubble, at all costs. *Avoid and pretend,* as Mags called it one night when I explained myself to her.

"I was on a job and would've been here sooner, but I suspect a business rival or one of Ellis's goons got wind of who killed E. And you being family of R.J. Turner, they wanted to send a message."

My heartbeat accelerates, and I swallow over the nausea building in my stomach. Someone is after me? Wants to kill me? Kill my baby.

*Oh, God.*

"Dad?" I don't know what made me call him that, but he is as shocked as I am. His head whips in my direction while trying to keep the highway in his line of sight. I blurt it out before I lose my courage. "I'm pregnant."

# CHAPTER TWENTY-THREE

## WES

I can't believe I'm doing this.

I cross my ankle over my knee in a failed attempt to stop it from bouncing—I'm making myself nervous. The whole motion is more than awkward because my six-foot frame does not fit comfortably in the last row of coach. I'm starting to question if this damn seat has less legroom than the ones ahead of me? I've never felt this claustrophobic on an airplane. My mind starts to chastise me: *That's what you get for waiting until the last minute to book your ticket—like, literally, the last minute.*

I went online last night to check if there were still any seats available. I told myself if the flight was full, I was not meant to go. Joke was on me: one seat left.

"First time flying?" the middle-aged man next to me asks.

I peer at him out of the corner of my eye. "No."

I'm a rude asshole, but that seems to be my usual setting these days. Plus, I haven't had a drink since last night, which doesn't help. I've grown used to the dark, numbing void that Kai's BFFs, aka whatever amber-colored liquid we can get at TMH, grant me each night. However, showing up sauced at my parents' house for the first time in two and a half years is not an option—certainly not on Christmas Eve.


DEN'S VISIT over Thanksgiving seems like a lifetime ago. To say she was shocked after I dropped the "my ex-girlfriend is the daughter of the guy who almost killed your best friend" bombshell would put it mildly. If King hadn't disappeared weeks ago, D would've chased her out of Stonebriar herself in her four-inch patent-leather winter boots—the sole *winter attribute* being knee high vs. ankle. There was nothing winter appropriate about those death traps.

It took several shots of Kai's private stash to calm her ass and prevent her from calling Lilly to sic George on King. If anyone could track her, it was The Ghost—the name George got after disappearing twenty-some years ago. He got injured in the line of duty and vanished *like a ghost* after that. Why? That's another story no one has been able to get out of him.

I still avoided everyone with a pulse, and the one person who knew King's secret was on my shit list—he had even replaced Rhys at the top. My feelings toward Devon "Kiwi" Kiwinski were... I needed to define them ASAP. The risk of sucker punching his pretty face steadily increased and would most likely end my friendship with Zeke.

During one of my clear(er) state of mind moments, I had concluded that Zeke was not to blame. He had no idea what kind of person Kiwi was when he first stuck his dick in. Kiwi's loyalty was to King—*and just King*—which Zeke probably had no idea about.

All in all, it was good to get out of Stonebriar. A few days ago, Kai threw a bitch tantrum about my avoidance tactics, and school and practice were on break for two weeks. Despite the extremely tempting option of drinking my way through the holidays, I chose to make my mom happy. I'd been a selfish prick for too long, and my parents deserved better. Den was the only one aware of me coming. She would pick me up from the airport and take me home to surprise my parents.

*Home.* I had no idea where that was these days. I hadn't belonged anywhere—until King. Was she what turned Stonebriar into home? There was a chance I would never know. She took that knowledge with her when she ran. My chest constricts, and I curl my fingers around the armrest of my seat.

*Goddamn her. Why did it have to be her?*

I can't wait to get back to practice in less than fourteen days. My hand is healed, and I got the official okay last week. The toned-down version of my workouts was getting on my nerves. I wasn't burned out when Coach blew the whistle, which led to restlessness and resulted in self-medicating myself to sleep. All of this would change when I got back, though. I promised myself I'd concentrate on football, even if I wasn't going to start any more this season. I lost that when I punched a hole in the wall next to Grizz's office.

New year, fresh start, and all that shit.

MOM INSTANTLY TEARED up when she opened the door, and the sense of peace that spread through my coiled muscles told me that I had made the right decision. I would not go another two years before coming back.

Dad and I spent Christmas Day lounging on the couch while my mother fussed over us. I could see that he enjoyed the special treatment as well. I don't think he had to get up once, which only happens when he's deathly ill. My mom is a very outspoken, "you have two feet, get your own stuff" kinda woman—and we love her for it.

I didn't venture out for the first few days. As much as I enjoyed being here with my family, it still felt weird to be back. Lying on my old bed brought back memories I'd rather forget— too much unfinished history.

The unknown of where Rhys and Lilly were spending the

holidays also kept me on edge. Were they in town or on the West Coast? I constantly expected Rhys to walk out of my bathroom like old times—when he lived with me. I would hold my breath and then...nothing. I was alone. What irritated me even more was when the realization hit. The space behind my rib cage would feel hollow, like I was missing something. Someone.

A TEXT from Den eventually answers the question to the McGuires' whereabouts.

**BK: Hi.**

Clue number one: no insult or faux sexual innuendo.

**Me: What's up?**

**BK: I saw Lilly last night.**

My heart stutters, but I refuse to acknowledge it. Instead, I squash the tingly sensation the same way King killed our future. No matter how short a time we had together, there was no doubt in my mind that we would've had one—if she wasn't the person she turned out to be.

**Me: Cool.**

**BK: ?**

**Me: What do u want me to say?**

**BK: I may have told them that you're here. They want to see you.**

I stare at the screen.

*Maybe it's time to forgive them*, King's voice reverberates in my head, and I squeeze my eyes shut. My chest feels tight while my body heat rises to the point of sweat pooling in my palms. Why does it have to be her that gets through to me? D has tried to talk me into moving past my anger and resentment for years, yet the girl I should despise more than Lilly and Rhys combined is the one that makes me consider it.

*Why can't I hate her for who she is? She lied to me.*

**Me: K**

The reply is instant.

**BK: K?**

The sensation of a thousand insects crawling up my stomach walls increases.

**Me: U heard me.**

**Me: Well, not heard. U know what I mean.**

The bubble pops up and disappears several times, and the little clock in the top corner shows that it takes her three minutes to form her response.

**BK: Do you want to meet at Magnolia's?**

**Me: Now?**

**BK: Maybe.**

That would be a yes. I catch myself smiling because I sense through her words that she's squirming. Am I ready? Probably not. Do I want to see them? Before I can talk myself out of it and send D another text, I push off my bed. Let's get this over with.

**Me: See u in 10.**

I borrow my mom's car and drive to the café we used to spend hours at in high school. When I walk in, it seems like nothing has changed—except for me. The guy who used to frequent this place and flirt with every female that looked at him longer than two seconds doesn't exist anymore. The place is packed with kids from Westbridge High on their winter break. One of the baristas recognizes me, and her eyes light up. She's in her mid-twenties and worked here the entire time I went to WH.

"Wes," she greets me. "What a surprise." Her smile is genuine, and some of my nerves ease.

"Hey, Piper. How have you been?" I plaster a fake grin on my face—one anyone who knows me would see right through.

"Great. How long are you in town for?" She scans me up and down, biting her bottom lip. Is she checking me out? My old high school self fist pumps in my head. *Hell yes, we always wanted to have a go with Piper*. Instead, College Wes wants to run for the hills—Montana mountains.

"Just a few more days, visiting my family." I've reached my socializing quota and want to order my drink. I'm about to ask for hot cocoa when two arms sneak around my waist. "Hey, grumpy."

Piper glances behind me, a frown wiping the flirty look away, and I chuckle. *Finally.* Twisting, I lift my arm and drape it around Den's shoulders. "Hey, BK." She punches me playfully in the stomach as I place a kiss on the top of her head. Two figures hover behind her, and I draw in a deep breath as I hold Rhys's stare. His expression is impassive, but his locked jaw gives him away. I know the guy better than myself sometimes. *Correction: knew him.*

My eyes flicker to the side, and Lilly smiles carefully at me. I force the corner of my mouth up, but then realize I don't have to put any effort into it. It feels...natural.

"Hi, Wes," she says softly and shuffles closer to Rhys, who interlaces their fingers.

"Lil." I should probably greet him as well. Facing my former best friend, I dip my chin in Rhys's direction, and he mimics my gesture.

"Well, that's almost civil. Next time, maybe try a verbal greeting with this manly head bobbing," D remarks dryly from somewhere tucked under my arm.

I shut my eyes and bite the inside of my cheek to prevent myself from bursting out laughing. Shaking my head, I face the three. "I'll order. What do you want?"

"Oh, you don't ha—" Lilly begins, but Rhys cuts her off.

"Let's go find a table, babe." Guess he can read me, too. That was my way of saying I needed a moment to collect myself.

Their drinks are not hard to memorize, Lilly asks for her signature Earl Grey, and Rhys wants coffee—black. Hesitating at first, Den follows the other two to a table by the window. My phone vibrates, and of course, I find Den's three-line-long custom beverage *demand* on my screen. We have to work on her using the word please.

With a chuckle, I place our order, and while I wait, I take stock. The emotional tsunami that sent me into a tailspin last time I was confronted with them is not present. *Huh, interesting.*

EVERYONE IS SIPPING THEIR DRINKS. How long have we been sitting here? This is beyond awkward.

My hands are wrapped around the mug, and I'm staring at the cocoa when Lilly's voice breaks the silence. "How have you been?" Her tone is careful, and Rhys stiffens at her attempt at small talk.

"Pretty good," I lie. Den clears her throat but doesn't make eye contact with anyone.

"That's good," Lilly replies.

Several more minutes of this deafening silence passes, and I can feel the vein in my neck throb. Am I wasting my time here? Every muscle in my body coils, and I swallow over the simmering frustration. Finally, I have enough. I came here for a reason—one that, up until this moment, I wasn't sure I was ready to accept. But I'm here. They're here. I had let the disappointment in my friends and their actions, as well as my pride, drive me to seclusion from everyone I cared about in my life. I miss my old self. I miss my friends. At that realization, my chest immediately feels lighter. "I understand why you did it," I say to no one in particular.

There are audible intakes of breath, and I lift my head. Meeting Rhys's gaze, I repeat myself. "I get it." Then I add, "But that doesn't change the fact that it was a shit move."

"I know," he agrees without breaking our stare down.

"I told you I didn't want the money. You made an idiot out of me." The more I say, the more my pulse turns to rapids in my veins. "Pine Hill would've never looked my way if it wasn't for your bribe," my voice rises. I snap my mouth shut, not wanting to cause a scene. All the hurt and humiliation comes flooding back and is magnified by the events of the last three months.

A hand lands on my thigh, and Den silently wills me to tell them—confide in Lilly and Rhys about King. I should, yet I can't. I shake my head, and she glowers at me disapprovingly.

"Wes." Rhys directs my focus back to him. When he has it, he leans with his forearms on the table and continues, "I made a mistake. I was selfish, and I want to make it up to you. Tell me what you need from me, man."

He sucks in his cheeks. I glance over at Lilly, who is chewing on her lip.

Picking up my mug, I take a big gulp of my cocoa, my throat suddenly feeling drier than Kai's latest conquest—his words, not mine.

"So, you're getting married?" I divert. I have no idea what he can do. It's not that easy.

*Baby steps*, a voice I don't want to hear whispers in my mind. I squeeze my eyes shut.

*Why won't she leave me alone?*

I count to five and blink. My...friends—yes, friends; this is my first stride in rebuilding and forgiving—study me with confused looks. I lift my brows, prompting them to answer my question.

Lilly stretches out her hand, and I whistle, peering at Rhys. "Dude, did you sell the R8 for that thing?"

Thanks to D and the countless fashion magazines she always carries with her, I've learned more about women's jewelry than I want to know. Lilly has a French Pavé diamond the size of a freaking hubcap on her ring finger.

Rhys smirks, his shoulders relaxing. "I got lucky with an investment. Marcus has been teaching me."

My brow hitches. Marcus? "He has more talents than protecting your future wife?" I remark, arching my mouth up.

"The dude is wicked smart. He could do so much with his life, but he refuses to leave *me*."

Lilly rolls her eyes. "The two are so obnoxious."

I chuckle at the exchange, then I notice Den next to me is stiff as a board. She has her drink in a white-knuckling grip, and it instantly triggers my protectiveness. Seeing her this way... I want to choke the answers out of Marcus, demand to know why he acts the way he does and why D is this rattled by it. Lilly and Rhys are oblivious or don't acknowledge it—I can't decipher which. Either way, I take that as my cue to change the subject—again. "Where is the wedding?" I'm making small talk, who would've thought.

*I knew you could do it*, the voice says.

*Shut up, shut up, shut up.* Jesus fuck, I'm losing my freaking mind. That's what I get for staying sober for almost five days.

"We were thinking of Stonebriar," Lilly says, eyeing me warily, and my jaw drops.

"Uh..." It takes me a second to collect myself. "You want to get married in Montana? Why?" I frown.

"We're kinda tired of the endless summer. I don't want to die of heatstroke in a suit because it's freaking a hundred degrees out," Rhys remarks dryly, but I see right through him.

"They do have something like air-conditioning, you know?"

"Okay, fine. It's supposed to be an olive branch, asshole." Rhys pouts, crossing his arms over his chest.

I can't hold back the laugh bursting out of me, and it feels... good.

"There is a chance of snow in April," I tell him.

"So you did look at the date on the invitation," the smug fuck exclaims.

"Right before I burned it." Two can play that game. Then, I see the hurt on Lilly's face. Shit. "I'm sorry, Lil. I—"

"It's fine." She genuinely waves me off, and tension I didn't realize I was holding releases. I draw in a deep breath. It feels... *good* to be here with them. Grouchily, I admit to myself that what the unwanted voice in my head said was true: baby steps.

I peer to the side at Den, who's been quietly following the

exchange. "What do you think, D? Should we let Kai lose on McGuire here?" I wink at her, and it does the trick.

She feigns outrage. "Don't you dare introduce the two without me." I wrap my arm around her shoulder and pull her close. We have a long road ahead of us to get back to where the four of us used to be, but who knows? If I've learned one thing, it's that the future is never set in stone.

I DIDN'T SEE Rhys or Lilly again. They left to meet up with friends in Colorado the next day. I wasn't too broken up about it, though. Magnolia's was the first step. I didn't regret meeting them, but it also brought a lot of old shit back to the surface—stuff I thought I had moved past. For whatever reason, the day Rhys let me in on their family secret—and his—kept replaying in my head. It was the first time I felt betrayed by him. He had lied to me since we met. That memory fucked with me more than him bribing my way into an elite school, and the craving for a drink became stronger by the day.

Den and I hung out a few more times, and then it was time to get back on the plane. Saying goodbye to my parents was harder than I expected. Mom blinked franticly when she hugged me during drop-off. I promised I'd be back over the summer, which made the tears spill over.

Placing a kiss on her cheek, I said, "I'm sorry."

She peered up at me, wiping under her nose. "For what?"

"For being a selfish dick and not coming home for two and a half years." I swallowed hard, guilt constricting my throat.

She cupped my face. "Oh, Wes, you did what you needed to heal. I would never hold that against you."

*Great, now I was tearing up.*

Thankfully, Dad limited himself to a quick handshake shoulder bump—no emotion there.

. . .

My 4Runner is waiting for me in the long-term parking lot. I didn't want to rely on anyone to pick me up. Kai should be back, but the chance of him arriving sober is slim to none—especially after spending two weeks with his family. I won't risk his or my life to save money.

Halfway through town, I come to the intersection that leads to King's house. Hesitating one second, I set the turn signal and wait for the light to change. Logic screams at me to keep going, go home, go to bed, drink myself to sleep if needed. I can't. The last time I drove down her street was when I slept in front of her place, avoiding home. I probably would've been back sooner— had I been capable of driving in the evenings.

It comes into view, and I stare at the two empty parking spots. I don't know what I was expecting. King took the Jeep with her, and Mags is at The Grizz.

*Why do I care?*

I'm almost past when I notice movement on the patio. I hit the brakes and reverse to get a better look. What the—?

I open the door and get out. "Echo!"

The dog's head whips around. Recognizing me, she takes off running. I kneel just as she slams into me, and I fall ungracefully on my ass—right into a pile of snow. Echo sits on my chest, covering me in dog saliva, and I laugh. Arriving in Stonebriar, I was cold and tired as fuck. Now, I'm wet and cold, yet my insides are warm.

I hug Echo close to my chest. "I missed you, too, girl."

She nuzzles her snout to my cheek and gives me one more lick.

"Off," I order her, and she instantly follows my command. A pang of pain slashes through my heart as I remember the after- noon King taught me how to use my voice to emphasize what I want Echo to do. She had explained that anyone could look up dog commands, but there is so much more to it. It's how you use them that makes a dog—your dog—follow you. Echo sits down next to me as I climb to an upright position. Glancing between Echo and the house, I ask, "What are you doing outside?"

I approach the front door, wiggling the knob. It's locked—the fuck?

I make my way to the side, noticing that the gate is open. Rounding to the back, I find a new addition to the patio door—a doggy door. Extra large to accommodate Echo.

"Why did King not take you?" I peer down at her, and she stares into my eyes as if to say, "Where is Mom?"

I lean down and scratch Echo's head. "I wish I knew, girl."

Echo huffs.

"I miss her, too."

*Neither of us should, though.*

She lied to me and abandoned Echo.

## CHAPTER TWENTY-FOUR

**KING**

THEY TOLD ME I WOULDN'T BE THIS EXHAUSTED UNTIL THE third trimester. Well, fuck all of them. Whoever spewed that bullshit didn't work two jobs at the time or have to be on their feet for twelve hours straight after puking for an hour every morning. Working at the diner has become my version of hell. Food aversions are legit. Who knew you could start retching by looking at the color green. And, of course, every other person wants a freaking salad. Or my newest form of gag-inducing torture: kale smoothies. They're green and already look like someone threw them up.

*Fuck my life!*

The temperature in this damn state is also proving my point. It's March, and according to the weather asshole on the diner's TV, it's the longest spring heatwave Arizona has experienced in ten-plus years. Just kill me already—figuratively ranting, of course.

I figured it wouldn't be that bad when Gray dumped me here in November. Not literally dumped me, but he didn't stick around for long. He called in a few favors and procured me a studio apartment, furnishings, and a job—more than I expected from him, given his track record.

His connections reach pretty far for a dead man. I guess if you have to remain under the radar wherever you go, you make other undead friends—or criminals.

Gray checks in every other week.

The news of becoming a grandfather had literally shocked him to silence for the remainder of our drive. He didn't mention it again until it was time to look at the apartment.

"This is temporary, baby girl."

We had passed one of my new neighbors as they handed another individual a baggie of white powder two doors down, and I nodded. I had lived in worse places. It would be fine—for now.

"I'm serious, Kingsley." He never called me King. "We will find something better before the baby comes."

I had held his stern gaze for a long moment. "Okay." I think I was still digesting what had transpired over the last seventy-two hours after peeing on the pink stick.

WITH THE AIR conditioning in the Jeep on full blast, I'm pulling out of the parking lot as my phone starts vibrating in the passenger seat. My heart instantly begins to race. Only a handful of people have my new number, yet every time I get a call, my thoughts immediately go to Wes. God, I miss him so much. Instinctively, I put my hand over my belly.

"Who do you think it is, Nugget?" I whisper, not sure if I'm asking her or me. My checkup is next week, and the ultrasound technician told me I'd probably be able to find out the gender. In my mind, though, I've been calling my little bean "her" since the day the two stripes appeared on the test.

I glance over and see Kiwi on the screen. I smile, but at the same time, my vision becomes cloudy. Blinking rapidly, I try not to lose sight of the road. The last thing I need is to get into an accident. I would never forgive myself if anything happened to our baby—*my baby*. I'll call him back when I get home.

Home being the studio crapshoot apartment I'm still renting in the apartment complex that's anything but safe. Gray hadn't mentioned finding a more suitable place in a while, so I promised myself—and Nugget—that I'd get us out of there myself. With the number of shifts I've been taking, I can save up enough to move the two of us into a nice(er) area. There is no way I'm going to let my baby grow up here. I turn the stereo on, and my beloved Jeep plays the last song I listened to on my phone's playlist. "Broken" by Jonah Kagen comes through the speaker, and I hit the steering wheel in frustration.

"Really?" I can hear the quiver in my voice. My eyes start watering instantly. There hasn't been a single time in the last few months that this song hasn't made me cry my eyes out. Out of control hormones, leaving behind the man I love, the fear of not being able to provide for my baby, but also reliving the moment he found out who I was...everything comes rushing back, and I have to pull over.

I go through an entire packet of tissues before I can keep driving. Glancing at the dash, it's already ten o'clock, and I'm covering the morning cleaning shift at the hotel—the other job I got *myself*. My alarm will go off at four thirty—that will be fun.

I pull into my designated parking spot at 10:13 and notice the black Escalade. My first thought is, *they found me*. Whoever killed Vic finally tracked me down. But then I remembered Gray's call three days ago. He was sure no one knew where I was.

A second thought hits, and I mumble to myself, "Fucking hell, the feds arresting someone else?"

*Wouldn't be the first time.*

I grip the Du Hoc in one hand, pull the car key out of the ignition, and slip two keys through my fingers, making me look like a piss-poor version of the Wolverine. Better safe than sorry.

It's the same ritual every night, and my skin prickles until I'm inside my apartment. Sliding out of the seat, I groan as my feet hit the cracked cement. There is no way I can keep this up for another four months—not at this rate.

Clutching the knife harder, I dip my chin and hurry past the parked SUV. If anyone is in there, I can't see them through the tinted windows. Hopefully, I can make it upstairs and inside before the shit hits the fan.

I take two steps at a time and fumble with the lock. Everything is quiet, which puts me more on edge. My hands tremble, and sweat creeps on my palms. My keys slip twice before I can complete this simple task. As soon as my door is shut, I flip the triple lock and lean my forehead against it. Sighing in relief, I let my bag drop to the ground next to me.

I'M HALFWAY to the galley kitchen when someone knocks at the door. My heart skips a beat, and my hand flies to my chest. What the—?

Whoever it is, it's not a forceful knock. Not like I'm used to from the cops when they're looking for one of my lovely neighbors. Yes, that has also happened.

*This is temporary*, I remind myself.

The soft tapping comes again, and I slowly swivel on my heels and walk back. I take a deep breath and peer through the peephole.

*Oh, God.*

I duck to a crouch, as if that would tell the person on the other side that I'm not here.

"King?" At her voice drifting through the piece of wood, I cover my ears.

*No, no, no.*

"King? We know you're in there. We saw you walking up."

*We?*

"We're not going to hurt you," her voice raises.

I can't leave her—them—out there. It'll draw the attention of my neighbors, and that's the last thing I want—no, having her in my apartment is the last thing. My head begins to throb from the internal battle. Neither alternative is any good—not for me. What is she doing here?

*Fuck, fuck, fuck!*

I untangle myself, my aching legs protesting as I straighten. Nugget probably isn't too happy with me either for squishing her between my thighs. I glance down at the slight but noticeable bulge under my uniform.

Inhaling through my nose, I close my eyes. Just get it over with. Worst case, I will deliver this baby in jail, and hopefully, her daddy will take care of her.

I release the locks and hesitantly turn the knob. *I can still pretend that I'm not here.* The small gap reveals the last person I ever expected to meet, let alone see knock on my bottom of the barrel, shitty studio door in the middle of the butt fuck, hot as hell Grand Canyon State.

"HI, KING." She smiles softly. Her gentle face stands in complete contrast to her all-black attire of skinny jeans, John Fluevog boots, and shirt. The leather jacket probably costs more than my entire wardrobe.

"Lilly."

No point in pretending I don't know who she is. I open the door wider and step aside.

She doesn't move. "May we come in?" Authority radiates off her, the same way I saw in the videos of the press conference. I glance behind her and notice the two men towering over her. I recognize both.

I nod my head and wave in an awkwardly jerky gesture for the trio to come inside.

Lilly slips past me, followed by her security detail: George Weiler and Marcus Baxter.

Jesus fucking Christ. The Ghost and The Shadow, as Wes called him once.

*Wes.*

My lips quiver for the second time tonight. The slightest reminder of him, and the hurricane of love, loss, and guilt threatens to overpower me. It's always there, simmering under the surface, and after my earlier breakdown, my emotional state has not yet recovered. Inhaling steadily through my nose, I focus on Nugget. She is my anchor to sanity. I'm doing this all for her. Calmer, and with my back to my visitors, I close the door, not bothering with the locks.

The arsenal on *them* is clearly visible. I don't know where I am safer: within my four walls with three armed-to-the-teeth individuals who essentially are my enemies, or outside in the courtyard with my drug-selling neighbors waiting for their next customer.

Biting the inside of my cheek, I straighten my spine and turn.

"I don't know where he is."

Lilly arches an eyebrow. "Who?"

I prop my hands on my hips. "My father."

She nods in understanding. "I'm not here for him."

*Huh?* "Oh."

"We will find him, though," Marcus barks out, which gets him a disapproving look from Lilly and George equally.

Somehow, this one sentence has broken me out of my stupor, and part of the old King rises to the surface. I draw my shoulders back. "What do you want, then?"

Lilly addresses George. "Would you mind waiting outside?"

Her head of security narrows his eyes.

"I'm fine, George. King won't hurt me."

Not that I could do much with my curved blade against the Glock 19 tucked in the back of her jeans.

"Lilly, I—" Marcus tries his luck as well.

"Get out," she orders, rolling her eyes. Her tone is easy, but it's an order, nonetheless.

Both men sigh heavily, but understand that this is not a negotiation.

"We'll be in the hallway," Marcus declares, scowling at me. George still has not said a word, but holds Lilly's gaze as he follows the younger man out.

I eye the girl in my living room, and she waves at the pull-out couch.

"May I?"

"Uh, sure." I hesitate for a second after she walks over and lowers herself down. This is my place, for fuck's sake. Get it together, Monroe.

When we're both seated, I open my mouth, but Lilly holds up a hand, and my jaw snaps shut.

"I apologize for ambushing you this late and unannounced. However, I didn't think you would've agreed to meet if I had called ahead."

"Probably not," I snort.

She smirks, and some of the tension melts away. Her personality makes you want to be her friend—cue, I feel like an idiot. I'm King Monroe *Turner*.

We sit in silence after that, and I wish I had one of my blades to keep my hands busy.

"I've known about you for quite some time," she says carefully.

Her tentative deliverance of the bombshell doesn't do anything to diminish the shock; the craving for my knife is forgotten.

"WHAT?" I squeak and choke on my saliva.

My vision blurs, and Lilly jumps up, filling one of the discarded glasses in the sink with water. She holds it out to me. "Small sips."

I drink half the glass before I can form words. "How long?"

She levels me with a look that tells me this is not going to be good. "Since the day your father disappeared—again."

My eyes widen to the point that I think they will bulge out of their sockets and land in my lap any second. "How?" My question is barely audible.

Lilly reaches into the pocket of her leather jacket and withdraws a piece of paper. She holds it out to me, and I'm not sure what to do. She nods, and I take the note from her.

Unfolding it, it reveals three words in handwriting I would recognize anywhere. My gaze flies to hers. I glance back down at my name written in my father's easily recognizable chicken scratch:

*Kingsley Monroe Turner.*

"It was chaos. I was bleeding heavily and barely coherent. I thought I had dreamed the whole thing until I found the note, days later, among my belongings in the hospital. Everyone was busy checking on Rhys. Gray had tucked it into my pants right before he disappeared."

"Why?" It seems my vocabulary has been reduced to one-word questions.

"His precise words were, '*No one betrays me. Our paths will cross again, but until they do...take care of her.*'"

"Betrays?" He had used the same word when he talked about his past. Who betrayed him?

She pauses and waits for me to look at her. "I assume you know where your father was all those years? With whom."

Slashing my mouth, I nod. "I found out after my mother's funeral."

"I see." Lilly stares at the wall opposite us. "I don't remember everything from that day. What we were able to figure out was that your father was cut off from the money. He had nothing left. We assume that was why he had *ended it* the way he did before he ran."

. . .

I THINK OVER HER WORDS. Things slowly fall into place. My father may have been the one to bring Lilly to that house, but he wasn't the only one there. His words echo in my ears: *I learned my lesson when the person I blindly followed betrayed me.*

"He took the shot?" A fact that was never publicly released.

Lilly nods. "Yes. He saved Rhys's life. Ended the standoff."

NEITHER OF US speaks after that. Lilly flips her thumb against her other four fingers, and I fidget with the hem of my uniform.

I don't look at her. "I didn't know he had faked his death until over a decade later. He showed up a week after my mother's funeral." I laugh, humorless, the earlier tension creeping its way back into my body as I remember the day. "I had just finished my shift and was walking to Mom's beat-up Honda in the parking lot. He was leaning against it, and—" I break off. "When I realized who he was, I punched him. Then I broke down in his arms." My shoulders slump, the shame of having taken comfort in his arms—after what he did—chokes the words I should say to her. Apologize for him.

A hand touches my knee, and my head jerks up. "He is your father. We can't control how we feel, no matter what our head tells us."

She never asked for my side of the events, yet I continue anyway. "He gave me my Jeep during his second visit. My car— Mom's car—had broken down completely. "'*Unfixable*,' the mechanic said," I imitate the guy's condescending tone with a sneer. The loser was one of the regulars at The Pole—a friend of a friend, otherwise he wouldn't have been able to get in. His knowledge of where I worked gave him a false sense of superiority, one I wanted to carve out with my knife more than my next breath.

"Then, Gray showed up with a brand-new MOAB. I accused him of bribing his way back into my life. I refused to take it, but he left the keys with one of the security guys at the club. I ignored it, took the bus to and from work. My best friend eventually had enough. He picked up the keys and drove the Jeep to my place."

"You don't need to feel guilty for accepting the car." She smiles gently. Her genuineness directed toward me makes no sense.

"Why are you here?" I don't think she is interested in my past or the gifts my undead criminal father, who was an active participant in the nightmare that ruined so many lives, gave me.

She shrugs. "He asked me to take care of you."

"What does that mean?" I'm so confused.

"Your mother gave you her maiden name as your middle name. With the note, it was easy to find out who you were. I, uh...*found* your original driver's license. When you started working at the club, you dropped your father's name, but your employer kept extensive records on everyone."

She's right. The fake ID I paid half a fortune for—the ID that made me three years older than I was at the time—was for Kingsley Monroe. Plus, E plastered my name and picture all over The Pole's website and social media. I was his star.

"She never took his last name," I mumble. "As fucked up as it was, it made me feel closer to her by changing mine to hers."

Lilly surveys me with an odd expression, and I tilt my head. "What?" I ask.

"Your father and Stephanie Monroe were never married."

My mind goes blank. I open and close my mouth. Nothing comes out. He—they—were—never— Black spots appear in my vision.

My shoulders shake. "King!"

*How is this possible?*

"King, breathe!" *Shake, shake.*

Something inside of me snaps back into place, and I inhale with a wheezing sound. Was my whole life a lie? No...no, there is no way. I refuse to believe that. The burning sensation in my chest slowly subsides, allowing for me to argue what I fell for being the truth. "They, uh...no. She was his wife."

My statement is less than convincing, forcing me to acknowledge that, deep down, I've already accepted the reality.

"Not legally," Lilly reasons.

I cover my face with my hands. Another lie. Another fucking lie. My eyes sting, but not because I'm sad. My hands drop to my lap and ball into fists. "And here I thought he had some good qualities," I growl, unable to form a properly articulated sentence.

"There is a lot I wasn't able to find out. Only your father can give you those answers."

"Why are you so...so fucking understanding? After what he did to you." I'm losing my grip.

Lilly takes my hands, her sincerity putting a lump in my throat. "I'm not defending him, King." She considers her next words. "I will make him pay for what he did to me, and to my family, but he is your father. He is not the reason I'm here." She squeezes my fingers, and I'm not upset at her volition to get justice—get, not demand. She will force it on her own. And she deserves it.

"When he asked me to take care of you, I had no idea what I would do with this information. I confided in George—and now Marcus. Rhys doesn't know. Not yet. I will fill him in as soon as I'm back home."

I wait for her to go on, careful not to withhold oxygen from my lungs again.

"I had watched you for a few months. Until you..." She levels me.

"Until I killed E," I admit to the murder of my boss. What am I doing? I'm pretty much begging to go to jail.

Lilly is not surprised at all.

"You already know," I state—not a question. How? Vic got rid of the body.

"I suspected it. Isaiah Ellis had a rap sheet a mile long and was accused of rape several times. Each time, the cases were dropped shortly after. He had a lot of people in his pocket. When someone reported him missing, I started digging. The surveillance videos of that night were wiped clean. There was no trace of him after he left the club before closing. However, you were caught on camera dropping off an injured girl at the local ER. And then you ran..."

"You really are a hacker, aren't you?" I shake my head.

Lilly smiles sadly. "It runs in the family. The town you were in was small. I checked the most likely places first and got lucky."

*Lucky.*

"E came back to the club. I forgot my phone and found him..." Saliva pools in my mouth as the scene replays in my head. "I called Gray," I admit to her. "I didn't know what else to do."

"I understand." Her tone is neutral.

"He made it go away." I don't want to repeat it.

"You are his daughter, and he protected you," she speaks matter-of-factly.

"Do you know what happened to the body?" I never dared to ask Gray, and if she can trace people...

Lilly's mouth twitches. "No, I'm good at what I do, but I'm not on that level. You were my focus, which is why I had you followed for a while."

"Followed?" My jaw drops. I was on the move for the better part of a year.

Lilly chews on the inside of her cheek. "George planted a tracker on your Jeep before it all went down. I knew where you were but didn't have to have someone trail you twenty-four seven. George checked on you every few weeks."

I don't know if I should be impressed, shocked, or furious.

"He saw Gray there twice. He was watching you."

"Excuse me?" I was aware that Gray trailed me; he admitted as much. *But she knew?*

I jump up and start pacing. Lilly regards me quietly as I try to make sense of it. My parents were never married. Gray asked her to take care of me. He protected me from the consequences of committing murder, then disappeared, but he and Vic followed me without my knowledge. The room is suddenly too hot. I make a beeline to the bathroom and strip out of my uniform. With my hands on the rim of the sink, I study my reflection. The deep circles under my eyes show the darkness of fear and confusion hovering above me. I quickly wash my face and throw on the oversized T-shirt and shorts I discarded there this morning. Emerging, Lilly is in the same spot, waiting patiently.

I stop in front of her with the question that hit me as I changed. "Why didn't you...take him?"

She answers without hesitation. "I was interested in his long game. It seemed you were important to him. He stopped checking in, though, right before you arrived in Stonebriar."

*When Vic took over.*

Stonebriar. My hand instinctively touches my belly, and Lilly follows the movement. I fight the urge to retract my arm.

"Does he know?" She glances between me and Nugget.

"Gray?" Yup, totally playing dumb.

She humors me. "Wes."

My eyes gloss over as she speaks his name, and my other hand flies to my mouth. I blink ferociously and shake my head at the same time.

Lilly reaches out and pulls me back down beside her. Sitting with her leg pressed against mine, she hugs me to her. I struggle against the embrace, but she's not having it. I give in. The weight of everything I've been carrying with me for the past months—no, years—becomes impossible to hold up. I've been hanging on by a thread as it is. Lilly's unexpected visit, her understanding and comfort, rips the little self-control I have left to shreds.

I fist her gazillion-dollar leather jacket as I bawl my eyes out.

She strokes my hair, murmuring to me, "Shhhh, it's okay. Get it all out."

When I regain some control over my tear ducts, I untangle myself. "I don't understand why you're here." I have no idea if I'm asking her or what.

"I'm here because you and Wes deserve to be happy. The three of you." She peers down at my belly.

"He would never accept us." Tears begin to run down my cheeks again.

Lilly takes my hands. "Did you give him a chance?"

"He wouldn't listen. He was so angry with me."

She lifts her hand and touches the side of my face. "King, he saw you with the man who was part of the night Rhys and I almost died. Not to speak of what else he did during that decade." She pauses for a beat. "Wes thought you played him. Betrayed him. He carried so much anger toward Rhys and me. You were the first person he let in after our...fight."

"He wouldn't l-lis—" I break off as new sobs overcome me.

"You should try again."

"Why would he want to be with me? My father—"

"Is not you." Lilly tilts my chin up until our eyes lock. "Our parents don't define who we are. Yes, they are part of us, where we came from. But we make our own choices. You gave everything up to care for your mother. You were the only one who was able to break through Wes's wall. A wall even Den hasn't been able to crack, and the two of them are as close as you and Kiwi." I don't ask her how she knows about him; of course she does. "You are special, King. And I know in my heart that Wes cares for you. And that he will care for your little one."

I want to believe her so badly my chest aches.

"I'm going to be in touch. My wedding is in one month—in Stonebriar. I would love for you to be there."

"I—what?"

*Did they make up with Wes?*

As if she's reading my mind, Lilly says, "Rhys is there, as we speak. I dropped him off before coming here. We met with Wes over winter break. I'm pretty sure I can thank you for him giving our friendship another chance."

I frown at her, but she simply shrugs.

"I—I don't know." This is insane.

"Think about it. I'll text you. The jet will pick you up. You shouldn't be driving by yourself."

"Of course you already have my number."

Lilly grins sheepishly as she gets up. On her way to the door, she turns again. "Oh, and King?"

I lift my gaze from my hand over my belly.

"No matter what you decide, you'll be safe from now on—in case you notice anyone following you." When I raise my eyebrows, she adds, "I don't like where you live, and I protect my family."

"Family?" I must've heard her wrong.

"You're carrying Baby Sheats. That makes you automatically part of the family. I don't care what the stubborn-ass daddy has to say."

And with those parting words and a wink, she opens the door and leaves.

## CHAPTER TWENTY-FIVE

### WES

AFTER I MADE SURE ECHO WAS INSIDE, I DROVE TO THE Grizz. With each light I passed, my irritation grew. At King for abandoning Echo, at Mags for not taking proper care of her, and where the fuck was Kiwi in all this? He was supposed to be King's BFF. Shouldn't he have been helping? *Why the fuck did she leave her here?*

By the time I parked behind the bar, I was fired up. My insides were buzzing, and I ripped the back door open with more force than necessary, causing it to slam into the brick wall. Whoopsie. Well, not my fault. Grizz shouldn't leave it unlocked.

How could King have left Echo? Who'd been taking care of her? Obviously, no one, since they relied on a fucking doggy door. What was Mags thinking, not double-checking the damn gate? What if Echo would've run off, or worse, gotten hit by a car? Again.

I reached the main room and immediately zeroed in on Mags. When she noticed me, she staggered backward. Guess she didn't expect me here.

I pointed at her and back to the corridor I just came out of. "NOW!" I shouted over the music.

She scowled, and I thought she was going to flip me off, but instead, she put the bottle she was holding down and said something to a new chick manning the bar with her.

They had replaced King. Of course they did, but seeing it, my fingers curled inward, which made my annoyance shoot to a new level—this time, though, because of my body's uncontrollable reaction when it came to *her*.

I turned, not waiting to see if Mags followed.

"What's your fucking problem, Sheats? Someone hiding your booze? We serve in the front—" she sneered at me as soon as we reached the employee lounge.

I spun around, not letting her finish the sentence. "My problem?" My pulse was thrashing in my ears. Rationally, I shouldn't have been this worked up. Echo wasn't my dog. "My problem is that I found Echo wandering the streets." Okay, a little exaggerated, but it might as well have happened.

"What?" she shrieked, the sass gone instantly. "Is she okay?"

Her genuine panic eased some of my rage. I didn't know if I was mad at her or at me—for caring. Caring about Echo. Wanting to know where King was and if she was okay.

"She's fine," I responded, calmer than before. "The side gate was open. She must've gotten out through there. I locked it after I put her back."

"Oh, thank God." Mags threw her arms around my neck, and I stiffened at the unexpected physical contact. Since King, my mom and Den were the only women I let come close enough to hug me. In my mind, I associated Mags with King. Memories came flying at me left and right: sitting in their living room during movie night, King stepping into the shower with me before I drove her to campus, laughing with everyone at our table at The Grizz.

My arms still at my side, she let go quickly. "Sorry, I, uh...

sorry." She blushed. Seeing Mags blush was a new sight, and it distracted me from what just happened inside my head.

I smirked. "It's all good."

We stood awkwardly in front of each other, and I tried to figure out what to say next. "I...um, if you need someone to watch Echo, I can do that." I quickly added, "While you work."

Mags looked stunned, opening and closing her mouth. She shifted back and forth on her feet and chewed on her thumbnail, all while staring past me.

"Mags?" I prompted.

"I don't know, Wes." She still wasn't making eye contact.

My shoulders sank, and my chest constricted. I didn't realize how much I wanted Echo with me until Mags shot me down.

"Cool." I wouldn't show her my disappointment. Maneuvering around her, I aimed for the door.

Her hand shot out and latched onto my wrist. "Wait!"

Mags pressed her lips together for a moment before she spoke. "I appreciate your offer." Her gaze flitted around the room again. "Kiwi and I are splitting our time with Echo, but between classes and work, it's not enough. Kiwi has a ton of projects. It's just—"

"Just what?" I interrupted. She was testing my patience.

"I don't know if King would be okay with that," she replied in a tiny voice.

"How would she know? She fucking abandoned us!" *Us?* "Echo, I mean." Fuck. The still simmering rage turned back to a boiling point, mostly at myself for showing my cards to the enemy. I glared at Mags, attempting to cover up my blunder, but then something shifted in her.

Her expression softened. "Wes, King couldn't take her. Echo still needed medical attention. She didn't know where she would end up. King would've never risked Echo's life like that. This dog means everything to her."

I held her gaze and let her words sink in. Something stuck

out, though. *She didn't know where she would end up.* "Do you know where she is?"

Mags went still, and I had my answer. "Where is she, Mags?"

She shook her head. "I can't."

I turned on my heels and left her standing there. I couldn't believe I did that. I basically admitted that I still cared about King. I didn't. Did I? No, she was Turner's fucking daughter. I couldn't.

*Goddamn it!*

THE NEXT FEW weeks flew by. Back to full capacity, I focused on training. It was the one thing that kept me sane—when I was sober. I went to class, practice, and even attended some of Kai's parties. Though, I would mostly stand in the kitchen, watching over the bar. Whenever Kiwi came around, which started to happen more frequently, I would call it a night. All in all, I was functioning.

Sometime in early February, Kai and the rest of the guys decided to head to The Grizz after practice. Apparently, Kiwi was celebrating another big deal at the Mountain Club. Waiting for my reply, they stared at me like I either was about to curl into a ball and cry or throw punches at whoever mentioned my ex-girlfriend's previous place of work. Sadly, I couldn't fault them. Instead, I surprised myself. I clapped Zeke on the shoulder and said, "Let's go celebrate your man."

I hadn't been back since I had confronted Mags. I couldn't. I was still embarrassed as hell for nearly begging her to let me dog sit. It was time to move on—at least, that was what I pretended for everyone else's sake. If they knew that I was doing regular drive-bys during Mags's shifts to make sure the gate was closed and Echo was safe, they would commit me.

The night at The Grizz went better than expected, and I found myself returning to my usual table at least once a week. Oddly enough, I drank less when I came here since I had to drive myself home. Taking an Uber all the time was becoming too pricey, and it was still too cold to walk the three miles.

The first Friday, when I sat in the corner and watched everyone have a good time, I experienced a wake-up call I could no longer avoid. I kept waiting for Rihanna's voice to come through the speakers. When it didn't happen, my throat tightened, and it suddenly was hard to breathe. With my elbows on the table, I intertwined my hands behind my neck, closing my eyes, and hung my head. Motherfucker, I missed her.

A few drinks later, I came to a decision. I marched over to Mags, who was in the process of mixing some type of pink concoction. I strutted straight behind the bar and ignored the new girl, who attempted to stop me.

"It's fine, Kira," Mags told her.

I snorted. What kind of name was Kira?

Mags scowled at me with her head slanted. "How drunk are you?"

"None of your fucking business. I want Echo." I swayed and steadied myself against the bar. I may have been drunker than I thought—probably shouldn't drive.

"Excuse me?" She looked at me like I had asked her to strip.

I scanned her up and down and settled on her tits. She probably has some—

My thought got cut off when she shoved me. "Weston!"

"Wha—?" I lost my balance and fell on my ass, disappearing behind the counter. A few customers leaned over the top like I was some type of free entertainment.

"Jesus Christ, Sheats." Mags looked past me. "Kira, get Kiwi. He just came in."

Oh, fuck no. I scrambled to push myself up, but slipped again. I hadn't had that much to drink. Had I?

Someone grabbed me under the arms and pulled me up. Mags shoved her hands in the front pockets of my jeans.

"Hey! Take your—"

She fished out my car keys and handed them to the person

holding me up. "Take him home." To me, she said, "We'll talk tomorrow."

Before I could reply, I was being dragged out of The Grizz. Outside, the fresh air hit me like someone backhanded me, and I stopped.

"Wes, dude, let's go," Kiwi said. He probably wanted to appear authoritative, but all I saw was the guy who had lied to me.

I rounded on him, and he stumbled back. "I'm not going to clock you, asshole," I barked then mumbled, "even though I really want to."

Kiwi sighed. "You have every right to—"

"SHE FUCKING BETRAYED ME!" I roared in his face.

His eyes narrowed, and he moved closer until our noses almost touched—emphasis on *almost*. He would've had to raise himself on his tiptoes to breach the gap. I was about to point that out when his next words shut me up. "Listen up, you dimwitted drunk. Roe-Roe *never* lied to you. She didn't advertise who her sperm donor was, but you got the version of herself she doesn't show anyone. And I mean, anyone."

He took a breath. "Neither of us had seen Francis for over a fucking decade. I mourned him with her for years. She had no idea what happened until her mom died.

"She went through fucking hell to survive and care for Stephanie. What do you think it was like? Watching her drive to The Pole every single night, putting herself on display for the scum of the male species. All to afford her mother's hospice care and pay bills.

"I was the one lying to her mother when she asked me if Roe-Roe took another double at the diner. *I*"—he stabbed his chest—"was the one who promised Stephanie I would take care of her and then fucking failed her."

"You're cursing a lot tonight," I observed.

This earned me a poke against the sternum. "Did you listen to a word I said?"

Man, I didn't think I'd ever seen this guy this worked up. I managed to nod. "Yeah, I got it all." And I did. I knew King had a rough life, not to mention what she did to save that poor girl from her boss, but hearing it from Kiwi...

"Okay, then pay close attention to what I have to say next." He leveled me with a glare until he was convinced he had my full attention. "Roe-Roe had no clue you were here when she stopped in Stonebriar. She never intended to stay either. It was all a damn fucking coincidence. Did she stay because of you? Yes. Did she have some weird, unhealthy crush on you? Also, yes. But none of that was planned on her part. Don't ask me what sparked this obsession of hers. Maybe it had something to do with what Francis did to your friend. Maybe she was curious. Maybe it was simple attraction—*you are a hottie*." He smirked, and I couldn't help but grin back. "But she never—NE-VER— had any intention of hurting you. You were the first person that made her truly happy. And that should say something. I've been her best friend since the day she was born. No one has made her smile the way you did."

The more he laid into me, the more it felt like being choked. Should I have let her explain?

"Where is she?" I rasped over my dry throat.

Kiwi's shoulders sank. "No clue, man."

My brow furrowed, and he explained. "I would be wherever she is in a heartbeat. Screw the business I built here. I've always put Roe-Roe first, which is why she refuses to tell me."

"Mags knows," I declared. She never admitted it, but she basically had a neon sign with the words "I know" hanging over her head.

"She does, but her loyalty is with King. Mags swears that King is safe. She'll give me the location when King is ready."

I rubbed my palms over my face, any type of buzz I still had completely gone. "FUUUCK!"

A hand landed on my shoulder. "Let's get you home. It's been a long night."

Without another word, I let him lead me to the 4Runner.

THE DAYS TURN TO WEEKS, but that saying about time heals all wounds is a big fat lie. Whoever came up with that should be sucker punched.

Kiwi setting me straight fucked me up more than seeing King with Gray. I didn't go on a bender or commit property damage, but I contemplated kidnapping Echo on multiple occasions. To be close to King, or get back at her—the verdict was still out. Every single time, I was only stopped by my inability to operate a vehicle. I still had enough brain cells to not do dumb shit like drive under the influence.

"BRO! You got a visitor," Kai hollers from outside my room.

*Huh?*

I'm not expecting anyone.

I've become a pro at pretending—around my friends, on the phone when D or Mom call, via text to Rhys. I push myself off the mattress and sway to the door.

Shit, this is not gonna be good, no matter who is here. I did not plan on facing my roommate or a visitor after I uncapped my —I peer back to my nightstand—fifth beer. *That many?*

I steady myself against the hallway wall and make it to the living room without embarrassing myself.

"Bro, what the fuck?" Kai sees me first, and it takes me a moment to focus.

"Dude, you look like shit." I zero in on Rhys standing next to my fuming roommate.

"Do I have to start taking your fucking keys again, asswipe?" Kai storms past me in the direction of my room.

I stare at Rhys, my brain slowly catching up to the visual cues my eyes give it. "What are you doing here?" Fair question.

That moment, Kai shoulders me to the side, then jiggles my car key in front of me. "This is mine until you get your shit under control."

"The hell it is," I growl and try to grab it, but miss it by a mile.

"Case in point, fuckface." He pockets my key. "You can catch a ride with one of the guys or me to campus. You are not turning into another version of...me." With that, he swivels on his heels and storms off like a little bitch.

"So, uh..."

My eyes fly back to Rhys. I forgot he was there when my entire attention span was on Kai.

I slowly make my way to the couch and let myself fall into the cushions. Rhys follows and lowers himself on the other end of the sectional. Leaning forward, he props his forearms on his thighs and studies me.

"What's going on with you?" He scans me with a wary lift of his eyebrows.

"Nothing, man. It's all great." I'm proud to say that I don't slur.

"Try again," he deadpans.

Why did he have to show up unannounced? "Why are you here?"

"Lilly dropped me off on the way to Elle. Something seemed off with you."

I frown. "You let her go somewhere alone?" I don't think he has left Lilly's side in two and a half years. Healthy? Probably not. But understandable.

"G and Marcus are with her." A little quieter, he adds, "It's an exercise my therapist ordered me to do."

*Ah, now that makes more sense.*

"Why did she bring both if she just went to Colorado?" The fact that both of their bodyguards are with her seems a little overkill to hang out with a girlfriend.

Rhys draws in a long breath. "She's been keeping something from me."

My brows shoot up. Lilly can't lie for shit, and the two made a pact years ago that they would never keep secrets from each other again.

"She's been...off ever since we came home from Christmas. She and G are having these hushed conversations, and then a week ago, Marcus joined their little club," he confides in me with discontent.

My adrenaline level rises, killing the nice and steady level of constant intoxication I had been maintaining. I'm surprised that he's come to me with this. We've been talking on and off since Magnolia's, but it's still nowhere near where our friendship used to be. His words have triggered a reaction I wouldn't have expected. My muscles coil, and my brain goes into high alert.

"Could it be wedding related?" I try to reason but know, at the same time, that this is a weak excuse.

"Why would she need both for some wedding shopping? Wes, she packed her gun—the one Dad gave her for Christmas a few years ago. She never carries it. She doesn't need to with Marcus having three on him at all times." He rakes his hand over his short hair.

*That is concerning.*

"Why didn't you ask her?" I fold my arms over my chest.

"I don't know, man. I want her to come to me. And at the same time, I'm...scared to find out what it is." His eyes are haunted, and I know that this is not easy for him to admit.

This is the first deep(er) conversation we've had in years. It feels natural to sit here and talk like old times. I don't like seeing Rhys like this.

"You have to trust that she has a reason for not telling you yet. Lil loves you. She would never intentionally hurt—" I break off because suddenly my chest feels like my heart is being ripped out.

*She never intentionally hurt me. She. King.*

"Fuck!" I close my eyes and shake my head.

"What?" Rhys asks inquisitively.

I open my mouth to confide in him as he did with me. Lilly would be able to track King. There has to be a trail, even if I would have to steal Mags's phone to get to her number. The words get stuck in my throat. Sweat builds on my forehead, and bile rises in my throat. What if Rhys freaks out and sends George after King to get to Gray? This would be his chance of getting even—however fucked up that may be. I can't do it.

"Nothing. Just, uh...girl trouble." I smirk at him in the hopes of coming across as semi-convincing. It's clear I've failed as soon as I look at him. His lips are in a thin line, and I wait for him to call me out on the lie, but he doesn't.

"What should I do about Lilly, man? We're getting married in a month." He returns to the original subject of our conversation.

"Ask her. Let her explain."

*Something I should've done.*

# CHAPTER TWENTY-SIX

**KING**

Lilly made good on her promises. For the past three and a half weeks, a black SUV followed me everywhere. At night, it was parked on the street, always in a different spot but never far away. It gave me a sense of security I didn't realize I was missing.

Yesterday morning, that pattern changed. I had just unlocked the Jeep when a tall figure—dressed in jeans, a black tee, and a bulletproof vest—approached me. Normally, I would've *reacted* accordingly, but he came from the direction the SUV was parked two houses down. This was the only reason I didn't pull one of my knives on him.

"Monroe."

I jumped at his voice. I did not expect it to be him. The urge to get in the car and speed off overwhelmed my senses, but I forced myself to remain in place. Slowly turning, I faced the man that scared the bejesus out of me: Marcus Baxter, Lilly's bodyguard. One would think that The Ghost would be more fear inducing, but Marcus, aka The Shadow, had darkness surrounding him. He was tormented by something—or someone. It takes one to know one.

I glanced around him at the car. Did that mean…?

He read my mind. "Lilly couldn't come. She wanted to, but something went wrong with the wedding venue. She is waiting for you in Montana." He stretched out a hand with an envelope, but all I could do was stare at him. What happened to this man? Except for the long hair he had tied back the same way, Lilly's bodyguard looked nothing like Wes. My heart grew heavy as Wes's face appeared in my memory.

"King?"

Hearing him address me with my first name snapped me out of my daydream, and I focused on the envelope he extended.

"What's this?"

"Lilly asked me to give this to you. The jet will be ready for you tomorrow at 1600 hours. I will be here to pick you up at 1400 hours."

I was about to take the envelope, while converting the military time in my head, when his words sank in. My eyes flew to his. "WHAT?"

Heart pounding, my head suddenly spun, and I supported myself against the Jeep.

Marcus took a step toward me, but I held up my palm. I couldn't have him touch me.

"Do you need medical assistance?" He eyed my growing stomach, and I automatically followed his gaze.

"No, I—" I what? What was I going to say? Lilly said she would send the jet, but somehow, I didn't expect her to do it.

He seemed to understand my internal battle. "May I speak freely, Monroe?" Marcus stood straight, his hands folded behind his back. One would think that him using my middle name—or, for all intents and purposes, last name—would come across as offensive or condescending, but it did the opposite. I couldn't explain it.

"Were you military?" I didn't know why I asked; it simply came out.

His mouth pressed in a thin line. "I was. But I've been

working under George for much longer." That was all I would get out of him. It was odd how I could read him.

"May I speak freely?" he repeated himself.

"Sure." I couldn't help the meek sound of my reply and tried to emphasize it with a nod.

"When Lilly sets her mind on something, there is no convincing her otherwise. She wants you in Stonebriar. She considers you part of her family, no matter how you feel about it or what will happen with you and Sheats."

I felt the blood drain from my face as my stomach dipped. This had to be a trick to get to Gray. "Why would she want to be my—"

"You carry one of her best friend's babies. On top of that, you two have more in common than most. You can relate to each other better than Rhys can probably understand at times. And the two of them are sickeningly in love. I never believed in soul mates until I met them." He chuckled at the last sentence.

"But I have a job." I couldn't just leave. A sensation all too similar to morning sickness began to spread through me. I needed all the money I could get to support us.

Marcus impassively waited for me to catch on. He reminded me of the videos I'd seen of George. I guess it made sense they'd have the same mannerisms if he has worked for him for years.

My shoulders dropped, and he saw it. The corner of his mouth quirked at the side as if he was waiting for me to concede.

"Lilly will meet you the day after tomorrow to discuss the future of you two. She won't let you come back to this dump; I can promise you that." His gaze dropped down to my belly again before he swung it to my decrepit apartment building.

"Do I even go to work today?" I asked him, furrowing my brows, feeling a mix of relief and dread at the same time. I hated it here, and I hated my job, but this was where Gray told me to stay until he came back for me.

"Collect your last paycheck, then go home to pack."

Quit? Pack? Like that? How could it be so easy for him?

Them? My nostrils flared at the sudden heat burning my cheeks. I didn't like being ordered around. My gaze dropped to the ground in an attempt to get my temper under control. I scanned the cracked and stained concrete—smears that looked too similar to what had coated the floor of The Pole that night. I left that life, that environment, behind when I went to Stonebriar—even before Wes came into the picture. I swore to myself that I would do anything to give my baby a better future. Decision made, I lifted my head.

"What about my Jeep?" I narrowed my eyes at Marcus. How could I trust these people? They were my enemies—or I was theirs.

"One of my men will drive it back. Give it two days, and we will leave it wherever you are staying." His tone was matter of fact.

*This was too good to be true.*

Marcus pressed the envelope into my hand and turned without another word. I watched him walk to the SUV and get in. I expected him to leave, but the car didn't move until it followed me to work fifteen minutes later. It took me that long to digest the letter Lilly added to her wedding invitation.


*KING,*

*I'm so sorry I couldn't come personally to pick you up. We have some issues with the venue, and I'm hoping to get it sorted out in the next few days.*

*I meant what I said. I consider you part of my family. Your father's choices in life do <u>NOT</u> define you.*

*Rhys and Wes have started talking again. While they have not been able to move past all their differences—these boys are so stubborn, can you believe it?—I'm confident things will get better. They're meant to be in each other's lives.*

*Of course, I hope you and Wes will work things out, but either way, Rhys and I will help you and your baby however we can.*

*Marcus will accompany you on the flight, and I'll see you the day after tomorrow to go dress shopping. (You didn't think you would get out of attending my wedding, did you?)*

*Have a safe trip, and don't hesitate to let Marcus know of anything you may need.*

*Lilly*

I READ the note four times while clutching the wedding invitation in my other hand. She sounded genuine. The same way Lilly appeared when she showed up at my doorstep. I wanted to trust her, but this was all too good to be true. Girls like me didn't get a happily ever after.

THE NEXT TWENTY-FOUR hours were a whirlwind. My boss didn't like me quitting very much. She immediately shouted about how I would dare leave her. We were on display for the entire diner to watch, and I swallowed hard. I didn't let people walk over me like that, but my current mental state was anything but clear. I had no clue what would await me tomorrow. When she began flailing her arms at me and coming closer, my mouth opened, yet still no words would form. The connection between my ability to form a coherent sentence—like, *"Fuck you, bitch!"*— and my verbal communication skills were severed. Suddenly, someone pulled me away from my boss, and a tall figure blocked my vision.

Marcus was in front of me while another guy in the same getup stood at my side with his hand on the small of my back. Lilly's bodyguard handed her a wad of cash, sneering, "This will compensate you for any potential loss you incur until you find a new slave."

My *former* employer gripped the wall beside her, but before I could utter a word, I was ushered outside.

After that, Marcus and his associate, who introduced himself as Ethan, packed up my apartment as I watched everything from the sofa-bed like a movie. This didn't feel real. The more they carried down to the Jeep or packed in boxes, the deeper the pit in my stomach grew, and a black hole was swallowing me. The two men loaded whatever they could into the MOAB, and by evening, Ethan was on his way. That way, I would have my car back sooner than planned, he explained.

I didn't know what to say. Was I really going back? I had to call Kiwi or Mags. I needed to let them know I was coming. Where would I be staying? My pulse sped up as question after question assaulted me.

I spent the night in a hotel room next to Marcus's, and on the way to the private airport, I finally gathered my courage and sent a group message to my friends.

**Me: Can I crash on one of your couches for a few nights?**

I didn't want to elaborate on why or how I was coming back, let alone make them think I'd be staying. Because let's be honest, I had no clue what would happen beyond the airplane ride.

Their replies were instant:

**Mags: FINALLY!!!!!!!! It's about time. You're staying here. This is your home, bitch!!!!!!**

I laughed out loud at my friend's overuse of exclamation marks.

**Kiwi: Are you okay?**

He was more hesitant. I had confided in him about Lilly's visit. While I kept in touch with both, my conversations with Mags were mostly pregnancy related—a fact I still hadn't divulged to Kiwi. I wouldn't be able to keep it a secret much longer, being five months pregnant and all, my belly was speaking for itself.

Avoiding a direct answer because I had no clue how I was, I typed: **See you soon.**

**Mags: ?**

I pocketed my phone without another response and concentrated on breathing in and out. My buzzing nerves and rapid heart rate could not be good for the baby. I gently placed my hands on my belly, rubbing small circles.

"Let's go home, little one."

MY FEET HAVE BARELY MADE contact with the sidewalk when both of my friends come running out of the house.

"Oh my God, oh my God, you're here! Whose car is this? How are you feeling?" Mags is talking so fast, I have to smirk. I've missed them more than I let myself admit while I was away, and I blink against the fog clouding my vision.

Marcus walks around the back of the car with my bag, and Kiwi's jaw drops. Of course he knows who Marcus Baxter is. He remains mute while Mags appraises him. "Who are you?"

Marcus ignores her and puts my bag next to me on the sidewalk. "You have my number, Monroe. Call if you need anything."

I nod, and he disappears to the other side of the SUV, gets in, and drives off. I watch the taillights disappear around the corner and turn to face my friends. Kiwi stares at me, his mouth hanging slack. No, not *me*—my belly.

*Fuck!*

"Roe-Roe?" His eyes slowly travel up to meet mine, and my cheeks heat.

"Can we take this inside?" I don't want to discuss my current state on the side of the road, plus my feet are killing me. It's true what they say about flying while pregnant.

Kiwi grabs my duffel, and Mags leads us inside the house. Stepping through the front door, I pause. "Where's Echo?" Why has my dog not come to greet me?

My friends hold their breath, and my heart stutters before taking off and pounding against my rib cage. "Where is my dog?"

*God, please don't tell me something happened to her.*

"Uh, well..." Mags stammers—something she never does.

Kiwi chews on his bottom lip, and he might as well be strangling me.

"W-where is Echo?" I repeat myself a third time.

Mags looks at Kiwi for...help? What the—

"She's with Wes," he rushes out so fast I do a double take.

*She's with Wes.* His words reverberate in my mind. She is with Wes. "WHAT THE FUCK?"

They jolt at my screech, but I couldn't care less. "Why the hell is *my dog* with my ex-boyfriend? You told me last week that she was fine." I level them with a glare that would've made my mother proud. I had asked them during every phone call how my baby—canine baby—was doing, and every single time, they assured me she was great.

"So, uh..." Kiwi tries to form words, but I'm past patience. Don't tell a pregnant girl her dog is gone. Let alone that she's with the one person who hates her most.

"Wes has been hanging out." Mags picks at her nails.

I bore my eyes into her. "Explain."

"He's been checking on Echo when I have to work. He's been coming to The Grizz again. But he's...he—"

"He what?" I throw my arms up.

"He's not been doing well. Especially after I set him straight," Kiwi tries his luck. "He drinks. His injury cost him his spot on the team for the season."

*Set him straight? Injury?*

I can't let myself ask about either. I thrust my hand out. "Keys."

"What?" Mags blinks.

"Roe-Roe, I don't think it's a good idea—"

"ONE OF YOU IS GOING TO GIVE ME YOUR FUCKING CAR KEYS RIGHT FUCKING NOW!" I'm bordering on hysteria. I'm overreacting. I could've asked one of them to drive me, but I am tired, hungry, and my baby has been sitting on my bladder for the past hour.

Kiwi digs out his keys, and I snatch them before he can say

another word. I will stop along the way to pee, even if it is in the bushes.

I PROBABLY BREAK HALF a dozen traffic laws on my way, which, in the back of my mind, I know isn't safe. There is still snow on the ground. I stop in front of the short driveway, blocking the garage of Kai and Wes's townhouse in the process. That way, no one can make a run for it.

Throwing the door open with more force than necessary, I exit the car. The light shining through the large windows illuminates the front walkway like a stadium, all the way down to the sidewalk. Do they have every freaking lamp in the house on? What a waste of electricity. Fucking rich people. And why the hell do I care? For a split second, as my foot hits the first step, I slow down. What if they're having a party? I'm not ready to face anyone. My trembling hands make matters worse. Is this nervous anxiety or plain rage? Curling my fingers into fists, I make the decision: rage. Before I can change my mind, I let myself in—ready to clock the son-of-a-bitch dog thief if I have to.

My eardrums are assaulted by a cacophony of sound. What the hell? "Numb" by August Alsina is blaring through the speakers of their club-worthy sound system. Something like gunshots accompany the bass, and when I round the corner to the open-concept kitchen-living room, I see the TV playing some type of action movie.

My anger disintegrates, and my heart freezes mid-beat. Wes is sprawled out on the couch, legs propped on the coffee table, head resting on the back, eyes closed. He's holding a bottle of... *something* in one hand, and the other rests on Echo, who is curled up next to him with her snout tucked between Wes and the couch.

I'm dizzy. I was so consumed by rage that he took my dog that I didn't consider for a second what it would do to me to see him again.

Despite the volume in the room, I tiptoe closer. Not that he would've heard me if I wore tap shoes attached to a megaphone while crossing the hardwood floor. With every step, my pulse increases from a slow jog to a full-on sprint, and I am unsure what to do. Wes doesn't move, and neither does Echo. I lower myself onto the other side of the L-shaped couch and wait. They don't stir as I watch them, drinking in Wes's gorgeous features. Finally, I take the universal remote and tap the mute buttons for both systems. Echo instantly jolts into a sitting position and presses herself against Wes protectively. Her eyes meet mine, and I swear she narrows them at me accusingly.

*Like I didn't already feel guilty enough. Or maybe it's the mother in me talking.*

"Hey, girl," I whisper low, not wanting to wake Wes. Yet.

Echo tilts her head, and after a moment of hesitation, she jumps the entire length of the sectional and lands next to me. Her front paws are on my shoulders, and she greets me with sloppy doggy kisses. A laugh bubbles up, and I attempt to ward her off and hug her at the same time. I've missed my fur baby so much.

"You're back."

Echo and I freeze at his slurred words. Oh God.

"It's been a few days."

*Huh?*

My dog leaves me to go back to Wes's side, and I frown at him. He blinks, and I can't decipher if he sees *me* or if he's asleep.

"I missed you."

His words hit me hard. Who was he expecting? Did he replace me? I didn't delude myself that he would wait for me, not after what I did to him, but fuck, this hurts. My throat suddenly is too scratchy to speak, and I swipe under my eye to prevent the tears from spilling over.

Wes frowns and pushes himself up in his seat. "Why are you crying, Princess?"

*Princess.* He even gave my replacement the same endearment. I can't do this. I need to— "I should go," I whisper as I shift my weight to my legs to stand. If he's waiting for someone, I don't want to be here when she comes.

"Don't!" He panics, and I halt with my palms pressing into the cushion. "Don't leave. This is the only time I get to see you."

I skim the room, confused, before I let my gaze settle on his gorgeous face again. "What do you mean?"

He lifts the bottle as if to say,' *See?'*

"Are you...drunk?" My brow creases as I scan him up and down. His clothes are wrinkled, his hair looks like he hasn't washed it in...weeks, and he's lost weight. "Wes, what's going on?"

"Of course I'm drunk, Princess. What do you think? It's the only time I get to be with you and don't feel like shit." Suddenly, his eyes focus on me, and I wait for him to realize that it's me. "You left me."

A flutter of hope forms in my chest. Do I engage in this conversation? I have no clue what to do. I rest my forearms on my knees, leaning far enough forward that my oversized sweater conceals my protruding belly. This is not the time.

"I didn't think you wanted to be with me anymore," I reply softly.

"I didn't."

My heart begins to break all over again when he adds, "But then Kiwi told me you had no idea until you came here. And Rhys...he and Lilly..." Wes trails off and takes another swig.

"Why don't you give that to me?" I wiggle my fingers in his direction. Wes looks between me and my hand before he slowly extends the bottle. I take it and place it on the table. I'm about to sit back when he grips my wrist. My gaze flies to his, and I hold my breath. Painfully slow, he shifts until he intertwines our fingers.

"You feel so real tonight."

*Oh, shit.*

I tug, trying to disentangle myself from him, but no dice. He's too strong, and if I'm honest, I don't want to let go. I've missed this man so much. Even if he thinks he's dreaming, I want to dream with him—pretend that there is a chance for us. Just for a few more minutes.

I scoot to the edge of my seat. Our knees almost touch, and he sucks in a breath.

"What are you doing to yourself, baby?" I can no longer hold the sadness inside. Seeing Wes so broken shatters my heart into tiny shards.

I lift my hand to the side of his face, and he immediately leans into my touch, closing his eyes.

"King?" he rasps.

"Yes?" My heart is hammering against my ribs. The proximity to him after so many months and the fear of him realizing he's not dreaming are pushing my adrenaline level through the roof.

"I never told you how much I love you."

*What?*

I try to pull away, but he holds on tight, and his lids pop open.

"What did you say?" Every inch of my skin tingles. Oh God, I've dreamed so many times of hearing those words from him, but he's drunk. It's the alcohol speaking.

"I said I love you. I wanted to tell you so many times before..." He lets the sentence hang, and I get it. We had only been together for a hot second. I knew that what I was feeling for him, even then, was not just a crush.

*Fuck it.*

"I love you, too." This must be the hormones and sleep deprivation—because what the hell?

He lifts our clasped fingers to his lips and places a soft kiss on my knuckles. "Thank you."

This conversation is confusing. "Um, you're welcome?"

Wes chuckles, then looks at Echo. "I'm gonna take her out."

He stands, and the sudden loss of contact rips open a void

inside of me. I want to shout at him to come back, but instead, I say, "Why did you take her?"

"Huh?"

"Echo." I tilt my head in her direction. "Why did you bring her here?" And why did Mags let him? But that's a *chat* I will take up with her.

"She was my connection to you." Those are his parting words before he leads my dog out the door.

I sit motionlessly. Stunned. What am I going to do with this?

Suddenly, my bladder signals that I never stopped to pee. Uh-oh. I jump up and speed waddle—there is no way this is considered walking anymore—to the hall bathroom. Shit, shit, shit.

I'm washing my hands when I hear voices, and I hold my breath.

"Ugh, some fucker is blocking our driveway again. I'm going to have a word with the asswipe from two doors down tomorrow. It's always his damn visitors." Pause. "Bro, did you drink alone again?" Kai.

"I have company." Wes.

"The dog doesn't count, dick," Kai retorts, but a laugh is audible in his tone.

"Whatever, I'm going to bed."

"Cool. Night."

Two doors close shortly after, and I sag in relief against the wall next to the sink. Time to leave. Opening the door a sliver, I peer outside. The light in the house is dimmed, and I tiptoe to the entrance. I'm about to turn the knob when the red blinking light catches my attention. Ah, fuck, they armed the security system.

I stand there for several minutes. If I trip the alarm, I'm going to have to answer to them both right now. I'm dead on my feet, but maybe if I hide in the media room, and one of them disarms the system in the morning before they find me, then I can sneak out.

Decision made, I grab a blanket off the couch and make my

way to my makeshift bed. I close the door, checking three times that it's indeed shut, and then curl up on the couch the guys put in here.

It's surprisingly comfy.

I have no idea what'll happen tomorrow. As of right now, Nugget and I don't care. We're both too exhausted.

# CHAPTER TWENTY-SEVEN

## WES

MY TONGUE FEELS LIKE I LICKED A CARPET—FUCKING GROSS. It's worth the few hours of oblivion, though.

Something wet swipes over my cheek, and I wrinkle my nose. I relish and despise Echo's wake-up calls equally. Okay, maybe I prefer it over waking up alone and hungover. Rolling to the side, I wrestle Echo until she's tucked under my arm. "We need to get you more of those teeth-cleaning bone thingies, girl. Your breath stinks."

Instead of being offended, she licks me over the mouth, and I can't help laughing. I scratch her ear. "Let's take you out before you leave Kai another present."

She had one small accident when I had first brought her over and we didn't have our routine yet, but Kai will not let me live it down.

I throw the covers back and walk over to the bathroom. If I don't pee first, *I'm* going to leave my roommate a surprise. After completing my business, I throw on a T-shirt and pad down the hall. I disarm the alarm and open the front door, but Echo is nowhere in sight—what the hell? She usually shoots past me and is on the little patch of grass in front of the house before I can take the first step. Glancing back, I find her with her nose pressed against the media room. I narrow my eyes. Kai better not have left old food in there again. That also happened, and poor Echo had the runs for two days.

I walk down the hallway and grab her by the collar. "Let's go, girl." But she won't budge and begins to whine.

*Jesus, this better be something good.*

"Let's take a look, alright?" I twist the knob and let the door swing inward. Before I can turn on the light, the dog takes off. I lift my hand to flip the switch when I notice a foot hanging over the armrest on one of the couches.

"What the hell?" I drop my hand again and step inside. I know for a fact Kai came home alone. That's something that always registers in my muddled brain, no matter how trashed I am. And walking past it, his door was still closed.

I round the edge of the couch and stop short.

I, uh—*what?* I blink once, twice. Nope, she's still there. My heart has stopped beating, or at least that's what the cramping sensation behind my ribs must mean. My chest hurts at the sight, and I can't make sense of it.

King is curled up, one foot out straight, which I saw hanging over, and her top leg thrown over one of the couch pillows. Most of her body is covered with a blanket that I'm pretty sure was in the living room last night when I started my nightly routine.

*Am I still drunk?*

I rack my brain. I came home from another useless training session, ate some leftover Chinese from...I think three days ago, then proceeded to watch TV and...drink.

*Why did you take her?* Her question sounds in my mind.

*Who?*

*Echo.*

*She was my connection to you.*

Fuck, was that real? I rake my hands through my hair and let them rest on the top of my head. King is here, in my house, and I—

"Oh fuck!" The other thing I said slams into my brain.

King jolts up, and the blanket drops off her body. Her sleepy gaze flits around the room, clearly disoriented, until her eyes settle on me, and her hands fly to her mouth. I only vaguely follow the motion because what the falling blanket revealed has all my attention: her stomach.

My fingers pull on the strands of my hair as my throat goes dry. My pulse thrashes in my ears, and I'm assessing what in this room I can destroy without it costing me a fortune. At least I have some rational thinking left. My girl is pregnant. No, she's not my girl. *But she is*. I tug harder, and the sharp pain on my scalp makes me wince.

"Wes?" At the sound of her voice, the red haze slowly disappears, and I study her closely. She's...scared.

"Who did you fuck?" *What the hell?*

"What?" She pulls the blanket over to cover herself.

"A little late for that, MOAB Girl," I sneer, and she lets it drop back in her lap.

"I'm going to ask you again. Who did you fuck?" Not *how did you get into my house?* Or *what are you doing here?* After no one had a clue where she was for almost five months.

"I didn't *fuck* anyone, Sheats." Her sass is back, and my cock twitches instantly.

"Well, someone put that bun in your oven," I mock her. Does she think I'm stupid? She jumped the next best dick as soon as she le—

"I'm five and a half months pregnant, you asshole! Do the math." She throws the blanket off and stands up, her hands on her tiny hips. She is still tiny. She's all belly. Belly. Stomach. Five and a half—I count back, and my eyes fly to hers.

"Five and a half?" I croak.

She sighs in resignation, and her chin dips forward.

I take a step toward her. "King, look at me." Cold sweat has formed on my forehead. I swallow, but it's of no use. I'm somewhere between puking and passing out. Maybe both. The remnants of the alcohol in my system are not helping either.

Another step, but then she jerks backward. "No." She holds her hands up, palms toward me.

"King, is this my baby?" I speak purposefully slow. Not because I think she doesn't hear or understand me, but because I'm trying to keep the two emotions currently battling for control from spilling out.

Happiness is too weak of a word for the sensation of seeing her in front of me. I've never missed anyone in my life as I've missed her. Even when I didn't want to accept it, when I still believed she had played me.

White-hot rage for having kept this from me. She ran away with my baby and hasn't bothered reaching out at all to give me the news.

"When did you plan on telling me?" I'm seething, and I can't fully pinpoint why. Do I want to be a father? I'm fucking twenty-one years old. I *legally* started drinking less than a year ago. I'm in college. We're not in a relationship. She lied to me about who she was. No, she never lied, but she also didn't tell me the truth.

"I found out the day Gray came back. I was going to tell you —" she starts, not meeting my eyes.

"Gray? You mean your father." Well, that escalated quickly. I guess we are doing this now.

"Gray is my father. But he hasn't been my dad since I buried him when I was seven." Her voice has dropped to an icy level. I hit a nerve.

I let myself fall on the couch and hang my head. I have no clue what to do.

"I came to get Echo. You told me you love me."

I can't look at her.

"Get your dog and go." I need space, need to think.

I hold my breath to see what she does next. I want her to wrap her arms around me and leave my house at the same time.

Footsteps indicate that she does the latter.

"Echo, heel!" Her command comes from somewhere down the hall, but *her* dog follows immediately.

I guess her loyalty lies with King, after all.


I STAY in the media room until Kai stumbles past the door, then backtracks.

"Uh, bro, why are you in here?" He peers around. "And where is Echo?" He scratches his naked chest, and something inside of me flips. I need to get out. I jump up and push past my roommate.

Where are my phone and my wallet? And maybe a hoodie, since it's still the fucking dead of winter in Montana. Two minutes later, I shove my feet in my boots next to the door leading into the garage. I'm down the stairs before Kai makes it two steps.

Where the hell am I going? King is probably at Mags's. No, I'm not ready to see her again. Den is not in town yet. The wedding is not until the fifteenth, another week. That leaves only...

I hammer at the door of their rental house. Well, house is putting it lightly since you could fit half the population of Stone-briar in this monstrosity.

"Open up, fucker! I know you're awake!" I shout as I bang on the door.

Technically, I don't, but whatever. The door swings inward and reveals Rhys in all his sweaty glory.

*See, I knew he was up.*

He lifts his eyebrows as I shoulder past him. Lilly comes down the stairs while Marcus appears from somewhere farther back in the house.

"Wes, what's—" Lilly starts at the bottom step.

"I'm having a baby!" I blurt out.

Rhys thins his lips, and I take in Lilly. "You knew." I'm not asking.

She lifts her chin, and I'm almost proud of her for standing up to me—almost. The pissed-off asshole in me feels blindsided once more.

"I knew, yes," she declares steadily.

"Babe." Rhys's tone holds a warning, and I round on him.

"Did you?" I swear to God, if he kept this from me, our friendship is officially over.

"He didn't." Lilly steps to her fiancé's side.

"She told me last month when we left here," he amends, not wanting her to take the full brunt of my anger.

"MOTHERFU—" The curse gets stuck in my throat. I cover my face. I should leave. Who can I trust these days?

A hand lands on my shoulder. "Let's talk, man."

*Talk.*

IT'S ALMOST noon by the time everyone is quiet. There has been a lot of yelling, cursing, and tears—on Lilly's side—since I arrived at their house.

Lilly spoke the most. She laid everything out, from when she found Gray's note, to when she left King's dump in Arizona. Ari-*fucking*-zona. At one point, I had to move. The longer I sat still, the twitchier I got—until it was too much. I jerked upright, and my chair toppled over in the process. I'm not sure how many miles I paced through their kitchen. When Lilly got to the part about King's apartment complex and how she had her followed for the past month for no other reason than their safety, I threw the closest thing I could find—a discarded coffee mug.

My already dry throat was closing up on me. *Their* safety. King's safety. My child's—holy fuck, I'm going to have a baby.

There went a glass that also sat on the counter. Neither of them flinched at my outburst. Lilly simply got up and started cleaning while I kept marching the length of the room.

During her recollection, Rhys mainly remained mute. His

expressions ranged from concerned, to livid, to—let's say, he was not happy about having been kept in the dark for nearly three years. That much was clear. I almost wanted to flip him off and say, "Sucks, huh?" I bit my tongue, though.

Marcus hovered in the attached sitting room. In the back of my mind, I was wondering, *why?* Was there trouble in paradise between Rhys and Lilly? Or was he there for a different reason? Was he worried I'd flip my lid on them?

Lilly mentioned that Marcus was the one that brought King back yesterday, and I found myself grinding my teeth at the thought of them being alone, him possibly laying a hand on her —even if it was to help her.

"I'M GOING BACK to the gym," Rhys announces out of the blue and pushes back from the table. When he passes Marcus, he barks, "Let's go, Shadow," but keeps going.

Marcus waits for Lilly to make eye contact, and she nods at him. That is her signal for him to go.

I'm leaning against the counter, watching Lilly load the dishwasher with slumped shoulders. Despite the turmoil raging havoc on my own emotions, I hate seeing her like this.

She knew who King was before I did. She was fully aware of me dating King, but still, she didn't say a word. Her behavior over Christmas break makes sense now. Especially because she knew every-fucking-thing!

I want to be angry with her. I deserve to be pissed the same way as when Rhys's actions blew up in his face. Somehow, I can't. Things have changed. *I have changed*, and all because of the few weeks I spent with one girl.

Every time I consider my next step—Do I confront King? Do I walk away from her?—my brain seizes up on me. I have no idea what's going to happen. It's like I'm stuck in an isolation tank. My mind works on overdrive to process the deprivation of senses, but at the same time, there's nothing. It's overload and starvation all at once.

I force myself to refocus on the girl in front of me instead. I have no clue what's going to happen with King and me, with our baby—zero fucking idea. But I care about Lilly.

"Are you two okay?" My heartbeat picks up, and I wait for her reply. I realize I need them to be okay. They're Lilly and Rhys. Nothing comes between them.

"Yes." She pauses with a bunch of utensils in her hand and locks eyes with me. "He's angry. Not because I kept King from him—he gets it—but that I went to her alone."

"Is he still...?" I trail off, remembering the time after Lilly came home from the hospital. I don't have to spell it out; she understands my question. Rhys would follow her everywhere. His fear of her being taken again was crippling him.

"Not like that." She shakes her head. "He trusts Marcus. He wanted to form his own opinion about King. He loves you, Wes, and he doesn't want anything—or anyone—to hurt you. Again." She sighs. "He regrets his decision. We both do."

"I know." Rhys has proven that on several occasions, and I believe him. Coming here today confirmed that. Rhys was the person I turned to when I needed someone—like old times. Does that mean I've forgiven him? It looks like it. Well, shit.

I surprise myself with my next sentence. "King wouldn't hurt me."

Lilly's mouth widens to a broad grin. "No, she wouldn't."

My stomach flips at her reaction. "You like her?"

She steps around the open dishwasher and wraps her arms around my midsection, peering up at me. "If you don't snatch her up, I will. And Rhys won't be happy taking you as my replacement."

I snort. "You're nuts."

"Runs in the family." She winks, but it wipes the smile off my face.

"Gray almost killed you," I choke the words out. King is his daughter.

"King is nothing like her father," Lilly says softly. "Your bloodline doesn't define who you are."

I cock my head at her, understanding the meaning. She is not talking about King anymore.

"Do you think she would've told me?" My pulse speeds up.

"Yes."

I squint at her. How can she be so sure?

As if reading my mind, Lilly deadpans, "Because this girl is so in love with you it puts Rhys and me to shame. You didn't see her when I asked her to come back here. She was scared to death that you would not want her."

Do I want her? I'm being pulled in so many directions. I don't know where top or bottom is. I love this woman. There is no question in my—for once sober—mind. But she knew who I was without telling me who she was related to.

*But when was she supposed to tell you?* a voice resembling Lilly's an awful lot echoes in my ears.

She left town with my baby. She knew all day and dodged my calls.

*Would you have listened to her?* Seriously? When was King replaced by Lilly in my head?

I need to think. So, I do the one thing that makes sense: I pull up the airline app. I'd be back for the wedding.

## CHAPTER TWENTY-EIGHT

### KING

"I don't think I've ever seen him speechless. I mean, he never talks much, but usually, there is at least a grunt or a disapproving glare," Mags whisper-shouts to me as we hover in Grizz's office door.

He took one look at me, and his jaw hit the desk.

Today marks two days of radio silence from Wes. Granted, I've been hiding at home, and he doesn't have my new number—as far as I know. My brain pauses, trying to process the picture that has painted itself in my mind. *Home*: a concept I can't wrap my mind around. Do I really plan to stay? I'm not ready to answer questions about my whereabouts the past five months or explain the medicine ball under my shirt.

Lilly showed up Saturday morning with Marcus in tow. She informed me that Wes went to see Denielle, and they'd be coming back together for the wedding. Fucking wonderful. Wes found out he was going to be a father and ran off to the one person who probably hated me more than my sister.

Marcus was loaded with garment bags, and the guy looked grumpier than normal. Having lost my train of thought at the sight, I hovered on the threshold.

Mags took charge and waved them into our small hallway. "Drop 'em there." She pointed to the living room and *ordered* him like it was the most normal thing in the world for Lilly and her security detail to walk into our little two-bedroom apartment. But this was Mags; why was I surprised? I wasn't—not really. Following at a slower pace, I watched the scene unfold. I had slept like shit the last couple of nights, thanks to Nugget's boxing routine between midnight and three—using my organs as a punching bag. When my baby finally exhausted herself, my thoughts wandered to a certain someone. My body and mind were running on fumes, and I couldn't even consume the necessary caffeine I needed to function.

"What's all this?" I gestured at the mountain overtaking our couch.

Lilly feigned innocence. "We need to get you a dress, and since I don't know your, uh, size"—her eyes flickered to my midsection—"I had a bunch of options overnighted."

My stomach flipped, and I peered over at Mags. Narrowing my eyes back at Lilly, I crossed my arms and rested them on my belly—*sorry, Nugget*. "Why would I need a dress?"

"For the wedding." The duh in her reply was silent.

As her words took root in my head, the previous somersault flip turned into a full-blown roller coaster, making the dizziness spread through every limb like a wildfire. "No, I— He would never— Uh, just no—" I spun on my heels and raced to my room. What the hell was this girl thinking? Yes, she had Marcus deliver the invitation to me, but I couldn't go to her wedding. Wes hated me. I would ruin everything. Echo took one glance from her doggy bed and sat up, alarmed. Since bringing her back with me, she had barely left my side. If we were sitting, her head would be somewhere in my lap or pressed against Nugget. If I was standing, she was in constant contact with my legs. I hadn't decided if she missed me or if she was protecting the baby—either way, she'll be a great big sister.

At a knock on the door, my heart slipped in my chest. *Go away.* "Come in."

I didn't know who I expected, but not Marcus. His head appeared in the gap, and he glanced around, uncomfortable.

"You won't find any embarrassing underwear lying around, so stop looking so constipated." I chuckled and shocked myself how at ease I was with him.

He pushed the door open, and I amended, "None of it fits anymore."

*What was I doing?*

Marcus choked for a second, gaping at me, then a smirk turned his mouth upward, and he shook his head. "You are something, Kingsley Monroe."

"Why, Marcus Baxter, you look almost approachable when you're not scowling," I shot back. Something in his presence made me feel lighter. Not because there was an attraction there —no one could ever compare to Wes. It was as if I recognized myself in him—my old, pre-Wes self.

He slowly walked into the room, eyeing Echo. "Will she attack?"

"Not unless you have the intent to hurt me." I glanced at my dog. "Echo." Her name was all I had to say. She scooted closer and sat pressed against my shins.

He lowered himself on my other side onto the mattress. "I asked Lilly to let me be the one to talk to you."

*Oh?* It was my turn to scowl. This would be interesting. Wiping my palms against my leggings, I didn't dare to breathe.

"Obviously, I know who you are and who your family is." He paused, waiting for me to show some type of acknowledgment.

The hammering in my chest increased in speed, and drawing in air became harder. I had no idea where this was leading. "Yes," I replied in a low tone.

"Do you know anything about me?" he inquired, and I shook my head. *Should I?*

"Let's leave it at: we both had a childhood no kid should ever go through." He exhaled. "But we did. And we came out the other side."

He wrung his hands together and talked toward the floor. This was new. I had seen Marcus Baxter arrogant, confident, condescending, not giving a shit, but this... He almost seemed uncomfortable. Like a little boy.

"It may not seem this way, but everything you...endured molded you into the strong woman you are today. You didn't let it beat you down; you fought. The same way you are fighting for your baby. You want to give it a good life. I watched you in Arizona."

"You did?" My surprise was audible. I didn't think he ever left Lilly's side.

"I was there for a few days before I came to pick you up." He turned his head and leveled me with a look that made me hold my breath. "Monroe, you are as fierce as they come, and you will survive this world no matter what happens. I don't know Wes—he's not been around for most of my time with Lilly—but I saw him before he left town."

*He did?*

"He came to the house. Lilly told him everything. Was he pissed? Hell, yes. Dude was fuming."

*That was encouraging—not.* My rapid pulse was making it hard to sit still.

"But who wouldn't be?" Marcus splayed his palms in a questioning gesture. "The guy didn't have a chance to get eased into either situation—your father or his baby."

"What if—" I started, but Marcus interrupted me.

"He will come around. Trust me. But even if his stubborn ass needs time, you can do this. Show the world who Kingsley Monroe is."

*Show the world.* A small smile formed on my lips. Who

would've thought that *The Shadow* would give me a pep talk and be decent at it? I slanted my head and glanced at him. "Who is Marcus Baxter?"

He mimicked my expression, then patted my knee and stood up. "That, little fighter, is a conversation for another day. Let's go try on dresses. I'm not carrying them all back."

And try on we did. Thirteen dresses, each one more beautiful than the last. Mags and Lilly had to help me while Marcus lounged on the couch like a king—no pun intended—commenting as if he had a say. Though, I found myself agreeing with him whenever he scrunched his nose at one of the outfits. It was almost eerie how alike we were.

In the end, we settled on number seven: a black, sleeveless, floor-length, A-line dress. It was simple yet elegant and the fanciest dress I'd ever had.

"I still don't think this is a good idea," I confessed to Lilly as Marcus loaded the rest of the gowns back into their SUV.

Lilly faced me head-on, taking my hands. "I'm the bride. I want you there," she stated, then softened her features. "You won't be alone for a minute, I promise you. Wes can go suck a lemon." She grinned, and a laugh bubbled up inside of me. How did this happen?

After I watched Lilly and Marcus drive off, I went to find Mags in the kitchen. We stared at each other for a long moment before we both burst out laughing. The reaction made no sense, and at the same time, was completely reasonable.

"I should probably ask Grizz if I can have my job back." I sobered. "At least for a little while." I needed as much money as I could get to support us.


AND THAT'S how I ended up shocking Grizz into silence a few hours later. "Grizz?" I prod carefully.

Still no reaction. I lean closer to Mags. "Should we call someone?" I chew on my lip. This doesn't seem normal.

"Yo, boss!" a voice hollers from behind me, and Mags and I turn in unison. Dean stops in his tracks, his eyes bugged out. "Holy shit! You're back." Then, his gaze drops lower. "And with a carry-on."

Mags snorts, and from inside Grizz's office comes a barked laugh. I peer over my shoulder and see that Grizz has recovered himself. Facing Dean, I say, "I am." I place a hand on my stomach, glancing down to my daily growing Nugget.

"That is...wow." He props his hands on his hips. "Who's the father?"

"None of your fucking business." Mags steps in front of me. I'm grateful for her taking over. I have no desire to hash out my fucked-up situation with a coworker before I get to speak to the father of my baby.

Dean holds his palms up. "Understood, Drill Sergeant Mags."

She lifts her fist as if to punch him, but he sidesteps her. Focusing on me, he pleads, "Please tell me you're back. Mags has been a raging bitch for months, and your replacement is useless."

My replacement. God, I hate that word. Grasping how my life was intertwined with so many, after having been on my own for the better part of fifteen years—Kiwi excluded—my heart sinks. Heaviness pulls on me like a weight drags one to the bottom of the ocean. I hollow my cheeks and shrug, pretending that this didn't affect me.

Mags, still in charge, addresses Grizz. "What's the verdict?" This would be the first time she would give him any say in a decision.

"Are you good to work on your feet?" His concern chases the dark blanket of guilt away and turns my insides to mush. This tattooed bear of a man has never been anything but kind to me.

"Yes, I've been working twelve-hour shifts in..." I trail off. It's not important where I was.

Grizz nods. "Okay, but you take breaks whenever you need them. We'll keep Kira on as a backup. She can help you grab stuff, and you focus on mixing. No heavy lifting." As he speaks, he stands and comes around his desk. I can't help my emotions spilling out and launch myself at my boss. We had never touched beyond a handshake when I first started working for him. But this moment, right now, I'm wrapped around his midsection, and it's where I'm meant to be. The Grizz is home. He drapes his arms around my shoulders, holding on tight. "Glad you're back, King."

MY DOOR FLIES OPEN, and I shield my eyes against the sudden glare coming from my ceiling light.

"Rise and shine, bitch!"

My pillow disappears from under my head and lands on my face. This means war. She has no idea what it means to assault a preggo with not enough sleep.

"WHAT THE FUCK?" I swat at the pillow.

My friend drops on the mattress next to me, propping her head with her hand. "We're going shopping. Get up!"

*Huh?*

"I don't need anything. I grow out of it in two days anyway," I grumble, trying to push her off my bed with my foot.

"Not for you, dummy. For your little bowling ball." Is dummy an up- or downgrade from bitch?

"I still can't believe you refuse to tell me the gender." Mags's toothy grin dims, and she juts her bottom lip out.

I push myself up to sit against my remaining pillow. I don't want to hope, but at the same time, I do. It's a constant tug-of-war in my heart. "Not until I talk to Wes, and who knows when that will be?"

My friend growls. "That drunk dimwit needs a good kick in the ass."

"Don't call him that!" I snap at her. I'm not happy with him running away either, but hearing her call him names instantly makes my body tense up. "Owww." I double over.

"WHAT?" Mags looks at me, alarmed. "What happened? Do you need a doctor?"

"Nugget didn't like you calling Wes names either." I grind my teeth as my baby goes to town on my full bladder. I don't even want to think about what she can do when she's bigger in there.

Mags leans close to my belly. "I'm sorry, little one. Your daddy needs to stop being a stubborn ass, though."

*Kick.*

"MAGS!" I wince and laugh at the same time.

She makes a zip motion over her mouth, eyes twinkling. Getting up, she scratches Echo's head, who lays in her bed in front of mine. "Get dressed. I want to buy my new little bestie some attire."

I blink several times. Damn hormones. "Give me a few. I need to shower."

"Okey dokey. I'll get your decaf ready," she quips, leaving my room.

"I hate you!" I want real coffee.


MAGS BUYS every gender-neutral baby item she can find in the one store we have in this small town. Everything is absolutely gorgeous, but when the cashier gives her the total, I want to throw up.

"Mags, that's too much." I stare at her as she hands over her credit card.

"Shut up."

"Seriously, this—" I try again, but she cuts me off.

"Kingsley Monroe, if you don't stop, I will also buy that gigantic, life-size giraffe you stared at for seven minutes." The girl behind the counter snickers, and I want the earth to swallow me whole. I'm not good at accepting gifts. I'm used to earning everything I have.

We haul the nine bags—NINE—to my Jeep, and Mags deposits them in the back.

"Let's go have lunch with Kiwi," she declares as she lifts the last one in.

"He's with Zeke today." Kiwi texted that the guys were all playing flag football in the park this morning, and he was going to watch.

"So?"

"They're Wes's friends." I fling my hands up. She can't be that dense.

"And Kiwi is your brother from another mother. Fuck 'em." That is the end of the conversation, and I know it. She'll drag me there by my hair if I put up any more of a fight.

Mags drives us to the park the guys are at. It takes less than ten minutes, but I can't help fidget with my Du Hoc the entire way.

She eyes me carefully. "We'll have to chat about your little tic when the baby is here. It's not safe."

"When did you become the mother hen?" I grumble, sheathing the blade against my urge to keep it out.

"Until you have a clear head, and you and asswipe sort out your differences, I'm your voice of reason. We also need to buy outlet covers and—"

"You want us to stay at your place?" I gape at her, my mouth hanging open.

Mags keeps glancing over while she maneuvers the Jeep into the parking lot. "I'm trying not to be insulted here. It is your place as much as it is mine."

I bark out a laugh. "You need to get your potty mouth under control then."

"Consider it done." She blows me a kiss, and my heart skips a beat. I am home. Now I hope Gray won't have anything to say against it.

The park actually goes better than expected. Kiwi and I lounge on a blanket, bundled up in coats with another blanket on our legs—April in Montana and all. As long as the sun is out, the temperature feels nice, but one cloud covering the sun, and it's freezing.

At one point, Zeke jogs over and drops down next to me. "It's good to see you, King."

His sincerity makes a lump form in my throat, and I croak, "You, too."

After a moment, he says, "Sheats will pull the stick out of his ass sooner or later." Before I can answer, he jumps back up and joins the game again.

Kiwi wraps his arm around my shoulder, and I lean into him, hiding in the crook of his neck. "Why is everyone so nice to me?"

A chuckle rumbles in his chest. "I'm not even dignifying that with an answer, Roe-Roe."

*BUZZ, buzz.*

I'm sitting on my bed, sorting through everything Mags bought today. Every single item is more than I could've ever hoped to provide for my baby. I had prepared myself for thrift-shop bargains because, let's be real, a decent roof over our heads (in a safe neighborhood) and food are more important than a onesie Nugget would grow out of in a week. And I was okay with that. You can find great items in thrift stores.

*Buzz, buzz.*

Eyeing my phone on the nightstand, I contemplate what to do. It seems too far away. Being out all day after not enough sleep has taken its toll. I'm dead on my feet—or ass since I'm parked in the middle of the mattress.

*Buzz, buzz.*

Jesus, what does Kiwi want now? He left an hour ago, and Mags is at work. I shift onto all fours and crawl over. Before I can take the device, the screen lights up with the repeat notification, and my stomach drops. My arms give out, and I plop onto the bed, followed by jerking back up. The last thing I want is to pancake my baby.

I programmed his name in just because. I never gave him my number, though. In slow motion, I reach out and pick up my phone. Swiping, I hold my breath.

**Wes: Hi.**

**Wes: U there?**

My heart is pounding in my chest, and the flutter in my stomach could be anything from happiness (he's reaching out) to dread (he's finally going to tell you he never wants to see you or your baby again) to heartburn.

My fingers hover over the keyboard. I don't know what to do. I type and erase the two words three times because I misspell at least one letter.

**Me: I'm here.**

The bubble pops up immediately.

**Wes: Hi.**

He said that already.

**Me: Hi.**

Nothing happens for two minutes, and the flutter in my stomach turns into a black hole. I place my hand over Nugget and rub circles. My phone goes dark, and I press my lips together to prevent them from trembling. I'm about to place it to the side when it buzzes in my hand. I don't think I've ever opened a message this fast.

**Wes: How are you feeling? Is the baby okay?**

"Your daddy is asking about you," I whisper to my belly. I don't want to get too excited, but the relief has me sagging against my pillows.

**Me: We're good. Though, she doesn't like to sleep when I want to sleep.**

I hit send and then realize my error. Shit.

Instead of another text, his face lights up the screen. He's calling—double shit. I had downloaded a picture of him from Kai's social media profile since Kai's is set to public. It is an old photo because, after I left, none of his friends shared one with Wes in it.

I swallow and answer the call. I can do this. I might throw up in the process, but I can do this.

"Hi." I hate how weak my voice sounds.

"I'm having a daughter?" His tone is equally low, but the awe and shock are coming through the speaker in waves.

"Yes." I haven't been this terrified since walking into The Pole that night.

Silence. Then, "Is she healthy?" I swear his tone cracks, and the stuffed animal I'm holding becomes blurry.

"She's perfect." I sniff and wipe under my nose.

I sit there, listening to his breathing on the other end, and watch the numbers on my alarm clock tick by.

"I want to—"

"I'm sor—" We both start at the same time and then laugh.

"You first," I blurt out.

"I, um... I want to be in her life." He speaks slowly, and when his words sink in, it's like he's stabbed me in the heart.

Her life. Not yours. Not both of yours. Hers. I close my eyes.

*You knew this was one possible outcome*, I chastise myself internally.

Forcing myself to draw in a slow breath and swallow hard, I reply, "I would've never kept her from you."

"Thank you."

"Uh, you're welcome?" I have no idea what to say.

"Can we talk when I get back to town? Figure out logistics?"

"Logistics," I repeat. "Yeah, sure." All I want is to get off this call so I can properly break down.

"Okay, I, um...I'll text you."

"Oka—" I click the end button so he doesn't hear my voice crack.

## CHAPTER TWENTY-NINE

### WES

DEN SITS ACROSS FROM ME ON THE JET. SHE'S HAD A FROWN ON her face since the wheels left the ground.

"What is it, D?" There are several options, and I don't feel like guessing. The last few days have taken it out of me. Also, my adrenaline level has been off the charts since Rhys informed me that King would be attending the wedding—with Marcus. What the actual fuck? Three days and I regret my decision to slow my alcohol consumption.

She is Lilly's guest. The two bonded even more, and since King didn't have a date and Marcus would be off the clock, Rhys's treacherous fiancée paired them up. I have my suspicion that this is all a ploy to piss me off. A successful ploy, but what the hell? And why would King go along with it?

Oh, I know why. I told her that I didn't want anything to do with her—only our daughter. Daughter. Jesus Christ, I'm having a baby girl. I've been trying to wrap my head around it since I read her words. The multitude of emotions that crashed down on me ranged from the urge to fist pump to throwing up. I tapped the call button so fast I didn't think about what I was going to say to her.


AFTER LANDING IN NEW YORK—DEN'S current hometown—my first stop was a liquor store. I arrived at her place sometime close to midnight, and to say she was displeased was putting it mildly. I was halfway through my first bottle of amber liquid, wrapped neatly in a brown paper bag.

"Really, Sheats?" If looks could kill. She shivered in her sleep shorts and tank top, but propped the door open farther. I stumbled past her with my duffel slung over my shoulder and clipped her in the process. She hurled several very explicit curse words after me as I headed down the hallway, supporting myself against the wall.

"I hathing babeee," I stated loudly—or at least I tried.

"Excuse me?" her pissed-off question echoed from the entrance to the living room. Despite my inner turmoil, my pulse was steady. A result of the heaviness that had been weighing me down since I left Stonebriar? I didn't know, the confusion driving me to block everything out with the help of my favorite liquid friend. I fell on Den's ostentatious sectional and peered up at her. My brain was full of cotton, and I closed my eyes to put the words in the right order. Speaking purposefully slow, I repeated myself, "I'm having a baby."

Squinting at her, Den resembled a fish the way her mouth opened and closed—no sound coming out. I pointed at her with the neck of the bottle clutched between the rest of my fingers. "Exactly my reaction." Then, a laugh broke free, and I couldn't stop. How could this happen to me?

After my manic moment subsided, I leaned forward, propped my elbows on my knees, and covered my face, still keeping hold of my paper-clad companion. The cushion beside me dipped, and the bottle was pried out of my hand.

"Did you say you're having a baby?" Her disbelief was audible.

I turned toward Den. "King's pregnant." My nice and comfortable buzz was quickly evaporating.

"She's back? How? When?" She scanned my eyes back and forth.

"Lilly brought her back." I couldn't help but throw D's BFF under the bus. I didn't feel like being the only one that had been kept in the dark—well, technically, Rhys had been as well.

"Come again?"

I reached for the whiskey that was now sitting on the low glass table in front of us, but Den beat me to it. She snatched it up and chugged. Lowering the bottle, she wiped her mouth with the back of her hand. "I need you coherent for this," she exclaimed before she took another gulp.

*Whoa.*

"Oh, but you are allowed to get trashed?" I scoffed.

"Hell, yeah. That way, I can't be held accountable for what I say to Lilly." A smirk pulled one corner of her mouth up.

*Now, that was my girl.*

It took until the sun rose behind the skyline surrounding her apartment before I was done. The longer I spoke, the calmer—no, not calm, numb—I felt. Was I in shock?

Oddly enough, Den didn't lose it as I had expected—like when I first told her who King was. She finally handed the bottle back over at one point, and we were in a similar state as three years ago—minus the urge to fuck my best friend. How could I? The only woman my body had craved in six months was several states away and pregnant with my child. Heaviness settled in my bones, replacing the numbness. As much as I welcomed the ability to feel, I was tired. From the lies, the betrayal, from fighting my way out of the hole I kept finding myself in.

"I have no idea what to say, Wes." She was sad.

"That's a first, BK. Help me figure out what to do?" I begged. I had no clue.

Her hand landed on my thigh. "Dude, this is beyond fucked up."

"More than what Lilly—"

"Different fucked up." She had her legs tucked underneath herself on the couch, her body angled toward me.

We stared at each other for a long time when I said the three words I wished were not true. "I love her."

Her mouth was in a thin line. "I know."

"What if I can't move past this?" I confess. One moment, I thought I could, then anger slowly seeped through my veins like venom. She was Gray's daughter. She ran away with my baby. Would she have told me about it eventually?

Den remained mute.

Glancing at the clock hanging on the wall, it was past six in the morning. Den slapped my knee. "Let's get some sleep. We can form a plan when we're both sober and I don't feel like throwing up."

I smirked at her greenish tint, but nodded in resignation. I couldn't come up with a solution in this state anyway.

Den slowly pushed herself up. "Ugh, I'm going to regret this later." She swayed on her feet, and I held on to her hips to steady her.

"Thanks."

I watched her make her way to her bedroom, shoulder sliding along the wall. Instead of going to the spare room, I let my body fall sideways and closed my eyes.

*This will do.*

"—THE FUCK, BABE?"

*Huh?*

"No, you let me talk."

*Jeez, my head hurts.*

"How could you do this? You knew about her all this ti—" Den whisper-shouted somewhere in the apartment.

I remained still on my back, fully aware that if I moved too fast, I would throw up on D's expensive rug. Plus, I wanted to hear where this conversation went.

"I get that she is not her father. That's not the point."

Pause.

"Babe," D growled. She was getting pissed. "No, you listen, Lilly. You fucked up. Wes is passed out on my couch. You have no idea how many times I've seen him like this since your dumbass fiancé pulled his stunt. And now this? How could you not tell him? King is FUCKING PREGNANT." She got louder, and suddenly, her head appeared out of her bedroom door, looking straight at me.

I saluted her. *Yup, heard it all.*

"Shit. Hold on." She dropped the phone from her ear and slumped into the living room.

"You look like shit," I remarked, maneuvering myself upright while consciously monitoring my puke radar.

"Have you looked in the mirror this morning, asshole?"

"You're always so polite when you're hungover." I couldn't muster getting pissed at her; I already had too many emotions battling it out inside my mind.

"Hellooo?" Lilly's tiny voice came from the phone as D dropped down next to me. She pressed the speaker button.

"We're here," Den barked. Man, she was livid.

"Hey, Wes."

"Liiil." A yawn made me draw out the I.

"How are you doing, Wes?" Lilly's question was hesitant.

"How do you think he's doing?" D wouldn't let me get a word out.

"I can talk for myself, BK."

Her eyes widened, and I averted my gaze. *Crap.*

I was about to open my mouth to answer Lilly when cold sweat began to cover every inch of my body. A wave of nausea rolled through me, and I clamped a hand over my mouth. Sprinting to the hall bathroom, I made it just in time before I expelled whatever was still in my stomach. The process repeated several times before I finally concluded that I had gotten everything out.

"You need to stop drinking."

I was on my back, feet flat on the bathroom floor. Den hovered above me, and her mouth was in a thin line. She didn't look angry, more concerned.

When I didn't respond, she held her hand out, and I reached up, interlacing our fingers. She helped me to my feet, then guided me to sit on the rim of the tub. She wetted a washcloth, and when she started cleaning my still sweat-covered face, warmth spread through every part of my body. Closing my eyes, I let her do her thing. Could I have done it myself? Sure, but it felt good being taken care of.

When she was done, she handed me the damp cloth. "Take a shower, and I'll order us hangover breakfast."

"Still not much for cooking, I see," I teased her with one side of my mouth up in a lopsided—and tired—grin.

She gently swatted the back of my head. "Not when it comes to cooking junk."

I REMAINED under the hot spray longer than necessary. Oh, the joy of never-ending hot water in D's fancy high-rise. Kai tended to be a girl when it came to bodily hygiene, and if we had to make it out of the house at the same time, I usually ended up showering cold. I pulled on a pair of sweats and a clean long-sleeve shirt and headed to D's living area.

A spread of various food items covered her granite countertop.

"I didn't know what you wanted, so I got a bunch of different options." She smiled at me with a knowing twinkle in her eyes. "You look much better. Kai still steals the hot water?"

I nodded, already having a massive bite of the breakfast burrito in my mouth.

Den sat down next to me on her barstool, sipping on a cup of coffee. She wanted to say something, but every time she opened her mouth, she ended up lifting the mug to her lips instead.

"What is it?" I mumbled, chewing.

I watched her draw in a long breath before she looked at me steadily. "You need to check on King."

*Huh?* My eyebrows shot up. That was the last thing I would've expected to come out of her mouth. All I could do was gape.

She lectured, "This is your baby. You both were there when it happened. So, man up and take responsibility." Her earlier hesitation was replaced by sternness.

*Responsibility? What was happening here?*

"Whose side are you on?" I snapped, squishing my breakfast in my fist, splattering its insides across the plate. White-hot rage engulfed the tranquil peace she had provided me with earlier in the bathroom.

Den ignored the mess, her sole focus on me. "You obviously didn't use protection, so..." She let go of her mug and splayed her arms wide in a "there you go" motion.

*Shit!* The heat fizzled out, and my stomach lurched. I wasn't sure if it was from dealing with a hangover from hell or that she wanted me to talk to King. I waited for the familiar signals of betrayal. How dare she take King's side? But instead of the crushing sensation of being let down by my best friend, my shoulders sank.

"I can't." My voice was a mere rasp.

She put a hand on my thigh. "Yes, you can."

How could she be so sure? I peered out her floor-to-ceiling windows. It was a perfect spring morning in the city. The sun was shining. The gray buildings appeared less dull. I glanced down at myself, engulfed in light. Shouldn't this feel...*good?* Yet, all there was, was a bone-chilling cold, as if the sky was covered in clouds. "Why?"

A hand rubbed circles between my shoulder blades. "Lilly

fucked up. I have your back on that. No questions asked." The rubbing stopped for a second. When it started back up, she went on, "But she is also right on one thing: King is not Gray. Our parents' actions don't define us unless we let them."

I glanced sideways at her. "Our?"

Den diverted. "From what you told me, she is nothing like her father, but everything like her mother." She cocked her head. I was still hung up on the *"our"* but let it slide. Something told me she was not just referring to the current topic.

"What am I supposed to say to her?" I needed help.

She shrugged. "Ask her how the baby is doing, how she's feeling. Start small. It's the right thing to do."

*Fuck.*

IT TOOK me two more days to work up the courage to send her a text. *Start small.* All that went out the window when she let the gender slip. It was clear she didn't mean to when she answered my call.

As soon as I heard her voice, my pulse started to race, and my hands became clammy. I wanted to hate her, hate her for who she was and that she ran, but at the same time, I couldn't. In the short time we spent together, she had become an irreplaceable part of my life. Little did I know back then how big of a part she would be. We would have a daughter together.

During one of our conversations—and there were many over the few days I spent in New York—Den metaphorically backhanded me by saying, "You didn't give her a chance to tell you her side. You could've told this Kiwi dude or her roommate that you needed to get in touch with her."

I was still convinced that something else was driving her sudden interest in pushing me toward King, but D wouldn't give anything away. She either dodged me or simply ignored me.

She also declared that I would have to be sober from now on. No one would want a drunk for a father. Another slap in the face. She was right, though. I had let my circumstances become an excuse to drink myself into oblivion—either to forget or to not care that I wanted King...wanted her with every fiber of my being. Because when I was sober, I didn't allow myself to go there. Which was how I asked her to meet me to talk about logistics. Lo-fucking-gistics. As if my daughter was a shipment. Jesus, I almost asked D to punch me after that.

IN THE END, Lilly punished me in a different manner, by making King her bodyguard's date.

My fingers curl inward again as I watch D stare out the oval window into the dark. We took off after a two-hour delay and wouldn't be landing in Montana until eight.

Just as the wheels touch down, my phone lights up.

**Rhys: We're at The Grizz.**

"What the fuck?"

Den quirks an eyebrow at me, and I turn the screen toward her. I can't read her; she simply nods.

My car is waiting for us in the long-term parking lot, as usual, and we drive straight to King's former place of employment. The former quickly gets scratched when we walk in, and my eyes zero in on my very pregnant (ex-)girlfriend behind the bar.

Mags is on the other side, and the new girl is also there. King is reaching for a bottle on one of the higher shelves but can't get to it. An arm appears out of nowhere and hands it down. King swivels and beams at her helper. Following the arm to a face that is now smiling down at her with a gentleness I've never seen before, my vision turns a deep crimson. Marcus laughs at something King says and pulls her into a side hug.

A growl builds in my throat, and I start forward.

My bicep is suddenly in a vise grip. "Whoa, slow down."

I jerk around and get into D's face. "Are you seeing this?" I point toward the bar with my free hand.

She doesn't move away. I can't intimidate her. But she does

let go of me and speaks calmly. "I am, but you told her that all you wanted was to be in your child's life, not hers."

"So, she replaced me with Lilly's shadow?" my voice gets louder, and I'm starting to make a scene. A group next to us stops talking, and their entire focus is on us. My pulse is thrashing in my ears, and Den's reaction to the show in front of us pisses me off even more.

"You guys made it." Rhys's overeager exclamation breaks our stare down, and D's eyes move behind me.

She gives him a curt nod and walks past us to a table Lilly and Elle are currently occupying. Seems everyone is starting to get to town.

Rhys opens his mouth, but I shoulder past him, aiming for the only person I have any interest in talking to.

As if there haven't been five months and two major secrets-slash-life events happen since the last time I saw her behind the bar, she senses my approach—that hasn't changed. Her eyes fly to mine, followed by her stepping out of Marcus's embrace. I shove my fists into the front pockets of my jeans in the hopes that I don't do anything stupid—like clock The Shadow. Marcus doesn't force her back into the hug, but he angles himself so that he shields King.

As soon as I'm within earshot, I can't stop myself. "Really, Shadow?" I seethe. "You think I would hurt her?" A mix of sarcasm and rage forces me forward until I'm almost nose to nose with him.

His exterior collected, he retorts, "With your recent track record of decisions, anything is—"

There goes my intention not to punch the fucker.

"Oh, my God!" King shrieks, but she ignores Marcus, who's cradling his jaw. Her whole attention is on me, her arms wrapped around herself.

Marcus drops his hand from his jaw and starts forward when a small hand lands on his chest. He halts abruptly, and when he realizes who has dared to touch him, he dislodges her in one lightning-fast motion. His snarl is menacing, and even I'm briefly distracted from my own drama. "Don't ever lay a hand on me, Keller." He pushes her out of the way and stalks off.

Before I can form a coherent thought, King is in front of Den. "Are you okay?"

My best friend's eyes water, and King pulls her into a hug. "Shhhh." She pats the back of Den's head, and I stand there, dumbfounded.

*What is happening?*

Rhys and Lilly have made their way over, and Lilly pries D from King. "I got her."

Den swipes over her eyes and lets Lilly lead her down the hall to the bathrooms.

Rhys lifts a hand, pointing his thumb behind him at Marcus, who is currently chugging a beer at their table. "I, uh...be right back."

*And then there were two.*

# CHAPTER THIRTY

## KING

My heart races in my chest as I stare at Wes like a deer in the headlights. Lilly told me he was coming back today, but I didn't expect him to show up at The Grizz—not immediately.

Lilly had brought her friend Elle with her, who flew in for the wedding, and as always, Rhys and Marcus were in tow. I worked tonight's shift, but carrying a small bowling ball in my stomach made it more challenging than expected, so I became the designated mixologist with my own barstool behind the counter when I got too tired. I never knew Grizz could be this warm and fuzzy, almost overbearing.

Marcus had sauntered over as soon as his charge was safely in her seat, surrounded by her fiancé and friend. "Monroe." He dipped his chin with a smirk.

"Baxter." I saluted him with the glass I took down for my next order.

Hanging out with Lilly automatically resulted in being around Marcus, and the more we talked, the less intimidating he was. For whatever reason, he let his guard down around me, which equally flattered and unnerved me. He hadn't made any advances, but I still wondered, why me? He barely talked to anyone besides Lilly and Rhys. Did it have to do with our similar childhoods, as he phrased it?

"I heard we're paired up for the big event." He walked behind the bar like he owned the place.

I eyed him leaning next to me against the counter. "So, I'm told."

Lilly informed me via text this morning that Marcus would escort me to the wedding. If I had learned one thing since meeting her, everything she did had a purpose, and it was easy to decipher this one.

I texted her back: **It won't work.**

**Lilly: Just wait.**

**Me: He told me flat out all he wants is to be in our baby's life.**

**Lilly: Just wait. ;)**

Oh, this woman was infuriating. At the same time, a sliver of hope formed in my chest, and I clung to it like a lifeline.

We'd been chatting in between orders, Marcus keeping me company and helping me get some of the more expensive bottles down from the higher shelves. Pre-Nugget, I would've jumped on the bar with ease, but my little one made that exercise impossible—which was exactly what he teased me about when he pulled me into one of his side hugs reserved only for Lilly and me. Even Elle only got a stern head nod.

Suddenly, the air in the room shifted, and I knew...knew without seeing him. Wes was here, and when I spotted him, he was pissed. My insides formed one giant knot.

The last thing I expected was for him to sucker punch Marcus. But what unsettled me more was Marcus's reaction to Denielle stepping between them. The hatred oozed out of his pores, and I almost burst into tears myself hearing his words directed at her. It wasn't what he said; it was *how* he delivered them—with such venom.

I didn't think anyone expected me to be the one consoling

Denielle, but seeing her that upset, I couldn't help myself. No one should have such disdain directed toward them. When Lilly took over, I could no longer avoid focusing on the man in front of me.

"Wes," my voice is barely audible over the noise level. By a miracle, the customers ignored what had transpired a minute ago.

"Princ—" His eyes widen, and he corrects himself. "King." His gaze drops to my stomach before it travels slowly upward, stopping at my boobs for longer than necessary. They've doubled in size since we've last been together—in November, not the five minutes at his townhouse. It also doesn't help that I'm wearing a work shirt running on the tighter side—Grizz was not prepared to hand out maternity clothes with the bar's logo on it.

Hearing him *almost* call me by his old nickname for me does things to my lady parts that I haven't felt in months. Until I saw him the other night, I hadn't considered being intimate with anyone since finding out about Nugget. Having Wes this close, I fight the urge to step into him, inhale the scent that's so uniquely his.

*He doesn't want me, though.*

The reminder forms a lump in my throat, and I blink rapidly. A groove forms between Wes's brows as he studies me. Then, he does something that shocks me to the core: he interlaces our fingers and leads me to the employee lounge. Where our hands are connected, a tingling sensation begins to spread until my entire body is aflame.

He lets go of me as he opens the door, and I pass him. Inside, I'm not sure what to do. Why did he bring me here? As a distraction, I aim for my bag sitting on one of the chairs, fish my phone out, and *un*-casually check my nonexistent messages. I'm acutely aware of him in the room. The soft click of the closing door is like a gunshot in my ears. I refuse to face him. I can't. My heart is pounding against my ribs, but suddenly, there is a new sensation.

"Oww!" I yelp, dropping my phone and cradling my belly.

"WHAT?" Wes is at my side before I can turn. He scans me up and down. "What's wrong? Is she okay? Do you need a doctor?" He fires his questions at me so fast it takes me a moment to comprehend.

Then, it happens again, and my eyes gloss over. Without answering him, I grab his hands and place them on the right side of my belly—just in time. He jerks back, staring at me slack-jawed.

"Is that—?" He breathes, and I nod, unable to speak. Hesitantly, he reaches out and puts a hand gently over the spot where Nugget just stretched my skin to the max—the stinging pain I experienced a moment ago.

Goose bumps spread over my back and neck, and I watch as Wes remains utterly still, waiting. Thankfully, our daughter doesn't leave us hanging. She pushes her little limbs out, and a bump forms under my shirt. Wes's gaze flies to mine, and the moisture in his eyes says it all.

"She hasn't done that before," I whisper. Speaking at a normal volume feels wrong.

"Never?" He studies me skeptically.

I shake my head. "I've felt her, and the doctor said she is perfectly healthy, but she has never stretched like this." I asked my doctor during my last visit if she was okay since I hadn't felt her kick too strongly yet. Her going to town on my organs had been the extent of it—until today.

Wes squats so he's level with my stomach. "Hey, baby girl. I, um... I'm your daddy."

*Stretch.*

His mouth forms an *O*, and I can no longer keep it together. Happy tears spill over, and I sob like a blubbery mess. "I'm sorry, I'm just—the hormones." I look at everything but the man in front of me.

"King." Wes straightens, but when I refuse to give in, he

takes my chin between two fingers, forcing my head in his direction.

If I see his distaste for me, after talking to his baby and getting a reaction from her, it will break me.

"King," he repeats more sternly.

*I don't want to.* I roll my lips under, staring at the framed picture of an ancient truck that hangs on the wall.

He grips my jaw tighter—not painfully but showing me that no is not an option. Once he has my attention, he surprises me. Ever so slowly, he begins to lower his face to mine. He pauses less than an inch from me, giving me a chance to move away.

I wet my lips, and his gaze dips, following the movement. I'm breathless. If he thinks I will stop him, he is delusional, but at the same time, I don't dare to breach the distance. Unable to bear the anticipation, I let my eyes flutter closed. I'm trembling and have to force myself to remain still.

The first thing I feel is his warm exhale, and my breath hitches. Oh God, oh God, oh God. Wes moves his hand from Nugget to my arm and lets it glide to my shoulder with the softest of caresses. He draws me closer, and then his mouth is on mine. Fireworks explode behind my closed lids, and before I can stop myself, I moan.

He opens up, his tongue darting out. As soon as he touches his to mine, I can no longer hold back. I cup his cheeks and draw him as close as I can, deepening the kiss. A soft chuckle rumbles in his throat as our little bowling ball creates a barrier between us. Instead of pulling back, though, he walks us to the couch without breaking the connection. He sinks down and pulls me onto his lap. I straddle his hips, and Wes groans as I unconsciously grind against him. My palms land on his chest, and I feel his thudding heartbeat under my touch, mimicking my own.

Wes pulls back slightly, and our eyes lock. He holds my gaze before he places one more kiss on my lips.

We sit in silence, and I can't help myself. I stroke my thumb over his cheekbone. I don't want to get my hopes up. I won't be able to recover if he rejects me again.

"What are you doing to me, Princess?" He studies me intently, and I fight the urge to slide off his lap. Better I decide than him telling me he doesn't want me—that this was a mistake. I start moving off, but he stops me.

"Don't," he orders, and I freeze.

"I—I just..." I stammer, not sure what I'm trying to say.

"Don't." He reaches up, placing his fingers on either side of my head. "I know what I said on the phone, King. This—"

I close my eyes, pressing my mouth together to conceal the quiver in my bottom lip—*he said King, not Princess.*

"Please look at me." A kiss is placed on my nose.

I cannot *not* obey. My nerves are buzzing with fear and excitement at the same time.

"You hurt me." The vulnerability he lets me see is almost too much.

"I know. I'm—"

"Shh," he shushes me. "Please let me get this out."

I nod, not wanting him to stop talking. The longer he talks, the longer I can pretend before it all ends.

Wes drops his hands and wraps me into an embrace around my mid-section. "When I saw you with...your father, I was convinced you had tricked me, made me fall for you. I just didn't understand why. I hadn't been in contact with Lilly or Rhys in years, and I had nothing you could take."

"I never—" I start, but he interrupts me.

"Kiwi set me straight weeks ago, but I was too proud to reach out to find you. I would rather drown in my misery. Then, you came back." His gaze drops between us. "And you were not alone. I felt...fuck, I don't know. Cheated? Betrayed? Tricked? I have no clue. Either way, it wasn't good."

I dip my chin, staying quiet this time.

"I'm still angry about how I found out. Especially because Lilly knew about you, about...her." He splays his fingers across

Nugget. "In my mind, you would've never told me about her." He searches my eyes. "Would you? Have told me?"

My heart squeezes, but I refuse to lie to him. There have been too many lies already. "I don't know," I whisper. "You hated me. I saw it written on your face that night. I didn't want to keep her from you, but I also didn't want to force you into anything." My eyes begin to water again. "I was scared."

Wes nods. "I want to be in her life. That hasn't changed." His tone is almost emotionless, and I can't read him. He's not pushing me away, but he's also not saying that he—

"I want us to try."

*What?*

"I can't promise you anything. We have a lot of damage to work through—on both sides. But I want to give this a shot."

I scramble off Wes's lap. "Please don't." I hold my palms out as if to warn him off.

He doesn't move, just stares up at me in bewilderment. "Princess?"

"Please don't call me that." *I can't breathe.* "I won't keep her from you, I promise, but please don't do this. I never meant to hurt you. I love you so much. You deserve more than—I'm not trapping you with a baby," I word vomit through a waterfall of tears, taking one step backward at a time. I need to get out of here.

Wes jerks up from the couch and grabs me by the wrists. "What did you say?"

*Huh?*

His tone softens. "Say it again."

A crease forms between my brows, and I go over my words in my mind. "I won't trap—"

"Not that, Princess." He chuckles.

"I don't—"

"You love me?" His gaze ping-pongs between my eyes.

*Oh.*

I can't form the words he wants to hear. I didn't mean to

blurt them out. Yes, they're true, but it also allows me to get hurt. He must realize my struggle because he releases my wrists and pulls me into a hug. My back stiffens, but he either doesn't notice or—more likely—ignores it.

Wes rests his head on top of mine. "Princess, I don't want this because we're having a baby." There is a pause. "I love you. And despite everything—who your sperm donor is, or you potentially never telling me that I was going to have a daughter—I can't deny what I feel for you. I've tried."

His words sink in. He loves me. He wants both of us. I grip his shirt with my fingers and shift to search his features for any doubt, but there is none. He lets me see it all. The pain, the confusion, the love—

*He loves me. Us.*

"I love you," I whisper.

He's suddenly serious. "You're not going to the wedding with the shadow."

I can't help but burst out laughing. Pulling him close until our noses touch, I challenge, "What are you gonna do about it?"

"You're going to be on my arm." And his mouth descends on mine once more.

WE STAY in the employee lounge until Mags comes to find me. She opens the door, takes one look, and closes it again. Before it clicks shut, we hear her say, "Fucking finally."

Embarrassment makes my cheeks burn, and I cover them with my palms. We are sitting on the couch, my legs draped over Wes's lap and his hands on my belly, rubbing circles.

I peer through my fingers. "What are we going to do now?" I'm not fooling myself into believing we will simply live happily ever after.

Wes draws in a long inhale, peeling one hand from my face and interlacing our fingers. "We take one day at a time. We date. I have questions."

*Questions?*

"What questions?" My mouth is suddenly too dry, and I swipe my tongue over my lips. It's of no use.

"Well..." He hesitates for a second. "Have you heard from Gray?"

Is he asking me this so he can hand the information over to Lilly and Rhys?

"I haven't spoken to him in weeks." Not a lie; it's been over three weeks since his last call.

"Do you have a way of contacting him?"

I narrow my eyes. "No. He always calls from a different number. Why are you asking?"

His expression hardens. "I don't want him around my child. He needs to be behind bars."

"I see," is all I manage to say. I'd been so focused on Wes and me that I hadn't considered Gray at all.

"Is that going to be a problem?" He watches me closely.

*Is it?*

"No." I don't have to think about it. Francis Turner was my father; Gray is a man I never had a relationship with. He has done unspeakable things, and he has to be held accountable for them—no matter what he's done for me these past few years.

"Are you sure?" Wes is not convinced.

I place my hand over his on my stomach. "I'm sure. If I knew where he was, I would tell you. He does need to pay for his crimes." Another thought slams into me, and my heart begins to race. My nails dig into the top of Wes's hand. "Promise me something."

Wes slants his head.

"If I get arrested for killing E, you need to promise me that you'll take care of our baby." I feel sick. "Promise me you'll keep her safe," I plead. I don't want to leave her—or Wes.

"You will not go to jail," he says with so much determination I want to believe him.

"I killed a man."

"You stopped a brutal rape. You are not going to jail." The way his mouth snaps closed, it's clear this conversation is over, which is confirmed by his following sentence. "I'm going to pick you up for lunch tomorrow."

"Lunch?" Is he serious? We just talked about—

"I told you I want to try. We need to start somewhere if we want to be ready when she comes. " He smirks, then peers down between us. "When am I going to meet my baby girl?"

"Her due date is July eleventh."

$$\overline{\phantom{xxxxxx}}$$

# CHAPTER THIRTY-ONE

**WES**

Wednesday morning, I get startled awake by a frantic Rhys. My door flies open, and he takes over the entire frame. "Dude, why are you in bed? I've been waiting for an hour." His tone borders on girly hysterical—no offense to any females.

*Huh?*

I peer at my alarm clock. Oh shit! The red digits tell me it's 11:13 a.m. I was supposed to meet Rhys at the venue at ten.

"I'm sorry. Shit. I didn't go to bed until, uh...two."

"What the hell were you doing?" He throws his arms up as if to say, *what's more important than my wedding?*

"I was with King." That shuts him up.

King had the early shift at The Grizz yesterday, and after lunch, I dropped her off to change, then drove her to work. We talked about everything and nothing all day. She showed me ultrasound pictures of our baby, and I teared up like a pussy. A week ago, I had no idea I was going to be a father before graduating college. I didn't know if I wanted to be a dad or part of her life—shitty ass selfish move, I know. Den chewing me out was the first step. I was prepared to be there for my daughter—do the right thing. Then, I walked in on Marcus with his arm around King, and it was clear that no matter what happened between us, the thought of another male touching her—now or in the future—was a *hell to the fucking no*. Not until I knew that there was no future for us. And here we are, giving it a shot.

I haven't kissed her since Monday night. The furthest we went yesterday was holding hands and her sitting in my arm on the couch. The way my pulse thrashed through my body made me feel like a teenager again that was getting his first feel of a girl's tits—and I didn't even get to touch anything. I couldn't help but notice the size of King's boobs, and dear Lord, if I didn't want to slip my hand under her oversized shirt and—

"Dude, you better tell me this is morning wood, and you're not this happy to see me." Rhys's mocked outrage makes me throw my pillow at him.

I blow him a kiss, and his eyes widen, then the biggest grin breaks free. "It's good to have you back!"

I laugh. "Get the fuck out. I'll be ready in ten."

*It's good to be back—feel like* me *again.*

THE DAY PASSES in a blur of wedding preparation. I check my phone regularly until Rhys threatens to confiscate it if I don't focus. But I made King promise before leaving yesterday that she'd text me if she or the baby needed anything. I am already whipped to my daughter's every whim, and she hasn't even asked for anything. I am in deep shit.

Rehearsal dinner passes smoothly, but when I call King on my way home, she doesn't answer. Every nerve ending instantly goes into overdrive, and I floor it to her house, all kinds of scenarios running through my head. By the time I throw the 4Runner into park, I'm at the brink of having vertigo. What if Gray took her (again), or something was wrong and she needed medical attention?

I burst into her house without knocking, and Mags jumps off the couch. "Where is she?"

"Excuse me?" She props her hands on her hips.

Her attempt to intimidate me is being drowned by the adrenaline coursing through my veins. "Mags," I growl.

She huffs, exasperated, rolling her eyes. "She's asleep, numb nuts. You kept her up way past the appropriate bedtime for a pregnant woman."

*There's a bedtime?*

Mags stares at me, dumbfounded, then cackles like a hyena on crack, pointing and circling her index finger at me. "That's priceless."

I flip her the bird and head down the hallway to King's bedroom. Echo is on her doggy bed on the floor and bolts up as soon as she sees me.

"Hey, girl." I squat down to greet her properly. When her wet kisses have covered every visible inch of skin, I try to gently push her off. "Enough," I chuckle.

"Wes?" a sleepy murmur comes from somewhere under a massive amount of blankets.

"Hey, Princess." I keep my voice low, not wanting her to wake up all the way. Being out cold at nine o'clock at night, she obviously needs rest.

Instead of going back to sleep, though, she pushes herself up to a sitting position and swipes her hair out of her face. "How'd goooo?" She covers the yawn with her hand.

I sink down on the mattress, facing her. "Good. Seems the best man is a bigger deal than the groom. All Rhys has to do is show up and look pretty."

She lifts an eyebrow but smiles sleepily. "Don't let him hear that."

"Nah, he knows. He enjoys being the spoiled trophy husband," I tease, and she shakes her head.

Her covers slip down, and without thinking, I lean down to

place a kiss on her belly. Straightening back up, I notice the shift in King's position.

"You okay, Princess?" I narrow my eyes at her.

"Mm-hmm." She avoids my gaze.

I place my hand on her blanket-covered legs, about to ask once more, when she shifts again, and her cheeks turn crimson. What the—? "What is going on with you?"

She whips her head in my direction and blurts, "I'm fucking horny, okay?"

*Whoa, what?*

My dick responds before my brain can catch up with her words, pressing against the fly of my jeans.

"You're horny?" I repeat slowly—I have to make sure I didn't misunderstand.

She covers her face with her hands. "Yes."

Apparently, I'm an idiot, because my response is, "But we wanted to take it slow."

Her hands land in her lap. "I know, but I can't help it. Ever since I saw you last week, it's all I can think about when you're around." She sounds as embarrassed as she does confident.

My ego drinks up her words. "*Only* when I'm around?" What the fuck am I saying?

She purses her lips. "Yes, Sheats. You're the only one who gets me wet. Happy?" She scoffs the last word.

My eyebrows shoot up. Is that a challenge to find out? I push my hand under the covers and between her legs. "How wet, Princess?"

King's eyes droop, and when I reach her core, I discover two things. "God, you're dripping. And where the hell is your underwear?"

"Is that really what you're concerned about?" Her question is breathy, and I can't help myself as I slip two fingers between her warm folds.

"Oh, God." She throws her head back into the pillow and arches her back. I groan at the visual she presents. *So fucking hot.*

My cock is painfully hard, and all I want is to sink deep inside of her.

I withdraw, and King whimpers in protest. "What are you doing?"

Standing, I unbutton my jeans in record time and shove them with my briefs down my thighs. "If you think all I'm gonna do is finger you after five months, you've lost your damn mind." My body buzzes with anticipation. I have no idea if it's from the time we were apart or that our entire relationship has changed since then. I had every intention of taking it slow, but that went out the window when I touched her.

I all but tear my hoodie over my head, and as I drop it, I find King biting her bottom lip, eyeing my dick. "Jesus, woman. Don't do that unless you want him in your mouth."

She doesn't respond. Instead, she moves to all fours and crawls to the edge of the mattress. She throws one daring glance at me before her small hand wraps around my length, and her tongue licks off the precum on the tip. My eyes roll back inside my head. My knees threaten to buckle, and at this rate, I won't be inside of her before I come.

She closes her mouth around me, and a shudder of pleasure runs down my spine. I grip her hair, and she moans as I guide her to take me as far as she can. With her free hand, she starts massaging my balls, and when she presses her tongue to the underside of my dick and sucks harder, I pull away before I reach the point of no return.

Sitting back on her haunches, she pouts. "What's the matter, Sheats?"

Her eyes peer at me innocently, and I smirk. "You'll see in a second, *MOAB Girl*."

Clasping the hem of her sleep shirt, I slip it over her head and throw it on the pile with my clothes. I watch the rapid rise and fall of her chest while pumping my cock with one hand. I step closer, letting my free hand caress her breast. "They've gotten so big." I grip myself as I lean down and suck her pebbled nipple in my mouth.

"Wes!" she shouts. "So sensi—oh, fuck." She breaks off when I roll it between my tongue and teeth.

Releasing it after another tug, I tease, "You like that?" before switching to her other side.

"Yesss." She fists my hair that's tied back and its usual bun. "More."

As much as I want to bring her to the brink of orgasm—several times over—my own desire for her does not allow for it. Not tonight. I let go of her tits and shift on the mattress to be beside her. King watches my every move with hooded lids as I lie down on my back and pick her up, maneuvering her on top of me. Even pregnant, she's a featherweight.

"Do you have any idea how gorgeous you are?" I let my gaze roam her body while my fingertips grip the smooth skin of her thighs.

She snorts, crossing her arms in front of her like a shield. I immediately let go of her lower half and circle her wrists, forcing her to bare herself to me. "I'm serious."

A soft blush tints her cheeks, and I let go. I grab her by the back of the neck and pull her down to me. She hovers on hands and knees as I draw her mouth close to mine. Her warm breath fans over my lips, and my hard-on twitches between us. I'm burning up, and the need to feel her everywhere overwhelms me. I breach the distance, nipping at the corner of her mouth. With the sexiest moan, she opens up, her tongue tangling with mine, and I groan. "I've missed you so much."

"Not as much as me," she confesses between kisses.

My dick throbs, and I pull her closer so my mouth aligns with her ear. "Now sit on my cock and ride me, Princess."

Her sharp intake of breath makes me think I've said something wrong. Then, King straightens, straddling my hips. "My pleasure, Mr. Sheats," she says with a gleam in her eyes that makes my length jerk in anticipation.

"That's a good girl." I wink at her, and she laughs.

Positioning herself above me, I help her by guiding myself to her entrance. The heat of her pussy radiates against my head. I'm about to tell her to take it slow—there is a tiny human growing inside of her—when she sinks down, and I'm buried to the hilt.

"FUUUUCK." My fingers dig into the soft flesh of her hips. God, she's so wet—so perfect.

"Ahh," King moans as she starts moving.

Her tits bounce as she grinds herself against me, creating the friction she needs—or wants. I let go of her sides and reach up to cup both breasts with my palms. Pinching her nipples between my fingers, she increases her speed, and I squeeze my eyes shut. It takes every ounce of concentration not to blow my load early; I want her to come with me.

"Wes," she breathes as I switch between massaging and squeezing her breasts.

"Yes?" I thrust my hips, meeting her halfway as she glides up and down on my shaft.

"Bite me."

"Jesus Christ." Those two words alone could make me come by themselves. This woman is going to kill me—but who am I to deny my girl what she wants?

We both halt our motion, and I lift her off of me, my dick glistening with her arousal.

"Lie on your side." I'm totally improvising, but I am pretty sure I've seen something similar in a movie once.

She follows my instructions, and I align myself behind her. I nudge my thigh between hers and she parts her legs farther. Entering from a whole different angle, both of us groan. Every nerve ending in my body is alive. My front is burning against her back. I can't get close enough. Resting my head on my arm, I wrap the other around her, trailing my fingertips up her belly until I reach her perfect tits. I begin to thrust harder, rolling her hard bud between my forefinger and thumb.

"Yes, just like that." Her praise is followed by a loud moan, and I'm on the brink of exploding. She brings one of her hands to her clit, and as soon as she begins to rub circles, I can feel her pussy clamping down on me.

"You feel so fucking good." I nuzzle my nose against her neck before I do what she asked me to. I trail kisses from her neck to her shoulder while thrusting into her from behind. Then, I bite down.

King instantly begins to shudder, and the hand that previously pleasured herself lands on my thigh, digging her nails in. "Oh, God, yes!" She's not holding back, and I follow her over the edge.

I groan and hold on to her as I ride out a new high.

We're both breathing erratically as we come out of our orgasm bliss, and goose bumps erupt on my body as the cool air settles on my flushed skin.

We're still lying there when there is a hard knock. "Hey, guys? Now that you're done, I wanted to let you know I'm heading to work." Mags's chuckle filters through the door.

King stiffens and bursts out laughing, covering her face with her hand. I turn toward the intruder. "Have a good shift, Mags."

King swats at me, and I shrug. "What? I'm simply polite." I pull the covers over both of us as King giggles, and I hug her to me.

"Are you staying?" she inquires sleepily, interlacing her fingers with mine on top of Nugget, as she's dubbed our baby.

"I can't leave my girls now, can I?" Sleep pulls me in, and I close my eyes.

NOT HAVING PLANNED THE SLEEPOVER, I had to hightail it home in the morning to get ready. Rhys would have my ass if I was late.

King drove with Lilly, Elle, and D. They would do all the girly stuff girls do before a wedding—whatever that was—and get dressed together at the venue. Lilly texted King the plan before I came over last night, and as much as I liked them including her, I was a little worried about how that would go. I was hoping for the best.

My best-man duties would keep me from seeing her until after the ceremony, but I made sure to text her once Rhys and I arrived. She promised that everything was great, and I told myself that Den would keep *BK* under lock and key—especially after King consoled her the other day. That had surprised all of us, and my best friend texted me that night that I better get my shit together because King was special. Elle had no mean bone in her body, so she was the least of my worries. The only unknown variable was Lilly's soon-to-be official mother-in-law, Heather. What had happened to Lilly hit her hard, and once she found out who King was... I hoped Lilly would stand up for King, as she had so many times before.

Lilly and Rhys ended up choosing a private property outside of town, set in the mountains. It was regularly used for weddings, and the view was breathtaking. A small banquet hall was attached to the main building and decorated minimally, but tastefully. Lilly never liked fluff, and it represented her and Rhys perfectly. We got fresh snow as well, and the whole scene was a winter wonderland—in April. The guest list was small, but that didn't keep the paps away. If there was something to report about Lilly, they found out about it—especially our all-time favorite stalker: Lancaster.

The guy was relentless. After he lost his life's purpose when Lilly's case was solved, one would think he would move on. He did the opposite. Lancaster became obsessed with everyone involved in the case. He even followed me for a month and a half after starting at MPU.

The good thing about this venue was that it was reduced to one access road leading up to it, and George had complete control. His men were everywhere. I had no clue he commanded this many scary-looking dudes in cargo gear. It also helped that the narrow access road was about three miles long and required all-wheel drive.

"If one of these vultures wants to track through the snow, they deserve to get a picture," Rhys had joked as we drove up. I didn't know how he could see it so lightly, but I guessed he'd also been living with this for years. It wasn't my wedding, yet I was the one with the twitchiness in every muscle at the chance of anyone crashing the event.

I was in my designated spot in the front when King walked in with Elle, arms linked together. Heat flooded my veins and went straight to body parts that had no business being awake right then. She was breathtaking. Her black gown emphasized every curve, and my mind was back in her bedroom the instant our eyes met. Her cheeks turned pink, and I smirked—guess she went there as well.

"Bro, if you have a boner while I'm getting married, I'm replacing you with Marcus," Rhys whisper-shouted in my direction.

Thankfully, only George and Rhys's father, Tristen, were in earshot. Both men barely glanced in our direction; they were used to worse.

Directing my focus back to my...girlfriend? Was she my girl-friend? The term didn't seem enough—she was carrying our baby —but I also couldn't come up with an alternative. We didn't get to have the relationship talk, other than we were trying. There was so much to figure out. Would we live together and where? Would I continue school? Would she work at The Grizz? How the fuck would I tell my parents? My mother was open minded, but making her a grandmother before fifty...she was going to have my balls. Shit.

My momentary panic attack of my mother whipping my ass got interrupted when King took her seat in the front. She and Elle were on the bride's side, with Elle's twin siblings next to them. Elle's brother, Hudson, leaned over his sister and said something to King, making me clench my jaw. She laughed and—

"Jesus, did you just growl?"

My head jerked to Rhys, who stared at me incredulously.

I narrowed my eyes. "Fuck off."

He smirked and shook his head. At that moment, a piano version of Canon in D started up, and I was no longer important.

---

# CHAPTER THIRTY-TWO

### KING

THE WEDDING WAS A DREAM. I'D NEVER ATTENDED AN EVENT this beautiful or fancy. From what I was told by Denielle and Elle —both coming from money—this was *nothing*. Lilly didn't care about any of it. All she wanted was to marry her soul mate.

Wes meets me at the entrance of the reception hall and immediately pulls me to the side and away from the other guests. He wraps his arms around me, and at his touch, my heart flips. Spending the day apart was torture. I kept envisioning his hands on me on more than one occasion, blushing ferociously when Elle checked if I was okay.

I'm about to ask why he's not with Rhys when his mouth comes down on mine. My knees weaken, and I hold on to the lapel of his dark suit. I've never been attracted to men in formal attire, but Wes has changed that. The way his broad frame fills out the dress shirt and jacket, my mouth waters at the sight.

He grudgingly breaks the kiss. "You look stunning, Princess." He places his hand on my belly. "Did she kick at all?"

I shake my head. "She knew you weren't around." Nugget moves, but she only stretches her limbs when Wes is with me. To say he's proud of that would be an understatement. Seeing him this excited makes me feel light headed and giddy. A massive weight has been lifted off me, though, even after falling asleep in his arms last night, I'm still not letting myself dream big—long term. But I have hope again. Hope that maybe we can be a family—in our own dysfunctional way.

"You're doing it again." Wes frowns, and I smooth out the wrinkle between his brows with my thumb.

"What?" *How does he read me so well?*

He rolls his eyes and interlaces our fingers together. "Come on. You're sitting with me."

I let him pull me forward and stop abruptly. "What do you mean?" I was supposed to sit with Elle and her family.

"Lilly changed the seating arrangement. Marcus took your seat, and you are with me."

I let my eyes wander and find Marcus at the far side of the room, next to one of the other security guards. They've been everywhere all day, and I should be scared—they're the enemy—but I feel oddly safe. Marcus's posture is stiff, arms crossed. The other guy talks, and it appears Marcus is listening, but his gaze bores into Denielle's back. She's at the head table, downing a glass of champagne. It seems almost purposeful how she's positioned herself to him.

I let go of Wes and touch his forearm. "I'll be right back."

His features harden as I dip my head in Marcus's direction. Then he nods. I can't explain the odd friendship developing between Marcus and me. There's nothing romantic on either side. It's as if we recognize something in each other, which Wes understands without me having to go into lengthy explanations I don't have. Plus, in its twisted way, Wes's possessive side is a huge turn-on.

I make my way over and position myself next to Marcus. He glances down at me. "Monroe." The strain on his face makes my jaw hurt.

"Baxter." I fold my hands in front of me, interlacing my fingers under my belly.

"You look beautiful." I'm about to thank him when he adds, "For someone with a soccer ball under her dress."

Without taking my eyes off the crowd, I whack him on the back of the head and then bring my hand back to its original position.

Marcus barks out a laugh. "That's why I like you, Monroe."

I shift my attention, and he arches his brows at me.

"Why do you *dislike* Denielle?"

"Don't go there, King." King, not Monroe. His tone is icy, and it's clear this is neither the time nor place.

I nod and turn toward my table when he stops me. "It's a long story. One I'm not ready to talk about."

"Okay." I give him a small smile. "I won't push. But I'm here if you need someone."

"Thank you." His expression softens.

WES DIDN'T LEAVE my side for the rest of the evening. We danced, laughed, and even Rhys's parents welcomed me as if I was not the daughter of the man who almost destroyed their family. It was surreal.

With Mags off on Thursdays, she ordered me to spend the night at Wes's. She would take care of Echo. In the follow-up text, she added that she couldn't find her earplugs and was still scarred from last night. I should have been embarrassed. I wasn't. I'd never been happier.

On the way down the mountain, Wes told me that Rhys and Lilly would stay a few more days. They had no plans to go on a honeymoon and no reason to return to LA. They could do everything from here. Hearing the news made me bounce in my seat. I'd never had a girlfriend until Mags. I liked Lilly a lot, and she quickly became my second female friend. *How messed up was all that?*

The night ended with us cuddled in bed. I was dead on my feet, and being curled up in Wes's arms was the perfect way to end the day. He put on a movie on his laptop, but I didn't make it past the opening credits.

OBNOXIOUS BUZZING SEEPS into the blissful void of sleep. What the hell is that? Every time it stops, it starts right back up.

"Weeees?" I whine. I'm on my side, with him at my back, his heavy-as-hell arm draped over my belly and keeping me in place.

He grumbles something incoherently. The buzzing starts back up once more, and I've finally had enough.

"Wes!"

That gets me a reaction—a sleepy one, but we're getting somewhere. "What, Princess?"

"Your phone," I snap.

"Huh?"

*Oh, for fuck's sake.*

I elbow him in the ribs, and he lets himself fall on his back, draping an arm over his eyes. I shift and climb over him to reach the bedside table. I may have pushed my knee into his abdomen in the process, which wakes him all the way.

"Owww, fuck."

*Ha!*

I grab the annoying device and peer at the screen. Thirteen missed calls from Rhys and one text. My stomach plummets, and a sour taste forms on my tongue. I don't have to read the message to know this is bad, and somehow, I know it has to do with me.

I shove the phone at Wes, who catches it before it impacts his face. He scans it without reading the text, immediately calling his friend back. It cannot have rung more than once because as soon as Wes has it at his ear, I can already hear Rhys's voice coming from the speaker.

"Finally, asshole. We're on our way over. Don't do anything

stupid." The line disconnects, and Wes holds my gaze. In slow motion—or so it feels—he peels the device from his ear and clicks on the one message. He taps again and then curses. His eyes scan something on the screen, and the more he reads, the redder he gets. An endless void opens in my belly.

"Wes?" My voice is tiny, and my nails dig into my palms.

His eyes jerk to mine, and he slashes his mouth. He drops the phone onto his chest and rakes his hands through his messy hair. He stares at the ceiling. "Fuck!" Then, he glances back at me, his eyes appearing darker than usual. "I'm so sorry, Princess."

"What?" I study his features but come up blank. He's unreadable. I grab the phone and scan the screen. I'm looking at a screenshot from a...blog? It's a personal website.

*Kingsley Turner attends McGuire Wedding.*

*You may ask yourself why this warrants a headline. I'll tell you why: Kingsley Monroe Turner is the daughter of Francis Garrison Turner. Ring a bell? I know. It's been a while since we got some news on this front.*

*The daughter of the man who almost killed Lilly McGuire—she finally carries the last name legally—was part of the very exclusive guest list. But not only that, she attended the event on the arm of the one and only Weston Sheats—previously estranged, but, as it seems, once again best friend of Rhys McGuire, as he was the best man. McGuire and Sheats had a falling out when he lost his scholarship over his friendship and involvement with the case.*

*Another surprise was Miss Turner's physical state, as you can easily see in the pictures taken at the wedding. This causes several questions. How did this transpire? Who is the father of the baby? How did Miss Turner get an in with the McGuires?*

. . .

"WHAT IS THIS?" My heart is beating in my throat.

Wes doesn't get to answer. He opens his mouth but is interrupted by banging at the front door. He scrambles out of bed, refusing to look at me. He bursts out of the room, and before I'm off the mattress, I hear Lilly and Rhys in the house.

"Dude, why didn't you—"

"Rhys, stop!"

"How the fuck did he get those pictures?" Wes.

Everyone is talking over each other. Only wearing one of Wes's shirts, I pull on a pair of shorts and pad down the hallway. They quiet as soon as I enter. I'm still holding Wes's phone in my hand. "Anyone care to explain?"

The fifteen steps it took me to get to the living room, I did something I never wanted to do again: I brought the old King back to the surface.

Three sets of eyes drop to my other hand—the one not holding the phone—and Wes slowly approaches me with his hands up. "Princess, give me the blade, please."

*Huh?*

I follow their line of sight, and sure enough, the Du Hoc is clenched between my fingers. *Shit.* Why does this keep happening? I stretch my arm out and let Wes take it from me. He interlaces our fingers and leads me to the couch, where Rhys and Lilly already took over one side.

"I'm so sorry, King." Lilly's sincere apology might as well have been her choking me. My throat constricts while the old King and the new King battle it out in my mind.

Wes pulls me down next to him, and I hand him his phone. I have zero desire to see the pictures of myself again. One as I'm walking to my seat with Elle before the ceremony. The next was taken during the reception—through one of the floor-to-ceiling windows. And the last one, where Wes has his arm around me, walking me to our transportation back into town.

"How the fuck did he get these?" Wes demands from his two friends.

"George thinks he came through the woods. They did perimeter sweeps, but let's be honest, who expected Lancaster to track miles through the snow for a picture? I'm not that *in the spotlight* anymore."

Rhys wraps his arm around Lilly as she speaks.

As soon as they mention the name, something clicks. "Wasn't that the reporter that was obsessed with your case?" I ask Lilly. I did get through some of his videos before I got cut off. He covered it all from start to finish.

"That's him," Rhys speaks up. "He's been a pain in the ass since, but always stays far enough away—knows exactly what to do to not break the law. Drives G insane."

"Do I have to be worried? What does this mean? I'm supposed to be in hiding." My pulse begins to throb. Gray is going to lose his shit over this. "I'm going to have to leave again." My eyes frantically start looking around the room. I need to pack, get Echo. Technically, I still have my lease in Arizona. I need to find a new—

"KING!" Someone shakes me.

—job. Maybe Eddie from the hotel can help. He was always nice and—

"PRINCESS! Jesus, look at me." Wes grips my chin and forces me to look at him.

When I finally meet his eyes, he continues, "We will figure this out. George is already looking for Lancaster."

"Marcus will take over your security for now," Lilly amends.

I gape at her. "What? What about you?"

"I'm fine. George has half his team here," she assures me.

I drop my head in my hands. Why? Why does this keep happening?

MARCUS SHOWS up with two of his team members shortly after. It takes some back and forth, but everyone eventually agrees for me to keep going as usual. No one asks me, though.

I become invisible as Wes and Marcus begin to form a plan, figuring out who would be with me when. Wes still has to attend class.

Lilly pulls out a laptop from God knows where, and Rhys is on the phone with first Denielle, then George.

As of now, there is no reason to suspect that anyone is looking for me for the murder of E. But Lilly promises to do some research regardless. Just because there have been no *Wanted* posters with my name on them, doesn't mean they are not searching.

"I want you to stay here," Wes announces.

"What do you mean?" My question is shrill, and I wince. A flutter in my belly makes me wrap my arms around my stomach and bend forward. It's not Nugget, but the sensation of being kicked in the gut/organs is almost identical.

Marcus had been leaning against the wall opposite the couch, scowling ever since Denielle walked in. His arms were crossed so tight I could see his bulging biceps under his long-sleeve shirt. He pushes off and comes over to where I'm still sitting on the sectional. Sinking down next to me, he explains, "The townhouse is easier to secure. The entrance is elevated, and there is no back door. The balcony in the back is too far off the ground for anyone to gain access unnoticed. I'm going to have someone on both sides of the property. We will look for reporters or anyone with interest to take pictures. If Wes can't be with you, I will."

The longer he speaks, the harder it becomes to concentrate. Adrenaline steadily rising, I itch for my knife. Where did Wes put my blade? A hand touches my knee, and I fling my head around.

"It'll be okay." Marcus levels me with a look that is meant to calm my ass. It does the opposite.

"This all seems like overkill." They are starting to freak me out with their overprotectiveness. I've taken care of myself for years and never felt this helpless. It was three photos, for Christ's sake.

"More reporters will show up, probably in the next day or two." Lilly puts her computer on the coffee table. "They'll try to get to you, figure out why you're here, how you and Wes got together, why I'm letting you into my inner circle when I've kept it to the same few people for years."

"They're vultures," Rhys interjects, and Lilly throws him a narrow smile.

"You're pregnant. I won't risk you or the baby's safety. We can go pack your stuff and bring Echo over later." Wes settles on my other side, interlacing our fingers.

I notice how everyone follows his movement. Lilly and Denielle have almost heart-shaped eyes and a goofy grin, versus how Rhys just smirks.

None of this makes me feel better, but my shoulders slump. There is no point in fighting them, and I see their point. "Okay," I concede.

THE NEXT FEW days continued as normal as they could. Reporters did slowly trickle into town. However, they kept their distance. Lenses the size of a small space telescope didn't require for them to come near me. Between Marcus, Wes, and Kai, who was ecstatic for Echo to be back, I was never alone. I anticipated for it to annoy me, but after spending my entire time in Arizona by myself, I enjoyed the constant company. Kiwi showed up with Zeke, and the guys would make a game out of getting Nugget to kick. I laughed a lot, and for the first time in...probably years, a sense of peace settled in my chest. There was no urge to run, no looking over my shoulder, no fear someone would find out about me. They kept me safe. I could just...be.

Lancaster was more determined, but even that didn't bother me. He would park outside the townhouse at night, follow me to work and to my checkup early the following week—for which

Wes and Marcus equally cursed him out. When Marcus threatened to forcefully remove him, Lancaster finally drove off—for a little while. Wes mentioned that he had camped out for weeks in Rhys's front yard three years ago. Not a comforting thought.

IT IS Friday morning when everything comes crashing down, and my safety bubble pops.

Wes leaves for class, and I plan to take Echo for a walk. Marcus is waiting for me outside, as has become our new routine. Lancaster is in his usual spot across the street.

Just as I reach the bottom step, Echo pulling me to get to our companion, a local sheriff's car and a dark SUV stop in front of us. Marcus immediately stiffens and reaches with one hand behind him.

"Marcus," I hiss. When his eyes meet mine, I shake my head at him imperceptibly.

A guy in uniform gets out of the first car, and the doors of the SUV open, revealing two men in civilian clothes. Despite their casual appearance, it's clear who—or what—they are: feds.

"Miss Turner?" the taller one addresses me.

I nod. No point in denying who I am.

"My name is Agent Oatis. Would you please hand over the dog to Sheriff Hansen?" My grip on Echo's leash tightens as the man in uniform steps forward.

"I'll take her." Marcus intercepts him by blocking me.

"Who are you?" The second fed scans Marcus up and down.

"A family friend, but I'm pretty sure you know who I am and want to act like you have a pair of balls," Marcus sneers and reminds me of the man who entered my apartment in Arizona.

"Watch your mouth, Baxter," the first one barks.

Marcus sends me a knowing glance. "See. Everyone knows Lilly's security detail."

His attempt to lighten the mood fails miserably as Agent Number Two—he still hasn't introduced himself—pulls out a folded piece of paper. "Miss Turner, we have a warrant for your arrest. I'm asking you to come with us willingly."

*Warrant?*

Dizziness forces me to reach for the rail. No.

"Warrant for what?" Marcus has Echo's leash in one hand and his other reaches behind me.

*When did I hand over my dog?*

I expect him to settle his hand on the small of my back for comfort, or maybe wrap his arm around my shoulders in a protective gesture. Instead, his fingers shimmy under Wes's oversized sweater I borrowed and between my leggings and bare skin. What the—?

He nudges Echo with his foot, who jerks toward the agents. She doesn't growl but is on alert. The three men stiffen and stare at my dog, waiting for her to attack. The sheriff even positions his hand over his gun, and I fight the urge to scream. Don't hurt her. Marcus shifts, his movement swift, and I don't realize what he's doing until the sheath with my knife has left my possession and is tucked in his coat pocket. That was his plan all along. As soon as the exchange is complete, he tightens the leash. "Heel." And Echo sits at his feet, looking at me for confirmation.

He leans in for what must look like a hug to the men across from us. "I got her. Do what they say. Don't talk. Stay quiet. Everything will be okay."

His words are for my ears only.

My heart jumps. *Do what they say?* Does he think I'm going to make a run for it? I'm fucking six months pregnant. My body temperature rises, and the pounding in my veins quickens. I'm as pissed as I am terrified. *Stay quiet?* I don't want to go to jail. I've finally found my happy.

On the other side of the road, Lancaster has gotten out of his car with his camera propped on the hood. Shit. My first thought is Wes. Because of his relationship with me, he will get dragged into this—his future potentially on the line again. Tears well in my eyes at the same time as my fingernails dig into the palm of my hand.

I turn and lock eyes with Marcus. "Protect Wes. Don't let him go down with me. He needs to be there for our baby when the time comes."

Marcus studies me before he eventually nods. Once I have his promise—his agreement is equal to a blood oath—a switch inside of me flips. The fear and anger dissipate, and a heavy hollowness settles in my chest.

# CHAPTER THIRTY-THREE

## WES

The second Rhys shows up in the doorframe of my class, dread settles in my stomach. Something is wrong. No, not wrong. I can feel my world being ripped from under me. King. My daughter. Something has happened to them. Kai straightens next to me. His gaze flits back and forth between Rhys and me several times before he stands up.

I'm frozen in place. The pounding in my ears muffles the question my professor directs at Rhys. There is movement at my side—Kai stuffing my shit from my desk into my backpack. All I can do is stare at my friend. My lungs begin to burn, and black spots appear in my vision. My girlfriend. My daughter. I can't lose them. A hand grips my upper arm, and I'm being dragged out of my seat.

"Mr. Raynolds. Mr. Sheats. What is going on?"

Marcus appears behind Rhys, and I notice a blonde head of hair behind him. My knees buckle, and Rhys races into the room, taking my other side. I can't form the question that the voice is screaming in my head.

*Where is King?*

. . .

OUTSIDE, Kai and Rhys let go of me, and I drop like a rag doll. I fall on my ass, not caring that I'm landing in a pile of snowy slush.

"What's going on?" Kai is the first to speak.

I peer up at the five figures above me. Five? Slowly, I scan everyone present and realize George has also joined the party. Lilly squats in front of me, waiting for me to give her my attention.

"Wes?" She reaches for my hand and squeezes.

I open and close my mouth several times before I ask the question that will determine what happens to me. "Are they okay?" The three words are no more than a rasped whisper.

Lilly hollows her cheeks and peers up at Marcus before she faces me once more. "She is healthy, Wes. They both are." She chooses her words carefully. "King has been arrested for the murder of Isaiah Ellis."

*Arrested.*

"Arrested?" I find Marcus's eyes. I've never seen this guy emotional, but at this moment, his expression ranges from worried to wanting to commit murder. He cares for King.

Hands reach under my armpits and drag me to my feet. Someone turns me to George, who starts to bark orders at everyone.

"Lilly, call Camden. She can find out what they have against King. Marcus, you stay with Lilly. Rhys and Wes are coming with me. We're going to the station." We're about to walk when he swivels around and levels Marcus. "I don't want Lilly anywhere near that place—not until we have more details."

"George, I—" Lilly starts, but he silences her with a hand motion.

"You will follow my orders, Lilly Ann. I will not explain to *him*..." He trails off. "I need to know you are safe."

Lilly's shoulders slump, and she bows her chin.

"Thank you." George's tone takes on a gentler note, and he looks at me. "Let's go."

THE DRIVE to the local police station seems to take hours when, in reality, it can't be more than fifteen minutes. I'm in the back seat of George's decked-out SUV, and I briefly wonder if they ship their tanklike vehicles to wherever they go or if one can rent a car like this. Anything to keep my mind off what's happening to my girls.

Fuck taking it slow. Fuck figuring out if we can make it work for our daughter's sake. When this is over, we will be together, and she will not just be my girlfriend.

The car comes to a halt, and I'm out the door before George can put it in park.

"Shit!" Rhys curses.

"Do not let him talk until I'm in there!" George shouts after Rhys, who is on my heels.

"Wes. Dude, you need to wait up."

I jerk around. My fists are so tight the skin over my knuckles burns. "Wait? How long did you wait before you followed George for Lilly, huh?"

Rhys halts, and his features harden. "You cannot compare—"

"THE FUCK I CAN'T!" I'm getting in his face, grasping the front of his jacket. "My family is in there." I point at the building behind us before latching back onto him. *Family.* My voice is shaky as I feel like my heart is about to burst out of my chest. "The mother of my child is somewhere in this building. What if something goes wrong with our baby because of what she's going through?" I'm nearly hyperventilating. I can't draw the necessary air into my lungs.

Rhys's hands land on either side of my head, and he forces me to look at him. "Listen to me. King will be okay. Your baby will be okay. We never leave one of ours behind." His hands drop to my shoulders, shaking me until my teeth rattle. "Do you hear me? They will both be fine." This situation can't be easy on him either. It's too similar to what we went through—almost losing one of ours.

Finally able to inhale, I force myself to jerk my head up and down.

"Good. I'm not going to fail you again." Several emotions cross Rhys's features, and I crumble. I step into him and let him hug me. Rhys and I have officially found our way back.

"Let's figure out what's going on." George's voice comes from behind us, and Rhys and I step apart.

I draw in a slow breath, but it's no good. As soon as we take one step toward the double doors leading to the station, I take off again.

INSIDE, George passes me quickly before I can lose it on the first person I see—a middle-aged, wannabe cop whose circumference is longer than he is tall.

"I would like to speak to someone regarding the arrest of Kingsley Turner," George addresses the man behind the glass.

"Are you her legal counsel?" the guy questions, not looking up from his phone.

"I'm Miss Turner's security guard," George deadpans.

That gets the asswipe's attention, and he does a double take. "Security guard? Why would a murdering stripper need a—"

"Watch your fucking mouth, you fat—" My palms are pressed against the barrier that protects the useless piece of shit from me wrapping my fingers around his triple chin.

A hand clamps over my mouth before I can finish my threat, and I'm dragged backward.

George blocks my view, and he says something in a low tone. I can't make out his words, which pushes my adrenaline level even higher. King is my girlfriend.

Rhys tightens his hold on me, and I strain my ears to hear what George and Fuckface discuss. When George turns toward us, Rhys loosens his grip slightly, although not enough for me to escape him.

*When did he become so freakishly strong?*

"He will locate the sheriff who was with the agents during the arrest. King is still being processed, but from what he knew, she was fine." He looks at Rhys. "Take him to the waiting room." He points down a hallway. "I'm going to call Lilly and see if she got ahold of Camden and then wait to speak to the sheriff or one of the agents."

Rhys starts manhandling me down the corridor. My legs won't cooperate, and he's switching between pushing and pulling until we reach the small room with two rows of plastic chairs. He deposits me in one and then plants his ass in the one next to me, clamping a hand on my shoulder again to keep me rooted.

We stay like this for *fucking*-ever until I finally can't sit still anymore.

I pull out my phone and stifle a curse. I have three missed calls from my mother. "Fuck!" I rake a hand through my hair and fist the strands.

Rhys leans over and peers at the screen. "Uh-oh. I assume you haven't gotten around to telling her?"

I glower at him, and he shuts his stupid trap.

Since we have no clue how long George will be, I hover my thumb over my mother's name before I draw in a breath, hold it, and press call.

It rings twice before a shrill voice pierces my eardrum. "Finally. Weston Sheats, what the hell is going on? Your father got a call from your aunt. She forwarded us several articles from gossip websites."

I grind my teeth. "Hi, Mom." And just like that, all my pent-up rage turns into a little boy who has disappointed his mother. My day is getting better and better.

"Don't you 'Hi, Mom' me, young man," she snaps.

"Is that Wes?" my father's voice comes from the background.

"Yes, our son finally graced us by returning my calls." She is pissed.

"Put him on speaker!" Guess he's not far behind.

"Please tell us what the press is saying is not true." Mom's tone softens.

"What are they saying?" I honestly have no idea. I have stayed off all social media and news pages since Lancaster's article.

"They say you are involved with Francis Turner's daughter."

I stand and start pacing the length of the room. Rhys doesn't stop me this time. I wanted to tell my parents in person, but had no idea when that would be. "I am."

"Weston!" Mom inhales sharply.

"Son, tell me this girl is not pregnant with—"

"She is." I don't have it in me to lie or draw it out.

There is silence on the other end, and I find Rhys's eyes. He looks at me with understanding. He's been through his own personal hell with his parents for years.

I glance at the ceiling and decide to lay it all out there. I don't have much more to lose at this point. "King and I met last year. I didn't know who she was since she doesn't use her father's last name. She knew who I was but was scared to tell me because—well, you can guess. We started dating"—okay, that's a stretch—"one thing led to another—you can guess that part as well. I figured out who her father was and drove her away for several months until Lilly found her, brought her back, and D told me to pull my head out of my ass and man up." I'm out of breath, I'm speaking so fast. "I didn't know she was pregnant until she came back, and even then, she never asked anything of me. She is the most selfless person I have ever met, and...and I love her."

More silence.

It's that moment that George walks in, and I disconnect the call before my father can chew me out for my irresponsible actions. I'll deal with that later.

"What did you find out?" My hands begin to tremble, and I cross my arms over my chest, tucking my phone into my armpit.

"They finished processing King. Lilly connected me with Agent Camden. She pulled some information—unofficially, of course. King is being accused of the murder of Isaiah Ellis, her former employer. His body was found by a hiker a few weeks after he was reported missing. Animals had unearthed the body." I fight the urge to gag at the visual forming in my mind, but George continues, unaffected. "Ellis was under investigation for gun trafficking and prostitution, suspected to be selling to a number of wanted individuals. Due to the damage the animals had caused, a thorough autopsy was performed. The cause of death was a stab wound to the neck. Ellis bled out. The knife left a unique mark on his C4 vertebrae, and it was determined that it was a curved blade." That's all George has to say.

*King's Du Hoc.*

"How did they tie it to King?" Rhys verbalizes what I can't.

George sighs. "She was the star attraction. She vanished around the same time as Ellis. The club's website featured several photos and videos of her dancing with—"

"Her knives," I finish for him. She told me that she was never without them. The room suddenly has gotten too hot. A sheen of sweat has formed on my forehead, and I wipe my hands on my jeans.

"Why did they not search for her publicly? Have the media do the work for them?" Rhys wonders aloud, and the mere thought of a public manhunt for King has my legs giving out. I flop into the chair behind me.

"From what I understand, it was kept a missing person case to continue the investigation of his customers and suppliers. They spun it in a way that he went into hiding."

"Genius, but fucked up," Rhys mumbles, and I want to clock him. Seriously?

"King and Ellis's right-hand man were the only employees

unaccounted for since his disappearance, and Victor Sidhrov was found with his throat slit last year."

I jerk upright again, my adrenaline level spiking at his insinuation. "Do they think she killed him, too?" That's ridiculous.

"We haven't been able to get our hands on his autopsy report. From what we learned, the knife is what connects King to Ellis's murder. And the witness."

"What witness?" Rhys looks between us like he's watching a tennis match.

I close my eyes. "The girl that was raped."

"Correct." George sounds almost apologetic. "She placed King at the club. The report says she confirmed that King dropped her off at the hospital. She did, however, state that she didn't see her killing Ellis. The girl was drugged and injured."

"Can't we use that?" A flutter in my belly gives me hope.

"Lilly contacted her legal team. Unfortunately, the knife is strong evidence," George explains.

My throat closes, and I can't swallow. "I want to see her. I need to know she's okay." The shadows in my vision are back.

"There is nothing we can do at this point. The jet is on its way to LA to pick up the family's attorney. But he already informed Lilly that he doubts anything can be accomplished over the weekend."

"WHAT?" He's got to be fucking kidding me. "They can't leave her in there over the weekend. She's fucking pregnant."

*Jesus Christ.*

I kick one of the plastic chairs with my boot, and it shoots across the room.

I peer at the clock on the wall. It's barely three on Friday. At the thought of her being in a cell for the next two-plus days, I can taste the bile coating my tongue.

"There is nothing we can do—" George starts, but I refuse to hear him.

"I'm not leaving."

"Bro," Rhys tries, but I plant my ass back down.

"Guess we're staying." Rhys plops down next to me, moving the chair next to him in front to prop his feet up.

I side-eye him, wanting to tell him that he can leave and needing him to stay equally. In the end, he makes the choice for me, and I am grateful for my friend.

"Okay, let me see what else I can find out," George relents and makes his way back out.


Saturday morning, I'm sandwiched between Den and Kiwi. Den showed up not long after I got comfortable in my plastic chair, and Kiwi joined us late last night. He threw a complete hissy fit that no one called him, and he had to find out from Zeke, who got texts from Mack, who was told by Chelsea, who heard it from Mags. Zeke was at practice, which delayed it even more. That being said, neither D nor Kiwi has left my side for longer than a quick pee.

Den is leaning against my shoulder, and I'm about to doze off again when Lilly and Marcus walk through the door. I'm out of my seat so fast D bumps into Rhys on her other side—who had been snoozing soundly—and he falls off his chair in a loud thud.

"What the hell?" No one pays his bitching any attention.

I scan both their faces. "Where is George?" If they are here, that means he is not.

"He got a call and had to leave," Marcus explains.

*Leave? What the—?*

Lilly's bodyguard has dark circles under his eyes, and it's apparent he hasn't slept either. He even lacks his usual hatred toward Den.

"Jaxon is meeting with Agent Oatis right now," Lilly says as she helps her husband off the floor.

"Jaxon?" Who the hell is that?

"My legal counsel for, uh...non-business-related matters." Lilly bites her lip, and I understand.

"Thank you." For once, I am grateful for her financial means and influence.

"He said he would come in here when he was done," she elaborates as she holds out a tray of coffee I didn't notice until now. She unplugs one cup from the tray and hands it to me. "Cocoa?" She smiles softly, and I take it, attempting to return the expression—unsuccessfully. I'm tired, and all I want is to see my girlfriend and feel my baby girl kick.

I never expected to feel so strongly for anyone, let alone two human beings.

It takes two more hours before Jaxon makes an appearance, and everyone stands at attention as soon as his foot is over the threshold. He is nothing like I expected a defense attorney to look. I expected a scrawny old dude, not a guy looking like a linebacker that just stepped out of a men's health magazine.

Lilly is the first to speak. "What did you find out?"

Jaxon takes his time to loosen his tie and sets his messenger bag down. I'm gonna strangle him with his fancy neck decoration if he doesn't start talking soon.

"Miss Turner—"

"King," I bark. I'm sick of hearing her referred to as Turner. "She has no affiliation with her sperm donor. She hasn't used that name in years."

He nods. "King and the baby are well. She is in a single holding cell with access to food, water, and a bathroom whenever she needs it. She was checked by a doctor earlier today, and I was assured that she would be treated according to her special circumstances."

"What about bail?" Den surprises me with the question.

"We won't be able to request bail until Monday morning."

"MONDAY?" I'm advancing on him when Marcus steps in front of me, placing his hand on my chest.

"Breathe." His tone is strained, which does the trick. I have no idea why, but it clicks that there is nothing we can do. Marcus doesn't like it either. He cares for King and also wants her out.

I close my eyes and let my head fall forward. Marcus grasps me by the back of the neck and pulls me into him. I let him, which probably surprises everyone as much as it does me.

"We'll get her out," he says so low that I'm the only one who can hear him.

"Wes?" I jerk away from him and look toward the door. The last person I would expect to see here stares back at me with her hands covering her mouth.

"Mom?"

# CHAPTER THIRTY-FOUR

## KING

"KING, MY NAME IS JAXON. I'M YOUR LEGAL COUNSEL."

I'm gaping at the man standing in the doorframe. *Legal counsel?* Is he shitting me? There is no way in hell this dude is a legit attorney; he looks like a male stripper. A high-pitched giggle bubbles up in my throat, and his eyebrows hitch. Why I find this funny is beyond me. Probably because I already cried myself out last night, and I'm running on two to three hours of sleep. Neither Nugget nor I were able to get any rest on the hard-as-a-rock cot. Hence, my sanity borders on unstable—it's definitely the picture I'm painting.

As sudden as it came, the laughter subsides, and I snap my mouth shut. I give *Jaxon* my best once-over. "I didn't ask for an attorney." My brain has lost its capacity for more words.

When I had refused to answer any questions and stared at the agents for what must've been hours, they finally gave up and led me to my current accommodations. Before they closed the door on me, I was informed with a smug expression that a judge would decide on the next steps on Monday. Agent Douche literally singsonged *Monday*. That was when the dam broke. It was freaking Friday. The old King was in charge until they dropped that tidbit on me. Three days. I would be in here for a minimum of three days. Even my former self couldn't suppress the emotional tidal wave of paralyzing fear for my baby and my future after that. I curled up in a ball and let it out until numbness set in.

Unfortunately, the void of feelings only lasted for so long. Sitting still ended in bouncing my leg until I made myself seasick with the motion. *Fantastic.* Next, I paced. Back and forth, back and forth. Eventually, assuming I had tired myself out enough, I took a break. As if on command, my lower extremities started their up and down routine again. Goddamn it. So, I jumped up, starting the marching process all over.

During lap number twenty-six, my thoughts started to wander. What would the news do to Wes? Did Marcus go and find him on campus? Where was he now? We had just started figuring things out between us. Would he be worried? Would this be his wake-up call? The final straw? No, I refused to believe that.

Agent O-hole wouldn't divulge to me what evidence they had. Clear strategy, since I refused to talk to them either. Did Gray not erase all the security footage? Did the girl I helped rat me out? I can't imagine that she would have; I saved her freaking life. But who knew? Maybe she thought I was as bad as E.

*Magic Mike* clears his throat, and I blink, focusing on him. Oh shit, I totally spaced out.

"I am on Lilly's legal team." He slants his head and waits for it to click.

*Oh.*

"Oh!" I chew on the inside of my cheek. "Did you—?"

"My team, yes. They handled the last family *situation*," he states matter-of-factly.

I nod and scoot to the end of my *bed*—I'm using the term loosely. "Would you like to sit?"

He gives me an appreciative but professional smile. Lowering himself next to me, he scans me up and down. "I was assured you were checked out earlier this morning, and both of you are well?"

I wring my hands in my lap before placing them on my belly. "Yes, the doctor said everything is fine."

He nods and pulls out a notepad. He asks me more questions about how I was treated, and I tell him that they didn't *mistreat* me. I wasn't coddled, but they also didn't abuse their power, if that's what he's fishing for. He writes down my answers and then some more. I try to get a glimpse of the novel he's jotting down, but no dice. He's had practice on how to position himself and obscure his handwriting—I wonder if he will be able to decipher it himself later. Jaxon is also cautious about how he phrases things, and I notice him glancing toward the door several times.

"Marcus did the right thing," he suddenly states, and my head whips in his direction. He holds my gaze steadily, and without saying a word, he conveys how serious the situation is. Marcus took my blade. He told me to stay quiet. Is my knife the evidence? My stomach hardens, and my mouth goes dry. No! I want to demand more details, more information, but another glance by my attorney toward the entrance to my current living quarters stops me.

What's going on? Is someone listening? He cannot leave me hanging.

"The evidence they have is pretty conclusive." He studies me as he speaks. "However..." He pauses, glancing down at his notes. "We received new information this morning."

"Information?" I whisper. What's with the riddles?

"Yes. That's all I can say at the moment." Putting his notes back into his messenger bag, Jaxon leans forward, propping his elbows on his thighs—almost too casually.

*So not attorney-like.*

We sit in silence until I ask the question burning on my tongue. "Have you seen Wes?"

He turns his head sideways. "No, I came straight here, but I do know he's at the station. Been here since yesterday."

*Yesterday?*

I don't deserve this man.

Jaxon gives me a small smile and pats my knee. "From what I gathered, your friends will camp out here until we get in front of the judge."

"Friends?" Who else—?

He huffs out a laugh. "I don't know all the names. Oatis is pretty annoyed by the number of people, though. It seems he thought this would be a cut-and-dry case for him. He didn't expect your...connections."

A flutter in my chest gives me hope, but then I remember that he said the evidence is conclusive.

"Can I see Wes?"

"Unfortunately not. I'm sorry." He is genuinely apologetic, then he reaches in his pocket and pulls out a card. Holding it out, he says, "This is my direct line. Call me anytime. I will be back tomorrow to check on you."

Jaxon gets up, and I want to scream at him not to leave me. He has almost reached the door when I blurt out, "Is Jaxon your first or last name?"

He glances over his shoulder. "Neither."

With that, he's gone. What the fuck?

I peer down at the card I'm clutching in my hand. All it contains is a phone number. I'm starting to believe this is all a cruel joke.

THE FOOD in this place is surprisingly edible, but then again, I've lived on a lot worse—or nothing at all. They leave me alone. I get to use the bathroom whenever I need it, but I try to hold it for as long as possible. This tiny room makes me feel safer than being in the company of the police officer on duty, which has changed several times since my arrival.

After Jaxon left, I sat cross-legged on the cot, rubbing circles on my belly, which equally soothed my baby and me. I was too exhausted to keep pacing. Going over every word of my wannabe attorney has left me with emotional whiplash. He gave me some of the information I needed. At the same time, he gave me nothing at all. What were my chances of getting out of here? Would I deliver my baby in jail? Trials could take months.

I rub my hands over my arms, trying to chase away the cold chill the realization brought on. I need a distraction. I'm not tired, but there is also nothing to do. In the end, I count every speck of dust on the walls and ceiling, but with no window, I have no sense of time. I go by my internal clock, aka Nugget, so when she settles down, I decide it is time for me to get some rest as well.

*I'M HAPPY. Wes and I are hiking at the reservoir, swinging our daughter between us. She giggles, and seeing the sparkle in her eyes makes my heart explode. The scene switches to the local park by the university. Wes is chasing her across the playground. Their laughter drifts over to me, and I smile. I'm about to call out to them when clouds roll in at an unusual speed—almost like fast-forwarding a video—and cover the sky. I reach out. I want to warn them to come back, but Wes and my little girl vanish in front of me like a mirage. No! The park suddenly turns to ash, and I spin in a circle. What's happening? Where are they? Come back. Breathing becomes harder, and I cover my mouth. The ash begins to rise around me and form walls. I try to run in the direction I last saw my family but slam against a solid barrier. I'm in a prison cell. Alone. Let me out. I can't breathe. I need my daughter. I need Wes. I cry out, but no one answers. I scream and scream for Wes and our daughter until my voice is hoarse—*

"MISS TURNER," someone barks. I jerk upright, heart thrashing in my chest. Cold sweat covers my face, and my clothes stick to my body. I shield my eyes against the light, but then I recognize Agent O-Hole standing in the door next to Jaxon.

*It was a dream. It was just a bad dream.*

"What's going on?" I rasp. My throat is dry.

Jaxon's expression is stoic, and my stomach quivers. Oh, God. He's here to tell me that I won't get out. I fight the urge to hide under the thin blanket I slept under.

Oatis glowers at me with his mouth pursed as if I forced him to suck a lemon. I peer back at my so-called attorney, who also doesn't say a word. My unease shifts, and something else rises to the forefront. I refuse to cower, not after the nightmare I woke up from.

I cross my arms, ignoring the still-present tightness in my chest. "If neither of you is going to tell me why you woke me up, I might as well go back to bed. Being pregnant sucks the life out of a per—"

"You're free to go."

Everything stops, including my heartbeat. "Come again?" Am I still sleeping?

"You are being released, Miss Turner," the FBI agent grounds out.

Jaxon steps forward and holds out his hand. "Let's go, King."

Time snaps back into place, and I'm off the cot, reaching for my legal counsel. My pulse is thudding and my fingers tremble as I place my hand in his. Not a gesture I would expect from a defense attorney, but I have a feeling nothing revolving around this man is normal.

The other agent stands in the hallway, frowning at me.

I stumble several times as I'm distracted by what is happening. Jaxon handles my release and then leads me toward a part of this place I haven't been before—not the front.

"Where are we going?" I'm having a hard time keeping up, plus I suddenly really have to pee.

"Back of the building. Lancaster and his friends are camping out in the front." He tugs on my hand, but I dig my heels in. Another thought slams into me like a wrecking ball.

"How do I know you are who you say you are?" My body

floods with heat. I have no proof that this guy really works for Lilly. "You said Jaxon isn't your name!" Oh shit, what if he works for one of the guys E supplied with...whatever he dealt with?

He stops and turns to me. "Jaxon is my middle name." He's about to start walking again when I bore my nails into his palm.

"What is your full name?"

Not that I have any guarantee that he's telling me the truth.

He sighs. Peering behind me, he contemplates, but visibly concludes I'm not going to make it easy on him. He's correct. "My name is Tanner. Tanner Jaxon Weiler. But I've been going by Jaxon my entire life."

*Weiler? What the—?*

The surprise revelation allows him to start pulling me forward again, and as soon as the metal door opens, I'm enveloped in a pair of arms.

"Took you long enough, Jax." Marcus hugs me to his chest, and I fist his shirt, holding on as tight as I can.

"Baxter," I breathe out, and a chuckle rumbles against my ear. The adrenaline that's been pushing me forward drops, and my body begins to shake uncontrollably.

"The car is waiting, Monroe. Let's take you home," he says gently. He supports me the rest of the way, as my legs have stopped functioning. Jaxon takes two steps at a time down to where Marcus's black SUV is parked. I'm being deposited in the back seat. Marcus slides in beside me, with my attorney in the front.

"Where is Wes?" my voice trembles, and I'm fighting to keep it together. I'm out. How did that happen? God, I want Wes.

"He's at home. He doesn't know yet. Lilly is on her way to him. She left a few minutes ago," Marcus explains as he keeps his arm around me, rubbing circles on my shoulder.

*Lilly was here?*

"Wes's mom dragged him home last night. The dude looked like shit."

"His mother?" I cough out the words. I'm going to be sick.

"Breathe, Monroe. It's over. You're safe."

Safe? I spent almost three days in jail and now am meeting my boyfriend's mother. I lean away from him to scan his face—or to sucker punch him; I haven't decided. What I see, though, is one-hundred-percent sincerity.

"What is going on, Baxter?" Using the same way we always address each other gives me a false sense of *normalcy*.

"Jaxon will explain everything when we get you home."

*Home.*

I can't decipher what he's keeping from me or why he won't just spit out why I got released. I doubt a judge randomly decided to let me go on a Sunday.

"You'll want Wes and Kiwi with you," he amends, averting his gaze.

My stomach flips. Why? What could be so bad that I need them both with me? Are the charges not dropped, and I got out on bail? Breathing becomes harder, and I close my eyes, concentrating. The little rational thinking I have left screams at me to keep it together, for Nugget's sake. No one will tell me anything, and I'm bordering between a panic attack and a temper tantrum.

The car comes to a stop. Opening my eyes, I recognize our surroundings. Jaxon parked the SUV in front of Wes's garage, another large SUV directly in front of us. Through the windshield, I see Lilly exiting the passenger side.

Marcus pushes open the door and shifts so he can take my hand and pull me out. My legs tremble, and I clutch his hand harder. He has to drag me after him. My body won't obey any mental cues. I'm home, yet I can't move. My feet hit the sidewalk when the door to the townhouse flies open, and Wes races down the steps—followed by my dog.

Tears instantly well up in my eyes, and all I can make out is a blurred form when I'm swept up in the pair of arms I have so desperately needed since Friday morning. I cling to him as sobs wrack through my body, and Echo whines at our feet.

"Fuck, Princess. What happened? Why are you here? Are you okay?" His words are spoken over an audible lump in his throat.

He pulls back and frantically scans me up and down. "Is the baby okay? Are you hurt?"

I shake my head, and his eyes widen. I realize his thought process, and I let go of him, cupping his cheeks with my hands. "She's okay. I'm not hurt."

He sags in relief. "Jesus, Princess." He leans his forehead against mine. "You almost gave me a heart attack."

"Let's take the welcome scene inside before we get an audience," Marcus exclaims from somewhere behind us.

Wes drapes his arm around my waist. He won't let go of me as much as I cannot lose contact with him. As he leads me toward his house, I find Lilly, Rhys, Denielle, Kiwi, Zeke, Mags, and a couple I haven't met waiting. My stomach plummets to my feet. I've handled everything life has thrown at me in the past, but the mere thought of meeting Wes's parents makes me want to run. A hand lands on my shoulder—Marcus—and Wes leans in to whisper in my ear. "You have nothing to worry about, I promise."

He lets go of my backside and interlaces our fingers. As we draw nearer, everyone smiles. Mags swipes under her eyes, and they start making their way back inside. I suddenly shiver, realizing how chilly it is.

The only people not following the rest are Wes's mom and dad. Both remain on the top step, waiting for us. With every step that brings me closer to them, I start squeezing Wes's hand harder until he grunts. I can't make myself let go, though.

Stopping in front of Mrs. Sheats, I look at everything but her. How can I face this woman? I'm pregnant with her son's baby because I forgot to take my birth control and just got out of jail.

A set of hands suddenly lands on my cheeks, and I involuntarily glance up. The woman's eyes are misty, and she smiles. *Smiles.* I don't know what to do.

"You are even prettier in person."

*Excuse me, what?*

She lets go, and I swivel to Wes with what must resemble a question mark.

He grins. "Told you. You have nothing to worry about."

INSIDE, I get sandwiched between Wes and Kiwi. Both have lost all sense of personal space. If they come any closer, Kiwi will end up in my lap with me on top of Wes. Mags is on Kiwi's other side and has her hand on me as well.

Denielle, Lilly, and Mrs. Sheats are on the other half of the sectional. Rhys stands next to Mr. Sheats behind the back of the couch. Marcus leans against the wall. He always keeps the entire room in sight—a trait I noticed long ago. I do the same.

Jaxon is the one remaining in the middle of the living room. He scrubs his hands over his mouth and looks at Lilly. "Have you filled them in?"

"No." Her expression is closed off. "I got here a minute before you and figured you should give everyone the report."

*Report?*

Jaxon shifts his attention to me. "I mentioned new information yesterday when we met."

My chest constricts.

He waits for me to confirm his statement, and I dip my chin. Where is he going with this? I lean farther into Wes, his hand between both of mine in my lap.

"I apologize that it took this long to verify the evidence, but we had to be one-hundred-percent sure. The coincidence was suspicious, to say the least."

I can feel my pulse pumping through my veins and wish he'd finally say it. Before I can voice my irritation, though, Mags does it for me.

"Spit it out, pretty boy. None of us have any patience left after the last few days."

Jaxon cocks an eyebrow, but not in an annoying way. He holds Mags's eyes for longer than necessary before he settles on me again.

"Isaiah Ellis's body was found by a hiker a few weeks after you...defended his victim." His words are careful, and I peer at Mrs. Sheats. She doesn't seem fazed, which is unnerving. What have they told her about me?

"His body had been unearthed by scavengers and used as their personal all-you-can-eat buffet—"

"Jax!" Lilly scolds.

"Sorry." He throws her a sheepish grin.

*How on earth did this guy pass the bar?*

"Anyway, due to the state his body was found..." He throws a *Is this better?* look at Lilly, to which she moves her hand in a go-on motion.

"A thorough autopsy was performed. The cause of death was a stab wound to the neck. The knife that was used nicked his C4 vertebrae, and forensics concluded that, based on the angle and marks on the bone, the blade was curved." He stares at me, and my stomach sinks—my Du Hoc.

I roll my lips under, unable to form words, and Jaxon continues. "Their investigation found that the security footage of the night Ellis disappeared was erased. The evidence found on-site showed a struggle and that the victim lost a lot of blood. They eventually tracked down the girl you dropped off at the ER, but she had been drugged out of her mind. All she could recall was coming into the club for a second interview, finding Ellis and his guard there, and that a woman drove her to the hospital."

Everyone in the room is tense as he recalls that part of the night, and I experience a wave of relief that the girl doesn't remember what E did to her. The scene will be forever burned into my brain.

"In short, she was of no help as to what had happened—until his body turned up. The police started interviewing staff and—I guess—regulars, and when a unique blade was mentioned, your name was dropped. There was a lot of footage of you on the club's website and social media presence, and despite you using a fake ID, Ellis had your full name in his records."

"Why did they not arrest me when I started working for Grizz?" I used the fake ID, but if they knew that name as well, wouldn't they've been able to track me down? Isn't everything online these days?

Jaxon's gaze lands on Mags, and I lean forward to get a good look at her. She fidgets under his scrutiny before she makes eye contact with me. "Grizz never filed your employment papers. The stuff you filled out... He never reported you as an employee. He paid you out of his own pocket. Don't ask me how he did the books on his end, but I know you are not on them. And you cashed the check every month, so...officially, you didn't work there."

*What?*

My jaw drops. "Why?" Why would he—?

"You need to ask him." Her gaze is back on Jaxon.

I need to figure out their relationship. This makes no sense.

"Anyway," Jaxon pulls everyone's attention back to him. "That's why you flew under the radar until last week."

"This is all my fault," Lilly speaks up. "I made you come to the wedding." Rhys places his hands on her shoulders in support, and Mrs. Sheats pats her knee.

"No, it isn't. I was living on borrowed time," I tell no one in particular. If they had E's body and knew about my knife, someone would've eventually found me—tied the knife wound to me.

"Why was I released if they knew that my knife killed him?" I don't have it in me anymore to talk around it.

Marcus steps away from his spot and positions himself next to Jaxon. "They found the real killer Friday night."

My heart halts. Everyone is silent. They all watch me closely while I stare at Marcus, then Jaxon. My brows pull together as I repeat his words in my mind. *The real killer?*

"I don't understand," I whisper.

Wes interlaces our fingers, and I keep my other hand wrapped around both of ours. His touch is the only thing that keeps me anchored.

Jaxon nods at Marcus, who first looks at Lilly, then back at me. "Lilly received an alert late Friday night. We have watchers in place for everyone involved in her case. The body of a male was dumped in an alley two blocks down from a police station in New Mexico. Then, a caller anonymously reported the body from a burner phone."

"A male?" My body temperature drops.

"Your father." Marcus's tone is flat. "Francis Turner is dead."

## CHAPTER THIRTY-FIVE

### WES

SEVERAL SHARP INTAKES OF BREATH REVERBERATE THROUGH the room. My chest constricts when his words sink in, but not because Gray is dead—he deserved whatever he got. For King.

Yes, she hasn't had a relationship with her father since she was a little girl, but he was her father. No matter what he's done, she didn't deserve to lose every member of her family.

An ache settles in the back of my throat as I scan the room. My mom covers her mouth, blinking rapidly. Dad mimics the sorrow I feel as he watches King closely. Lilly reaches back, placing both hands on top of Rhys's on her shoulders, and Den's nails dig into my thigh. I can't see Mags or Kiwi, but I'm sure I would find similar displays. King sits rigidly as her fingers have mine in a crushing vise. She stares at Marcus, unblinking.

I peer over at Kai's obnoxious scoreboard-style clock next to the flat-screen TV. Even the blinking dots seem to have slowed down. Echo presses farther against King's shins from her spot at our feet. We're all waiting for her reaction.

King parts her lips, but no sound comes out. Minutes tick by before she finds her voice. "Gray...is...dead?" There is an elongated pause between each word.

Jaxon and Marcus nod.

"Yes. George flew to New Mexico as soon as we got the news. He identified the body," Marcus elaborates.

That's why he had to *leave*.

"What happened?" I decide to take over. King doesn't have to carry the burden of this on her own. I want to be the one she leans on. She isn't alone anymore.

Jaxon bends down and pulls a folder from his bag. He takes a photo out and places it on the coffee table. King and I scoot closer to get a better look. In front of us is a picture of her Du Hoc blade. It looks like an evidence photograph, with a ruler on the side and smudges on the blade—blood? I'm studying the picture when *the knife* appears on the table next to it.

*King's Du Hoc.*

My eyes fly up to the two men in front of us. What the hell is this?

"I don't understand." King exhales, glancing between me, Marcus, and Jaxon.

"Gray was stabbed multiple times. With this knife." He points at the photograph. "A note that read, '*What goes around comes around,*' was pinned to the body, along with a copy of an article that reported the murder of Victor Sidhrov."

Pinned? As in—? Saliva pools in my mouth, and I swallow hard. I have no love for the man, but *pinned?*

King shakes her head. "Vic worked for Gray."

*He did? I missed that memo.*

I peer at King, who has her eyes narrowed on Jaxon.

His chest rises and falls once before he nods.

"George has been pulling strings for the last thirty-six hours. The knife contained traces of Gray's and Sidhrov's blood, as well as Ellis's." Everyone's attention shifts to Marcus. His arms folded in front of him, he holds his chin high.

"How is that possible?" Den queries, and for the first time, Marcus answers without hatred lacing his words.

"We can explain Gray's and Vic's blood, but Ellis's was obviously planted."

*Obviously?*

"How?" Kiwi joins the mix, and I clench my teeth not to tell the room to shut the fuck up. The only thing, or person, holding me back is King. She doesn't seem to mind letting our friends find the information out for her. Is she in shock? Does she care that he is dead? Does she not care? I can't ask any of this in front of an audience. It becomes harder to follow the conversation. My sole focus is on my girlfriend and the deep-rooted urge to know what she needs from me.

"We're not sure," Jaxon responds.

"Do we care?" Mags blurts out, and several sets of eyes turn to her—except King's. She's still studying the photo, with one of her hands now on the blade. *Her blade.*

"We helped solidify the evidence." Lilly's quiet confession makes my heartbeat falter.

"What do you mean?" King has a slight quiver in her question. Her gaze remains locked on the items on the table. I untangle one of my hands to pull her into my side.

Instead of Lilly, Marcus answers, looking as innocent as a choirboy. "The girl you helped was the mere tip of the iceberg. We may have nudged the authorities in the direction of what went on inside The Pole."

"What happened..." King slowly repeats. Her head lifts, and she first peers at Lilly, then at her attorney, and last, at Marcus. We're all waiting for them to let us in on what they cooked up to save my girlfriend.

I've never been more grateful for the people in this room than I am at this moment, yet the conflicting signals my brain sends me throw my mind into a tailspin. Relief and happiness are in a synchronous dance with guilt and sorrow. Gray is dead. He's gone and no longer a threat to my family and friends. I want to high-five Rhys. Then, the guilt for having such a euphoric emotion chokes me. He was King's father. King dealing with another loss splits my insides open, and I want to shield her from every negative emotion ever again.

"Gray found out that Ellis had planned to do to King what he'd been doing to all his other girls, for which Gray killed him. E's bodyguard ran, but Gray tracked him down here in Stonebriar. Sidhrov was following you." Jaxon regards King carefully before continuing. "When Gray found him here, he killed him as well. Ellis had his hands in many business *ventures*, one of which took his death personally and retaliated—using Gray's weapon against him."

*Makes sense.*

"But Gray didn't kill Vic," King exclaims, moving closer to the edge of the couch. I can sense her need to jump up, and I tighten my hold around her shoulders, slowly tracing circles on her arm.

"He did now." Marcus juts his jaw and emphasizes his opinion on the matter with a blank stare directed at King.

I'm with Marcus on that. I'm sure she wants to understand what really transpired, but as long as it keeps her out of prison, I don't give two shits who killed whom.

"Gray believed one of the others was behind Vic's murder," King mumbles as she meets my eyes for the first time since the bomb was dropped on her. "Which is why he came here last year."

I lower my forehead to hers and let the world around us disappear. It's the two of us, and we lean on each other. She holds my gaze, squeezing my hand in her lap. I place a gentle kiss on her lips, and when I pull away, the corner of her mouth tugs upward.

"Gray left the knife to you when he faked his death," Jaxon states point-blank, and our bubble of solitude bursts.

King's head jerks around. "How did you know that?"

"I think besides Francis Turner himself, not many people—

alive—know more about him—*or Gray*." He drops the folder on the table and shoves his hands in his pockets. "My team interviewed his Ranger buddies, and they provided us with old pictures—one of which had him displayed with this knife."

King traces the blade with her fingertip. "It was a gift when he graduated boot camp. I don't know from who."

Marcus widens his stance farther. "Who knew about the blade? "

Why does it always seem like every answer comes with more questions?

"I always had it with me. You could say everyone knew about it, but not where I got it from." King furrows her brow.

"You have someone on your side, that's for sure. We just have no idea who," Marcus confirms her suspicion.

And Jaxon adds, "Yet."

"It's like we're always followed by the dark," D murmurs next to me, too low for anyone else to hear. I eye her sideways, wondering if there is something my best friend is keeping from me.

"What am I doing now? This is all too...I don't know. Convenient." King splays her free hand. I'm not letting go of the other.

"Officially, you gave the knife back to *your father* when you last saw him before Ellis disappeared," her attorney advises. "Don't let anyone see you with it. George will remain in New Mexico until Gray's body can be brought back to LA. Camden is meeting him there tomorrow. Gray was still considered a fugitive in Lilly's case. Camden will make sure that no one questions that he was the one who killed Ellis."

"You have an FBI agent in your pocket?" Mags explodes, her shrill tone making everyone jerk around.

Before one of the guys can respond, Lilly explains calmly, "Not in the way you're thinking."

"We're not blaming an innocent person for a random crime. Gray was a dangerous criminal. *Scum*." Rhys flicks his gaze to my girlfriend. "Sorry, King."

The only acknowledgment she gives him is a slight tilt of her head.

Rhys trains his eyes back on Mags. "King doesn't deserve to be punished for this. She rescued a girl from a heinous crime. Victor Sidhrov stood by as this girl was—" He breaks off, throwing a glance in my mom's direction. "Gray got rid of the body. Someone got rid of both. If it was revenge or to help King, we'll find out. But for now, this is over."

*Over?*

"Do you really think so?" I challenge my best friend.

Rhys looks at Marcus, then Jaxon. It's Marcus who answers my question. "Yes. No one will come after King for what happened."

*It's over.*

HOURS LATER, the house is empty, and King and I are lying in my bed. My head rests on her chest and my hand on her belly. Nugget is in high form and kicking up a storm in there, which brings the biggest grin to my face. I poke King's belly, and a limb pushes out.

"Would you stop that?" King tries to sound annoyed, but the laughter in her tone contradicts her words.

"Why? She likes to play with me." I push my finger into King's side again.

"Ow, Sheats. I'm serious. Quit it." She shoves me off her, and I bark out a laugh.

EARLIER, when my parents were the only ones left, King had excused herself.

"Are you okay?" I held her by the wrist, halting her retreat.

She twisted out of my grip, lacing our fingers together. She was tired. I wasn't sure if it was from the lack of rest the last two nights or the emotional roller coaster. Probably both.

"Yes." She smiled softly. "I just need to...process. And take a long-overdue shower." She wrinkled her nose.

"Do you want me to come?" I was turning into Rhys, not wanting to leave my girl's side.

"I won't be long." Her eyes pleaded with me to let her go.

That would be a no. She had always dealt with life on her own, and I guess it was a hard habit to kick.

"Call if you need anything." The strain in my voice was audible to my own ears—most definitely to my parents'. But on that note, embarrassment had exited a long time ago with, "My girlfriend is pregnant and currently in jail."

Surprising me, she leaned down and placed a lingering kiss on my mouth. "I'll always call for you," she whispered against my lips.

Before she left the room, though, she stopped and hugged my mom. After she disentangled herself from my mother, who was reluctant to let go, eyes glossed over, King padded down the hall.

I watched her until she disappeared through the door. Focusing back on the room, I found my parents both gaping at me with expressions I did not expect from them under the current circumstances. They had remained mute the entire time the others were here. Now, I was looking at them and was not sure if I was facing my parents or some body snatchers.

"Why are you smiling at me like that?" I frowned at Mom.

"I'm proud of you, Wes."

*Definitely body snatchers.*

"For what, exactly?" I inquired slowly. It couldn't have been for accidentally impregnating the daughter of a fugitive. My mom was open minded, but that would be pushing it even for her. Slanting my hand, I waited for their skulls to split open and reveal an extraterrestrial entity.

She relocated to the spot on the couch King had vacated. "You fucked up, son."

*There was my mom.*

Then, she placed a hand on my leg. "But you're dealing with it. You lost a lot three years ago and still found your way."

I snorted. "By drinking and developing a temper?"

"We all did that during our time in college. Your dad was the campus bully."

My head jerked in the direction of my father, who glowered at his wife. "Really? You had to bring that up, Laura?"

Mom waved him off. "Oh, come on, *Charles*." She looked back at me. "It's part of becoming your own person. I was worried about you; I won't lie. I hated for you to be lonely. You might not have wanted to admit it, but you and Rhys had been inseparable for most of your life. You missed him."

"I'm not sure I like where this is going," I grumbled.

Dad chuckled, but remained mute.

"King changed that. You were different when you called last fall. Then, you met with Rhys over Christmas break. I didn't want to push you. I could sense that something was still *off*, but you were more yourself than the previous years."

"Have you always been this insightful?"

"I'm your mother," Mom deadpanned.

"You can't tell me that you were happy finding out about King." I peered toward the hallway. With my luck, she'd show up right then.

"Was I happy to find out from your aunt? Who had read it in some gossip magazine, of all places? No. No parent would. But then I called Denielle and Heather."

"YOU DID WHAT?" My voice went several octaves higher —a pitch I didn't realize I was still capable of. Den was in deep shit.

"You didn't give me a chance to ask questions. Heather called Lilly to send the jet. She met us at the airport and told us about King while we waited. She had spoken to her during the wedding last week. Heather had nothing but kind words for the girl."

A whoosh of air left my lungs.

"Did I picture being a grandmother at forty-seven? You can guess that answer."

"But?" I didn't dare inhale fresh oxygen.

She pursed her lips. "But nothing. I still think I'm too young to be a grandmother. But I will make the best out of it. I'll be the coolest grandma this baby girl can have."

"Cool?" I spluttered. *Jesus Christ.*

She swatted my arm. "You know what I mean. You made your bed; you will sleep in it. Though, from what I've observed, the two of you have found each other for a reason. King is good for you, and you for her. And this baby will bring out the best in both of you."

Warmth seeped through my chest the longer she spoke.

"It won't be easy. Especially with you still in school," Dad stated sternly.

I opened my mouth to defend myself, but he held up a hand.

"With that being said, I have no doubt in my mind that everything will work out in the long run. Your girl is a fighter, and so are you."

Between both of them, I had to swallow over the lump forming in my throat. This day turned out nothing like I had expected when I woke up alone this morning.


I PROP myself up on my elbow and peer down at her. Drink her in. "You are so beautiful."

"You're not so bad yourself, Mr. Sheats." The corner of her mouth turns up.

"We haven't had a chance to talk about—"

"There is nothing to talk about," she interrupts and pushes a strand of hair from my forehead.

I study the crease between her brows.

"I'm okay." She softens her features. "Nothing has changed from when I agreed with you that Gray needs to be in jail." She draws in a long breath and peers at the ceiling. "I lost my father a long time ago." She turns back to me. "I mourned him."

"How do you feel about his..." *God, why can't I form the words?*

"Murder?" She pulls her brows up.

I press my lips together, unable to even confirm the word.

Her thumb strokes over my cheekbone, and the motion sends a tingling sensation down my spine. "No one deserves to get their life cut short, no matter the evil they harbor inside. Gray should've faced a trial and gone to prison for his actions. That fact will always make me sad. But I cannot mourn a man I didn't know."

*This woman.*

I stare into her ice-blue eyes, my heart fluttering in my chest.

"When Rhys showed up in class, I thought I had lost you. Again."

Her smile vanishes. "I know. Me, too."

"I never thought I could feel this way about someone. Two someones," I correct myself, nudging my baby girl inside her mom.

"You're stuck with us." She nips at my bottom lip.

"Is that a promise, MOAB Girl?" I smirk.

Instead of answering me, she moves her hand to the back of my neck and pulls me down to her. Her mouth presses against mine once, twice.

"Promise, Tight End."

## EPILOGUE

### WES



*THREE YEARS LATER*

"DADDY, AGAIN!" Haddie squeals, strapped in her life vest, as she bobs up and down in the waves of the Pacific Ocean. We arrived in LA two days ago and are leaving tomorrow with everyone for Lilly's family vineyard to celebrate their daughter's first birthday.

Arms wrap around my neck from behind, and lips leave a scorching trail on the skin underneath my ear. "Yes, Daddy. Again," King whispers, her warm breath causing goose bumps to erupt on my neck and back, making my cock instantly stand at attention. She is not talking about me playing with our daughter in the water. I turn my head so I can properly kiss my wife.

"I like when you call me that," I murmur against her mouth.

Her eyelids are hooded, and she swipes her tongue across my bottom lip. "Maybe we should take D up on her babysitting offer."

I lean in. "Maybe we shou—"A wave of saltwater hits me in the face, and King splutters, having gotten a mouthful as well.

"Get a room!" Den exclaims, faux exasperated, from behind us. She scoops Haddie up and twirls her around.

"Faster, faster," my little girl screams with joy, and heat radiates through my chest. So much has changed in the last three years.

I didn't get to fulfill my dream of becoming a professional athlete. I got something better. I played on the team my entire time at MPU, but in the end, I majored in finance and partnered with Kiwi. Together, we started *Stonebriar's Urban Chair*, a custom furniture company.

After his first few contracts with the Mountain Club, more and more requests came in. Rich people talked, and soon, he couldn't keep up. His old business partner left, and one night during dinner, I blurted out, "Why don't I take over the operating side, and you focus on designing and building?"

Kiwi and King stopped eating mid-chew and stared at me like I had sprouted a third eye.

"What?" I shrugged. I was graduating that year, Kiwi needed help, and football had become a hobby long before then. I looked at King. "We've talked about it. We both want to stay here. You can finally get your degree once Haddie starts preschool, and everyone wins."

They both eyed each other, and for a second, I questioned if I had spoken English—not that I spoke any other language.

As if on cue, the biggest smile formed on King's face. "Yes!" Her head whipped around to Kiwi. "Say yes!"

"Dude, better say yes. She wasn't this enthusiastic when I asked her to marry me," I mumbled, taking another bite of my dinner to hide my smirk. The proposal was not what I had planned, but thinking back, I wouldn't have had it any other way.

"Excuse me? I was in the process of pushing a human being out of my vagina, asshole," she shoved my shoulder, laughing.

"Ewww, Roe-Roe. TMI." Kiwi wrinkled his nose.

She flipped him the bird and kept glowering at me.

"What are you thinking about? That would mean I'd finally get to see you more than just five minutes a day," Zeke piped up from the fourth chair at our table.

Kiwi held Zeke's eyes for several breaths before his gaze swiveled to King, then to me. He held out his hand in my direction. "Let's do it."

And we did.



KING IS about to start her second year at MPU, and her passion has not changed. She is her professors' star student—her having attended their lectures for nearly five years now. Haddie is almost four and the sassiest little girl I've ever met. She puts her mother's smart mouth to shame.

When I arrived in Montana, I was lonely, angry at the world, and had no real future. Nearly six years later, I own fifty percent of one of the most lucrative custom furniture businesses in the state, and I have a gorgeous wife and a daughter who wants to be exactly like her mom—knife-wielding and all.

King still carries a blade with her wherever we go. Though, the Du Hoc has been retired to the safe in our house. Separating her from her safety blanket during our flight to California was a challenge. Haddie picked up her mom's passion for sharp objects, but when it came to teaching her skills—as King phrased it—I put my foot down.

I stand in the water, watching King and Den swing Haddie between them toward the beach. Every time they pretend to drop her in the water, she shrieks in delight. She'll be dead tired later.

And to think that I almost didn't get to experience this.

. . .

"SHE'S OUT COLD." King straddles my lap. I'm sitting on our king-size bed in one of Rhys and Lilly's spare bedrooms, running numbers for a new project. She takes my laptop, moves it out of the way, and scoots closer until she rubs up against my cock. Placing her hands on my shoulders, she pushes me farther into the pillows and leans close. Our lips almost touch, but instead of making contact, she trails the tip of her tongue along my jaw to my ear.

She swivels her hips to create more friction. A tingling sensation shoots through my spine, followed by a flush of heat to my lower half. I'm already painfully hard. "I want you inside of me," she moans as she repeats the motion.

*Jesus fuck.*

I wrap my arms around her and, with one swift move, flip us over. Hovering above her, I touch my nose to hers. "Is that so, Princess?"

Her eyes gleam with desire. She interlaces her hands behind my neck and pulls me close enough to capture my mouth with hers. She nips on my lower lip, followed by soothing the sting with her tongue. I groan as the metallic taste registers in my brain. She learned a long time ago how much this turns me on.

It's my turn. Sitting on my haunches, I hook my fingers in her sleep shorts and slide them down her legs. "Tsk tsk, Princess. Commando again? That was mighty presumptuous of you." I attempt to keep a serious expression, but my mouth waters as I stare at her bare pussy.

She feigns innocence, tipping her index finger to her lips. "I was hoping you would make good on your promise from the shower."

*The shower.* I close my eyes and inhale slowly in an attempt to calm my jutting pulse. This morning, King slipped into the shower with me after Lilly took the kids downstairs for break-fast. With my eyes closed and soap all over my head, I was not prepared for what my wife had planned. One hand around my dick, the other stroking my balls, and before I could wash the suds off, her lips closed around me. Her tongue swiveled my tip as she moved up and down my length. I let my head fall back, the water spraying directly in my face. I wouldn't have cared if a marching band would've paraded through our bathroom at that point. I fisted my fingers in the wet strands of her hair, motioning for her to take me deeper.

*Jesus, so good.*

Picking up her pace, it didn't take long for me to come. She knew exactly how to push me over the edge.

Peering down at her exposed lower half now, I pretend to think about it. She places one foot against my chest and pushes playfully. "Sheats," she growls.

"MOAB Girl," I shoot back before I dive between her legs, and her moans fill the room.

Later that night, her spent body is tucked under my arm, and I draw circles with my fingers on her shoulder. "I don't want to miss a second of it this time." I can't see her face and keep my voice low in case she fell asleep.

She tilts her head up, and our eyes meet. "Not a second?"

"Not one," I confirm.

"You're going to hold my hair back when I puke my guts out?" she challenges.

I grin. "Bring it on, Princess."

We found out last week that King is pregnant. We weren't trying, but we also weren't preventing it. We're going to keep it to ourselves for a little longer since it is still early. This week is to celebrate someone else—two someones, if you count *his* return.

"How was the beach?" Hudson asks me from across the aisle on the private jet. He and Elle made it today; his sister and the rest of their gang would come tomorrow. I haven't seen him—or the others—in almost two years and am looking forward to catching up with everyone at the party.

"Oh, you know. The girls played in the ocean until they

passed out from exhaustion, and then I had to take care of myself—even cook my own dinner," I counter with a grin.

*Smack.*

"Ouch! Woman!" I rub my bicep where King sucker punched me, throwing her an accusing glare.

"Who took care of you last night?" She tilts her head, daring me to give the right answer.

Hudson cackles in his seat, and I hear Elle chastise, "You guys never learn. Don't antagonize the women who feed you."

That makes King blush, and it's my turn to laugh out loud. I lean close to her ear. "You fed me, alright."

"What did Mommy make you for dinner, Daddy?" an innocent voice comes from somewhere between us, and we both wince at the same time.

"Yes, Daddy, what did Mommy make you?" Hudson mocks.

"Why don't we go check if Heather wants to do some color by numbers." King rummages through her massive bag until she finds Haddie's pencil case and coloring book and stands from her seat. Before she takes our daughter's hand, she slugs Hudson against the shoulder and then marches past Elle, who's kneeling next to Lilly, talking in hushed voices.

I grin at Hudson, who scowls. "Your wife has a mean punch."

"Don't I know it." I turn forward and take in the thundercloud over Marcus's head. He glowers at something behind me—correction, someone. It's been years, and I'm still clueless about what his deal is. He's as closed off as George's secret hideout on the East Coast. I have a feeling that King knows—at least part of it. She and Marcus have a bond like Den and me, but I've never asked my wife. If it's something I need to know, she would tell me—or Den would. Besides being a huge dick to Den, he has always been nothing but good to my family.

After we land, two SUVs take us to the vineyard. Marcus drives with Tristen in the passenger seat. Elle, Haddie, and King take the middle row and leave Hudson and me to climb into the third.

Everyone chats among themselves when Hudson nudges my knee with his. I meet his eyes, and in a low tone, he asks, "Have Rhys and Lilly said anything about how *he's* doing?"

I shake my head. Lilly has been unusually quiet about the topic, and I didn't pry. No one expected him to be back after just six years. With the legal team Lilly had at her disposal, and the blame being pushed onto the pharmaceutical companies for his erratic behavior, they managed it somehow.

After we arrive at the estate, Lilly and Rhys separate from everyone, heading into the house right away. Heather starts directing us to our rooms. King leads Haddie into the main building, and I call after her, "I'll grab the bags."

"Okay," King's voice drifts back to me.

I unload our rolling duffels and follow everyone into the house. I reach the landing to the second floor and—shit, did Heather say our room is to the left or right? I'm about to turn left, where more of the guest rooms are, when out of the corner of my eye, I notice a blonde head ducking into the room at the end of the hall of the west wing. By the time I turn, the person is gone. Weird.

Shrugging to myself, I set out to find my girls. It was probably Lilly.

"Daddy, here!" Haddie pops into the hallway just a few feet from me, and King follows, smiling.

"There you are. We were about to start a search party."

"Well, you found me." I walk past them and drop the bags in the corner.

I plop down on the edge of the bed. King eyes our daughter, who has a mischievous twinkle in her little ice-blue eyes.

"Ready?" King grins at her.

"Ready," she mimics her mother.

"Girls," I warn, but it's already too late. Both pounce on me with a war cry.

*My family.*

Dear reader,

If you enjoyed Wes and King's story, please consider leaving a brief review (or star rating.) Each review helps a book to be considered for audiobook deals and other amazing opportunities. I would appreciate it so much.

Make sure to keep turning the pages for **exclusive BOTD bonus scenes only available in this paperback** or through my website.

**BUT FIRST,** keep reading for an exclusive preview of *Followed by the Dark*, Book Five in The Dark Series.

**Followed by the Dark
(Prologue)**

## MARCUS

I cross my ankle over my knee in a failed attempt to stop my leg from bouncing. All I achieve is for the itch to switch to my other limb. My knee starts to bob up and down, and I swallow the growl that's been steadily building in my throat since boarding the jet. I glance at the Garmin on my wrist and calculate our remaining flight time—one more hour.

*I shouldn't be here.*

I'm not afraid of flying. At thirty-seven years old, there is not much that scares me. I was thrown into hell well before I was legally an adult. I fought and clawed my way out of the black pit that kept my soul hostage since I last held her. I'm alive, but I'm not. I'm in purgatory. To the clueless observer, I am having a case of aerophobia as my nails dig into the buttery soft leather of the armrest. I'm not. My heart rate has been somewhere around one-twenty, and the oxygen supply to my lungs is as delayed as the restocking of toilet paper during the pandemic a few years ago. None of this should be the case when your ass is planted on a private jet approaching a multimillion-dollar vineyard in Northern California.

I'm a mess.

I'm not supposed to be working. I've never worked this week—not in the fourteen years I've *served* under George Weiler. He knew the date when he hired me for his security team. It was my one and only condition.

When Lilly and her husband, Rhys, informed me that they decided to move their daughter's first birthday party to the family's private estate, it was a win-win situation. The place is a fortress. Ever since becoming Lilly McGuire's bodyguard before she came out to the public and took over her family's empire six years ago, I've felt guilty about leaving her side for a whole week. She and Rhys are not just my employers; they are my friends. The closest I will ever get to having a family again. Knowing she would be shielded during my absence was a huge relief.

Then, I got the call.

George was not able to accompany Lilly on the jet as planned. He is the head of security for Lilly's family, including the business side. He runs the show. Being his second-in-command for almost a decade—and Lilly's *Shadow*, as I was named—it would fall on me to make sure the family arrived safely. Everyone under George is qualified. He trained us all. But neither he nor I are *able* to give up control when it comes to Lilly's safety. It's personal for us.

I've replayed the phone conversation in my head numerous times, searching for a clue as to why George would force me to be here. I came up blank. It could only mean one thing: something came up with Lilly's brother. If George doesn't want to talk about it, you'd have more success digging through a three-foot-deep concrete wall with a plastic spork than getting answers out of him.

Don't get me wrong, this job saved my life, which is why I will never refuse an assignment. I care about the McGuires and, of course, want to make sure their guests are secure. But being in *her* vicinity for longer than I already have had to be since her arrival in LA—

*Her*. Denielle Keller. Lilly's best friend since the two were prepubescent teens.

I lift my head, and my eyes immediately zero in on the perfectly curled, dark-brown hair spilling over the backrest two rows up. I purposefully chose the single seat in the front in order to limit having to face the woman to boarding and deplaning.

I attempt to be courteous with her, but ninety-nine percent of the time, that goes out the window. Her presence triggers a deep-rooted hatred I didn't know existed for more than one person. Most still believe it is because she clocked me in the nuts six years ago, and I had to physically restrain her for hours—I let them believe that. The last thing I want is to lose my position because of my dislike for Denielle *"The Bulldog"* Keller. This week, though...I have no fucking clue how I'm going to do it. I can't escape the same way I can in LA.

She laughs at something Rhys says to Lilly, and my jaw clenches of its own volition. A wave of heat spreads through my body—the unpleasant kind. Besides the physical assault, which I can somewhat excuse, given the circumstances, her presence sets me back years—not something I ever thought I'd have to go through at this age.

A ripping sound redirects my attention to the present, and I close my eyes in resignation when I take in the tear in the leather where I've dislodged it from the seat.

*Well, fuck. This is going to be a long trip.*

# BONUS SCENES

*Wes takes Denielle to the airport.*
*(This scene takes place between chapters eleven and twelve of Because of the Dark.)*

## DENIELLE

I PICK AT MY MAROON-COLORED NAIL POLISH. PERFECT COLOR for fall, right? All I can see now, though, are flecks of dried blood. I never considered how close the tints are. Peering at Wes out of the corner of my eye, the knot in my stomach expands, turning to a vise around my heart. He is white-knuckling the steering wheel of Kai's Rover with a deep groove between his brows. He wouldn't explain why we didn't take his car, but with how his overall mood was this morning, it wasn't important.

Lilly texted me when she was on her way to the airport: **Marcus & I will meet u on the field. We'll take right back off since we don't need to get gas. See u in a bit.**

She knows about my *strained* (cough, cough—understatement of the year) relationship with her shadow. Hell, everybody who has spent more than thirty seconds in the same room with *him* and me is aware of something being seriously fucked up between us.

Yet, I still don't believe Lilly has all the details—if any. Her talent allows her to get information, but she puts her friends' privacy above it all, especially after what happened between Rhys and Wes.

Weston Sheats. My best friend. In high school, he was the funny guy. The boy every girl fell in love with but couldn't keep. He was cocky, aware of what his looks could get him, and he used it to his advantage—until two years ago. Losing his dream and his oldest friend at the same time broke him. Watching it, unable to do anything about it, split my heart in half. He had been my rock since I had found my cheating boyfriend doggy-styling a sorority slut and, later, when the four of us went through hell and back. It was my turn to be there for him, and I have been since. I will do almost anything for my friends, but at the same time, I don't give them everything about me. I can't.

I refuse to talk about certain parts of my life. No one knew about it until Marcus. My entire childhood, I kept telling myself that none of that had anything to do with me. Little did I know, it had everything to do with me. And Marcus Baxter lets me feel it every chance he gets.

I can sense him before I consciously know he is there. A bone-chilling cold creeps through my veins and turns my insides to ice. My hands tremble, and The Bulldog tucks her tail and runs, hiding in the farthest part of my mind. I'd never cowered to anyone until Marcus Baxter. His deep-centered hatred comes off him in waves, and no one understands why. I'm not going to tell them. This secret will remain in the dark for as long as I can keep it there.

We pull into the small parking lot of the airport's private aviation section. The building is not part of the main terminal, and one can just walk onto the airfield and board their mode of transportation. The jet is easy to spot, the red-and-gold emblem of Lilly's family empire glistening in the early morning light. My heart squeezes before growing in speed until I fight the need to press my palm against my sternum.

*They're early.*

"You look like you could use a drink—or ten," Wes remarks non-comically.

I've caught him staring at his phone several times since last night, his mood souring every time it remains blank.

"So do you. And I'm not the one with the drinking problem," I snap and then instantly turn my gaze back out the window. Fucking great. This is what he does to me. I turn into a raging bitch and treat the one good guy in my life like crap.

"I'm sorry," I whisper as I swipe away the mist in my eye.

"D?" Wes's tone is gentle. Guilt chokes me as I curl my lips under to prevent it from trembling. He has his own shit to deal with—more than I was aware of until arriving in Stonebriar last night. Who was the girl? *King.* Seeing them together burned a hole in my stomach. I'm not the jealous type—never have been —which is probably part of the reason I didn't notice what Charlie was up to (or into) until he literally flashed it in my face. But Wes has been mine for the last two years. Does he whore around? Yes. Everyone needs to get the itch scratched—so do I. Last night, though, it only took one look to see that this was different. Wes was different. I didn't like it. He was my constant.

Lilly's text had distracted me from interrogating him further. **George had to leave. Family emergency. It'll be just Marcus and me tmrw. Can't wait to hang this next week with you.**

All I could see was, *'It'll be just Marcus and me.'* Marcus and me. Marcus, Lilly, and me.

*FUCK!*

"One of these days, you will tell me what's going on," Wes states with a confidence I don't have the heart to crush.

"Sure." *Never.*

I need to get a grip. This is going to be hard for Wes as well.

He hasn't seen Lilly in years. And Rhys's ambush last week already unhinged him. I knew it was going to happen but promised Lilly not to interfere. I picked up the phone numerous times to give Wes a heads up but never hit dial or sent the text. The guilt of letting him go in blind had been gnawing on me like flesh-eating bugs on a carcass since I heard that Wes had kicked Rhys out of his house. Hence, my spontaneous trip to the treasure state. It worked out with my already planned vacation in LA —except for George screwing it up. With him, Marcus would've been distracted. Now...

Wes comes around the Rover and opens my door. His jaw is so tense the skin stretches as he grinds his teeth. As soon as I'm out of the car, he slams the door shut. My shoulders scrunch to my ears, and adrenaline shoots through my body like it is powered by a nitrous-oxide engine. *Shit.*

"Let's go, D." Wes has already turned toward the double doors, the gravel crunching under his boots.

"You don't have to come with me," I croak. I was selfish to ask him.

He snorts and keeps marching, forcing me to pick up my pace if I don't want to cause more attention by arriving last.

Side by side, we step out on the airfield. Lilly and Marcus are outside the jet, chatting. Lilly turns toward us, but her usual sunshine smile is missing. She has one arm draped around her midsection. Letting my gaze drop, her trademark tic is on full display on her other hand. One of these days, she will pop a joint out of its socket.

The closer we get, the slower Wes's steps become. Marcus follows our approach without really looking at us. It doesn't minimize the contempt slithering across his features.

I reach over and interlace my fingers with Wes's. Squeezing his hand, I draw strength from him as he is from me when he returns the motion. We're only a few feet away when he halts us.

"Wes," Marcus greets him.

"Marcus." His palm is clammy in mine, but it might as well be my own.

I inhale, forcing the dizziness down, and turn the corners of my mouth up. "Hey, babe. Thanks for picking me up," I chirp too brightly, and all three can see through my cringe-worthy performance. Thankfully, though, none of them call me out.

Lilly mimics my faux display of happiness and steps closer. She hugs me to her, which forces me to let go of Wes. "Anytime. I'm glad it worked out."

Wes instantly backs up, and an invisible chasm divides the concrete below our feet. Lilly drops her arm but leaves it draped around my waist. I fight the urge to escape the embrace. This is all wrong. She hasn't come face to face with Wes since he sucker-punched Rhys. This must be as nerve-racking for her as it is for him, but I can't help but feel like I'm taking sides.

Wes's hands are shoved into the pockets of his jeans, and his shoulders are hunched.

"Hi, Wes." She tilts her head with a quiet smile. Her fingers dig into my side as we wait for what happens next.

"Lil."

At his nickname for her, Lilly's grip loosens, and I straighten my spine.

"How are you?" she probes carefully.

*Dear God, make the awkwardness go away.*

"Fine." After a pause, Wes adds, "You?"

"Good," she breathes the word out with a whoosh. "I'm good."

More silence, and my eyes drift over to my enemy. Marcus mimics Wes's stance. The only difference is, he scans the surroundings, whereas Wes's attention is on Lilly.

"I better—"

"Listen, Wes—"

They start simultaneously then stop.

"You first." Wes motions with a hand gesture.

Lilly slashes her mouth and peers everywhere but at the person she just addressed a second ago.

"What is it, Lilly?" His hollowed cheeks and the twitch in his left eye are clear indicators. I know him better than most.

"I, um...I wanted to run something by you." She shuffles and finally drops her arm from me.

I blink between my two best friends, unease simmering in my core.

"What's that?" Wes keeps his tone neutral, but the movement of his fist clenching and unclenching in his pocket is visible.

"I heard that your dad's company was not doing so, um...good. I, uh...wanted to offer my help. To you or your parents."

*She did not go there.*

I want to throttle her. What is she thinking? This is not common knowledge. I'm aware of it because Wes confided in me a few months ago when his guilt of not going home was becoming too much once again. He wanted to be there for his family but couldn't bring himself to get on a plane. Charles and Laura Sheats are private people. They wouldn't have advertised that to anyone.

Wes's spine is ramrod straight, and his stare bores into Lilly. The vein in his neck flexes, and so do his biceps under his long-sleeve shirt. He left his jacket in the car. His eyes flick to mine, then back to Lilly.

He slants his head. "And how would you know about my parents' financial situation?" The threat in his tone draws Marcus's attention.

"I—"

"You fucking dug into my personal life. AGAIN!" He's seething.

Lilly flinches. "I—"

"You what? What excuse do you have this time? Wasn't it enough for Rhys to invade my home uninvited? Now you have to show me once more what a charity case I am to you?"

He slams his hands in his hair and turns his back to us. "FUCK!" he roars into the cold morning air.

"Wes." I need to do something. Defuse this ticking bomb.

He holds up a hand. "No, D."

He takes one step toward the airport building. Without turning, he states, "I'll call you, D. Have a safe flight."

Those are his last words before jogging toward the gate.

## THE CONFESSION

*Lilly tells Rhys about King on the way home from Montana. (This scene takes place after chapter twenty-four of Because of the Dark.)*

### LILLY

"You're doing it again." Rhys scowls at me.

*Huh?*

I peer up at him over the top of my laptop screen. I've read the same paragraph a hundred times. Attending college in the middle of what is my life is taking its toll. Following Rhys's line of sight, I glance at my hand resting next to the keyboard on the small table separating our seats.

*Oh.*

I curl my fingers into a fist, stopping myself from flicking my thumb. My stomach dips as a flush creeps across my cheeks.

"Talk to me, Calla." He reaches over, placing his hands on top of mine.

*Calla, not babe.*

I fight the urge to rub the heat on my face away. Shit, I didn't plan on having this conversation in the air.

I chew on my bottom lip and find George on the other side

of the aisle—one row of seats down. He is facing me while Marcus sits with his back to us.

George meets my gaze and dips his chin in the slightest nod. He wasn't happy with me for leaving on our trip without filling Rhys in—or for keeping *it* from him in the first place. It.

The secret has been eating away at me for almost three years —thirty-five months, to be exact. We had promised to never keep anything from each other again, yet I could not confide in him about this. Mainly because I had no clue what to do with the information.

What if he won't forgive me? No, he wouldn't leave me over this. Not after everything we've been through. Right? With every thought, my breathing increases until I can't get enough air into my lungs.

I had kept the note hidden in my old journal for months before starting my research. It only took about a week to find out everything there was to know about Kingsley Monroe Turner, daughter of Francis Garrison Turner—the man who drugged and kidnapped me—and Stephanie Monroe, his twelve-year-younger girlfriend. Why did he ask me to look out for her? What kind of game was he playing? I had my assumption of why he had killed *her,* the person he abandoned his girlfriend and daughter for—not that it would change anything. What he did to my family and me was unforgivable. But why Kingsley? Was she important to him, after all? He left her behind when she was a little girl. I had a gazillion questions and no answers. I couldn't talk to the person I wanted advice from. If he were here, he'd be able to dig deeper. Maybe find what I was missing. But our conversations were monitored, and the media still followed my every move. In the end, one night, after everyone was asleep, I sought George out and confessed what I had found in my bag of belongings the hospital handed me.

George remained silent for almost ten minutes after I

presented him with the evidence. The hollow sensation in my stomach grew with every passing second.

"What did Rhys say?" was his first question.

I pressed my lips together, the sinking feeling in my stomach turning to a bottomless pit.

George narrowed his eyes at me. "Lilly Ann."

Lifting my chin, I pushed back. "Don't you *Lilly Ann* me, George Weiler."

That gave me one of his rare chuckles. This man could scare the worst of criminals, but he'd been nothing but good to my family. He'd become the father figure I needed when Tristen was not around.

"Why?" If there was a record for using as few words as possible to communicate, George would hold it.

"He would want to use Kingsley to get to Gray," I admitted. Rhys had been in a bad headspace—especially since his fallout with Wes. He refused to talk to his therapist, wouldn't leave my side for longer than five minutes, and the paps constantly followed us. It was wearing on our relationship.

"It would be an easy way to draw Turner out." I was talking to my head of security now.

"His daughter had nothing to do with what happened the last ten-plus years." Anger flooded my veins, and I could feel my face burn. "She's worked at a freaking strip club since she was sixteen to make ends meet and support her sick mother—who *died* when she was eighteen."

George simply nodded, and that was that. I'd made my case. After that, he'd followed King over the years and planted a tracker on her car, which allowed us to find her whenever it was time for another check-in. The first time he reported that Gray was trailing his daughter, we spent hours discussing what to do. Take him in custody or wait it out? George wouldn't turn him over to the authorities; that much he made clear. He and Tristen had that planned out before I had even left the hospital—details I wanted nothing to do with.

"Babe." Rhys brings my attention back to him.

"I wasn't in Colorado," I blurt out, and Marcus's head whips around. He glowers at me over the back of his seat. I'm throwing him under the bus as well. He and Rhys are close, and Marcus had lied to his face and on the phone while I was with King.

Rhys stares at me impassively with his arms crossed over his chest.

*He knew. How?*

"I guessed as much. There was no reason to bring both of them"—he tilts his head toward our security detail—"with you for a girls' night out—not with Elle having her own guard dogs."

I blink and try to breathe through the tightness in my chest. Did I make a mistake?

Inhaling slowly and squaring my shoulders, I face Rhys. I believe in my decision. "I met with Wes's ex-girlfriend. Girlfriend, if I can convince her to come back."

A crease forms between his brows.

I count to five before saying, "Her name is Kingsley Monroe *Turner*."

At first, there is nothing. Rhys holds my gaze, and I begin to question if he heard me. After a moment, he places his hands on the tabletop and pushes himself up with such force the table dips. He storms to the back of the cabin, and I hear the door to the small bedroom open and close. Then, there is silence. The only sound in the cabin is from the jet's engine.

*Shit, shit, shit.*

I fold into myself in my seat, barely able to see George and Marcus. A blurry form stands and comes toward me.

"Do you want me to talk to him?" Marcus. His tone is soft, not something I get to hear often. He's always angry.

I shake my head. "N-no."

He lowers himself in Rhys's vacated spot and takes one of my hands in his. I wipe my eyes with the sleeve of my shirt and peer out the window into the dark. Guilt, embarrassment, and fear are choking me.

"Go. Talk to him," my shadow nudges.

I remain unmoving until he squeezes my fingers, and I nod. Without looking at either man, I follow my fiancé. My heart trembles, and I can barely get a grip when I try to turn the knob.

Rhys sits on the edge of the queen-size bed. His elbows are propped on his knees, and his head is in his hands.

Letting the door click shut, I lean against it—waiting.

"How long, Calla?" His tone is raspy.

"How long what?" My voice is no more than a whisper.

"How long have you been keeping this from me?" he accuses.

I try to speak, but the words are stuck in my throat. I cross one arm over my chest and lift the other to my neck, feeling my thrashing pulse under my palm.

"HOW LONG, LILLY?!" His head whips up, and the moisture in his eyes makes them glisten.

"Three years."

Rhys jumps up and reaches for the first thing he can get his hands on: the iPad I put in here to charge, which is laying on the bed next to him. It crashes against the wall next to me, but I force myself to remain still.

Turning away, he rakes his hands through his hair. "JESUS FUCK!" He kicks the bedframe.

A strong knock on the door makes me take a step into the room.

"Everything okay in there?" George's tone is authoritative.

"FUCK OFF, G!" Rhys roars, and my shoulders scrunch up. This is so not good.

"Open the door, Lilly." George is in protection mode now. He loves Rhys like his son, but my brother and I will always come first.

"It's fine, George. Please give us a minute," I call through the barrier, attempting to sound confident.

"Lilly." Marcus inserts himself into this clusterfuck.

Rhys finally meets my eyes. I hold his gaze, and some of his rage evaporates. "We're good, G." His tone has calmed, and I exhale with a whooshing sound.

Rhys suddenly opens his arms, and with a flutter in my belly, I step into his embrace.

"Please don't leave me," I mumble against his shirt, letting my own tears flow freely now.

His hand comes to the back of my head, and he tightens his hold. "I'm not leaving you. But I am pretty fucking pissed," he growls.

"I know." I lean back without letting go and scan his face. "Please let me explain."

He doesn't speak, then he pulls me down to the mattress so I am sitting sideways on his lap. He drapes his arms around my waist.

"Talk." It's an order, and I comply.

I tell him everything. From the day I found the piece of paper between my clothes, to the moment I left King's apartment two days ago. He listens quietly the whole time.

When I finish, Rhys exhales a sigh. My hand rests on his chest, and he pulls me closer to him.

"I'm done with fucking secrets."

"I know."

"We don't have secrets, Calla. No more!"

He's silent again, and I amend, "I promise."

"We'll talk about it more when we get home and away from your shadow with his ear pressed against the door." He raises his voice toward the end.

There is a thud outside, and I curl my lips under. *Busted*.

"She is the reason Wes is drinking so much?" Rhys brings my focus back to our conversation.

"I think so, yes."

"I don't like seeing him like this." His concern for his friend makes my insides warm.

"Neither do I. Which is one of the reasons I went to see her."

"What are the other reasons?" Rhys shifts, studying me intently.

I chew the inside of my cheek, and he cocks an eyebrow.

"She has nothing to do with what her father did to us. We can't blame King for any of it. It's as much *her* doing as—" I break off. I hate talking about *her*.

"I get it." He turns my face to him with his index finger under my chin. "You always see the good in people, and from what you've told me, this King girl genuinely cares for Wes."

"She does." I smile so hard my cheeks hurt.

"What's the next reason?" Rhys eyes me curiously now. I didn't think he had caught that.

I interlace my fingers with his. "She's pregnant."

"WHAT?" His eyes bug out, and he jerks to a stand, dropping me ungracefully on the floor in the process.

"Ow," I wince, rubbing my tail bone.

"Oh, shit, babe. I'm sorry." He lifts me up like a little kid and puts me on my feet.

"It's fine." I rub my butt.

Leveling me with one of the most serious expressions I've seen in a long time on him, he asks, "Are you telling me Wes— our Wes—is going to be a father?"

"He is."

He swipes his hand over his mouth. "Well, shit. Does he know?"

"Not yet," I reply quietly.

$$\overline{\phantom{xxxxx}}$$

# UNKNOWN

$$\overline{\phantom{xxxxx}}$$

*This scene takes place on the evening of King's arrest in chapter thirty-two of Because of the Dark.*

## GRAY

I EYE THE GLASS IN FRONT OF ME. THE NEED HAS LESSENED over the last few months, but I'd be lying if I said I didn't want to feel the burn at the back of my throat. Eventually, the burn would numb, and so would everything else. The voices, the faces...it would all disappear—for a little while. I slant my head and watch as my hand slowly inches toward the tumbler on the bar top. The itch that makes my fingertips tingle with anticipation slowly moves through my arm and keeps spreading until my entire body feels like I have a million tiny insects crawling through my veins—all craving the same thing.

*Fuck, I want it.*

Right before my fingers can wrap around the glass, I repeat what I do every Friday night, then I push away from the counter and leave the bar. The location changes, the liquid content differs, but the routine stays the same—ever since King asked for my help.

And now a grandchild. Never in my wildest dreams would I've seen that coming. Stephanie would have been ecstatic, even if King is only twenty-two. Steph was younger when our daughter was born. It never stopped her from being the perfect mother, though. The dim light in my chest that King put back into me over the last three years gets snuffed out whenever I think of her. Stephanie Monroe. I didn't appreciate her when I should've. King was an accident, not a mistake, but I also had never planned on being a father. In my high-as-a-kite mind, paying the bills was more than sufficient.

We weren't married—not that Steph didn't want to. I couldn't. She would mention in passing how women try to be subtle without saying what they want. Couple it with her doe-like eyes, and every man would've fallen to their knees to make her theirs. Not me. My heart would come to a complete stop before taking off at breakneck speed. Cold sweat would build on my neck, and I did what I had to do to deter her. I went to my brother for a fix. It was easier than telling her the truth. Linking her and King to me legally would've turned the targets on their backs to flashing beacons of light. King carried my last name, but as long as I was not officially tied to her mother, everyone in the business assumed I didn't give a shit about them. Despite how I treated my family—I cannot blame it all on the drugs and booze—I never wanted them to get noticed.

I push the door of the bar open and turn in the direction of where I parked the old beat-up SUV I *borrowed* a few days ago. It would be time to switch vehicles again soon. As I get closer, I notice a silhouette leaning against the side of it. A few more steps, and I recognize the person. How did this fucker find me? I've been on the move for months, avoiding Mara's calls for just as long. He's her lapdog, nothing more.

"Gray," he greets me, acting all tough and shit. He's a fucking pussy.

"Why are you not with *her*? She let you off the leash for once?" I jut my bottom lip out and lace the insult with mocking sadness.

His jaw ticks, and I know I struck a nerve. Good.

"You made quite the mess for your little girl, *Francis*."

Blood immediately begins to hammer in my ears. How dare he bring King up? My hand shoots out, and my fingers wrap around his throat. I lean in until my nose is an inch from his. Surprisingly, he doesn't flinch or piss his pants.

"What did you say?" I sneer.

He lifts his arm and wiggles his phone between his thumb and forefinger. "Lookie, lookie."

I peer at the object out of the corner of my eye. Even from this angle, I see who's on the screen. I let go of his neck, no matter how much I'd like to squeeze his miserable little life out of him for good, and snatch the device. I tap on the photo and minimize it. What the fuck? He has dozens of pictures. Enlarging one, I swipe through them. With every new one, my vision narrows until I see nothing but her face. My chest cramps. There is a handful from the McGuire wedding. I knew it was happening in Stonebriar, but I made sure to be at the other end of the country with all their security *and Weiler* there. The next ones are of King outside her house, on her way to the bar, some with Weston, and even one with Lilly. I'm not surprised she took King in. That girl is nothing like—

My stomach drops at the last photo. King is being led into the local police station by two men whose appearance screams feds.

My gaze flies up to his, and his smug grin tells me that he had something to do with it. I drop the phone, and it clatters on the sidewalk. My hands are back on this throat. This time, I don't ease on the pressure. My nails dig into his skin, and a gurgling sound bubbles from his throat.

"What have you done?" Spit flies out of my mouth, covering his ugly mug.

Instead of cowering, though, his expression shifts. I can see the emotion run off his face like pelting water on a window. Then...nothing. His eyes are empty, soulless.

A sharp pain punctures my side, and I let go of him. What the—?

My gaze drops to the spot where my insides are on fire, and I see a handle sticking out of my body.

"Whoopsy. Didn't think you were this easy to get, old man. I'm disappointed." His tone is detached, not at all how I've known him for years.

My arms hang by my side. I'm...stunned. There is no other explanation for my inability to take him out. His arm shoots out, and he pulls the knife out—only to stab it back in.

"Argh!" The sting from the first stab turns to agony. My knees threaten to buckle as black spots appear in my vision.

"And that would be your left kidney." His free hand clamps over my mouth, and he twists the knife.

I howl, but it's muffled by his palm. My eyes dart around the empty street, but there is no one. We're in a shitty part of town, and even if someone was here to witness this, I doubt they would help. I scramble for the gun I have tucked in the back of my pants, regretting not having drawn it from the start. I underestimated the fucker.

He swipes my legs out, and I crumple to the ground.

"You disappoint me, *Francis*. I would've expected more of you when you had Vic dump Ellis's body. You're getting sloppy. Losing your touch in your old age, eh?"

His boot steps on the handle of the knife. I try to push him away, but my arms won't move how my brain signals them.

"I'm here to fix your mistake." He applies more pressure to the blade, and bile rises in my throat.

"Unfortunately, that means you will take your precious daughter's place."

The last thing I see is him pulling a piece of paper out of his jacket. Then, he straightens, lifts his boot, and—

## CHANGE OF PLANS

*This scene takes place two months after chapter thirty-five of Because of the Dark.*

### WES

"Jesus Christ, Sheats. Stop pacing," Den snaps at me. "I'm about to head down to the pharmacy and beg for Xanax. For you *and me.*"

I round on my best friend. "You didn't get kicked out of that room by an angry pregnant woman in pain who's about to get a three-and-a-half-inch needle shoved in her back, BK!" I fire back. My pulse has been a constant 125 since I got the call six hours ago.

She lifts her hands, wiggling her fingers. "Oooh, someone did his homework."

*Is she fucking mocking me?*

I advance on her when a set of arms wraps around me from behind. "Deep breaths, bro."

I was in the middle of a class when Marcus's name flashed

across the screen. My phone is never far from me these days, but today I didn't have it out because of concerns for my pregnant girlfriend. The doctor assured us last week that everything looked great, and our baby girl was right on track.

Marcus was supposed to pick King up for brunch and keep her busy until tonight. He was in town, but King didn't know why. For all intents and purposes, he was visiting her—the two spoke several times a week. King was the only person, besides Lilly and Rhys, that Marcus Baxter did not treat like a nuisance. Little did she know, *everyone* was in Stonebriar.

I had it all planned. The Grizz was closed tonight—also a fact King was unaware of. She no longer worked, being due in three weeks, but I told her we would meet Mags and Kiwi for drinks after I was done at the gym.

I bought the ring weeks ago, but the right time hadn't come. All I knew was that I wanted her to be *officially* mine before the baby came. I was pushing it close—too close.

"Everything will be fi—" Rhys is cut off when an ear-piercing scream echoes through the hallway. All eyes are on King's door, and Rhys snaps his trap shut.

My stomach rolls. I'm gonna throw up. I scrub my palms over my face and into my hair. Making eye contact with Denielle, she's chewing on the inside of her cheek.

*Not such a bitch now, huh?*

I start walking half the length of the corridor again. If I stand still much longer, I'm going to punch a hole in the nearest wall— or face.

Footsteps pound against the linoleum floor, and I turn in the direction of the sound. Mags followed by Grizz and Jaxon are racing down the hallway. She's out of breath, and her hair looks oddly disheveled, but I dismiss that fact. If it were any other situation, I would comment, but I'm about to be a dad. *I'm not ready.* My daughter has decided to meet the world twenty days early. Is that safe? They told me it is. But is it really? What do I know? Maybe there is a reason she needs out now. Something is wrong with her. Fuck, what if something *is* wrong?

Black spots appear in my vision. I can't breathe. *Fuuuck.*

"You're doing it again." Mags steps in front of me. She has dark shadows popping up on her face and all around her. She places a hand on my chest. "Breathe with me."

*I'm trying.*

"You're no good to your soon-to-be fiancée if you pass out. Focus on me." Her tone is soothing—her psych classes working to my advantage for once.

I follow her inhales and exhales, and my thundering pulse begins to calm. Behind her, Lilly and Rhys come back into focus, both having identical creases between their brows.

"Better?" Mags scans my face with a soft smile.

"Better," I confirm and hug her to me. "Thanks."

A chuckle comes from behind me. "I kind of would've enjoyed seeing you pass out because King is giving birth in there." Marcus—the Asshole—grins and slants his head toward the door.

"Fuck off. I want to see you when it happens." I flip him off.

"Never going to happen," he states with utter conviction before his gaze flicks behind me. I don't have to turn to know who he is glowering at.

The voices in King's room get louder again.

"Mrs. Sheats, you—"

"HE HASN'T PROPOSED YET, YOU B—" King shrieks but catches herself before she insults the person providing her with the pain meds.

"Uh oh, better whip out that ring of yours," Kiwi sing-songs.

*One of them will be clocked today.*

We wait a few more minutes before the door opens, and a slightly flushed nurse pokes her head out. "Mr. Sheats, you may come back inside now."

She looks at me apologetically. I dip my chin at her, clenching my jaw. What the hell am I walking into?

She glances at my entourage. "May I ask you to wait in the waiting room down the hall?"

One by one, they nod and shuffle away, and I follow the nurse inside King's room.

I approach her slowly. "Hey, Princess." My hands are up as if to fend off a rabid animal. I hope they took her knife away when she was admitted.

King looks exhausted. She doesn't curse me out for accidentally putting a living being inside her body any more, so I take it that the epidural is working. The first time I was in here, I made the mistake of responding that she was the one that forgot to take her pill, which resulted in more insults and a plastic cup being hurled at my head. Lesson learned.

"Hey." She smiles.

"How are you?" Dumb question, but I don't know what else to say.

She cocks an eyebrow and—

"Five centimeters, King. We'll keep checking." A head pops up from under the sheet draped over her propped-up legs.

I jump because I didn't see the person there, which makes King snort. *Jesus.*

"Was that Rhys and Den out there?" She studies my face. How she was able to hear us through her own verbal abuse of the medical staff, I'm not sure.

"Um, yes." I interlace my fingers with hers.

She slants her head. "Want to explain?" Her tone is soft, and guilt floods me for not having done it sooner.

"Not sure if we should wait until after, uh..." I glance at the person diving back under the sheet. "You might change your mind," I stammer like an idiot, suddenly terrified she might say no.

King squeezes my hand. "I told you, you're stuck with me, Sheats. Now get down on one knee and ask me before I pop this baby out." She has her devilish smirk on her face that I love so much.

I reach into my pocket and pull out the small satchel that I haven't dared leave at home since I picked it up. King presses her lips together, suppressing the broad grin she wants to let out. We haven't talked about marriage—not directly. Out of the corner of my eye, I notice the two nurses in the room take a step back, giving us a false sense of privacy.

I draw in a deep breath and lower myself to one knee. King has to lean a little to still see my face. Our fingers still connected, I place the little velvet bag next to them and put my other hand on top.

"Princess, this is definitely not how I planned this, but from the moment you almost ran me off the road last year, nothing has been normal or ordinary for us. You came into my life when I didn't know I needed you. You broke down my walls and made me fall for you—hard. We had some minor hiccups—"

King laughs. "That's quite the understatement, baby." Her IV hand reaches over and caresses the side of my face.

I lean into her touch. I love when she calls me baby, which is not often. "It was all part of getting us here," I state, convinced. "Now let me finish, MOAB Girl."

Her eyes crinkle, and she nods.

"Kingsley Monroe, I've never felt for a person what I feel for you. From the first time you threw your trademark smirk at me, I knew you were special. I couldn't get you out of my head. We both fought against what was meant to be, not believing we deserved what fate gave us—literally." I peer at her swollen belly. "But there is no doubt in my mind that we were meant to meet one way or another. I can't wait to watch our daughter grow and spend the rest of my life with you."

I untangle our hands and take the little satchel, emptying its content into my palm. Her eyes widen as I hold up the elongated cushion-cut diamond ring I bought after selling my bike. I told King that I wouldn't need it anymore, since our focus was on Nugget, and an infant seat didn't fit on my Harley. She accepted the explanation, and once Rhys connected me with the jeweler he used, I put the money to good use.

"Princess, will you do me the honor of being my wife?" I choke over the last word, the entire situation surreal.

Tears are streaming down her cheeks, and she nods ferociously. "Yes. Yes!"

"Mr. Sheats?" one of the nurses addresses me carefully.

When I turn, I find one with her hands over her heart, the other swiping under her eyes. "She won't be able to wear the ring until after giving birth. I'm so sorry."

You'd think she had told me King wouldn't be able to marry me, she looks that distraught. "She is not allowed to wear any jewelry in case we have to perform a c-section."

I glance back at King, who doesn't seem upset. "Just let me see it for a second, and then you're going to keep it safe until after we meet our daughter." She radiates happiness.

I hand it to her, and she stares, not touching it. "I love it, Wes." She looks up at me. "You sold the bike for this, didn't you?"

I dip my chin, and she reaches for me. "Come here."

I lean in and place a gentle kiss on her lips.

"I love you," she breathes.

"I love you more."


It takes three more hours before King is ready to push. From what I'm told, it could've taken a lot longer, but my fiancée is beyond exhausted when the first scream erupts in the room. I stay by her top side the entire time, holding her hand. I wanted to see my daughter meeting the world, but the one time I took a peek under the sheet, a wave of nausea instantly hit me, and cold sweat covered me from head to toe. King rolled her eyes, and the doctor suggested I hold King's hand instead.

"Mr. Sheats, Miss soon-to-be Sheats, you have a beautiful baby girl," the nurse announces and places a little bundle on King's chest.

Her eyes gloss over, and she reaches for me with one hand while placing the other on our daughter's back. My vision becomes blurry, and I press my lips on King's forehead.

"We have a baby," King whispers.

"She is perfect, Princess." I can't decipher what emotions are raging inside of me, looking at this tiny human. Everything from the purest love, to gripping fear, to the fiercest protectiveness.

"Have you picked a name yet?" someone asks, but I cannot look away from my two girls.

King peers up at me, and I smile at her. We decided on the name a few weeks ago.

"Haddie Monroe Sheats."

# ACKNOWLEDGMENTS

You guys, I am crying. Again. Is this normal every time one finishes a book? I wrote the prologue while I was still in the writing cave for *Out of the Dark*—almost two years ago. A similar scene played out in front of me during a late grocery run, and all I could see was Wes and King in my head. I came home and wrote it down, knowing this was how Wes's story would begin.

**If this was your first encounter** with **The Dark Series**, thank you so much for picking up Wes and King's story. While I did my best to keep their story separate from the first three books in the series, you received some hints about Lilly and Rhys. If you want to find out how it all began, check out ***In the Dark,*** available on Amazon.

   (***Please note***: *Lilly and Rhys's trilogy is considered a mature, <u>slow-burn</u>, new adult, suspense romance. While there are steamy scenes, the intensity increases gradually throughout the books.*)

**For those of you who have been with me from the start**, thank you from the bottom of my heart. What a wild ride it has been. It is still mind blowing to me that people read the stories that play out in my head.

   You get to experience how everyone has grown—is that the right word?—over the last few years. Wes is no longer the guy you met in Lilly and Rhys's books. What do you think about grown-up Wes? :-)

You also got a glimpse into what's to come. **Denielle and Marcus are next**. The dark has been following everyone, and as you can probably guess, Denielle has secrets of her own. I'm so excited to give you their story.

**Bonus Scenes!!** Make sure to sign up for my <u>newsletter</u> to receive bonus scenes for each book in The Dark Series. The exclusive newsletter content for *Because of the Dark* are the following scenes:

- The Airport (Wes drops off Denielle at the airport)

- The Confession (Lilly's confession to Rhys that she kept King from him)

- UNKNOWN (A small glimpse into what happened to Gray)

- Change of Plans (Meet Haddie Sheats)

Once again, I'm aware that there are still some **unanswered questions**, but I can <u>promise</u> you they will be answered. Bear with me and the series.

- **What happened to Gray in New Mexico?**

Make sure to sign up for my newsletter. (Bonus scene: UNKNOWN)

(If you missed the newsletter, don't worry. All bonus scenes will be published in ***Behind the Dark*, A Dark Series Novella** when the series is complete)

- **Tanner Jaxon Weiler!!**

I didn't see him coming either until I wrote his name. George will get his own novella, which will have more backstory to Jax, but you will find out more in books five and six.

- **What's the deal with Grizz, Mags, *and Jax?***

Once I figure that out, you will be the first to know. Grizz's backstory is set, and he will get a book (or novella) of his own.

If there are any other loose ends that you would like to know when they will be tied up, **message me**. I'd love to hear from you.

Okay, now to the thank-yous. WOW, I need to thank so many people for their assistance with this book. I have such an amazing team behind me. I couldn't do this without all of you!!

**My husband & daughters:** You are my everything. Chasing this dream would be nothing without you by my side. I love you!

**My family and friends:** Thank you for your continuous support in my dream and for cheering me on every step of the way.

**Mary:** My PA, plotting partner, beta, and friend. She always throws curve balls at me that trigger new plot twists or brand-new book ideas in my head. Thank you for your daily voice messages, letting me rant when Wes or King went quiet or didn't do what I had planned for them. I couldn't do this job without you.

**Sammi:** You are my sanity. I cherish our daily conversations and texts. Your friendship and support means the world to me. Love you to pieces!

**Cara**: My wonderful alpha. Who would've thought that one dinner with our men would lead to this? You were the first to get the full story of Wes and King, and I was TERRIFIED sending it to you. Thank you so so much for all your feedback and help in polishing this book up. To many more books together.

**My betas**: Lyndsey, Maggie, Jenn, and Arika. Thank you for taking time out of your busy lives to beta read Wes's story. You are such an integral part of my process, and I can't begin to tell you how grateful I am for you.

**Jenn** from Jenn Lockwood Editing: Thank you for once again working with my crazy schedule and making my words clean and pretty.

**Rosa** from My Brother's Editor: Thank you so much for

proofing *Because of the Dark* and making sure Wes's book is ready for the world.

**My ARC Readers & Street Team**: THANK YOU!! Thank you for reading and reviewing my books before they're out in the wild and for spreading the word. I'm blown away by your support and wouldn't be here without you!

And finally, **you**, **my Readers:** Thank you for reading my words and escaping with me into the world(s) my crazy head cooks up. Seeing you fall in love, like (or even dislike) my characters makes me so happy because it means I created something you can identify with in one way or another. I can't wait to give you many more books and to hear what you think about them.

Denielle and Marcus, let's see what your story brings.

See you all at the end of book five.

xoxo
Danah Logan

Born and raised in Germany, Danah moved to the US, where she met her husband, eventually trading downtown Chicago's city life for the northern Rockies.

She can be seen hanging with her twin girls and exploring the outdoors when she's not arguing plot points with the characters in her head.

But it's that exact passion that has produced *The Dark Series* and continues to keep her glued to her laptop, following her dreams.

Scan the below QR code to sign up for my newsletter and be the first to know about upcoming releases, sales, and new arrivals.

Add me on Facebook
www.facebook.com/authordanahlogan/

Follow me on Instagram
www.instagram.com/authordanahlogan/

Visit my Website for more content
and other places to stalk me
www.authordanahlogan.com

Or scan this second QR code for all the links:

# ALSO BY DANAH LOGAN

**The Ghost**
*The Beginning.*
A Dark Series and Davis Order Novella
(George & Lou)

**The Dark Series**

**In the Dark**, Book 1
**Out of the Dark**, Book 2
**Of Light and Dark**, Book 3
(Lilly and Rhys)
A Dark, New-Adult, Romantic-Suspense Trilogy

**Because of the Dark**, Book 4
(Wes and King)
A Dark, Hidden-Identity, Romantic-Suspense Novel

**Followed by the Dark**, Book 5
(Denielle and Marcus)
A Dark, Enemies-to-Lovers, Age-Gap,
Romantic-Suspense Novel

**I Am the Dark**, Book 6
(HIM)
A Dark, Age-Gap, Romantic-Suspense Novel

<u>**The Davis Order**</u>

**Rezoned**, Prequel
(Ethan)
A Dark, Hate-to-Love, Second-Chance,
Romantic-Suspense Novel